Oh, Brother!
BRAT ATTACK!

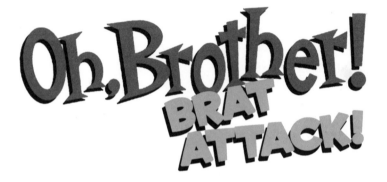

Oh, Brother! BRAT ATTACK!

Bob Weber Jr. and Jay Stephens

Andrews McMeel Publishing®

Kansas City • Sydney • London

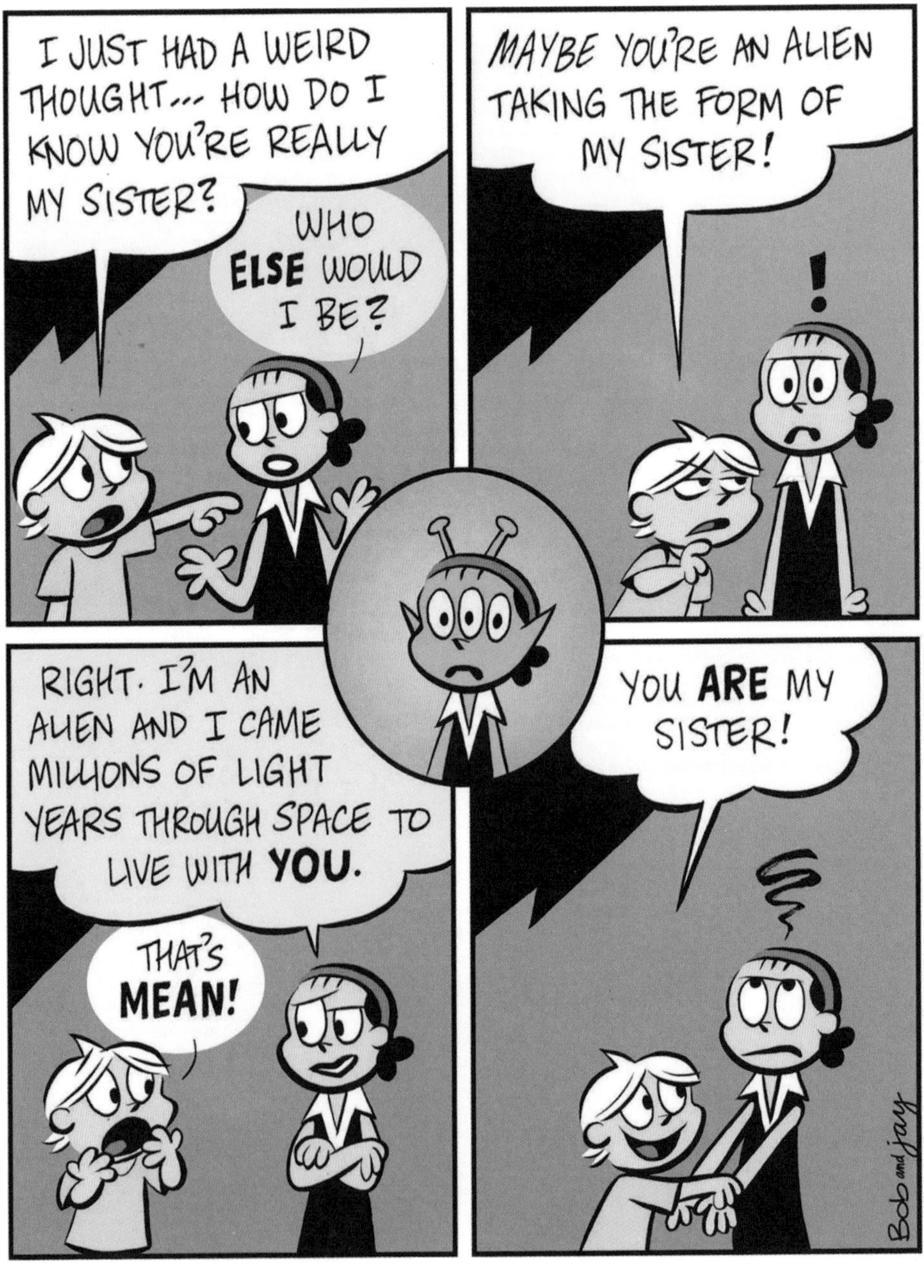

I JUST HAD A WEIRD THOUGHT... HOW DO I KNOW YOU'RE REALLY MY SISTER?
WHO **ELSE** WOULD I BE?
MAYBE YOU'RE AN ALIEN TAKING THE FORM OF MY SISTER!
!
RIGHT. I'M AN ALIEN AND I CAME MILLIONS OF LIGHT YEARS THROUGH SPACE TO LIVE WITH **YOU**.
THAT'S **MEAN!**
YOU **ARE** MY SISTER!
Bob and jay

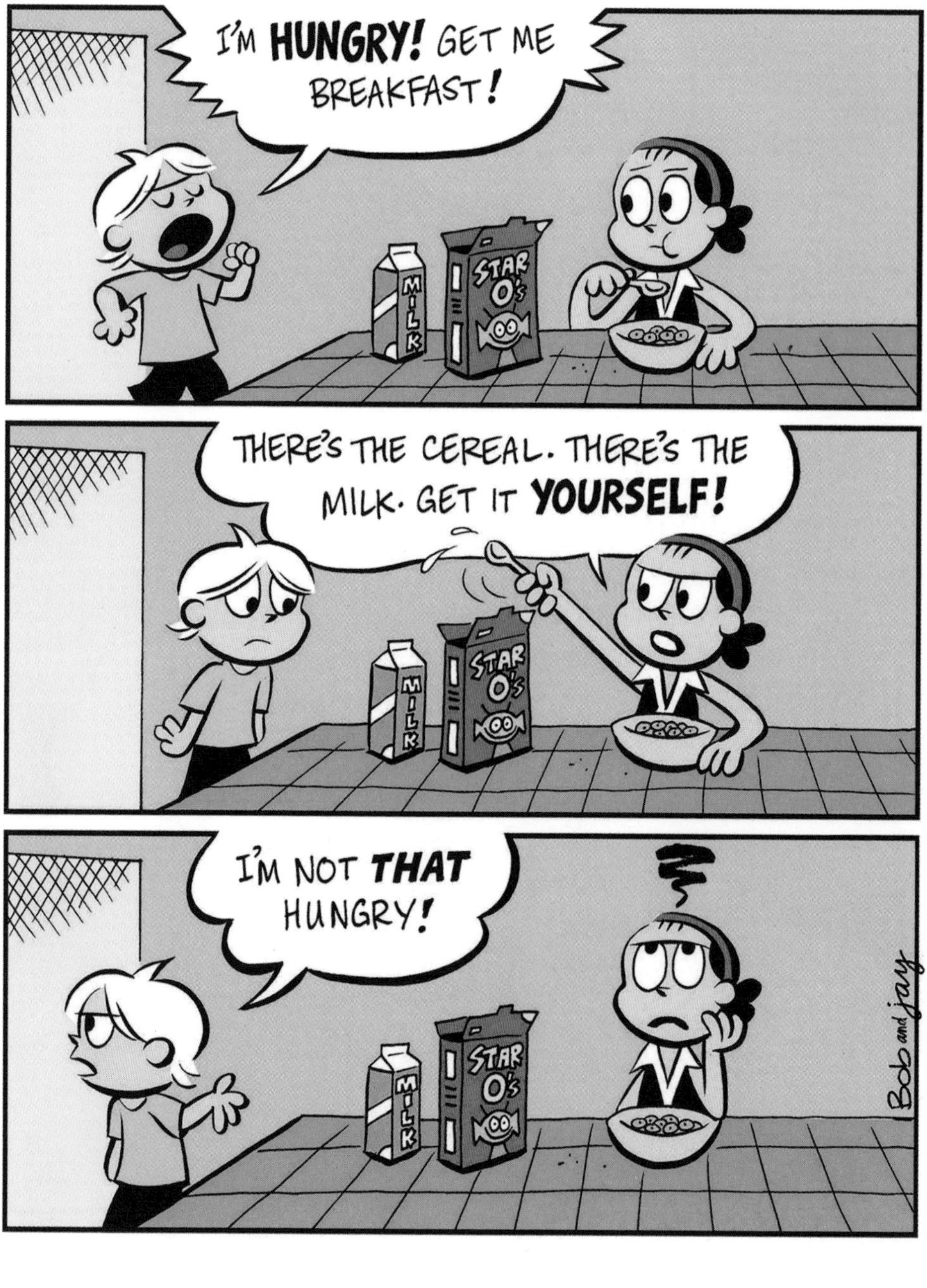
I'M **HUNGRY!** GET ME BREAKFAST!
MILK
STAR O's
THERE'S THE CEREAL. THERE'S THE MILK. GET IT **YOURSELF!**
MILK
STAR O's
I'M NOT **THAT** HUNGRY!
MILK
STAR O's
Bob and jay

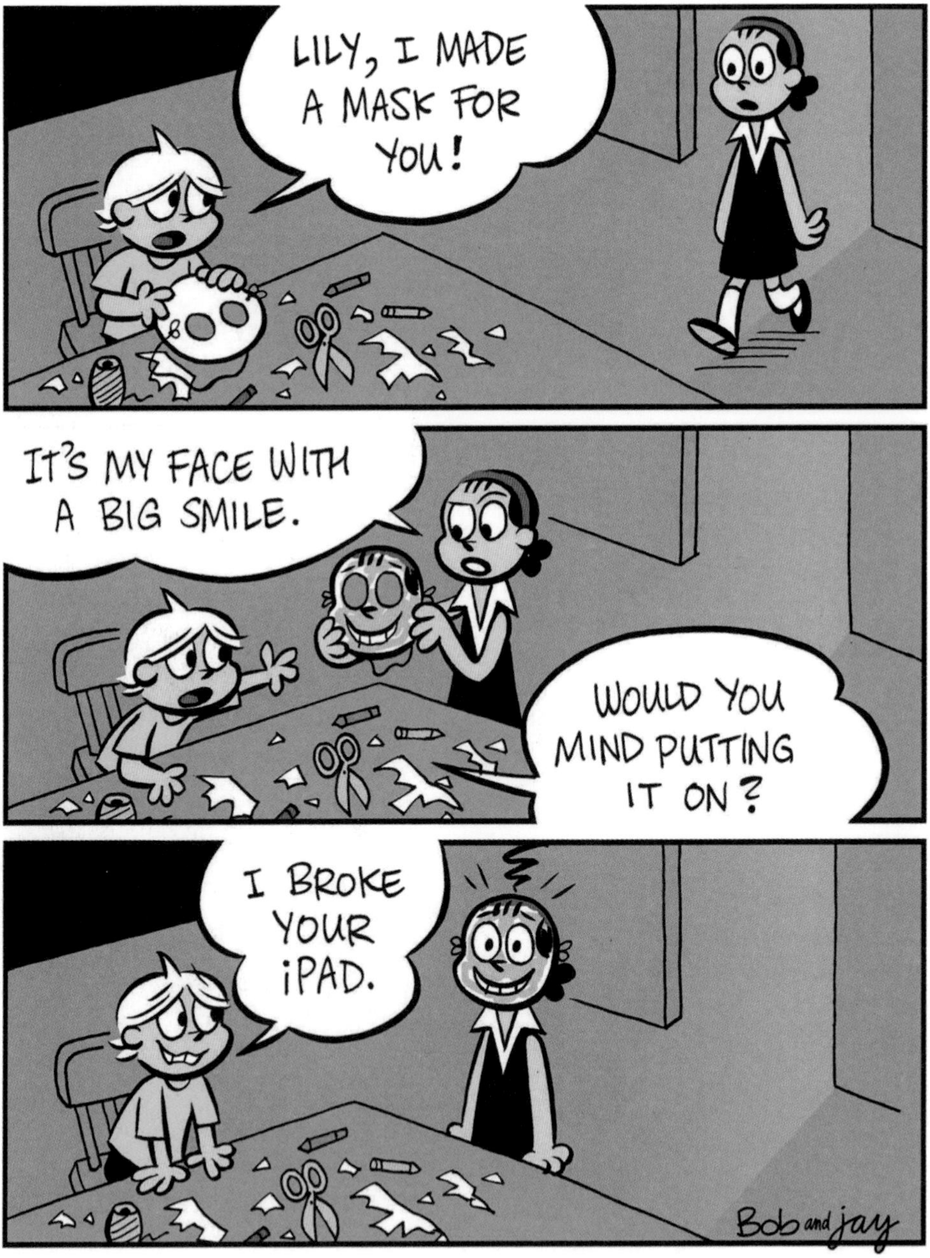
LILY, I MADE A MASK FOR YOU!
IT'S MY FACE WITH A BIG SMILE.
WOULD YOU MIND PUTTING IT ON?
I BROKE YOUR iPAD.
Bob and jay

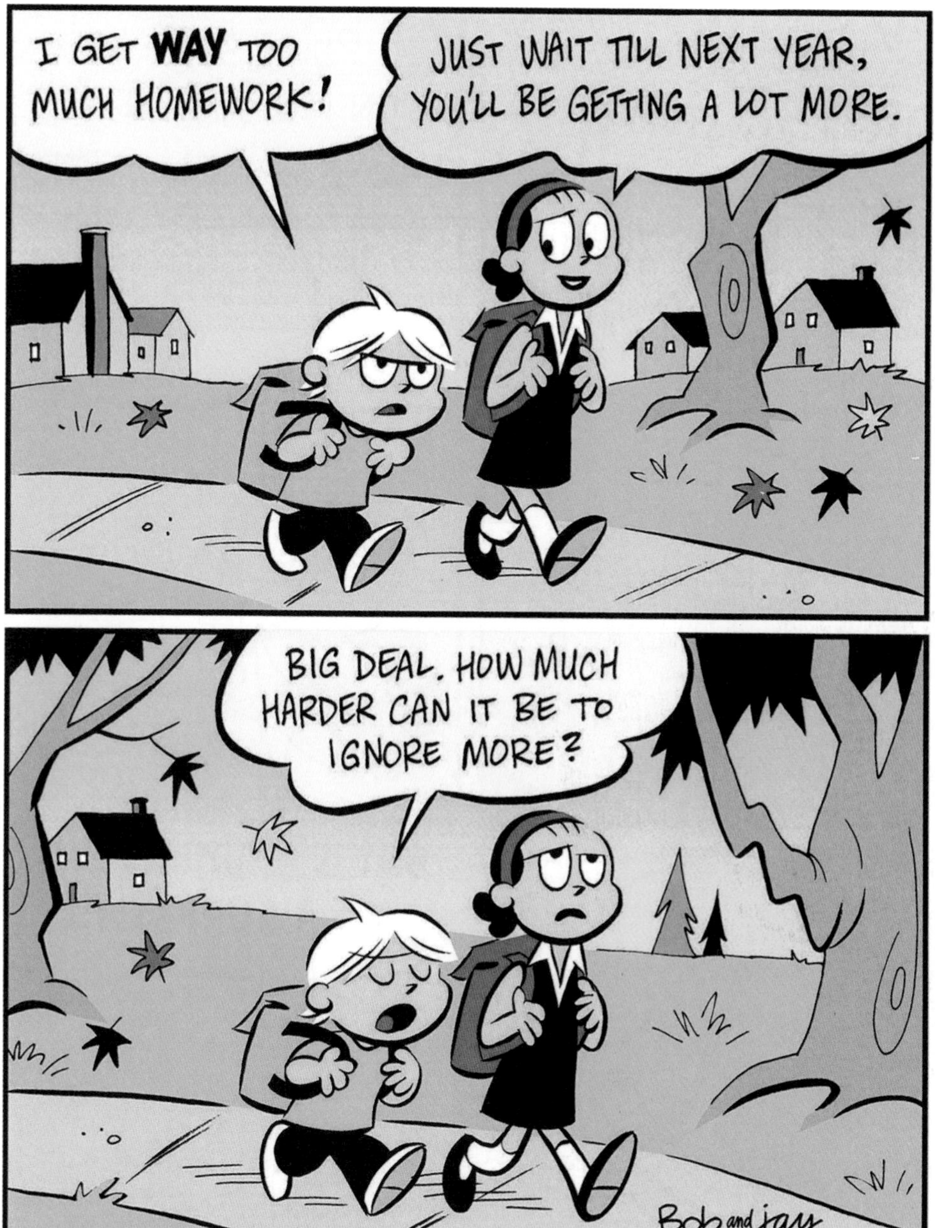
I GET **WAY** TOO MUCH HOMEWORK!
JUST WAIT TILL NEXT YEAR, YOU'LL BE GETTING A LOT MORE.
BIG DEAL. HOW MUCH HARDER CAN IT BE TO IGNORE MORE?
Bob and jay

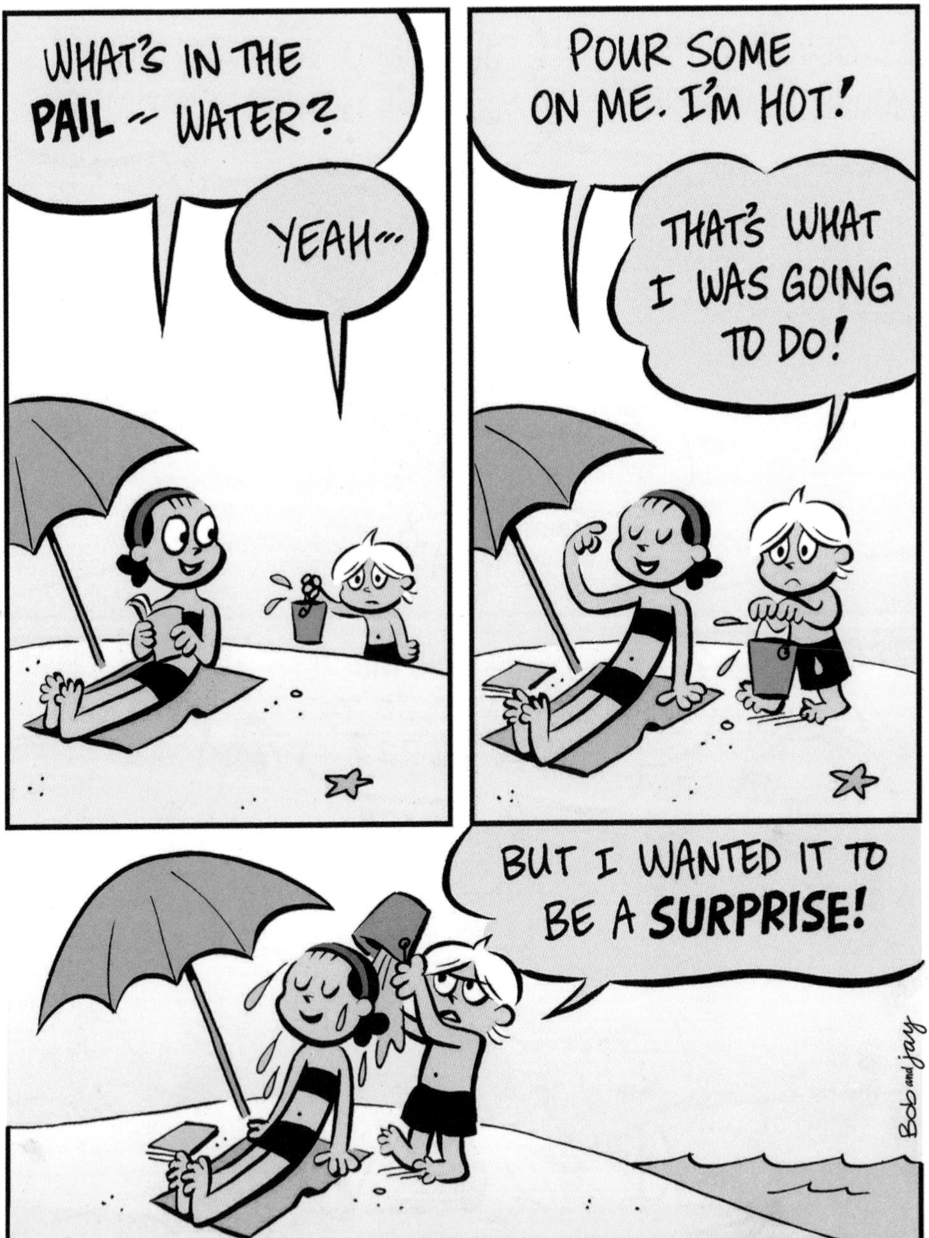
WHAT'S IN THE PAIL -- WATER?
YEAH...
POUR SOME ON ME. I'M HOT!
THAT'S WHAT I WAS GOING TO DO!
BUT I WANTED IT TO BE A SURPRISE!
Bob and jay

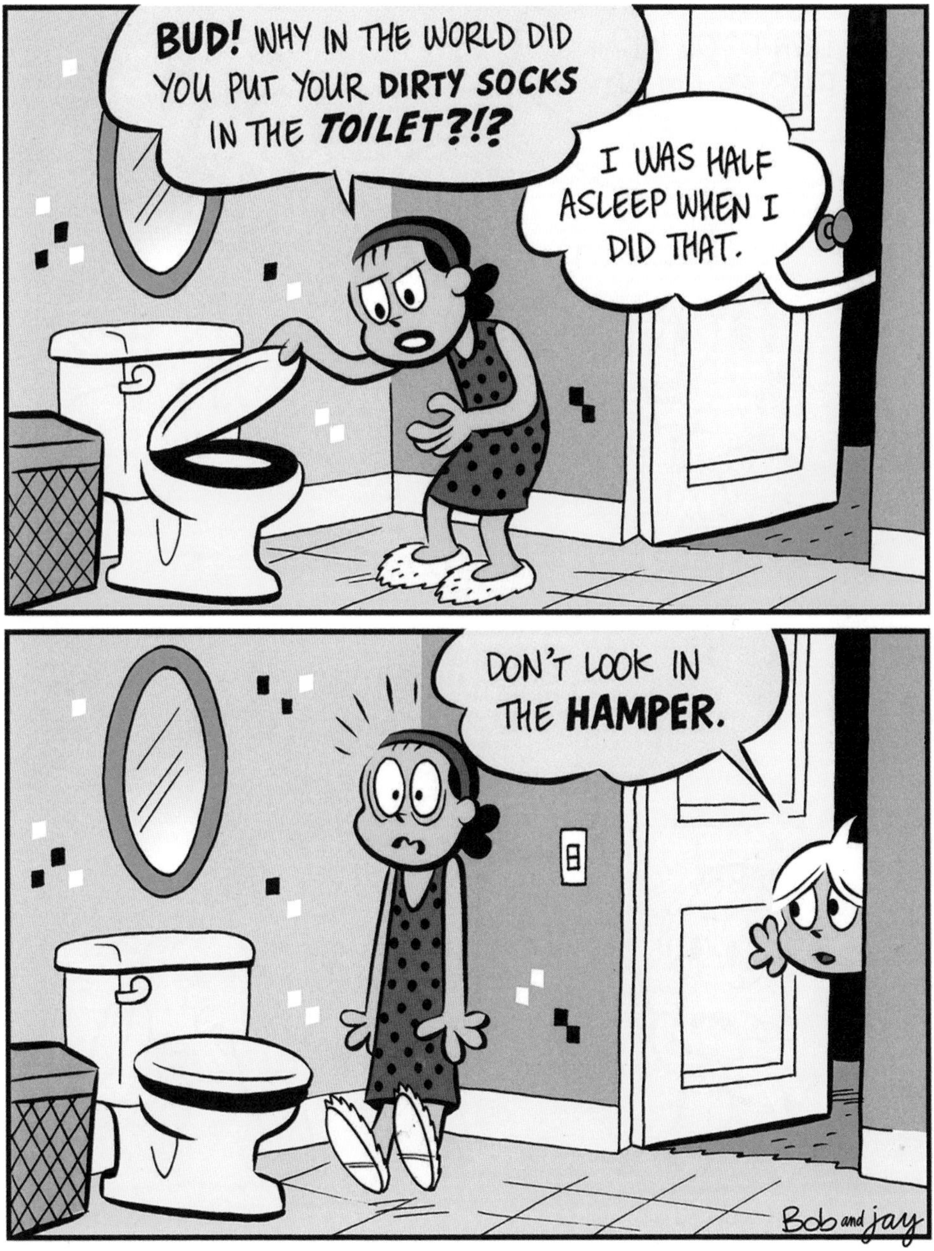
BUD! WHY IN THE WORLD DID YOU PUT YOUR DIRTY SOCKS IN THE TOILET?!?
I WAS HALF ASLEEP WHEN I DID THAT.
DON'T LOOK IN THE HAMPER.
Bob and jay

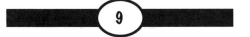

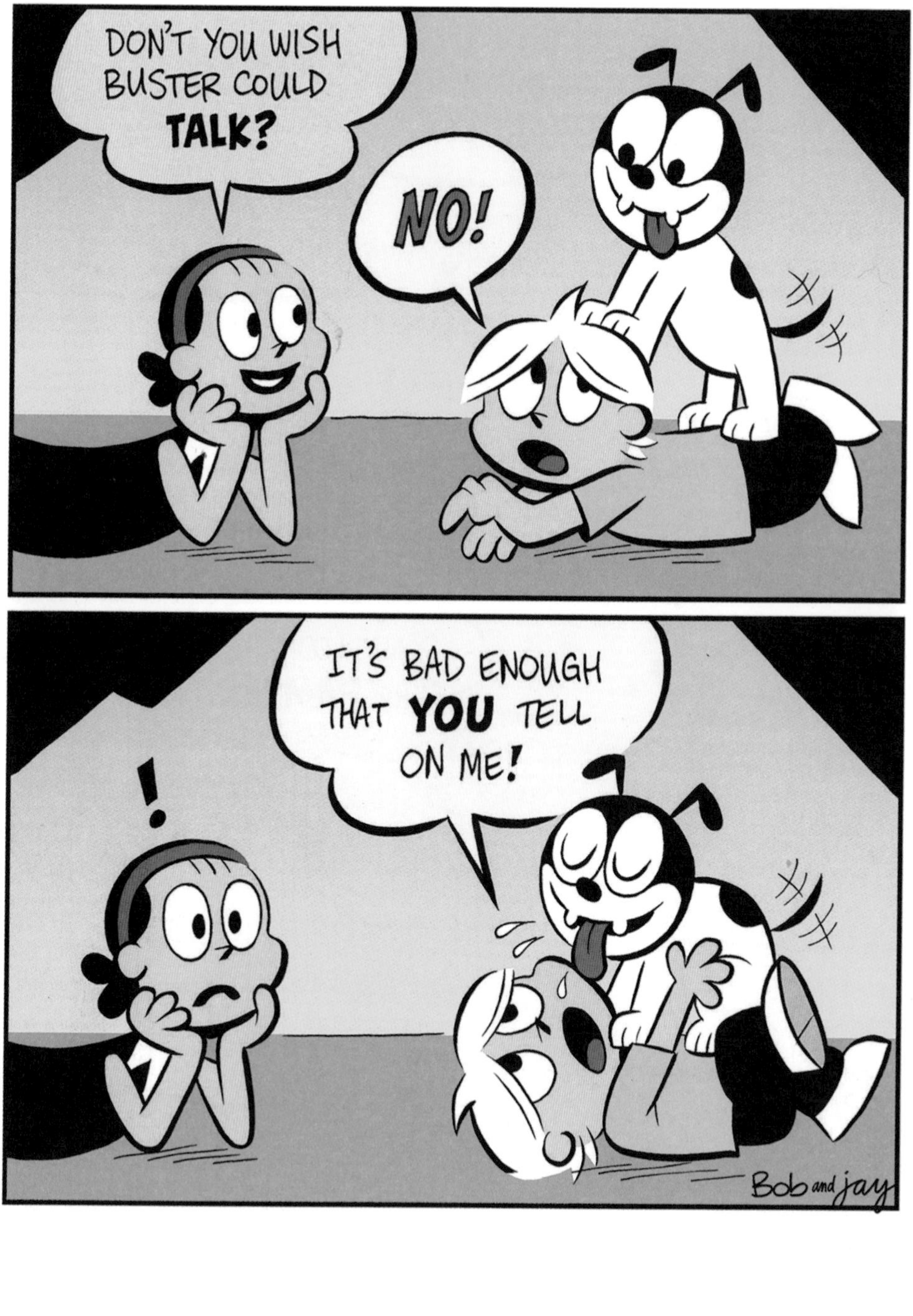
DON'T YOU WISH BUSTER COULD **TALK?**
NO!
IT'S BAD ENOUGH THAT **YOU** TELL ON ME!
!
Bob and jay

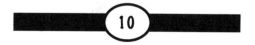

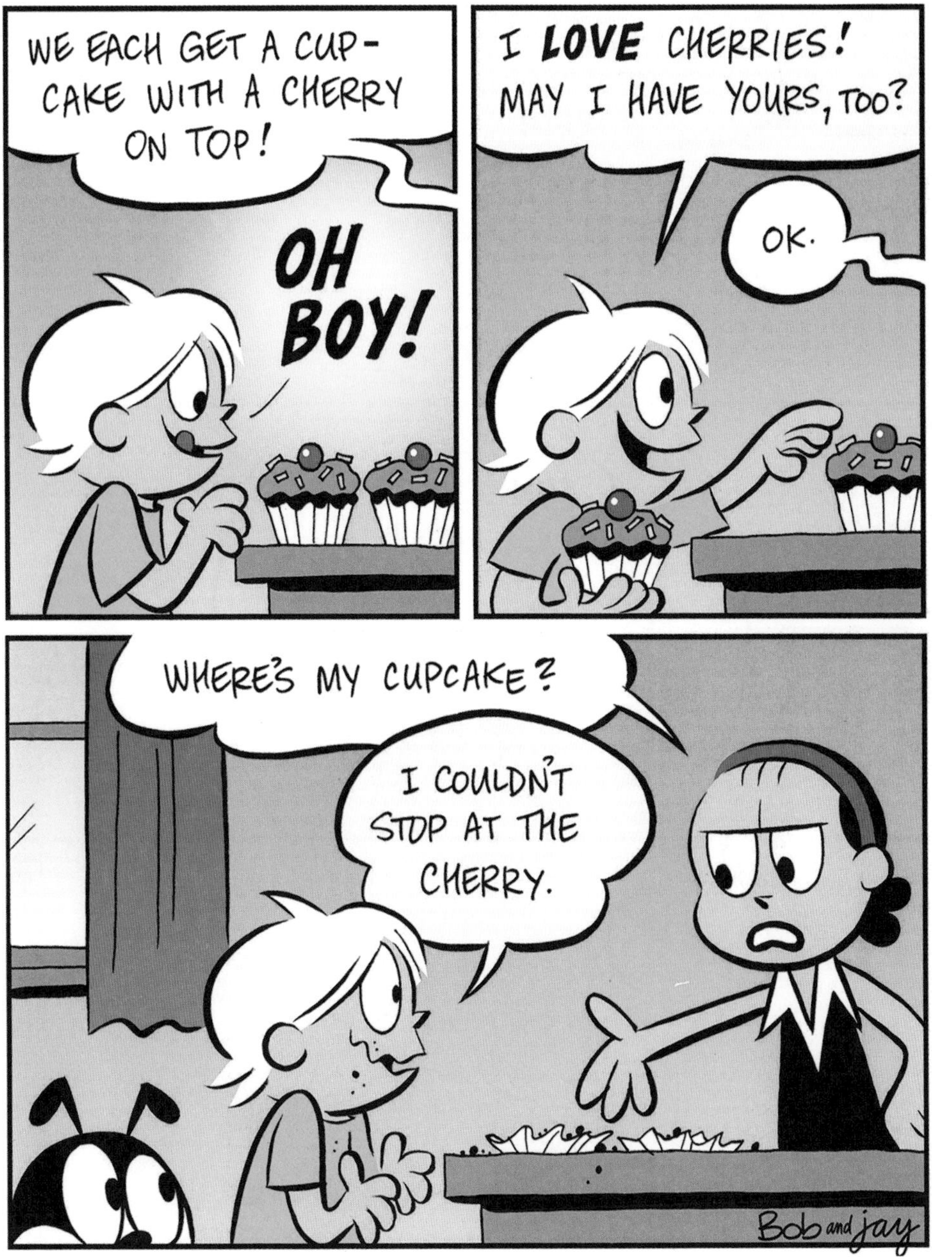
WE EACH GET A CUP-CAKE WITH A CHERRY ON TOP!
OH BOY!
I LOVE CHERRIES! MAY I HAVE YOURS, TOO?
OK.
WHERE'S MY CUPCAKE?
I COULDN'T STOP AT THE CHERRY.
Bob and jay

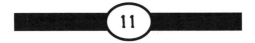

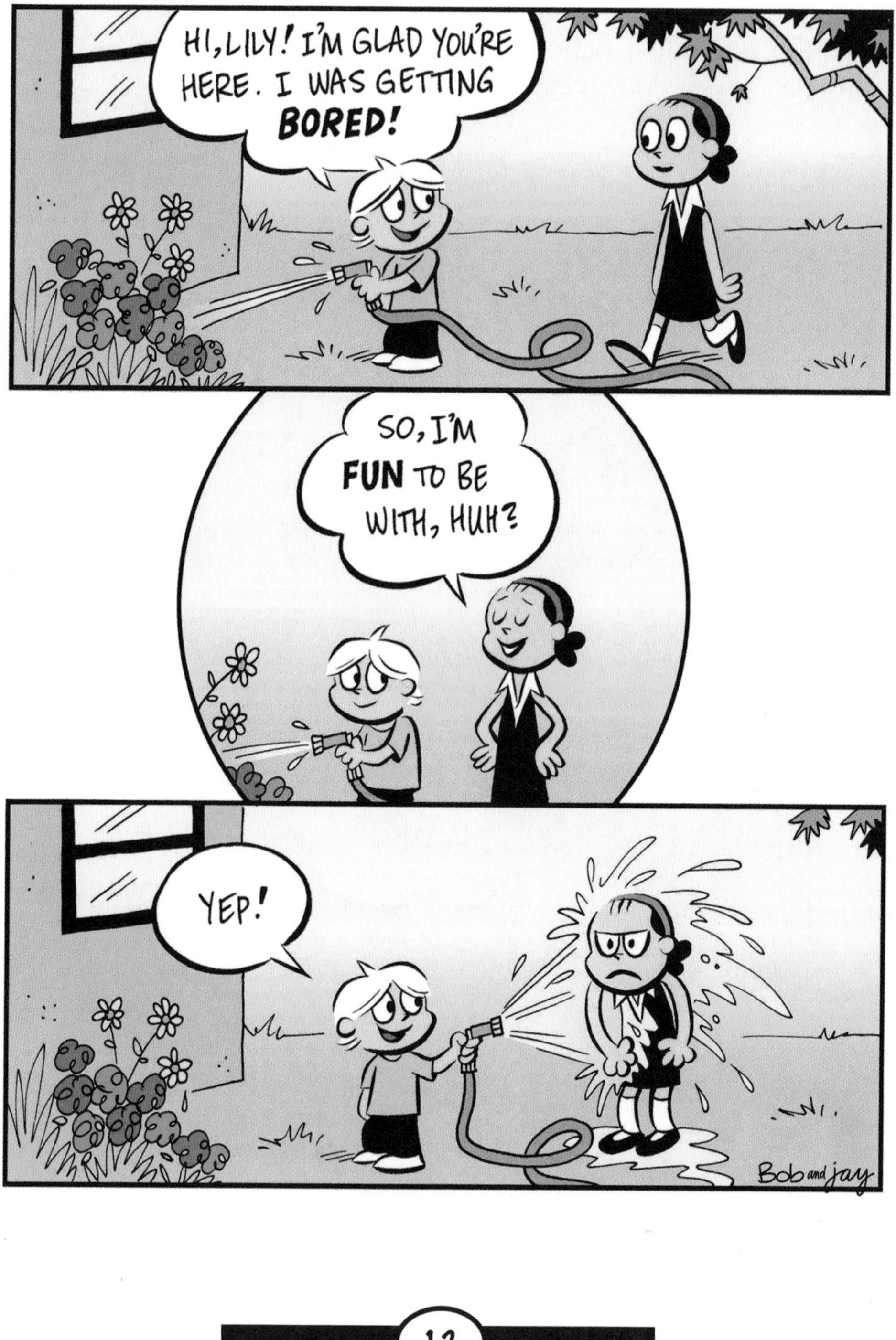
HI, LILY! I'M GLAD YOU'RE HERE. I WAS GETTING **BORED!**
SO, I'M **FUN** TO BE WITH, HUH?
YEP!
Bob and jay

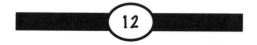

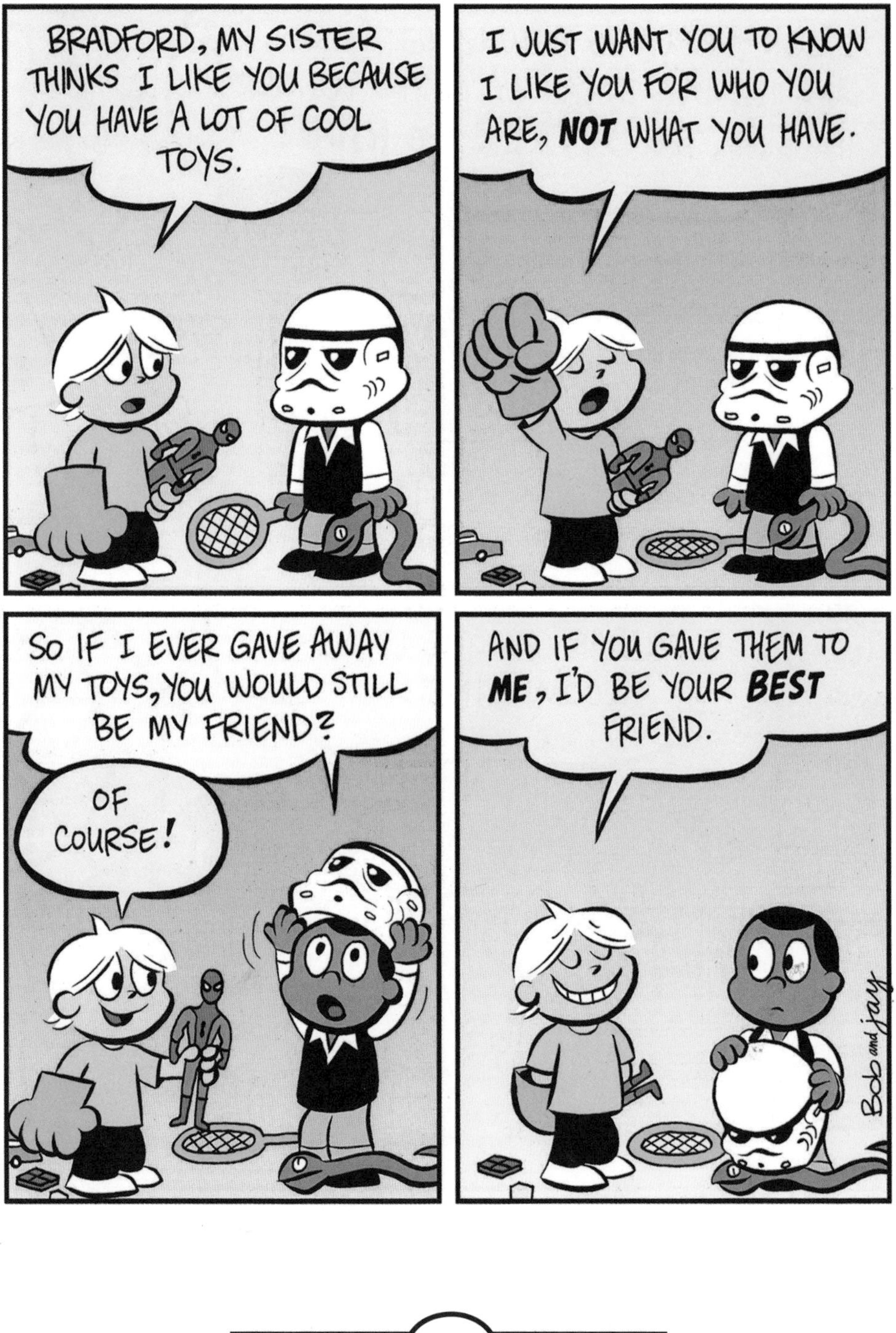
BRADFORD, MY SISTER THINKS I LIKE YOU BECAUSE YOU HAVE A LOT OF COOL TOYS.
I JUST WANT YOU TO KNOW I LIKE YOU FOR WHO YOU ARE, NOT WHAT YOU HAVE.
SO IF I EVER GAVE AWAY MY TOYS, YOU WOULD STILL BE MY FRIEND?
OF COURSE!
AND IF YOU GAVE THEM TO ME, I'D BE YOUR BEST FRIEND.
Bob and jay

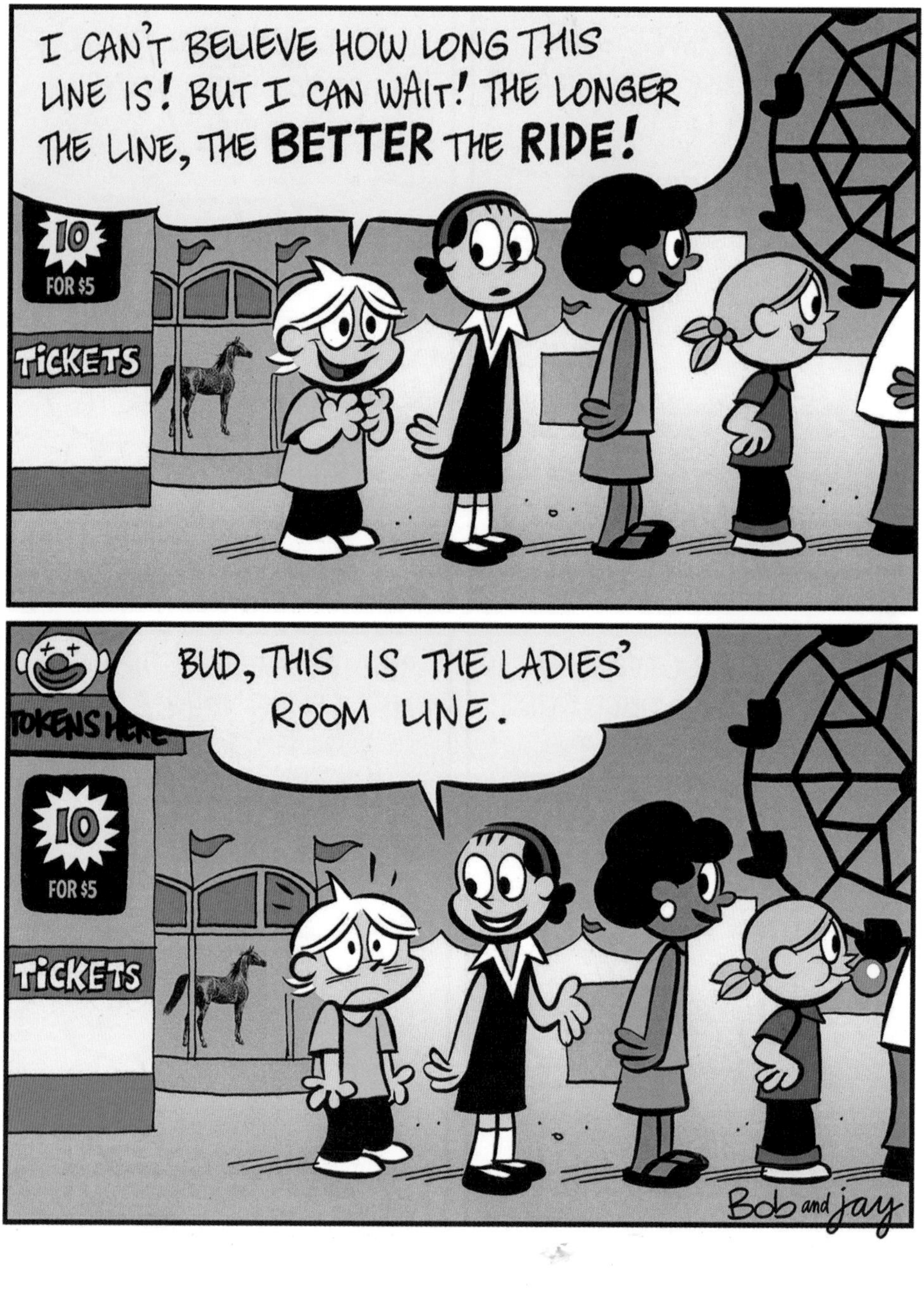
I CAN'T BELIEVE HOW LONG THIS LINE IS! BUT I CAN WAIT! THE LONGER THE LINE, THE BETTER THE RIDE!
10 FOR $5
TICKETS
TOKENS HERE
BUD, THIS IS THE LADIES' ROOM LINE.
10 FOR $5
TICKETS
Bob and jay

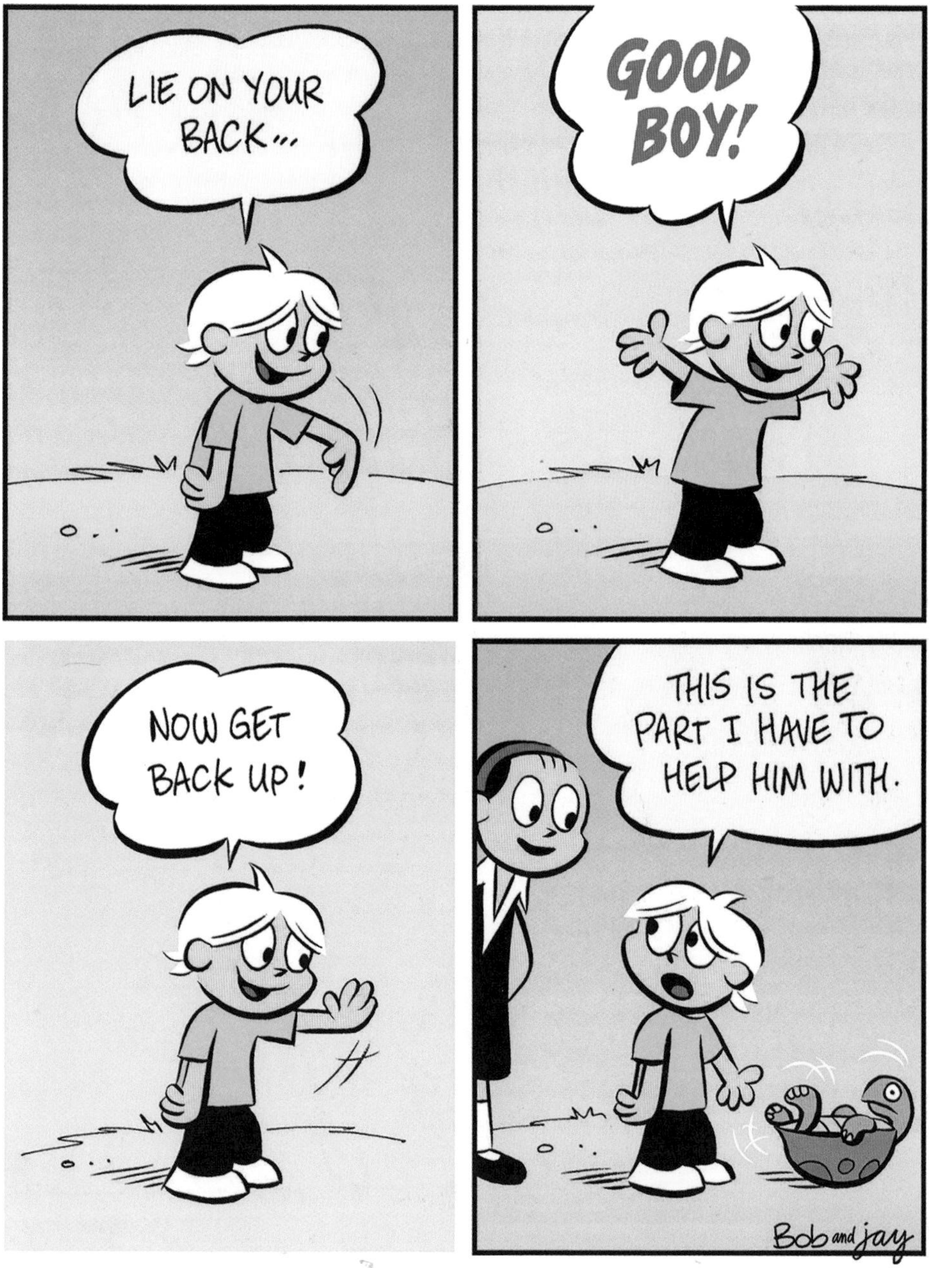
LIE ON YOUR BACK...
GOOD BOY!
NOW GET BACK UP!
THIS IS THE PART I HAVE TO HELP HIM WITH.
Bob and jay

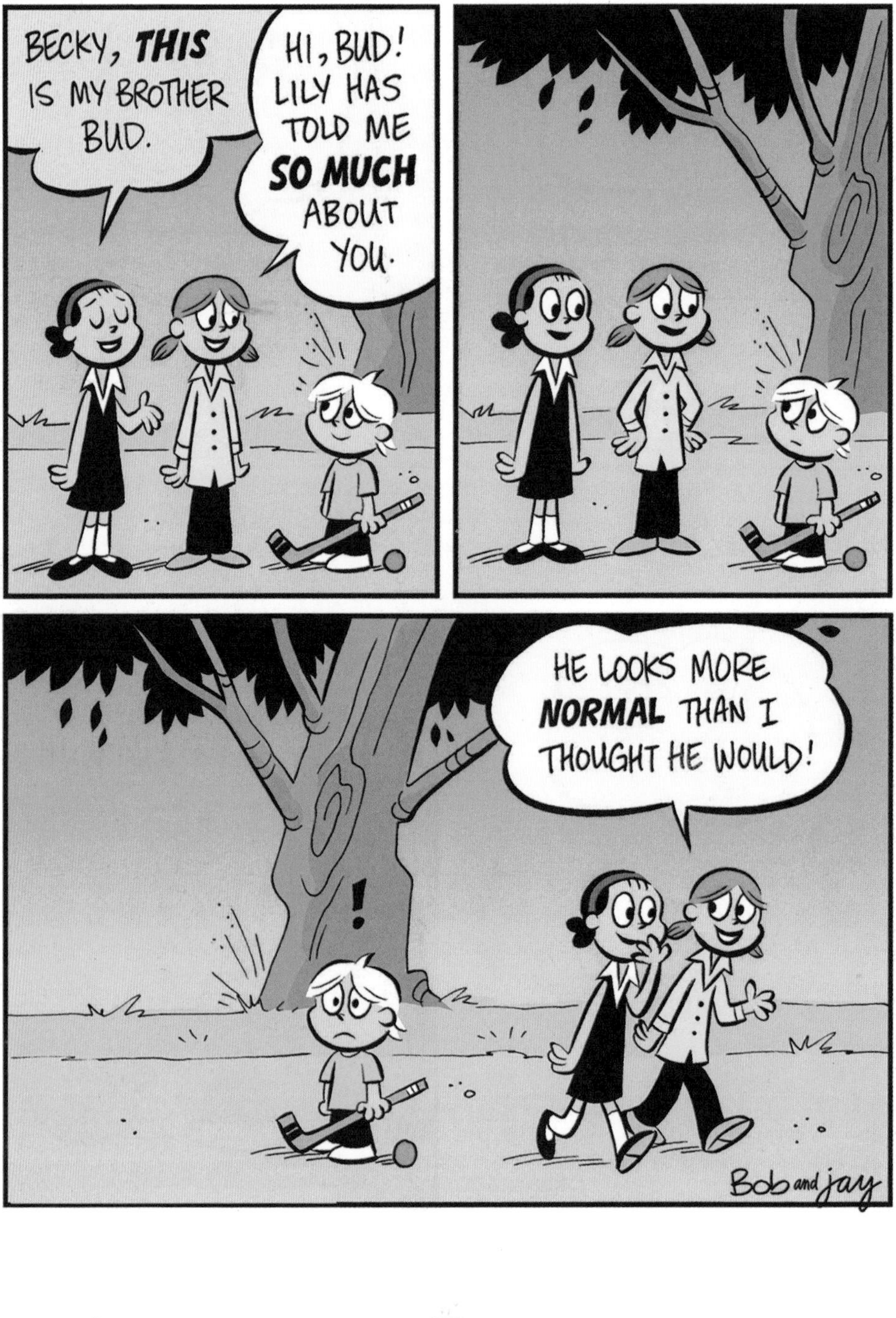
BECKY, **THIS** IS MY BROTHER BUD.
HI, BUD! LILY HAS TOLD ME **SO MUCH** ABOUT YOU.
!
HE LOOKS MORE **NORMAL** THAN I THOUGHT HE WOULD!
Bob and jay

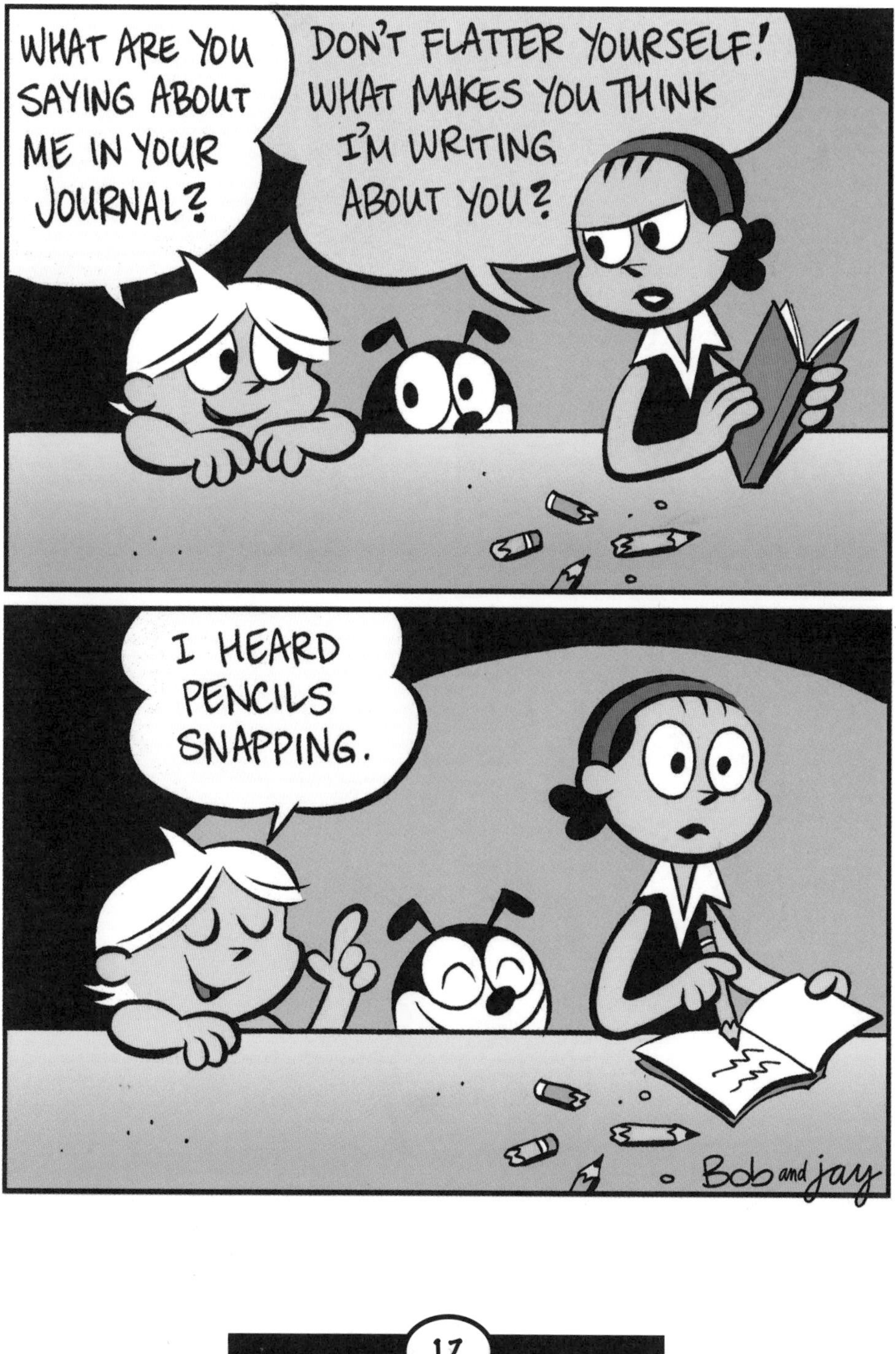
WHAT ARE YOU SAYING ABOUT ME IN YOUR JOURNAL?
DON'T FLATTER YOURSELF! WHAT MAKES YOU THINK I'M WRITING ABOUT YOU?
I HEARD PENCILS SNAPPING.
Bob and jay

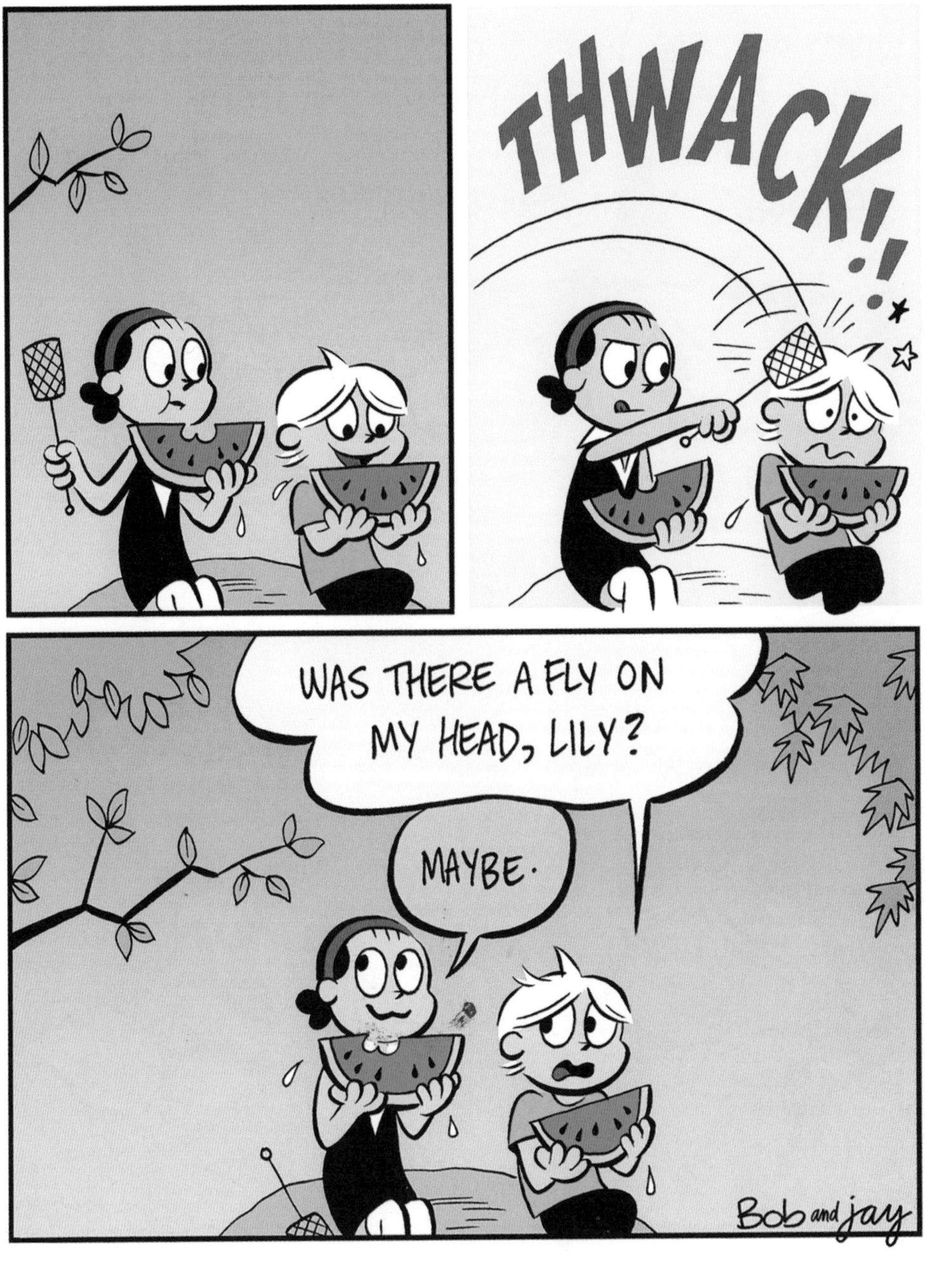
THWACK!!
WAS THERE A FLY ON MY HEAD, LILY?
MAYBE.
Bob and jay

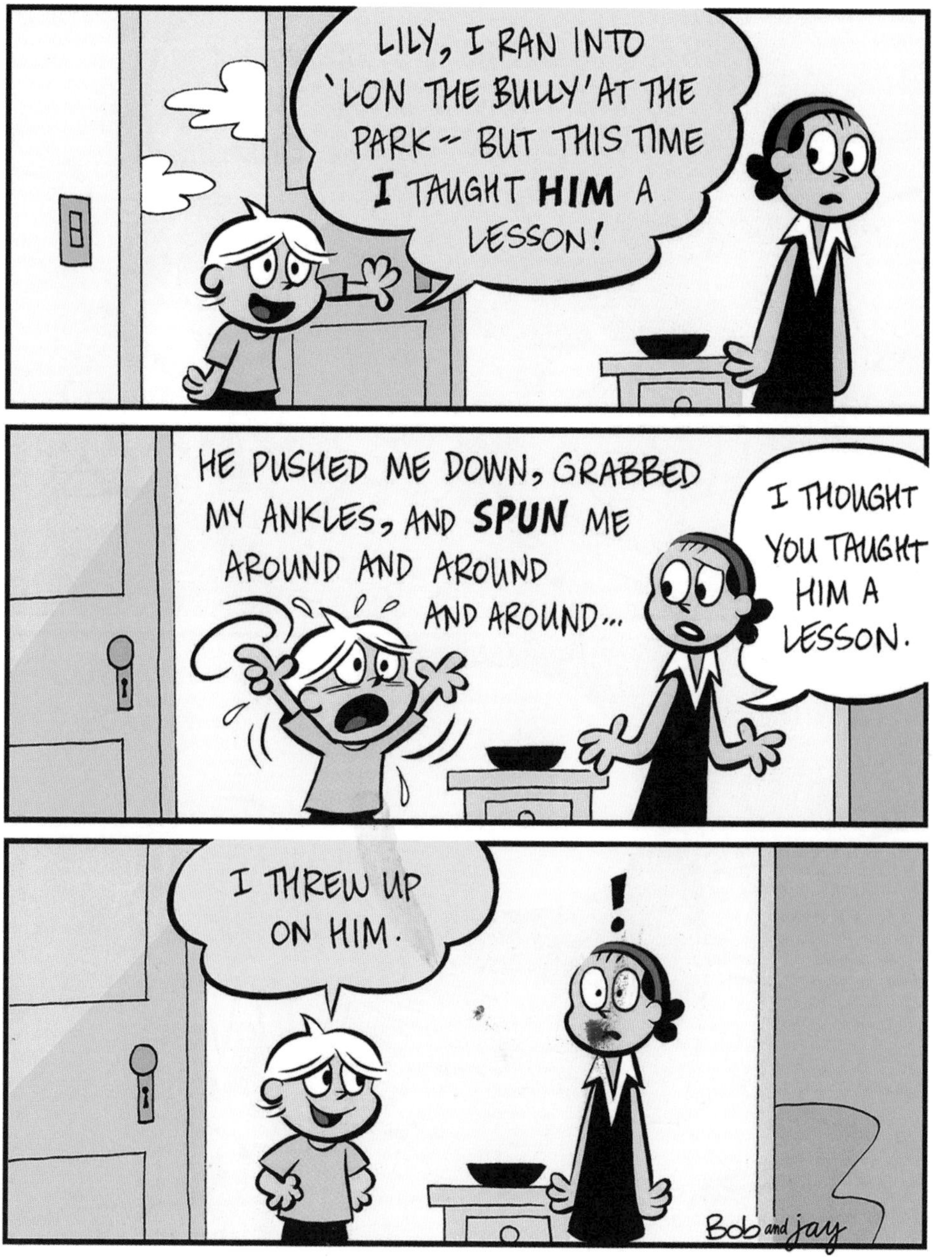
LILY, I RAN INTO 'LON THE BULLY' AT THE PARK -- BUT THIS TIME I TAUGHT **HIM** A LESSON!
HE PUSHED ME DOWN, GRABBED MY ANKLES, AND **SPUN** ME AROUND AND AROUND AND AROUND...
I THOUGHT YOU TAUGHT HIM A LESSON.
I THREW UP ON HIM.
!
Bob and jay

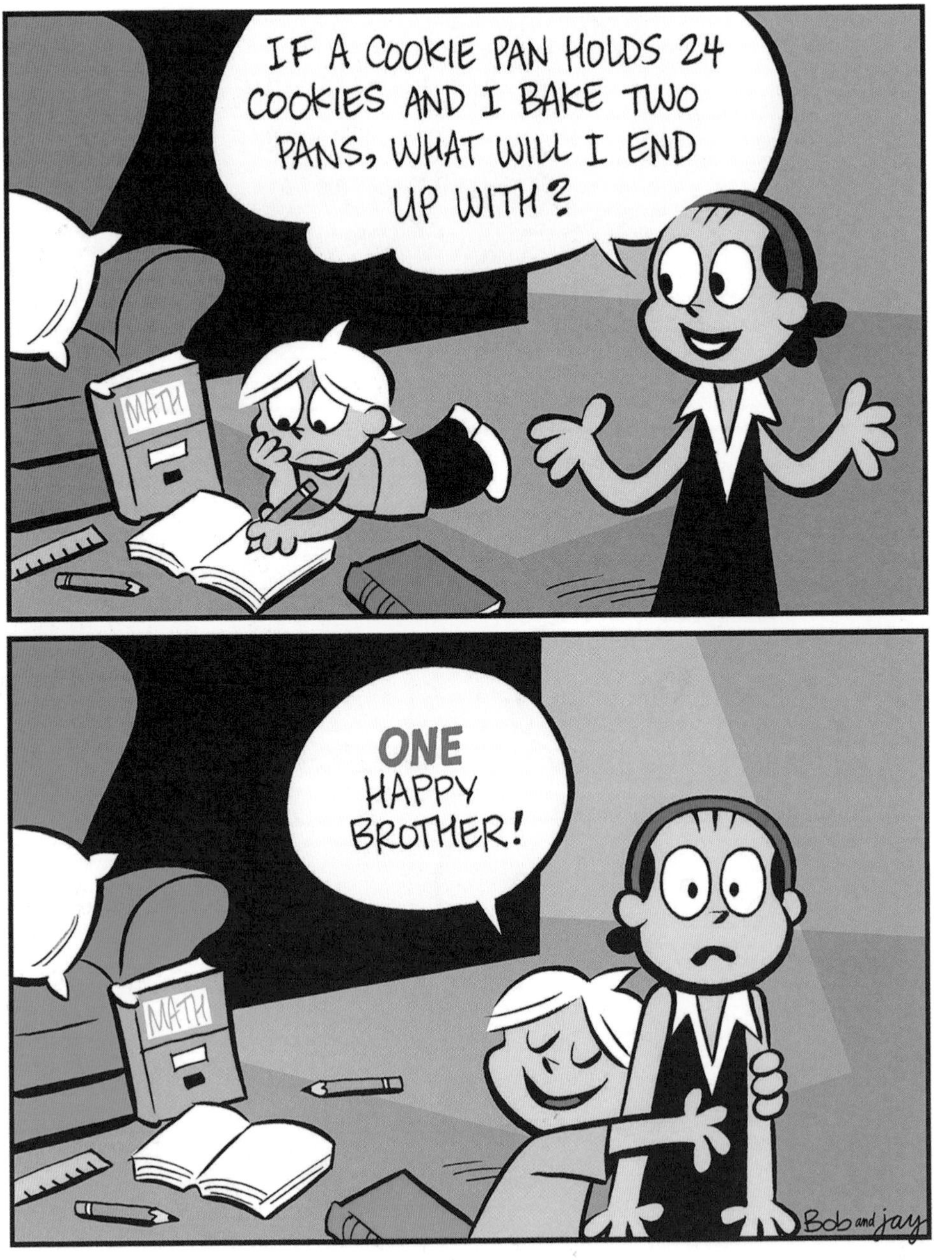
IF A COOKIE PAN HOLDS 24 COOKIES AND I BAKE TWO PANS, WHAT WILL I END UP WITH?
MATH
ONE HAPPY BROTHER!
MATH
Bob and jay

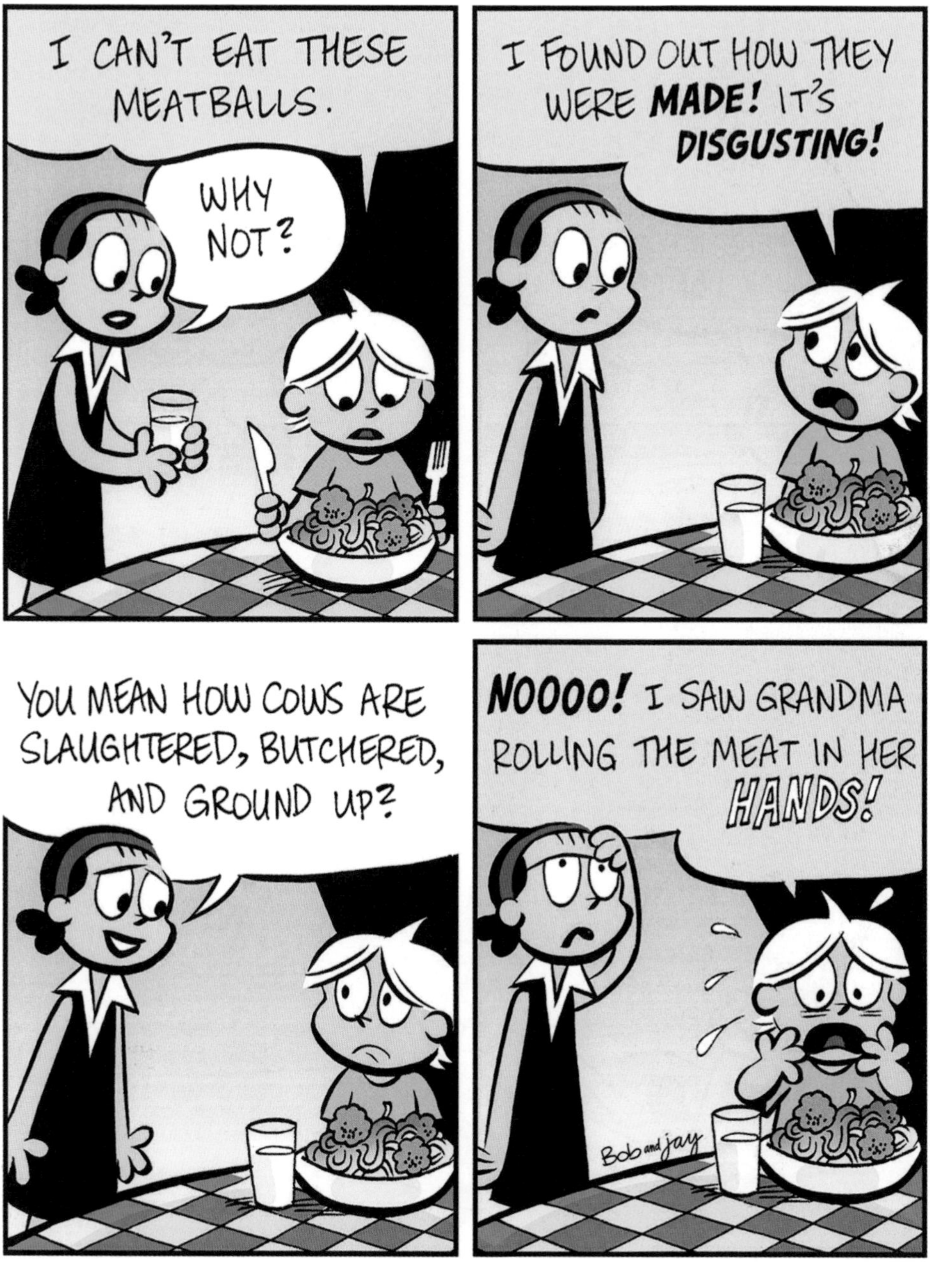
I CAN'T EAT THESE MEATBALLS.
WHY NOT?
I FOUND OUT HOW THEY WERE MADE! IT'S DISGUSTING!
YOU MEAN HOW COWS ARE SLAUGHTERED, BUTCHERED, AND GROUND UP?
NOOOO! I SAW GRANDMA ROLLING THE MEAT IN HER HANDS!
Bob and jay

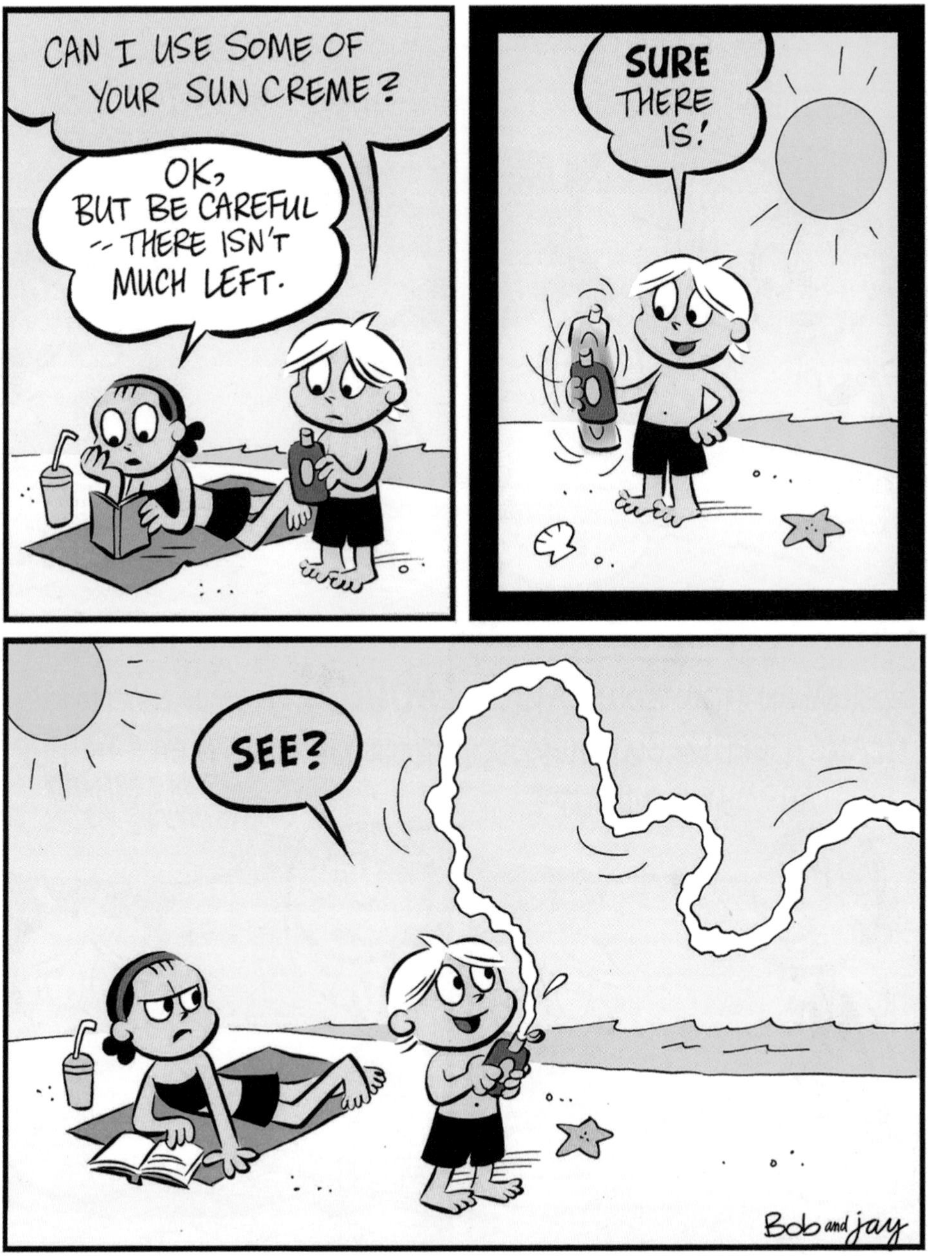
CAN I USE SOME OF YOUR SUN CREME?
OK, BUT BE CAREFUL -- THERE ISN'T MUCH LEFT.
SURE THERE IS!
SEE?
Bob and jay

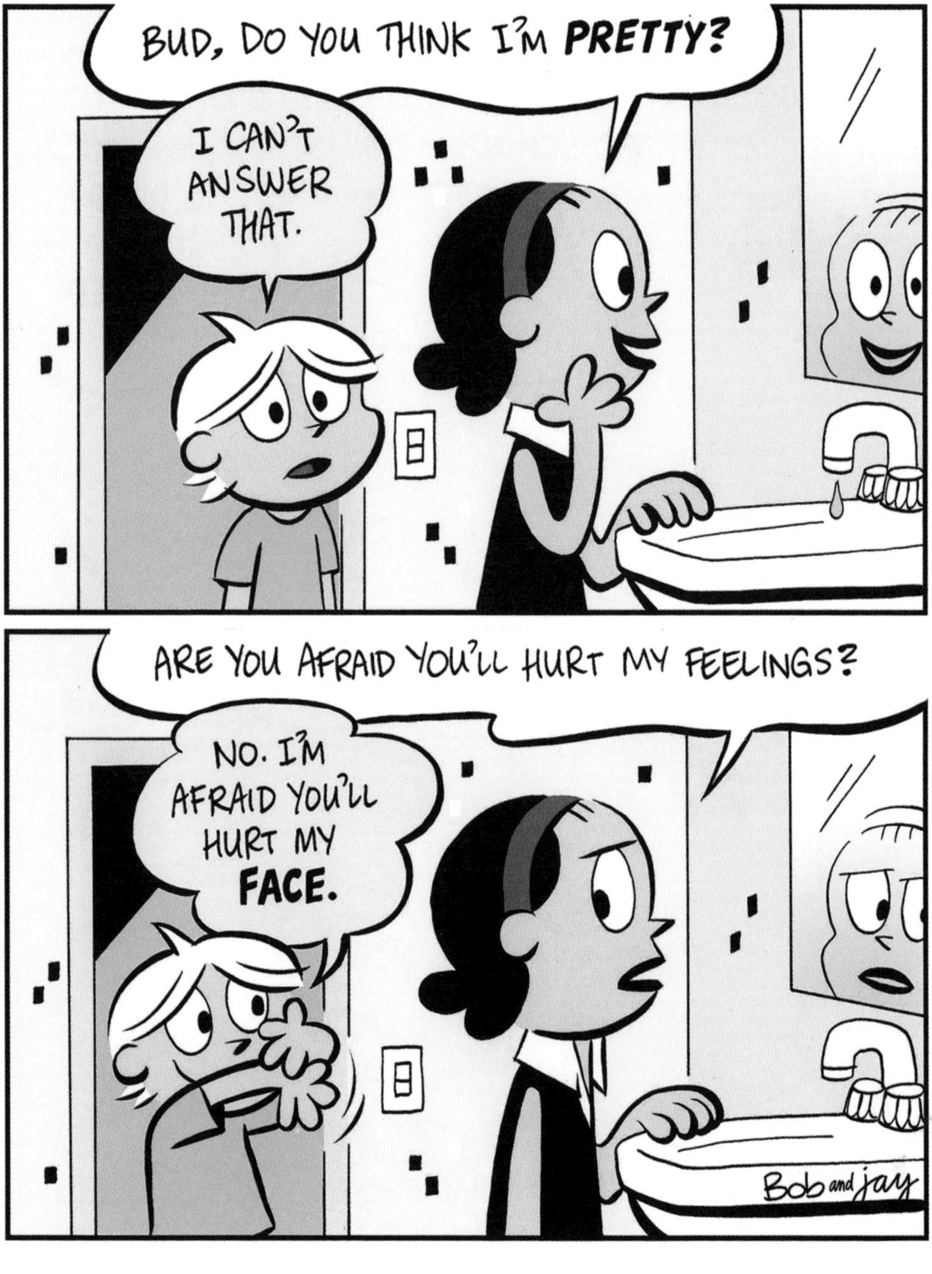
BUD, DO YOU THINK I'M PRETTY?
I CAN'T ANSWER THAT.
ARE YOU AFRAID YOU'LL HURT MY FEELINGS?
NO. I'M AFRAID YOU'LL HURT MY FACE.
Bob and jay

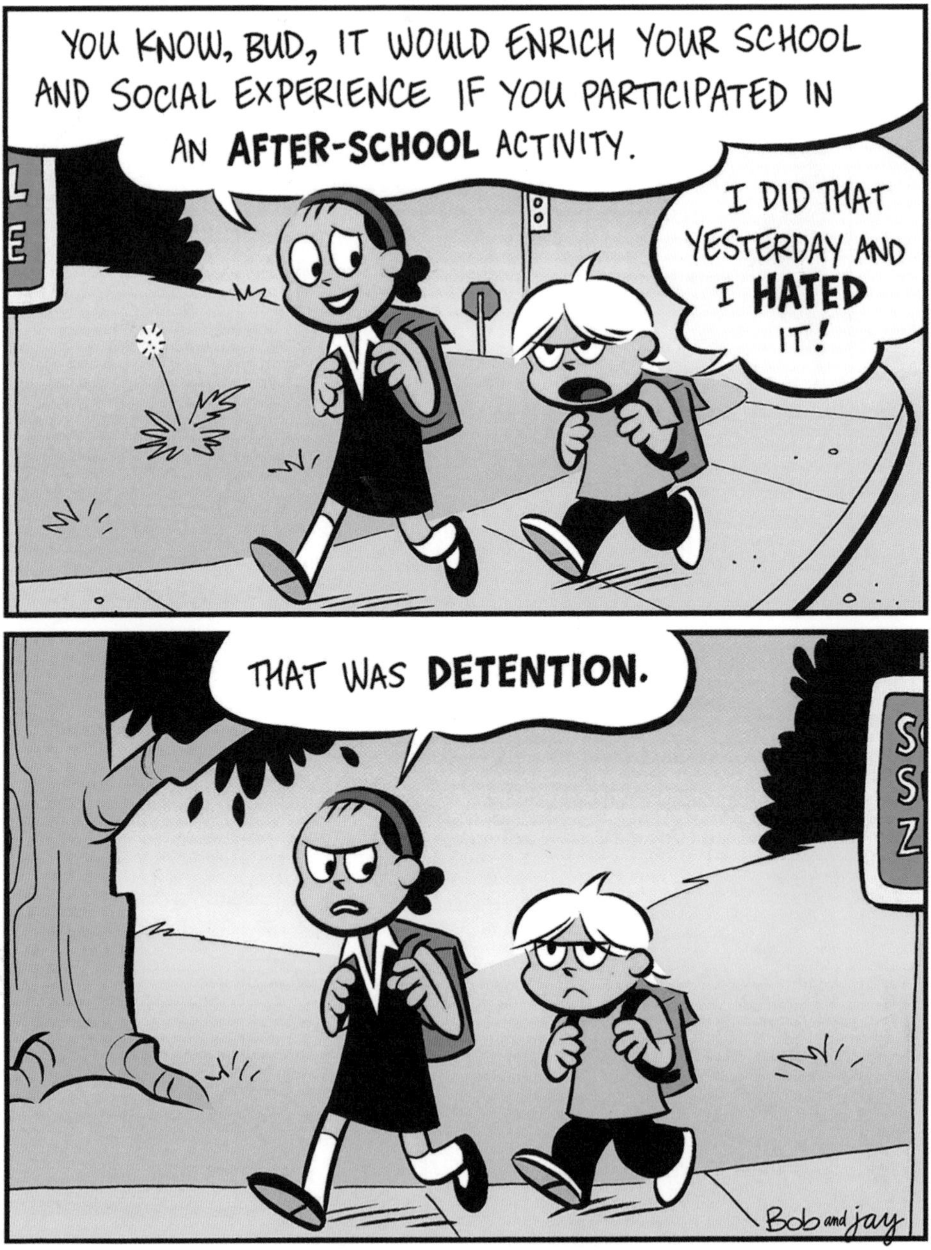
YOU KNOW, BUD, IT WOULD ENRICH YOUR SCHOOL AND SOCIAL EXPERIENCE IF YOU PARTICIPATED IN AN **AFTER-SCHOOL** ACTIVITY.
I DID THAT YESTERDAY AND I **HATED** IT!
THAT WAS **DETENTION.**
Bob and jay

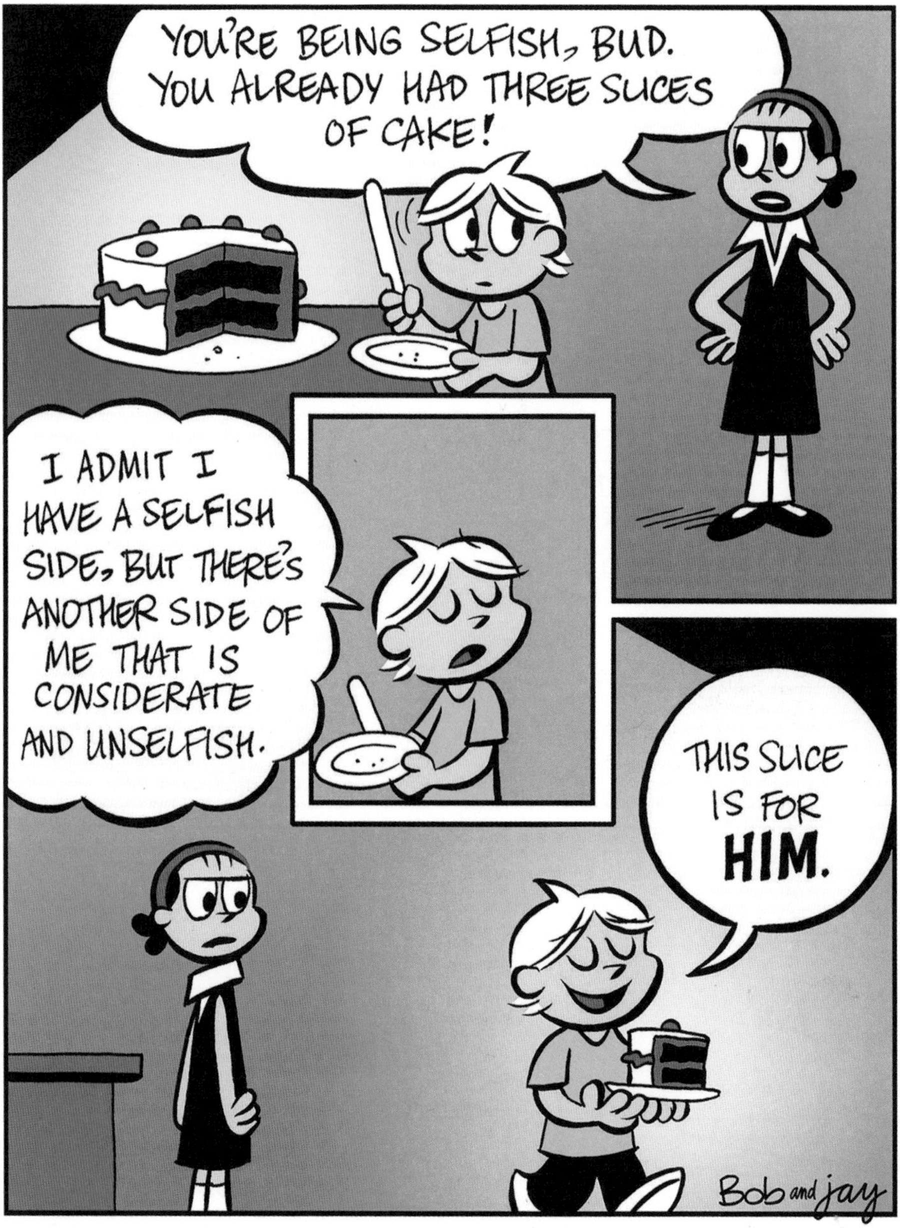
YOU'RE BEING SELFISH, BUD. YOU ALREADY HAD THREE SLICES OF CAKE!
I ADMIT I HAVE A SELFISH SIDE, BUT THERE'S ANOTHER SIDE OF ME THAT IS CONSIDERATE AND UNSELFISH.
THIS SLICE IS FOR **HIM.**
Bob and jay

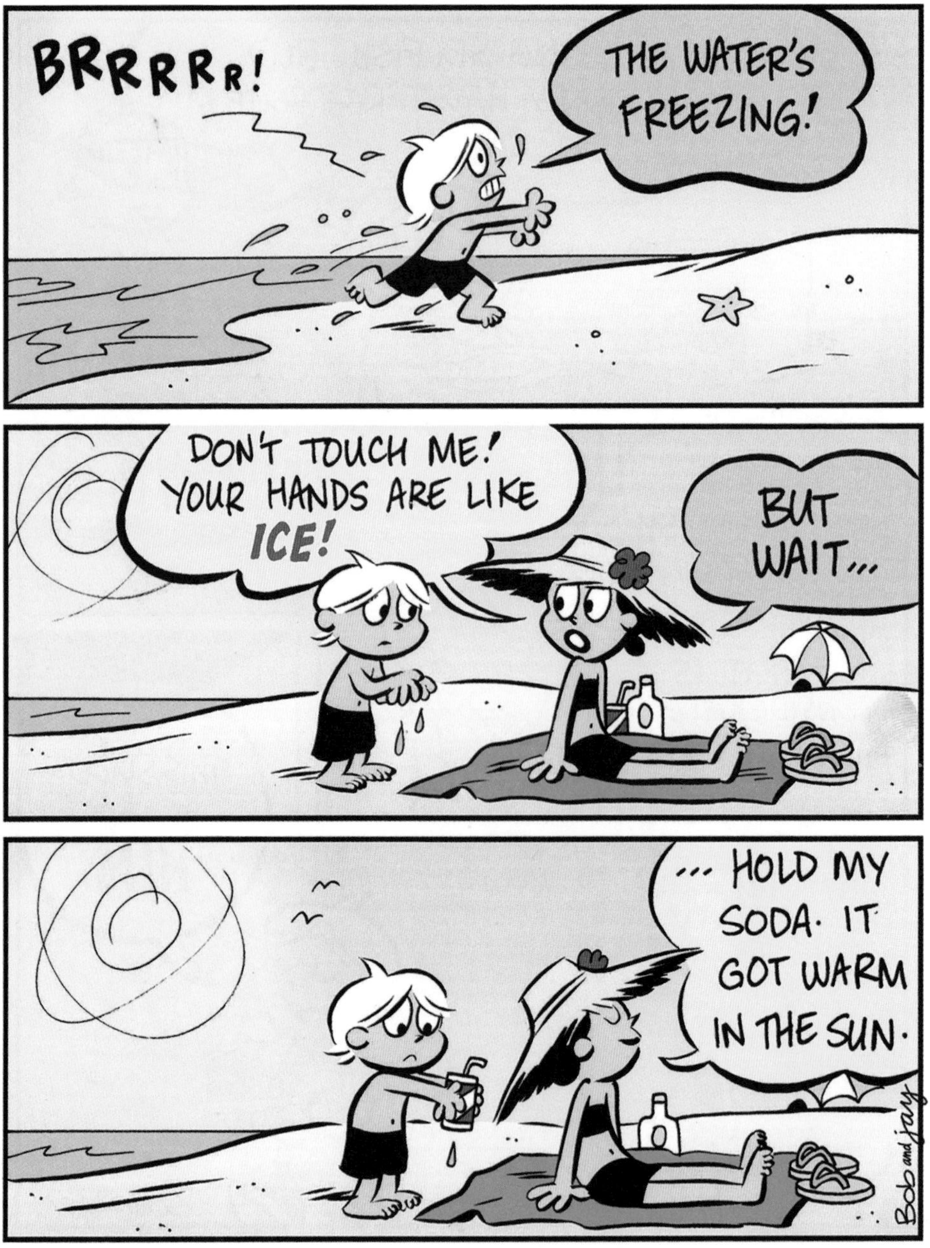
BRRRRRR!
THE WATER'S FREEZING!
DON'T TOUCH ME! YOUR HANDS ARE LIKE ICE!
BUT WAIT...
... HOLD MY SODA. IT GOT WARM IN THE SUN.
Bob and jay

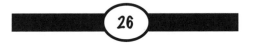

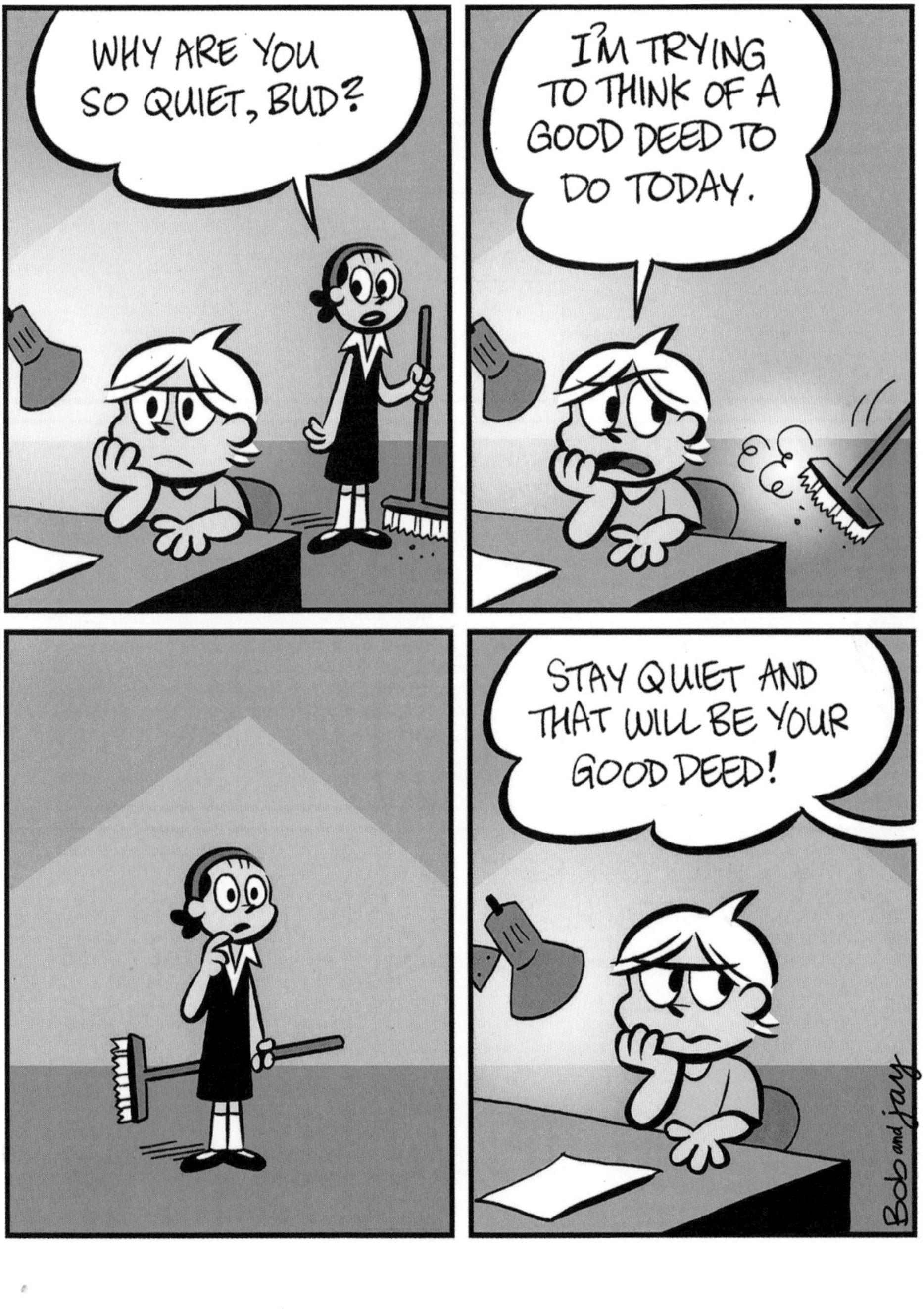
WHY ARE YOU SO QUIET, BUD?
I'M TRYING TO THINK OF A GOOD DEED TO DO TODAY.
STAY QUIET AND THAT WILL BE YOUR GOOD DEED!
Bob and jay

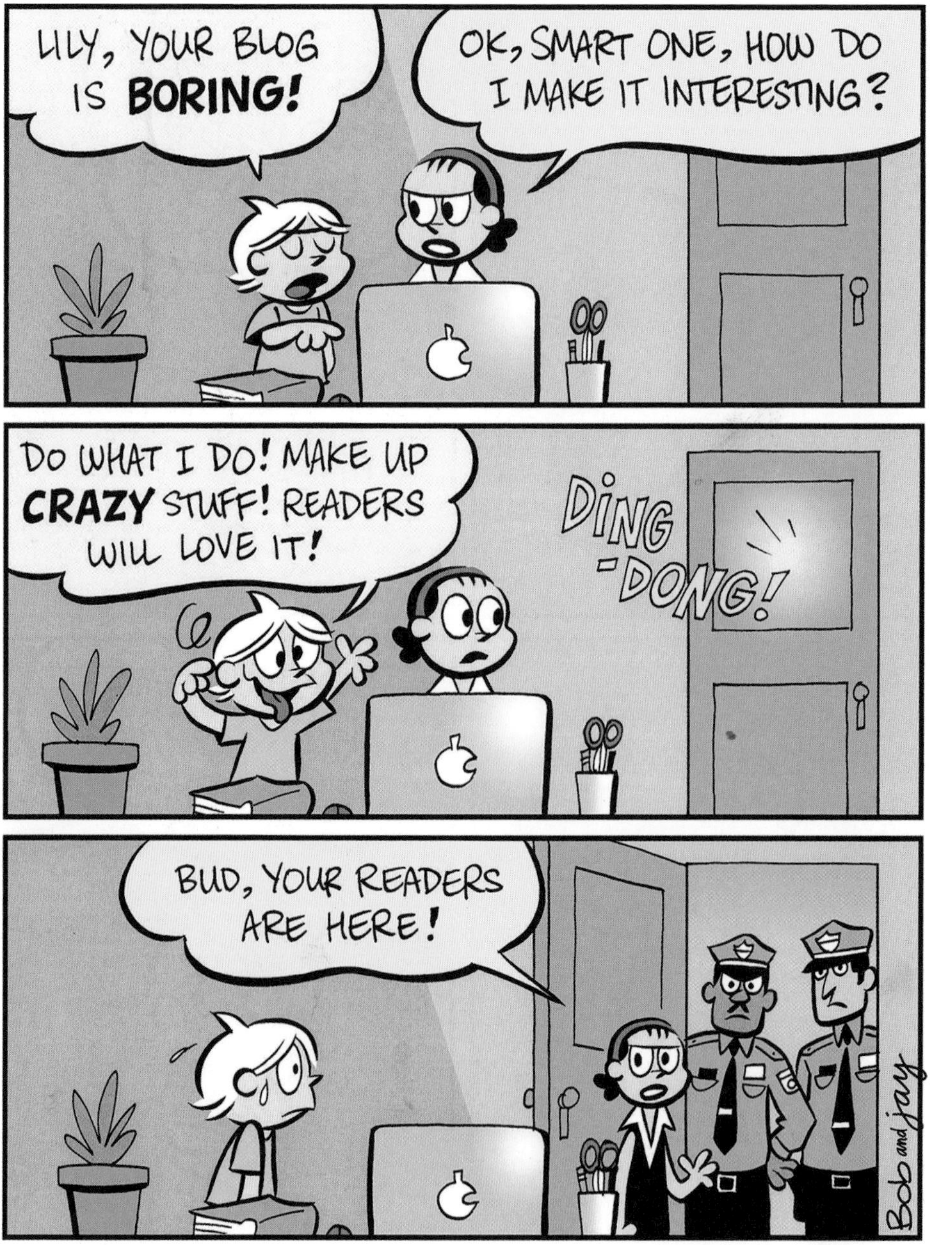
LILY, YOUR BLOG IS BORING!
OK, SMART ONE, HOW DO I MAKE IT INTERESTING?
DO WHAT I DO! MAKE UP CRAZY STUFF! READERS WILL LOVE IT!
DING-DONG!
BUD, YOUR READERS ARE HERE!
Bob and jay

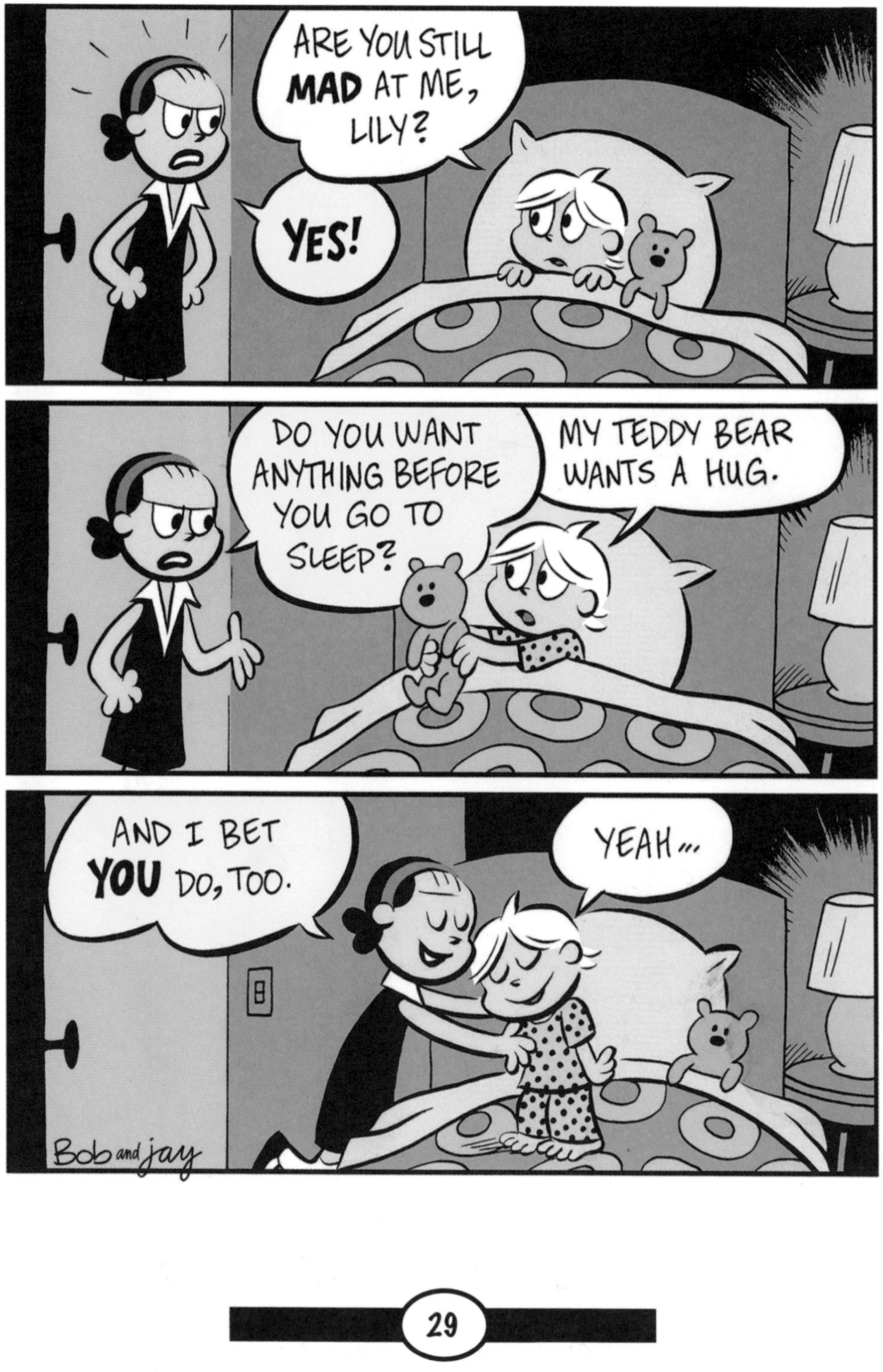
ARE YOU STILL **MAD** AT ME, LILY?
YES!
DO YOU WANT ANYTHING BEFORE YOU GO TO SLEEP?
MY TEDDY BEAR WANTS A HUG.
AND I BET **YOU** DO, TOO.
YEAH...
Bob and jay

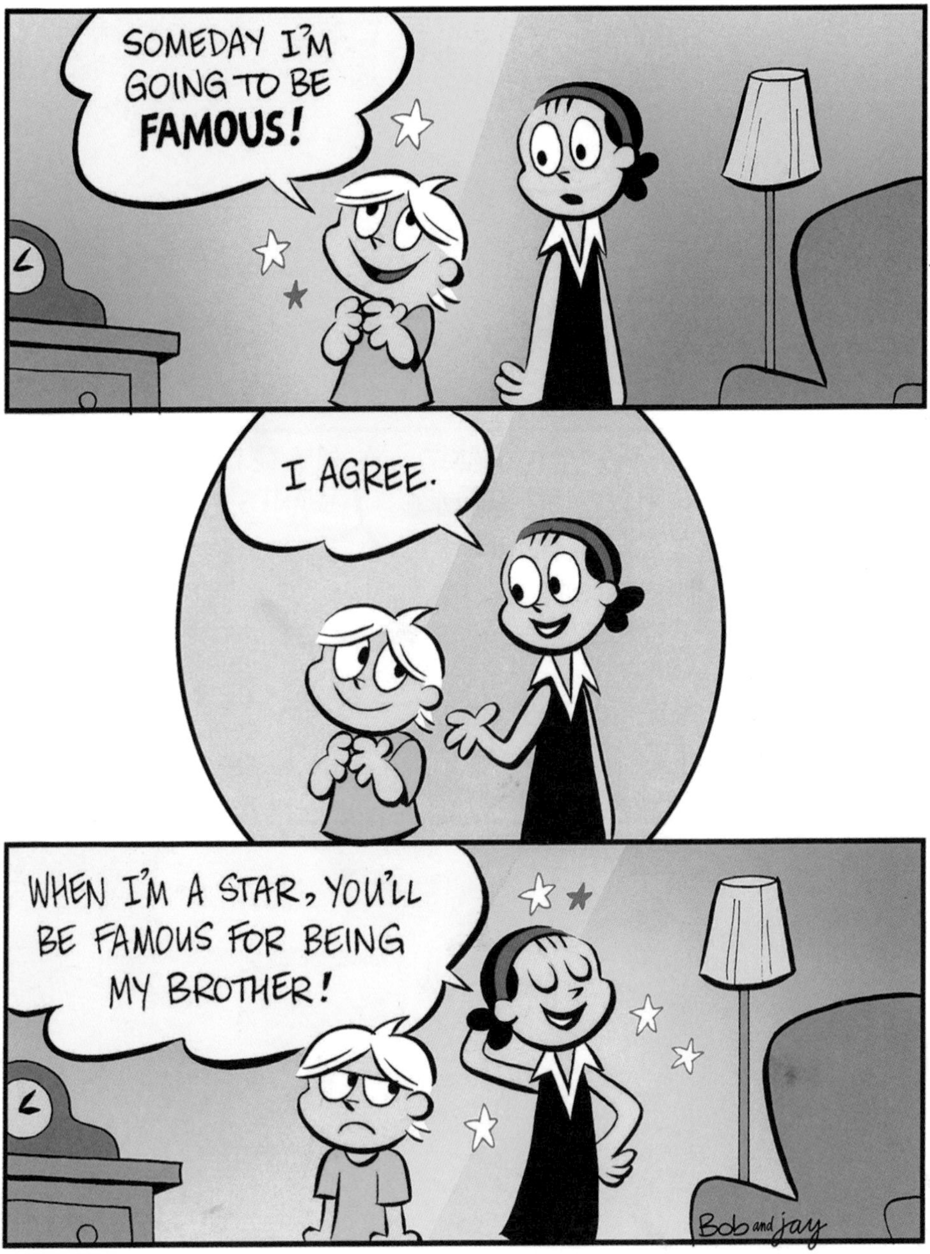
SOMEDAY I'M GOING TO BE FAMOUS!
I AGREE.
WHEN I'M A STAR, YOU'LL BE FAMOUS FOR BEING MY BROTHER!
Bob and jay

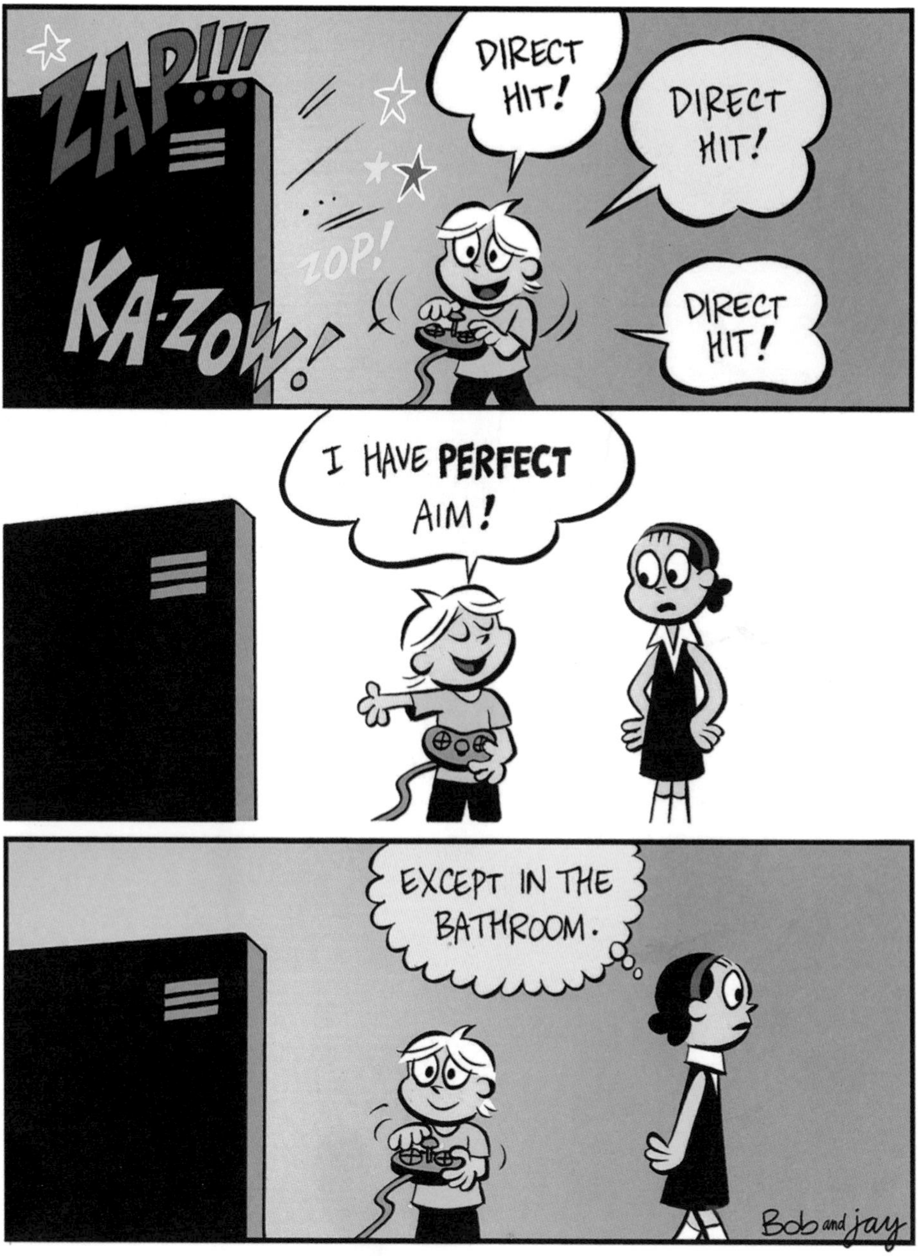
ZAP!!!
KA-ZOW!
ZOP!
DIRECT HIT!
DIRECT HIT!
DIRECT HIT!
I HAVE **PERFECT** AIM!
EXCEPT IN THE BATHROOM.
Bob and jay

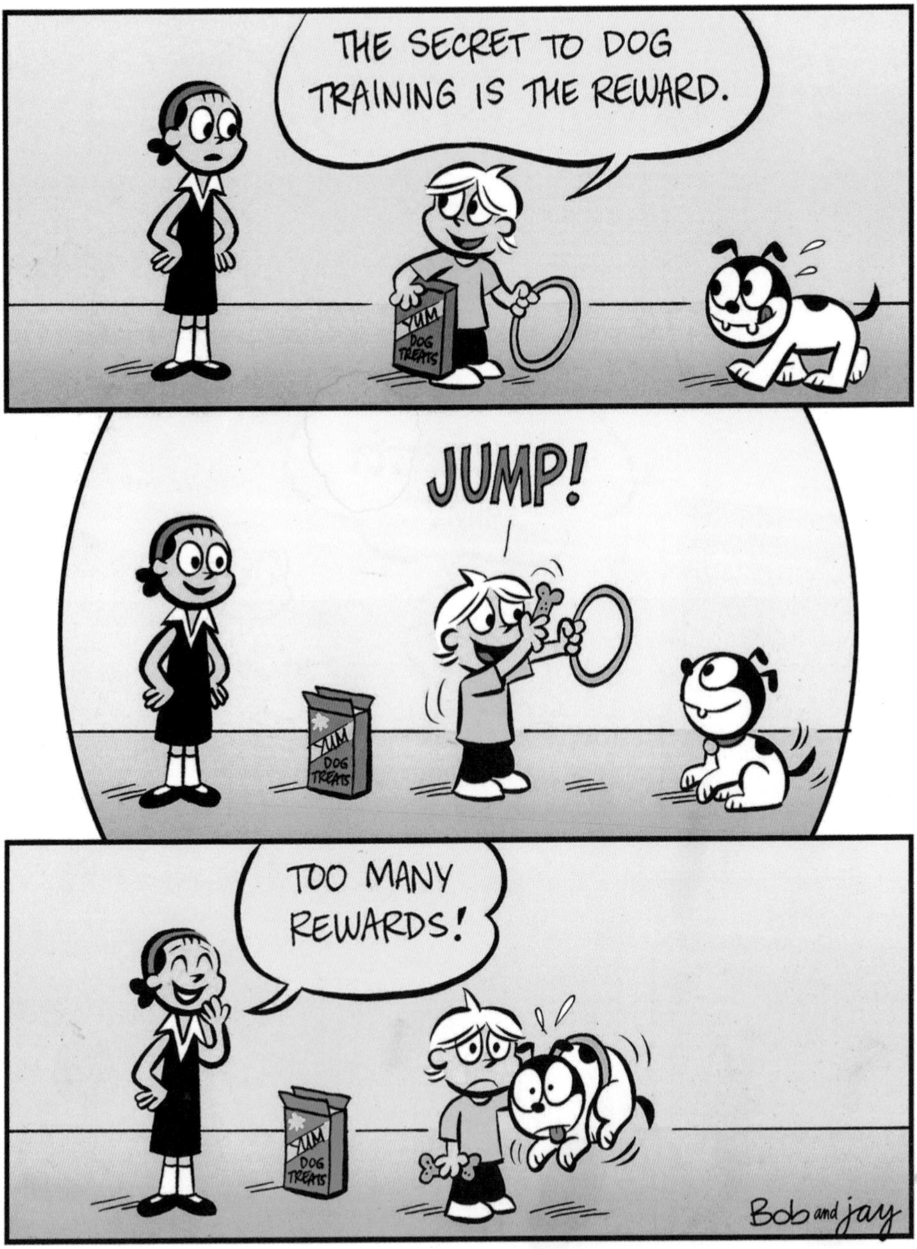
THE SECRET TO DOG TRAINING IS THE REWARD.
YUM DOG TREATS
JUMP!
YUM DOG TREATS
TOO MANY REWARDS!
YUM DOG TREATS
Bob and jay

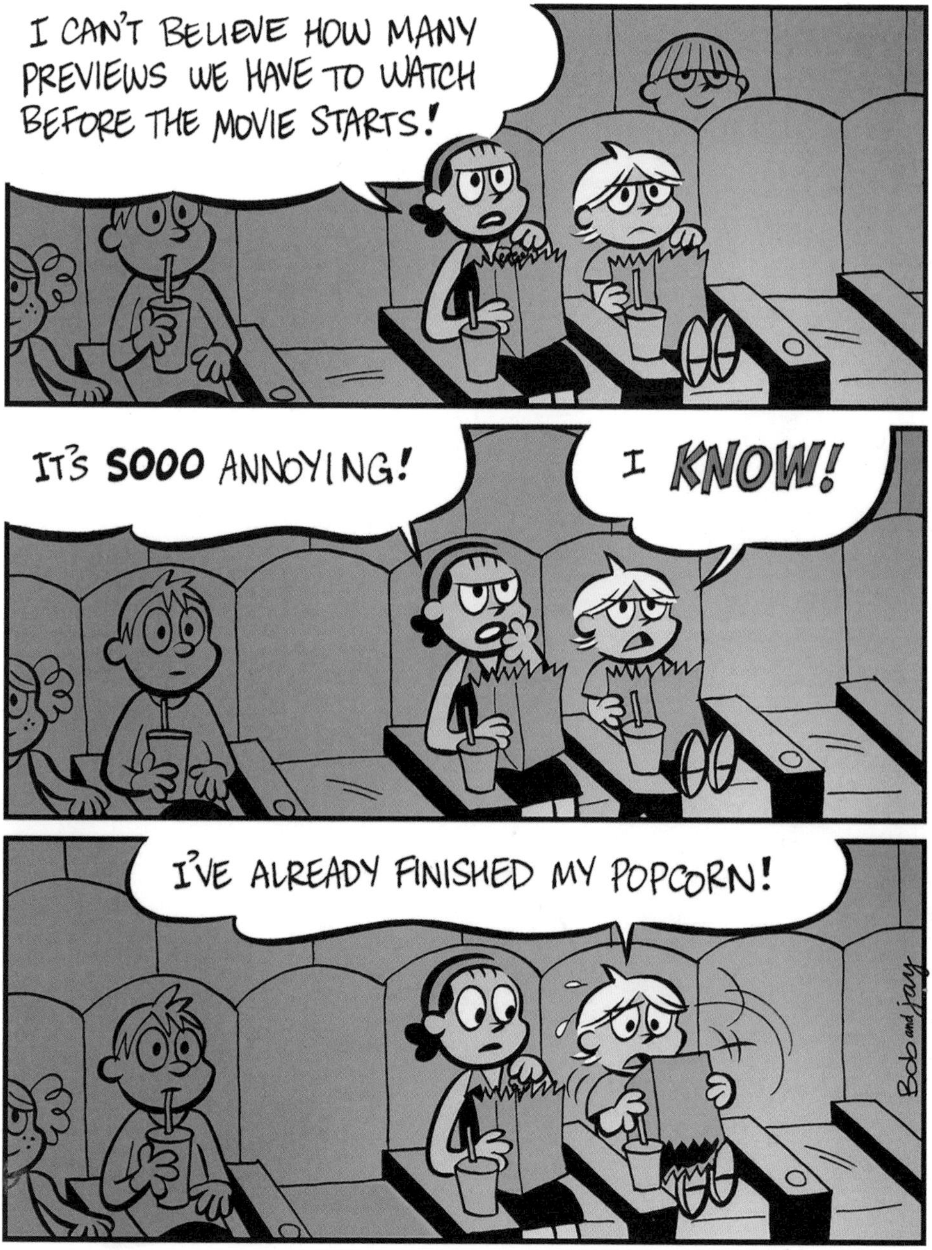
I CAN'T BELIEVE HOW MANY PREVIEWS WE HAVE TO WATCH BEFORE THE MOVIE STARTS!
IT'S **SOOO** ANNOYING!
I **KNOW!**
I'VE ALREADY FINISHED MY POPCORN!
Bob and jay

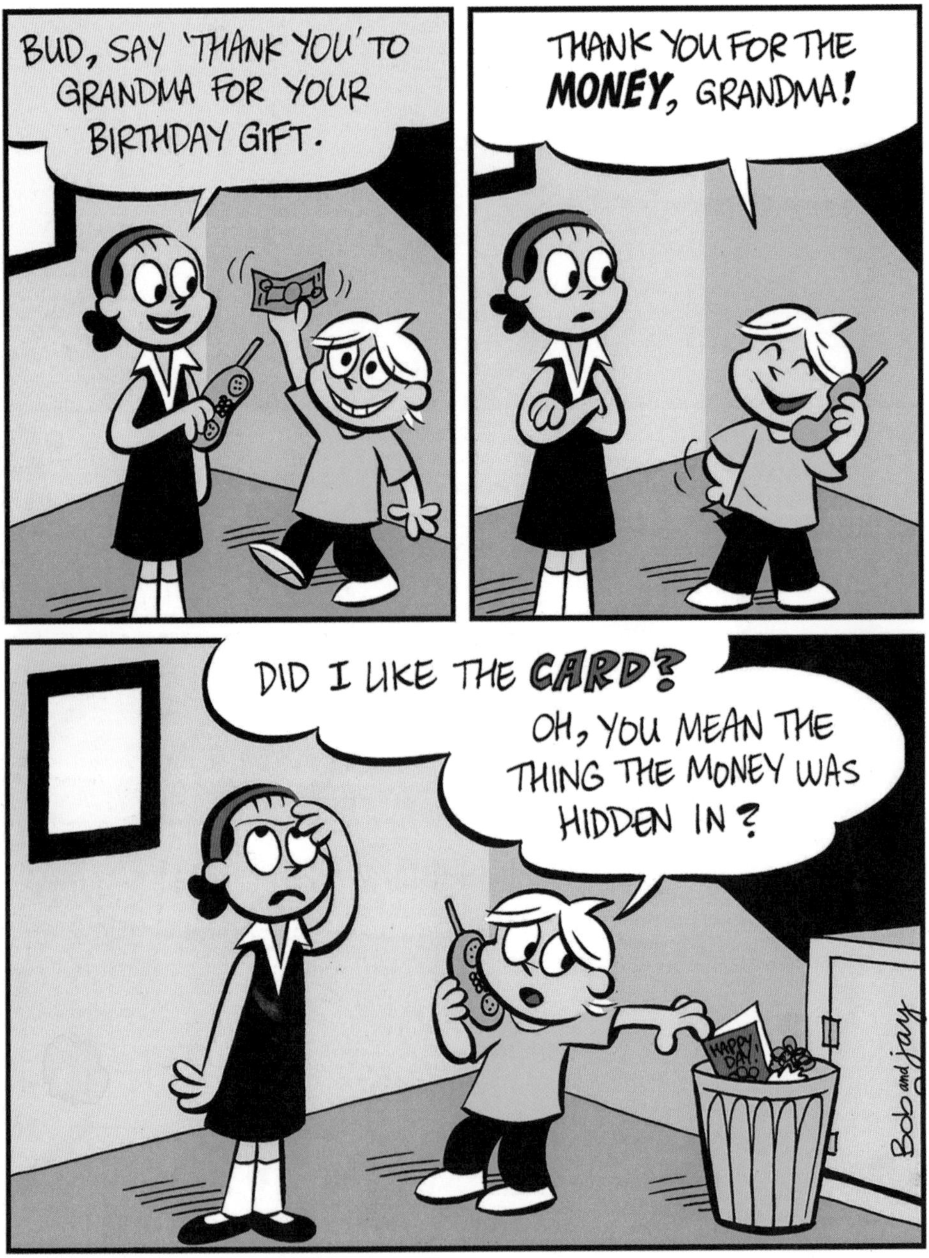
BUD, SAY 'THANK YOU' TO GRANDMA FOR YOUR BIRTHDAY GIFT.
THANK YOU FOR THE MONEY, GRANDMA!
DID I LIKE THE CARD?
OH, YOU MEAN THE THING THE MONEY WAS HIDDEN IN?
HAPPY DAY!
Bob and jay

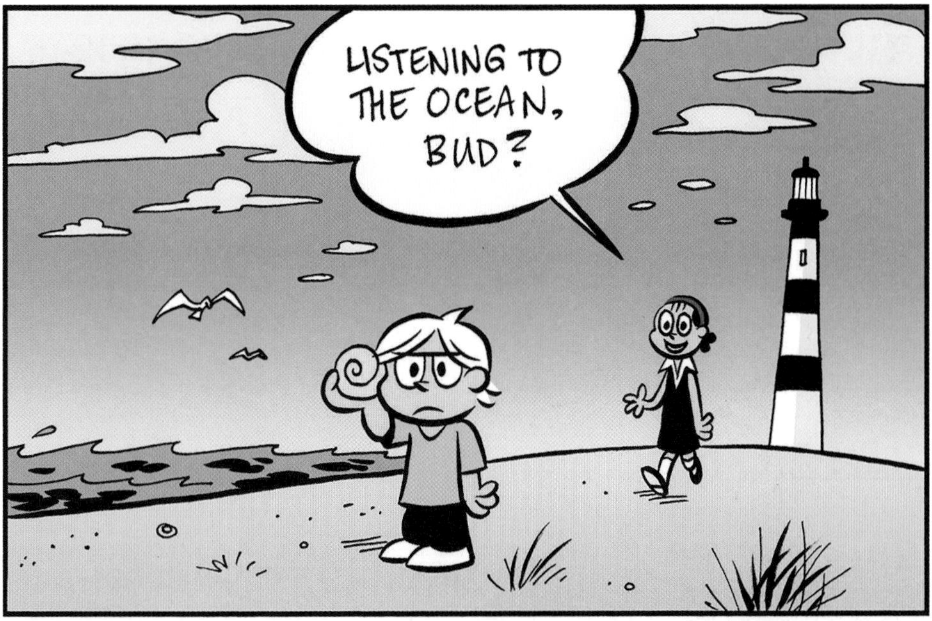
LISTENING TO THE OCEAN, BUD?

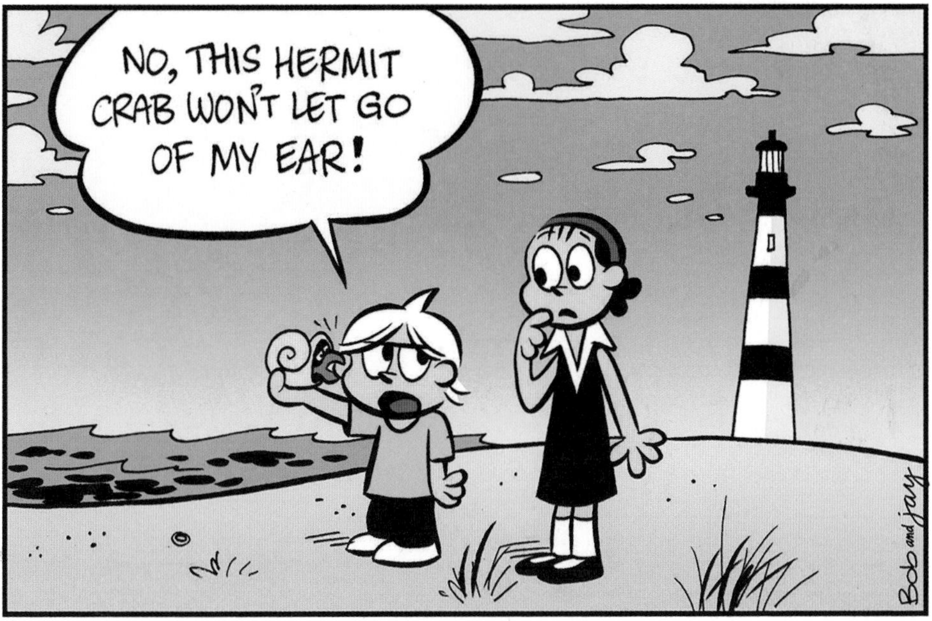
NO, THIS HERMIT CRAB WON'T LET GO OF MY EAR!
Bob and jay

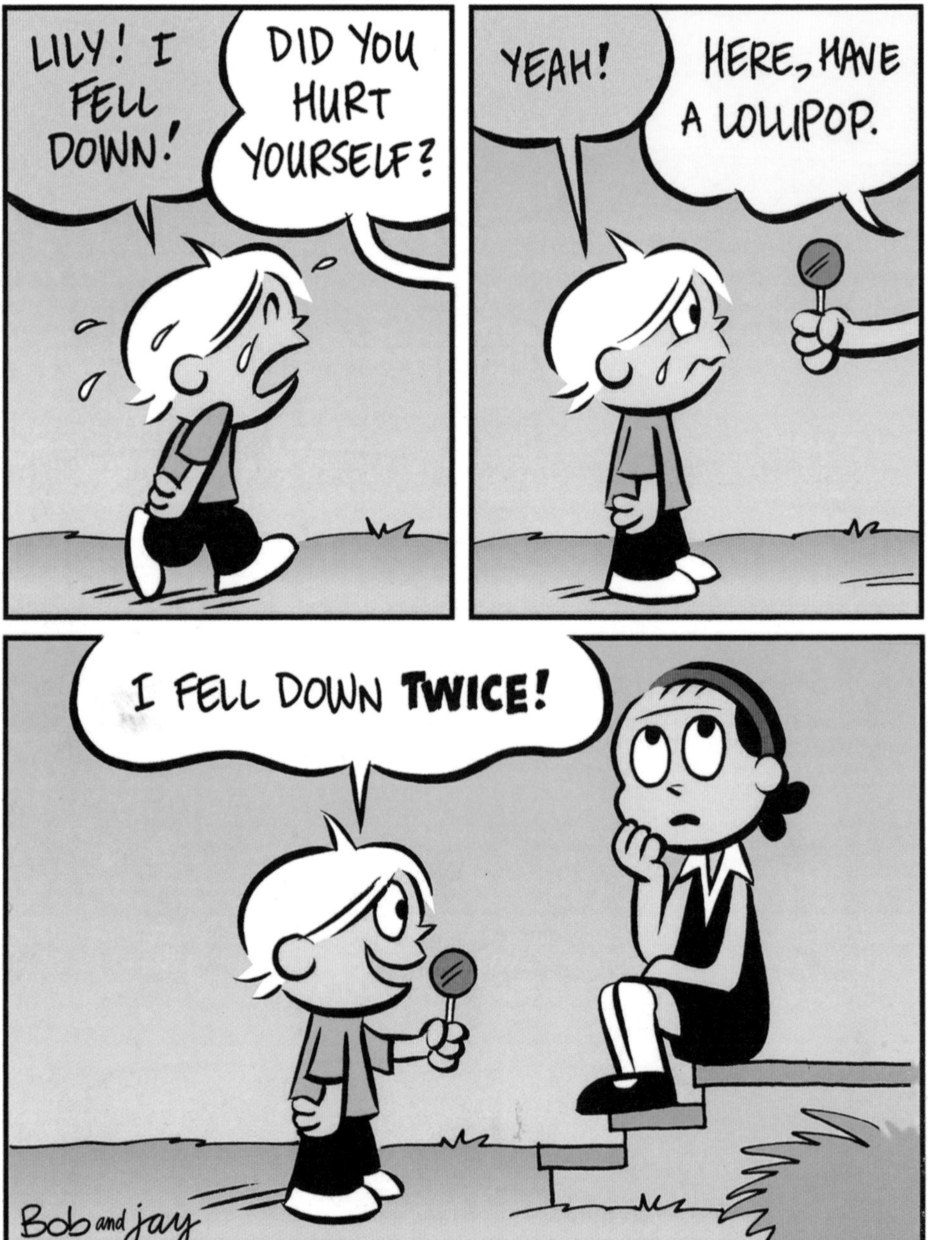
LILY! I FELL DOWN!
DID YOU HURT YOURSELF?
YEAH!
HERE, HAVE A LOLLIPOP.
I FELL DOWN **TWICE!**
Bob and jay

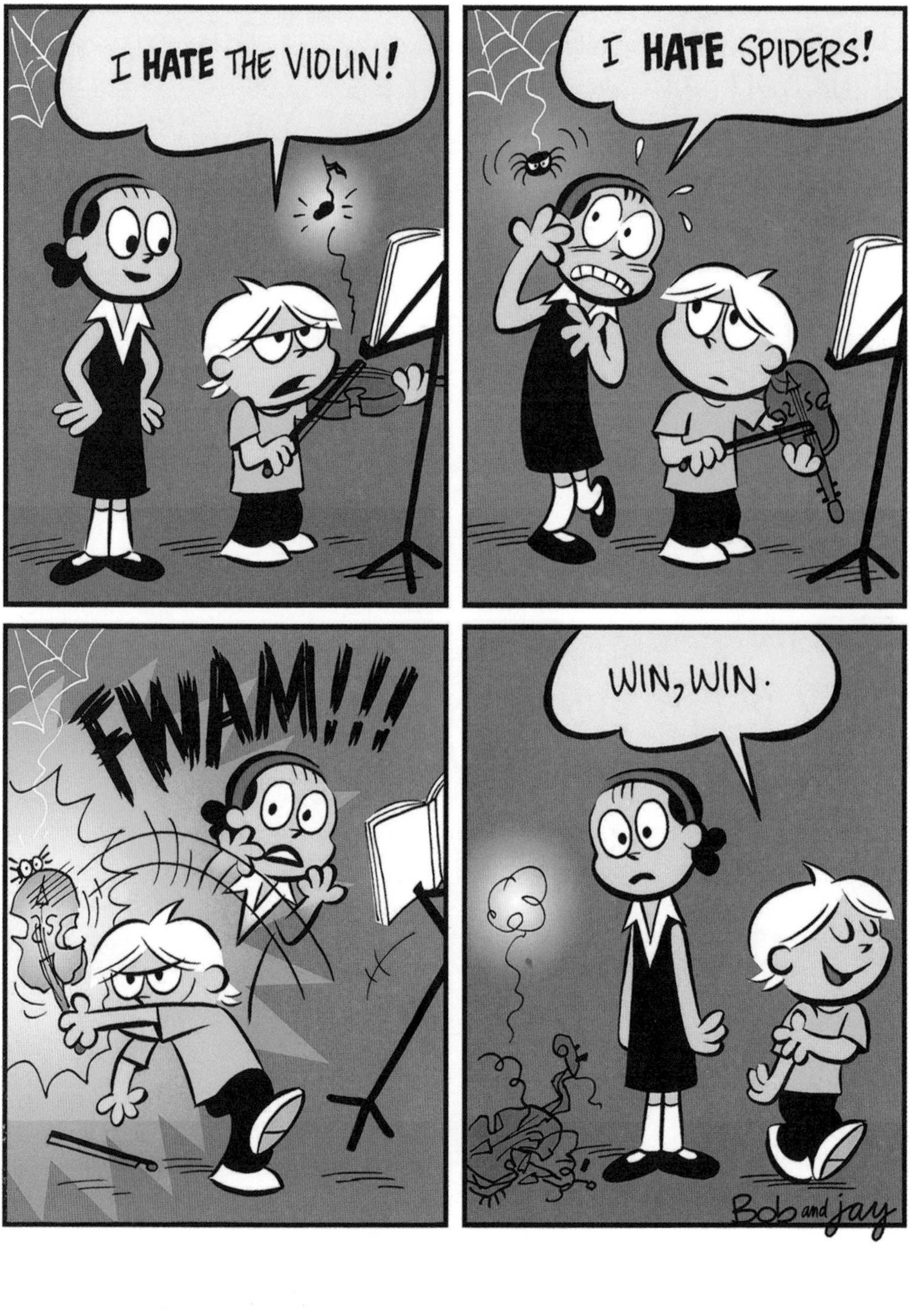
I HATE THE VIOLIN!
I HATE SPIDERS!
FWAM!!!
WIN, WIN.
Bob and jay

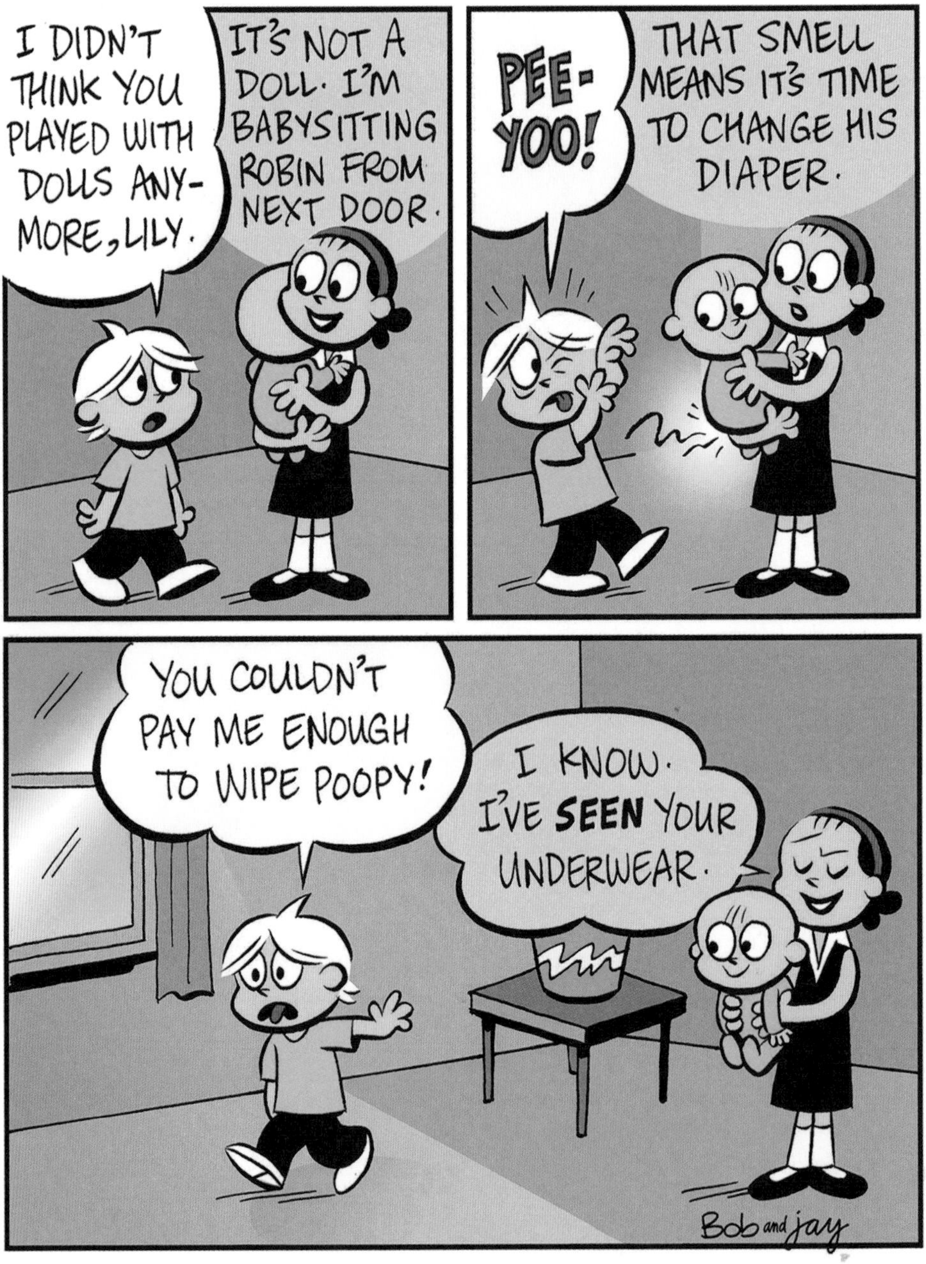
I DIDN'T THINK YOU PLAYED WITH DOLLS ANY-MORE, LILY.
IT'S NOT A DOLL. I'M BABYSITTING ROBIN FROM NEXT DOOR.
PEE-YOO!
THAT SMELL MEANS IT'S TIME TO CHANGE HIS DIAPER.
YOU COULDN'T PAY ME ENOUGH TO WIPE POOPY!
I KNOW. I'VE **SEEN** YOUR UNDERWEAR.
Bob and jay

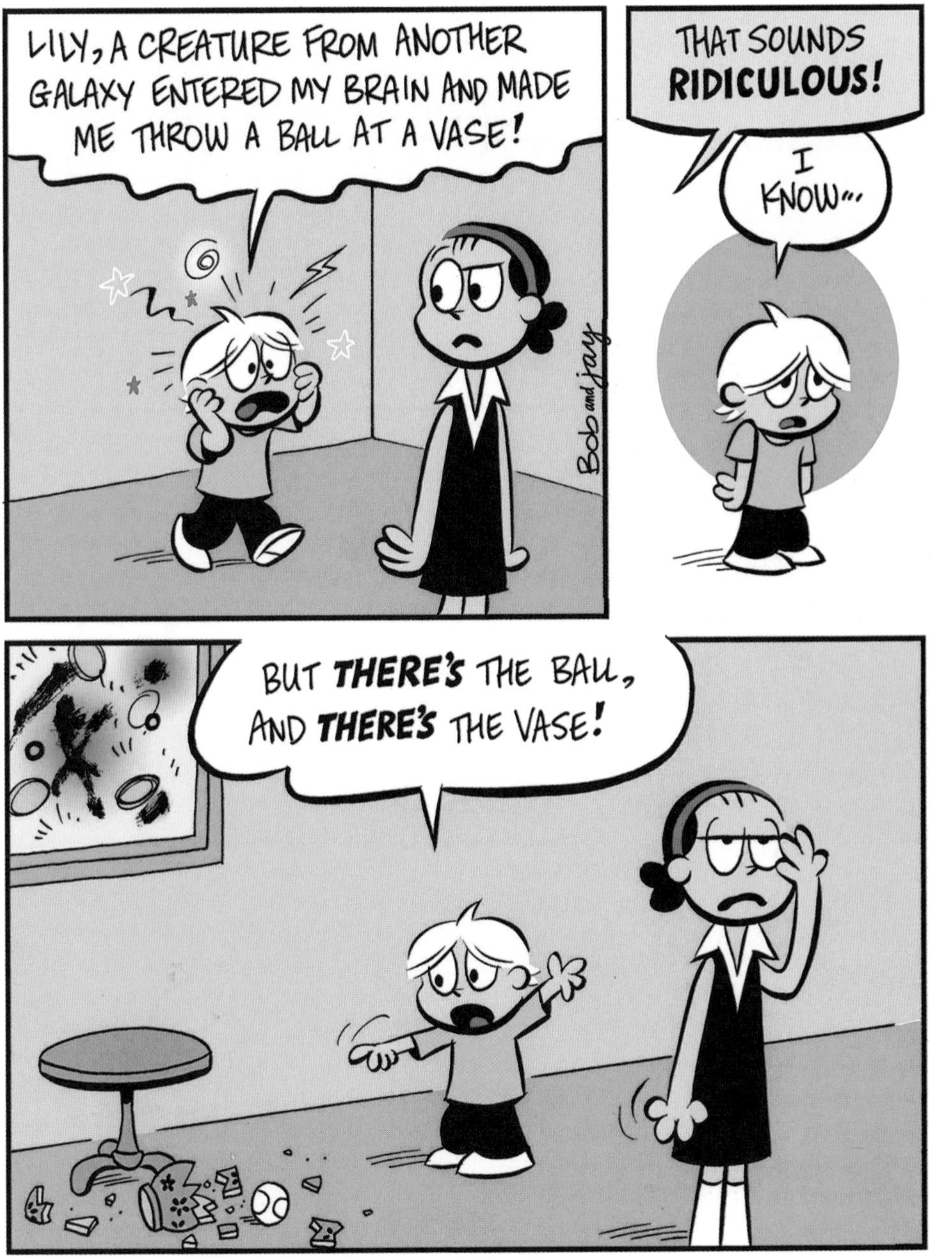
LILY, A CREATURE FROM ANOTHER GALAXY ENTERED MY BRAIN AND MADE ME THROW A BALL AT A VASE!
Bob and jay
THAT SOUNDS **RIDICULOUS!**
I KNOW...
BUT **THERE'S** THE BALL, AND **THERE'S** THE VASE!

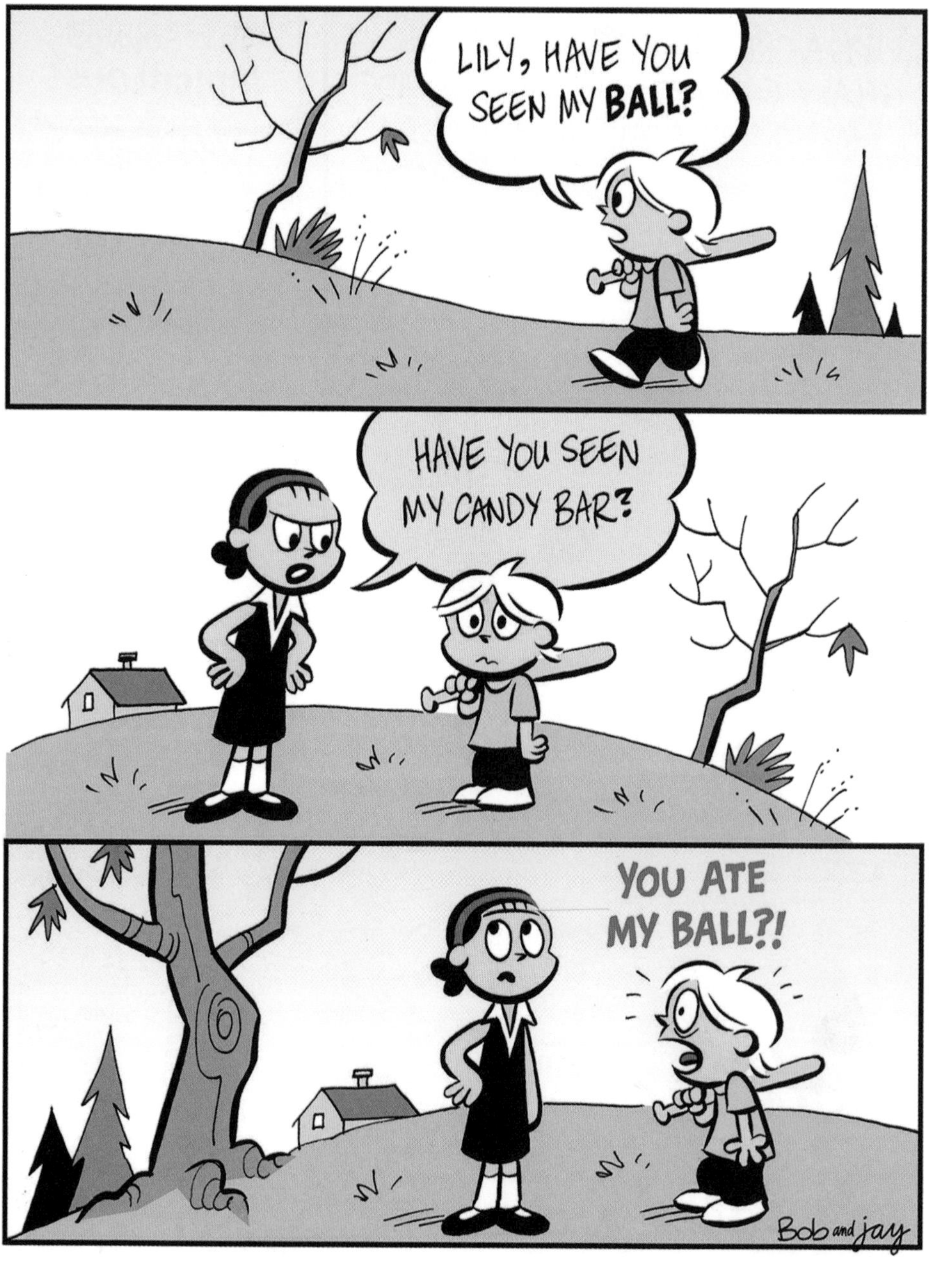
LILY, HAVE YOU SEEN MY BALL?
HAVE YOU SEEN MY CANDY BAR?
YOU ATE MY BALL?!
Bob and jay

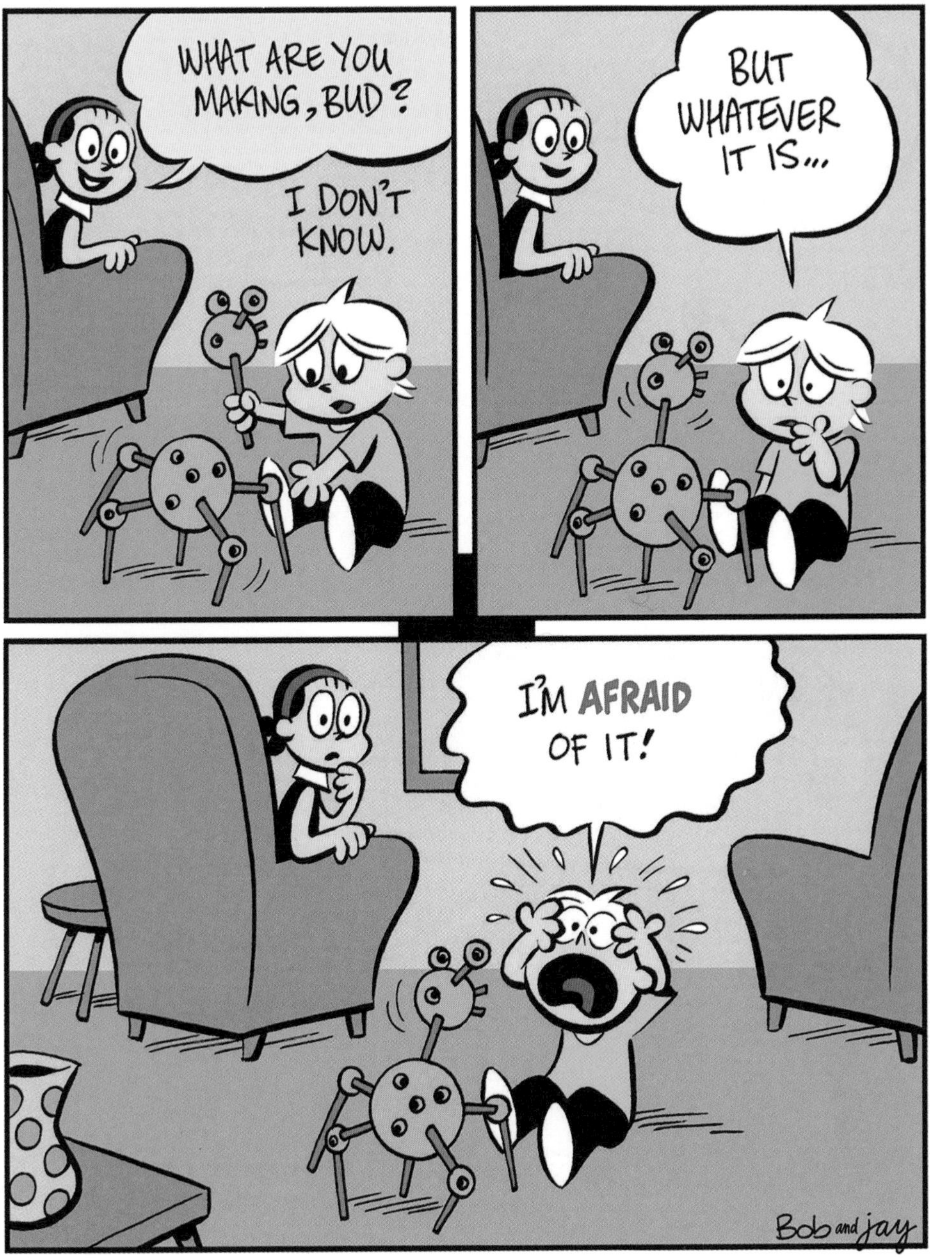
WHAT ARE YOU MAKING, BUD?
I DON'T KNOW.
BUT WHATEVER IT IS...
I'M AFRAID OF IT!
Bob and jay

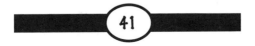

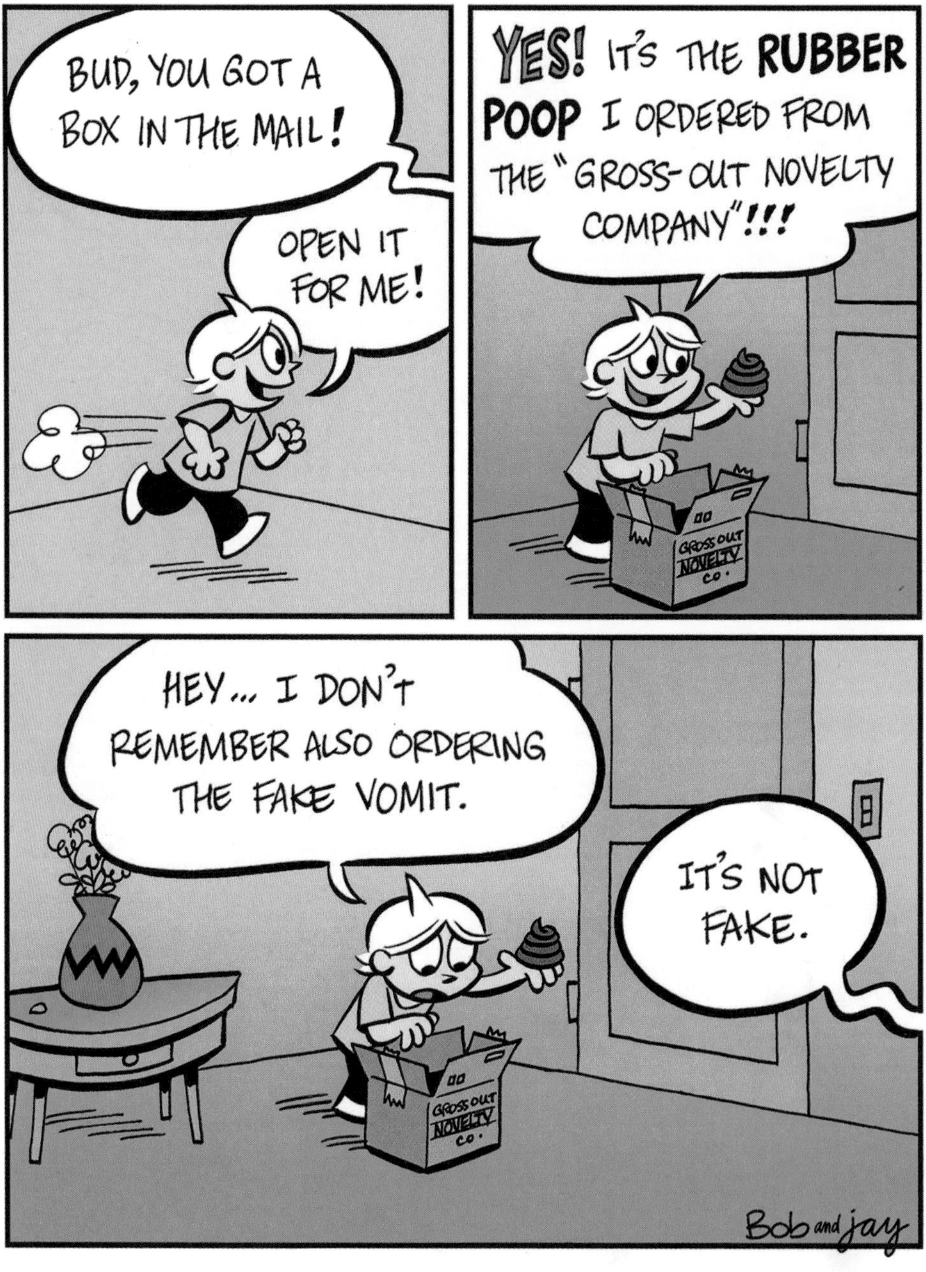
BUD, YOU GOT A BOX IN THE MAIL!
OPEN IT FOR ME!
YES! IT'S THE RUBBER POOP I ORDERED FROM THE "GROSS-OUT NOVELTY COMPANY"!!!
GROSS OUT NOVELTY CO.
HEY... I DON'T REMEMBER ALSO ORDERING THE FAKE VOMIT.
IT'S NOT FAKE.
GROSS OUT NOVELTY CO.
Bob and jay

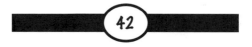

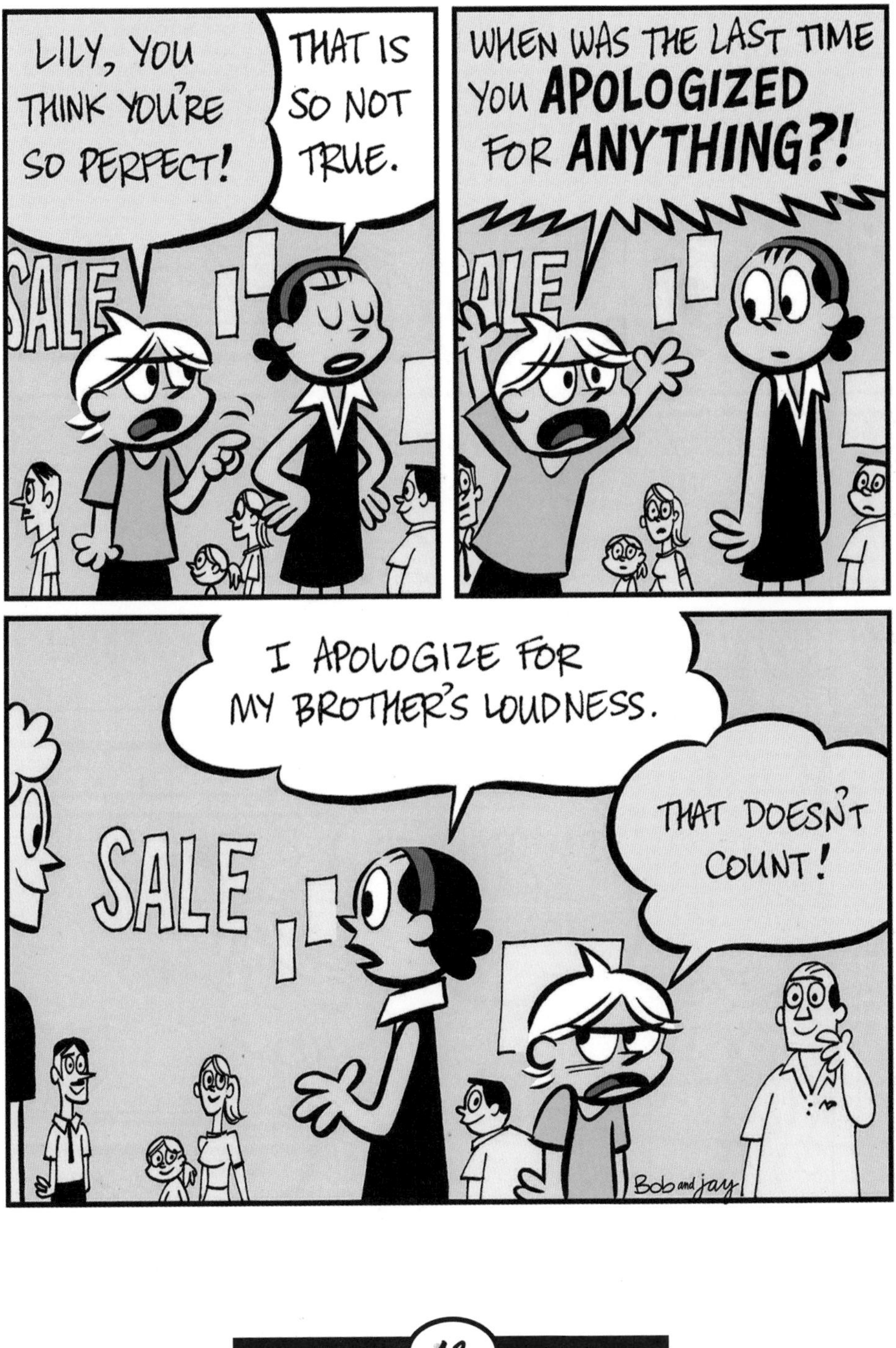
LILY, YOU THINK YOU'RE SO PERFECT!
THAT IS SO NOT TRUE.
WHEN WAS THE LAST TIME YOU **APOLOGIZED** FOR **ANYTHING?!**
SALE
I APOLOGIZE FOR MY BROTHER'S LOUDNESS.
THAT DOESN'T COUNT!
Bob and jay

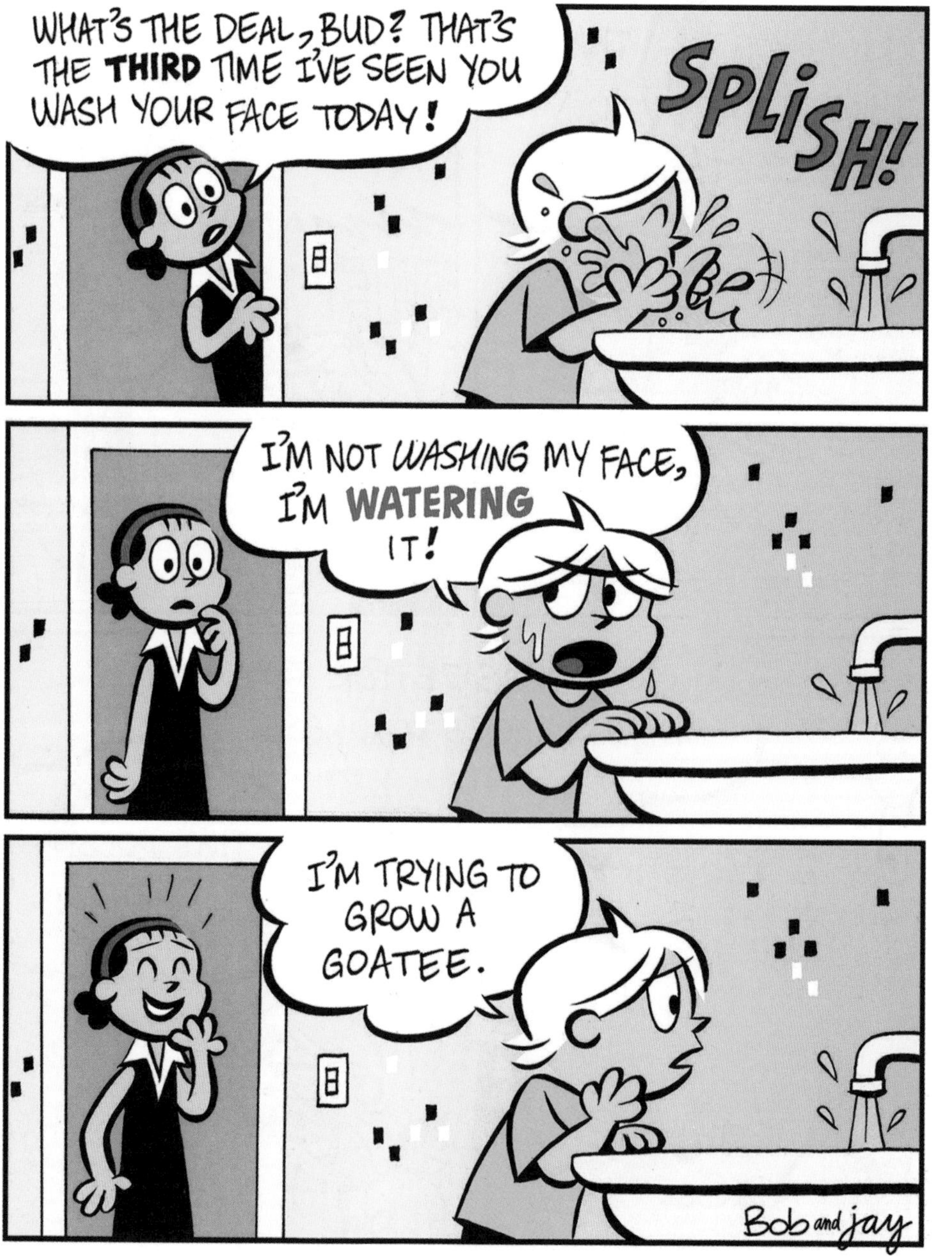
WHAT'S THE DEAL, BUD? THAT'S THE **THIRD** TIME I'VE SEEN YOU WASH YOUR FACE TODAY!
SPLISH!
I'M NOT *WASHING* MY FACE, I'M **WATERING** IT!
I'M TRYING TO GROW A GOATEE.
Bob and jay

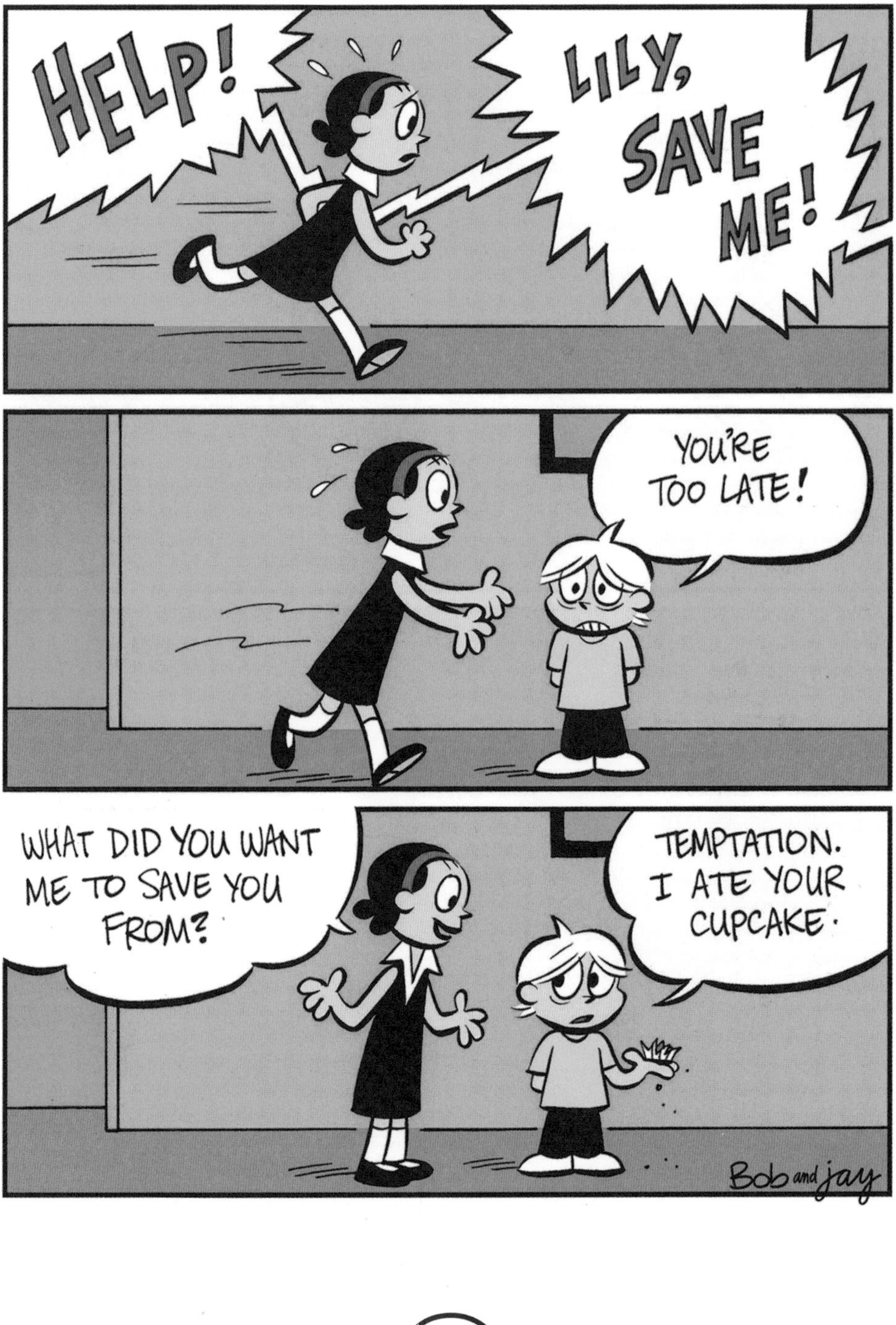
HELP!
LILY, SAVE ME!
YOU'RE TOO LATE!
WHAT DID YOU WANT ME TO SAVE YOU FROM?
TEMPTATION. I ATE YOUR CUPCAKE.
Bob and jay

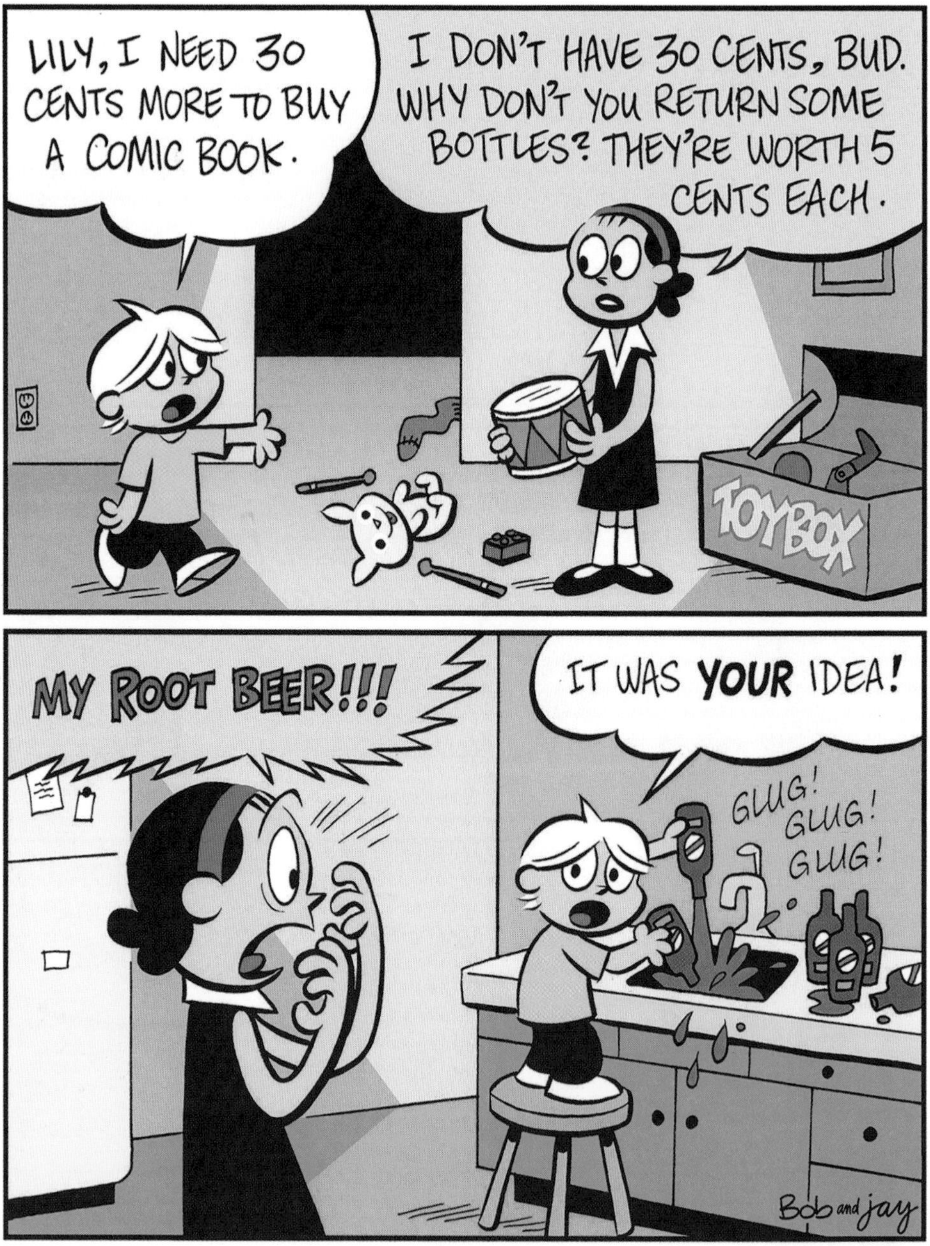

LILY, I NEED 30 CENTS MORE TO BUY A COMIC BOOK.
I DON'T HAVE 30 CENTS, BUD. WHY DON'T YOU RETURN SOME BOTTLES? THEY'RE WORTH 5 CENTS EACH.
TOYBOX
MY ROOT BEER!!!
IT WAS YOUR IDEA!
GLUG! GLUG! GLUG!
Bob and jay

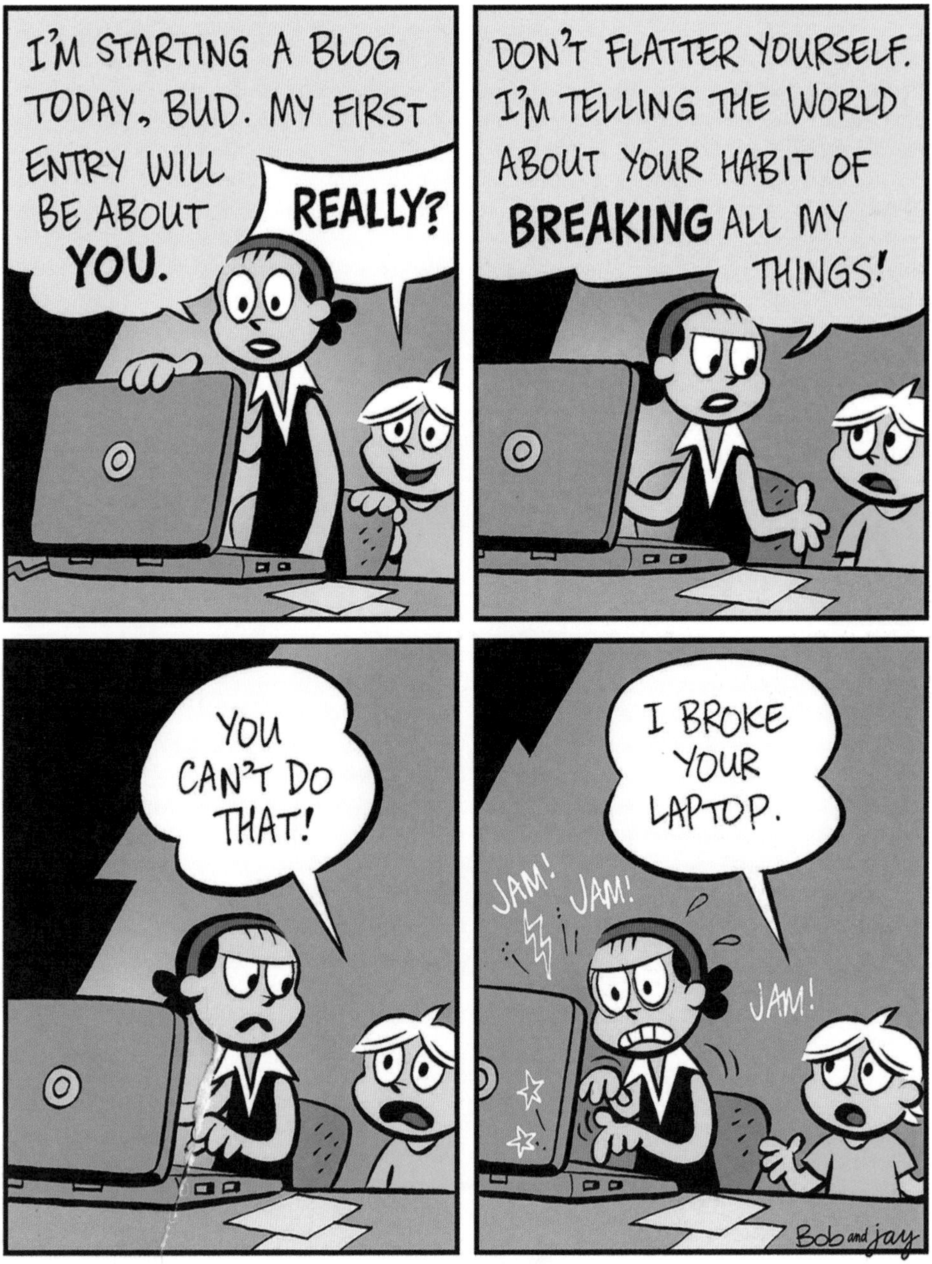
I'M STARTING A BLOG TODAY, BUD. MY FIRST ENTRY WILL BE ABOUT YOU.
REALLY?
DON'T FLATTER YOURSELF. I'M TELLING THE WORLD ABOUT YOUR HABIT OF BREAKING ALL MY THINGS!
YOU CAN'T DO THAT!
I BROKE YOUR LAPTOP.
JAM!
JAM!
JAM!
Bob and jay

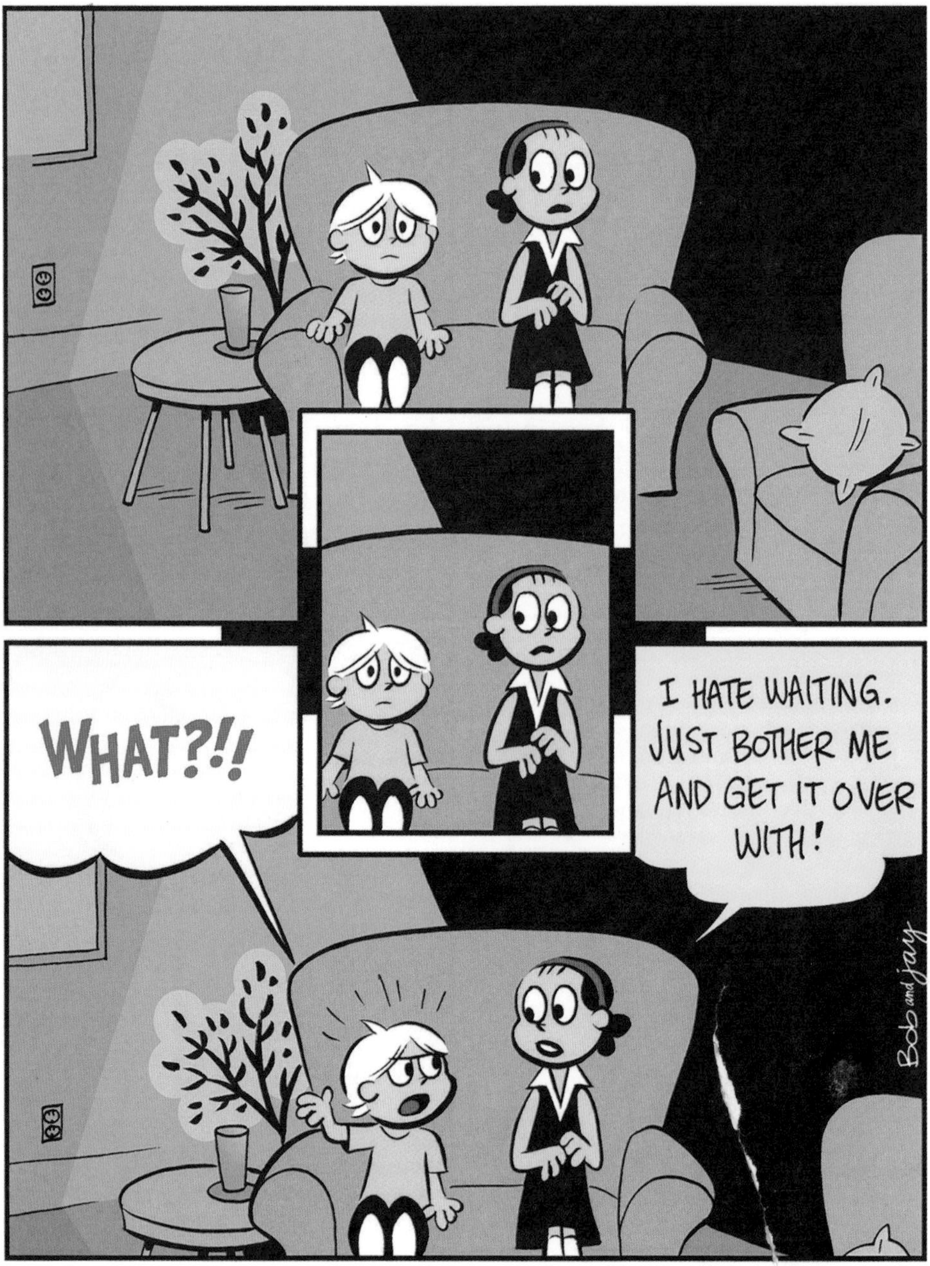
WHAT?!!
I HATE WAITING. JUST BOTHER ME AND GET IT OVER WITH!
Bob and jay

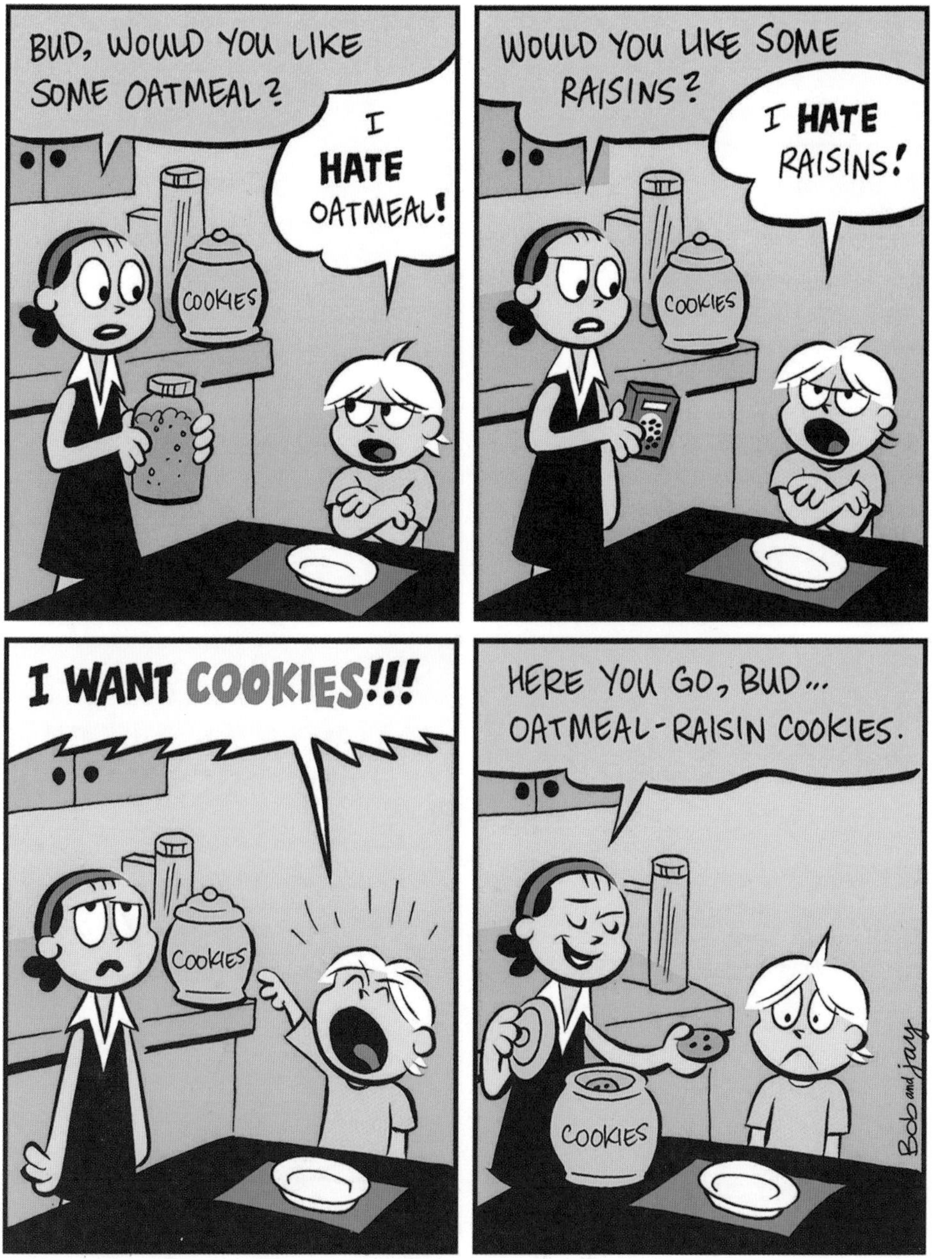

BUD, WOULD YOU LIKE SOME OATMEAL?
I HATE OATMEAL!
COOKIES
WOULD YOU LIKE SOME RAISINS?
I HATE RAISINS!
COOKIES
I WANT COOKIES!!!
COOKIES
HERE YOU GO, BUD... OATMEAL-RAISIN COOKIES.
COOKIES
Bob and jay

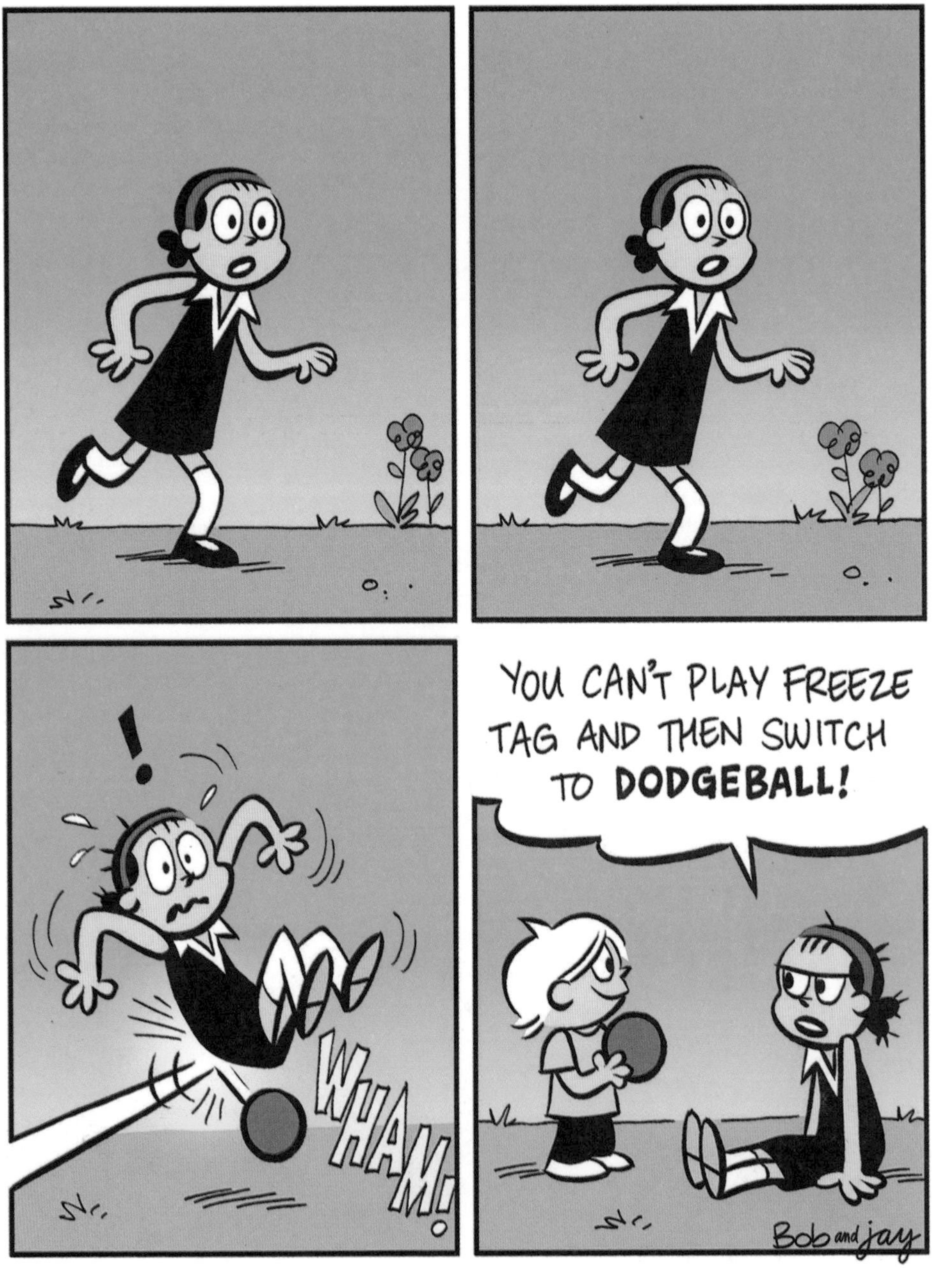
!
WHAM!
YOU CAN'T PLAY FREEZE TAG AND THEN SWITCH TO DODGEBALL!
Bob and jay

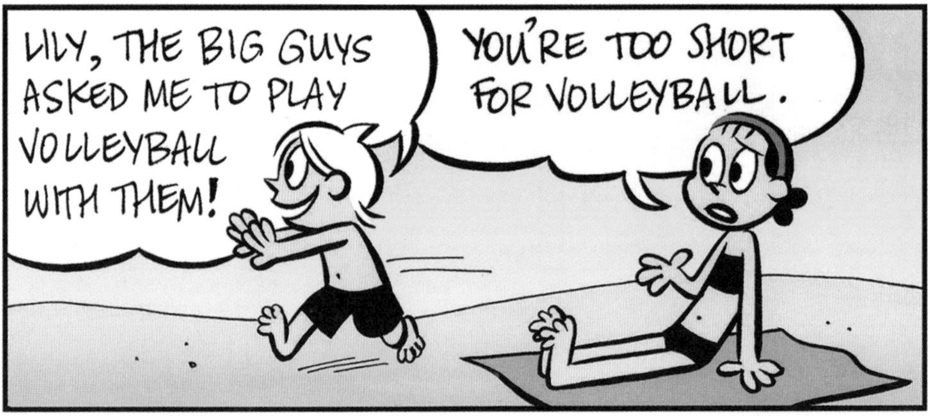
LILY, THE BIG GUYS ASKED ME TO PLAY VOLLEYBALL WITH THEM!
YOU'RE TOO SHORT FOR VOLLEYBALL.

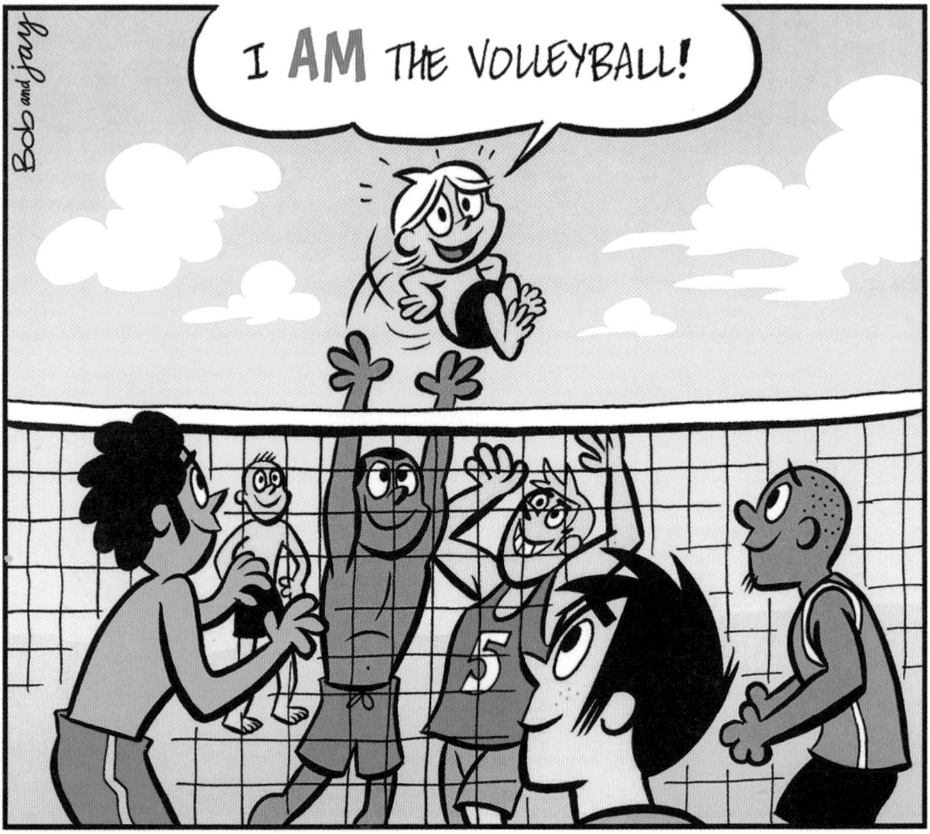
Bob and jay
I AM THE VOLLEYBALL!

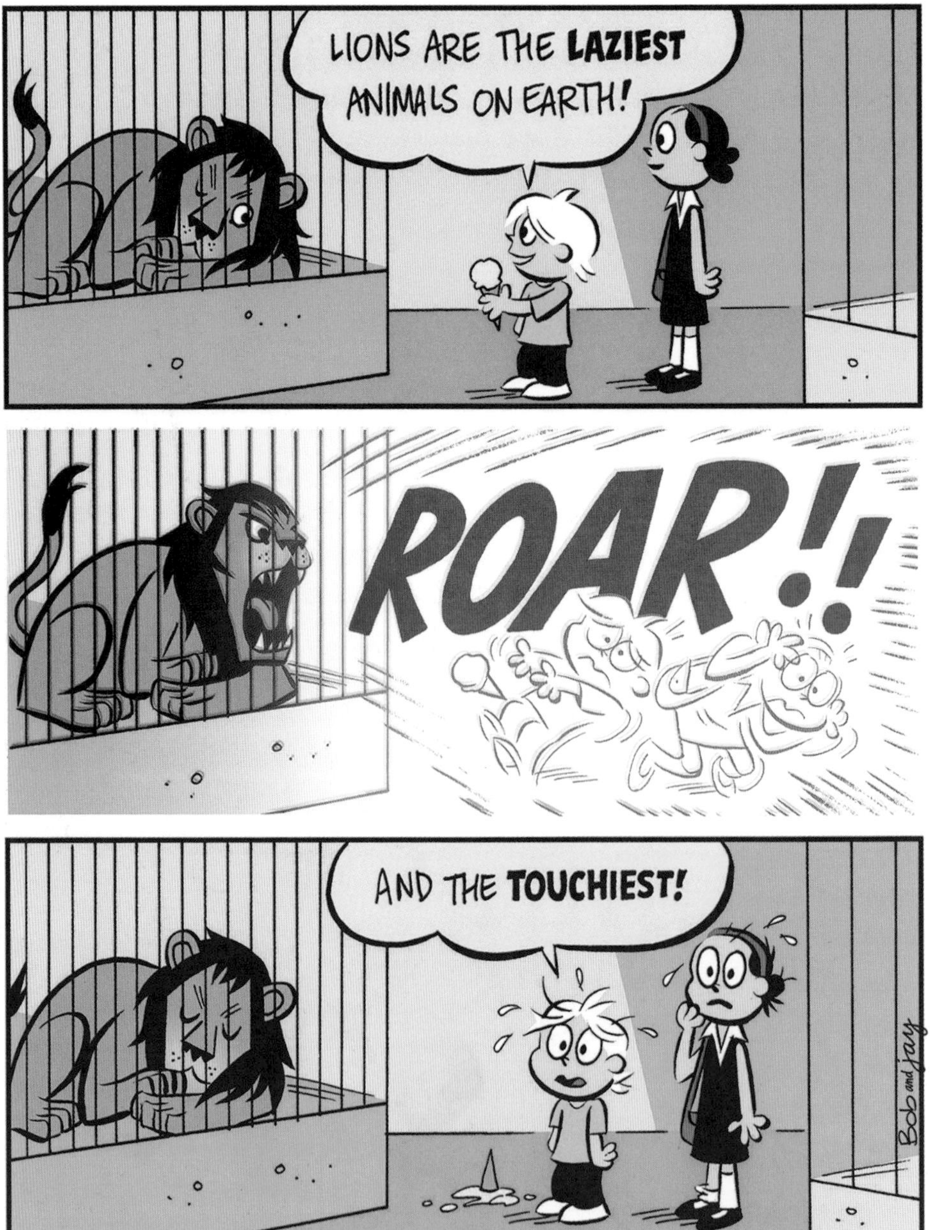
LIONS ARE THE **LAZIEST** ANIMALS ON EARTH!
ROAR!!
AND THE **TOUCHIEST!**
Bob and Jay

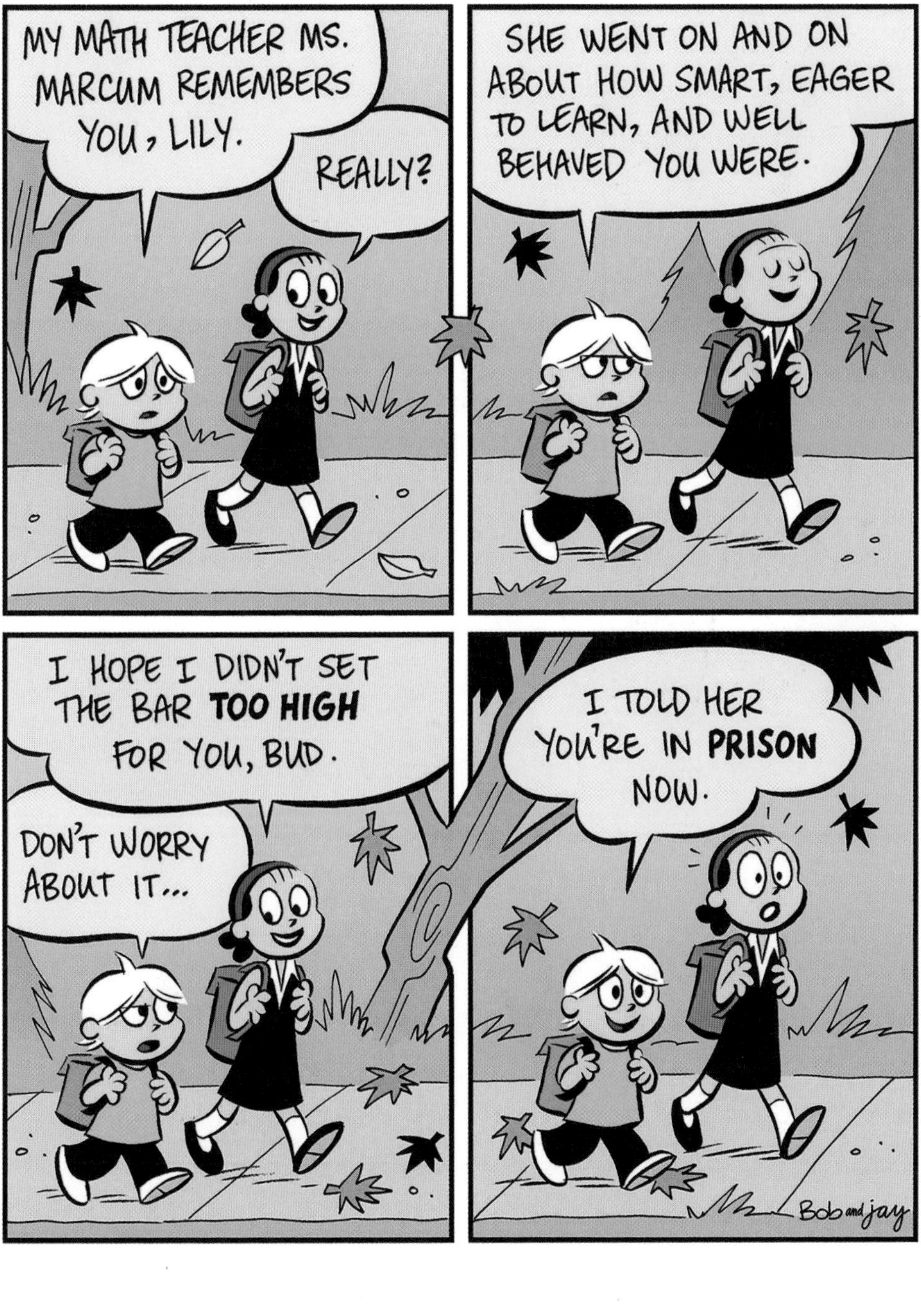
MY MATH TEACHER MS. MARCUM REMEMBERS YOU, LILY.
REALLY?
SHE WENT ON AND ON ABOUT HOW SMART, EAGER TO LEARN, AND WELL BEHAVED YOU WERE.
I HOPE I DIDN'T SET THE BAR **TOO HIGH** FOR YOU, BUD.
DON'T WORRY ABOUT IT...
I TOLD HER YOU'RE IN **PRISON** NOW.
Bob and jay

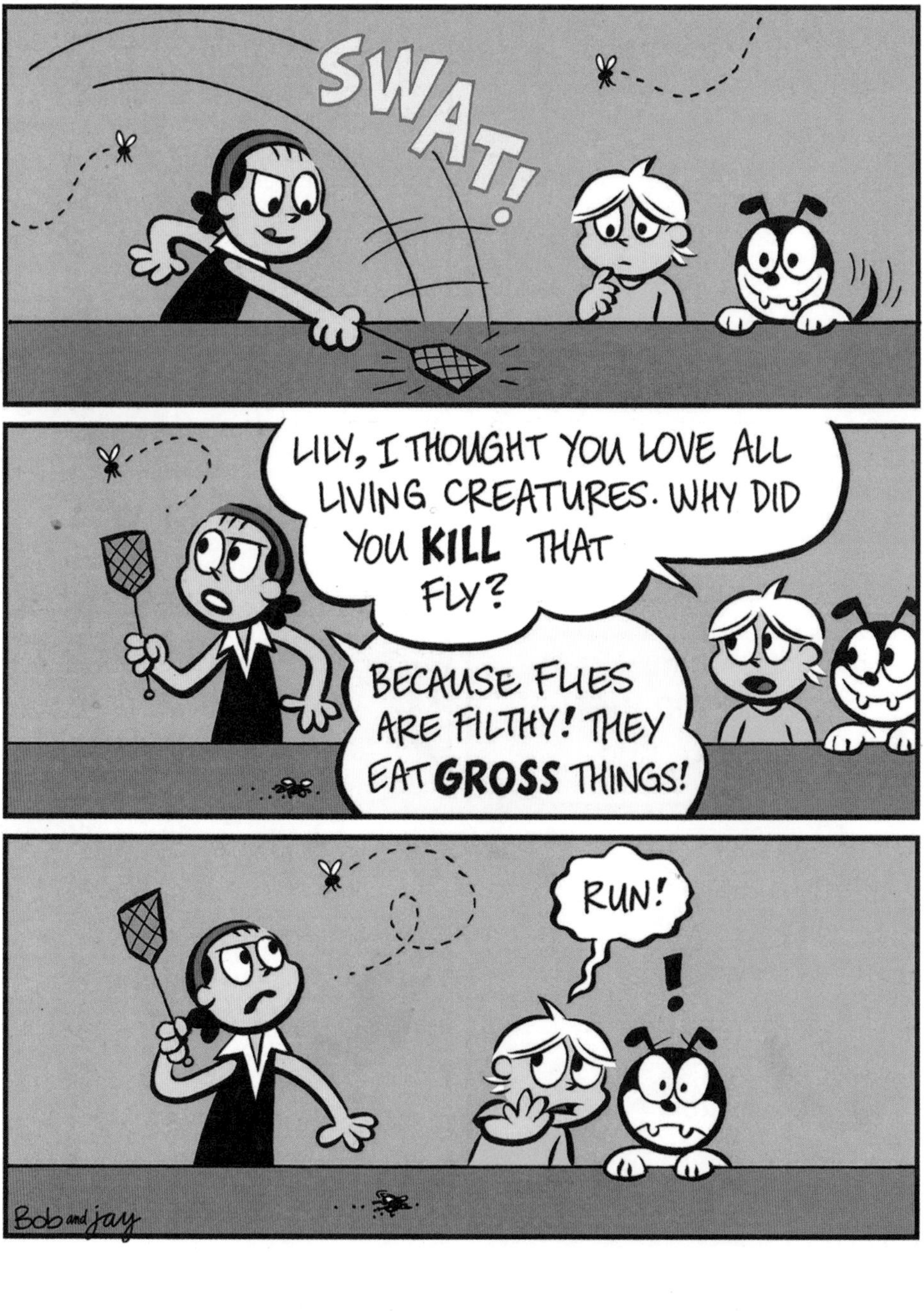
SWAT!
LILY, I THOUGHT YOU LOVE ALL LIVING CREATURES. WHY DID YOU **KILL** THAT FLY?
BECAUSE FLIES ARE FILTHY! THEY EAT **GROSS** THINGS!
RUN!
!
Bob and jay

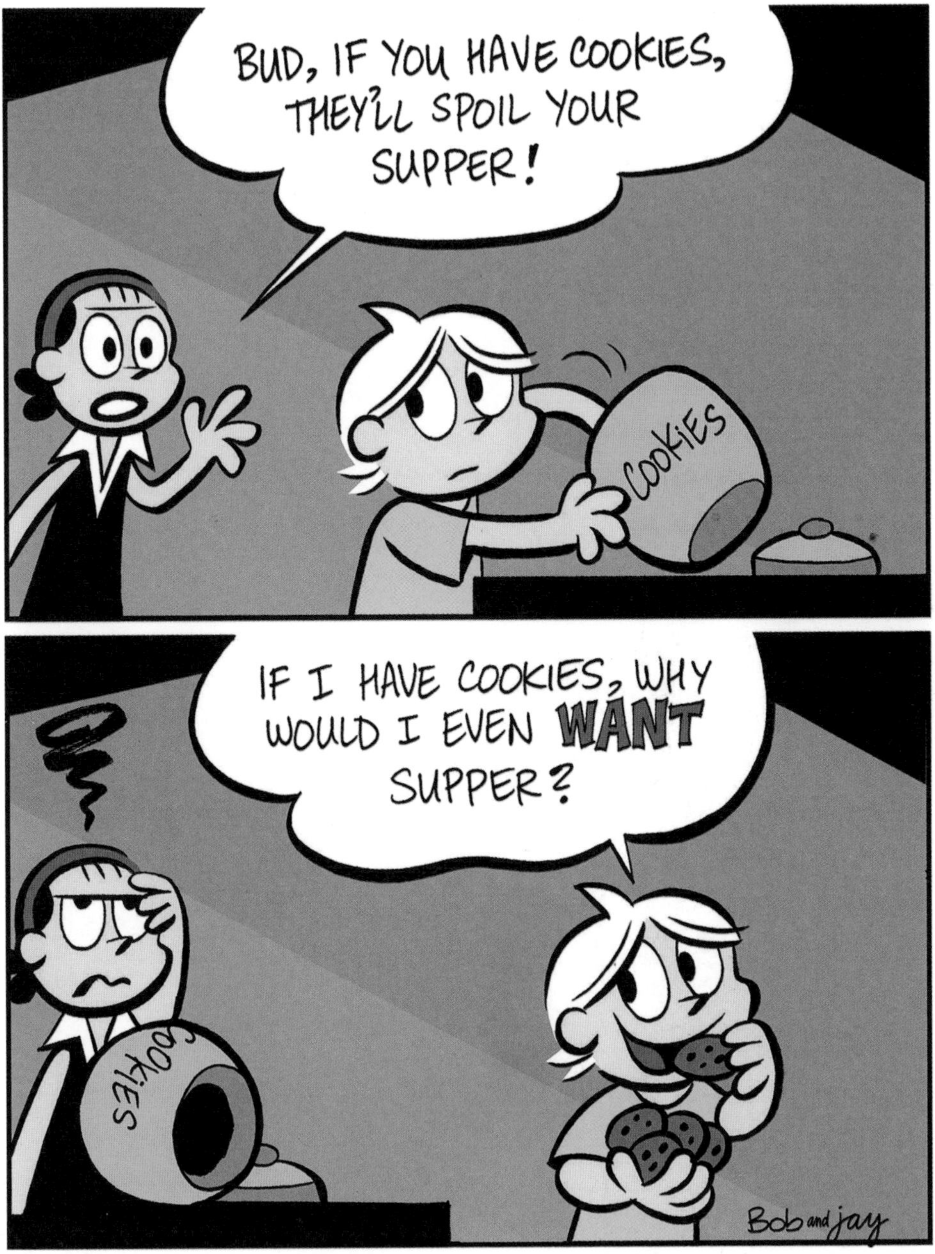
BUD, IF YOU HAVE COOKIES, THEY'LL SPOIL YOUR SUPPER!
COOKIES
IF I HAVE COOKIES, WHY WOULD I EVEN WANT SUPPER?
COOKIES
Bob and jay

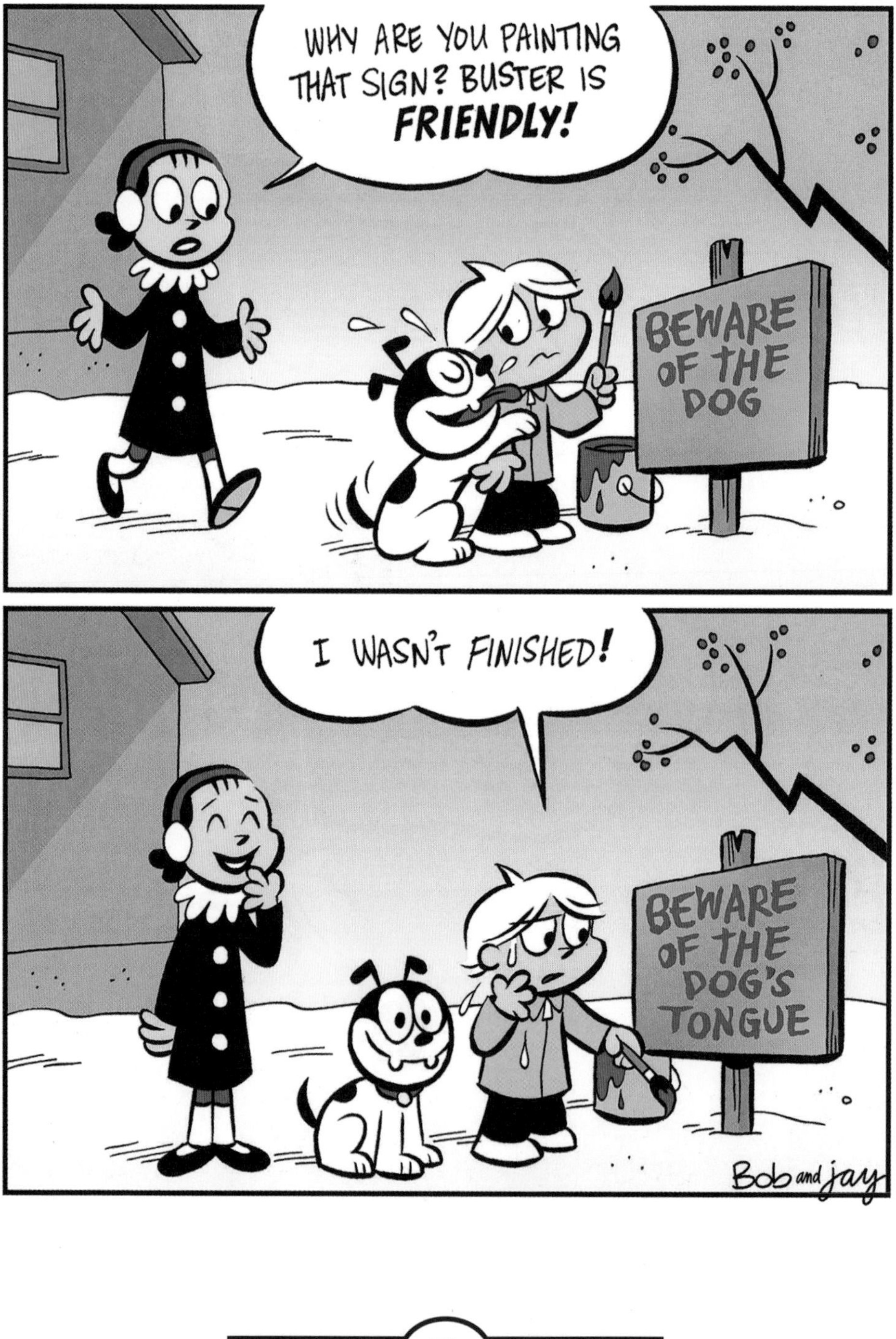
WHY ARE YOU PAINTING THAT SIGN? BUSTER IS FRIENDLY!
BEWARE OF THE DOG
I WASN'T FINISHED!
BEWARE OF THE DOG'S TONGUE
Bob and jay

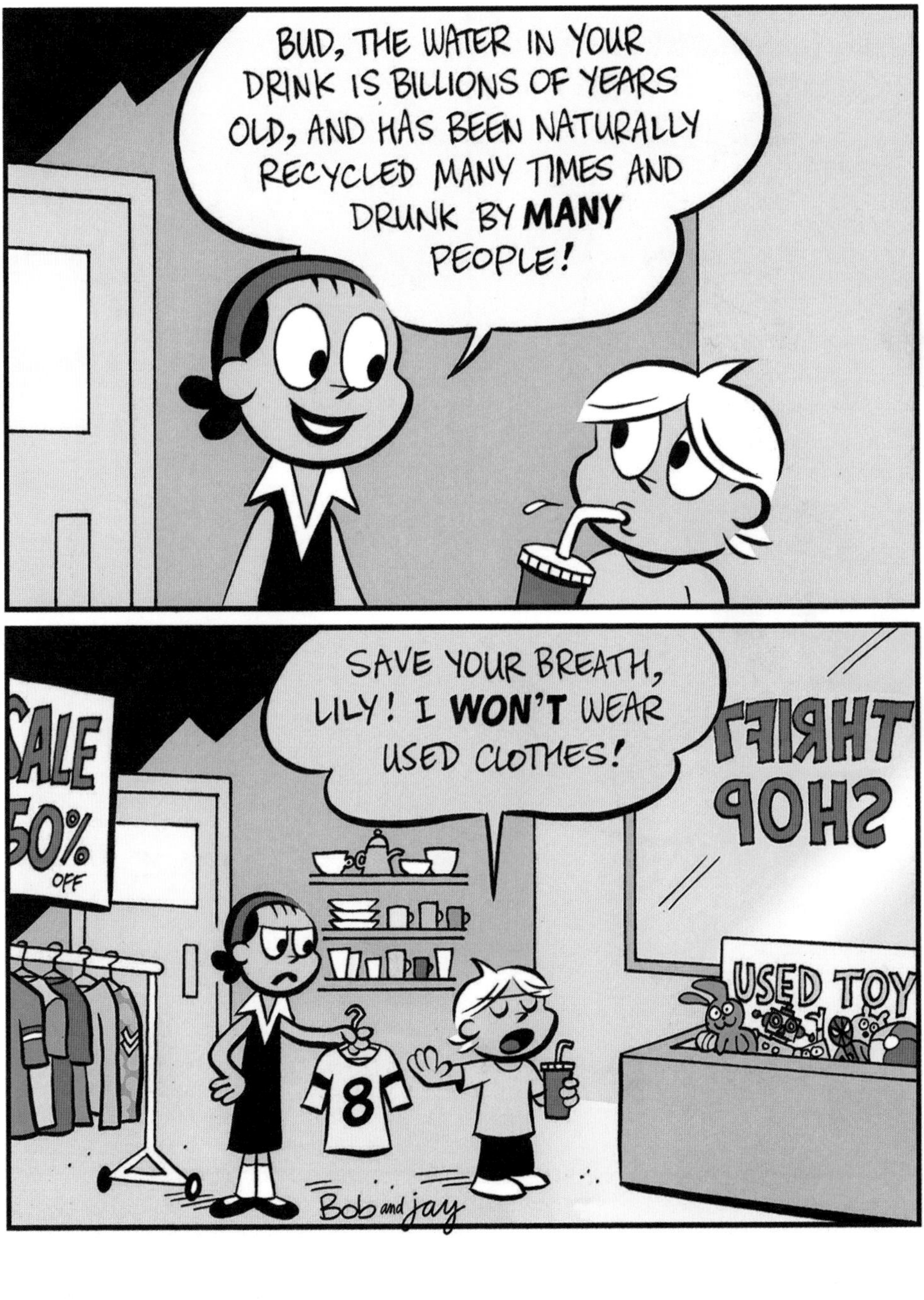
BUD, THE WATER IN YOUR DRINK IS BILLIONS OF YEARS OLD, AND HAS BEEN NATURALLY RECYCLED MANY TIMES AND DRUNK BY **MANY** PEOPLE!
SALE 50% OFF
SAVE YOUR BREATH, LILY! I **WON'T** WEAR USED CLOTHES!
THRIFT SHOP
USED TOY
8
Bob and jay

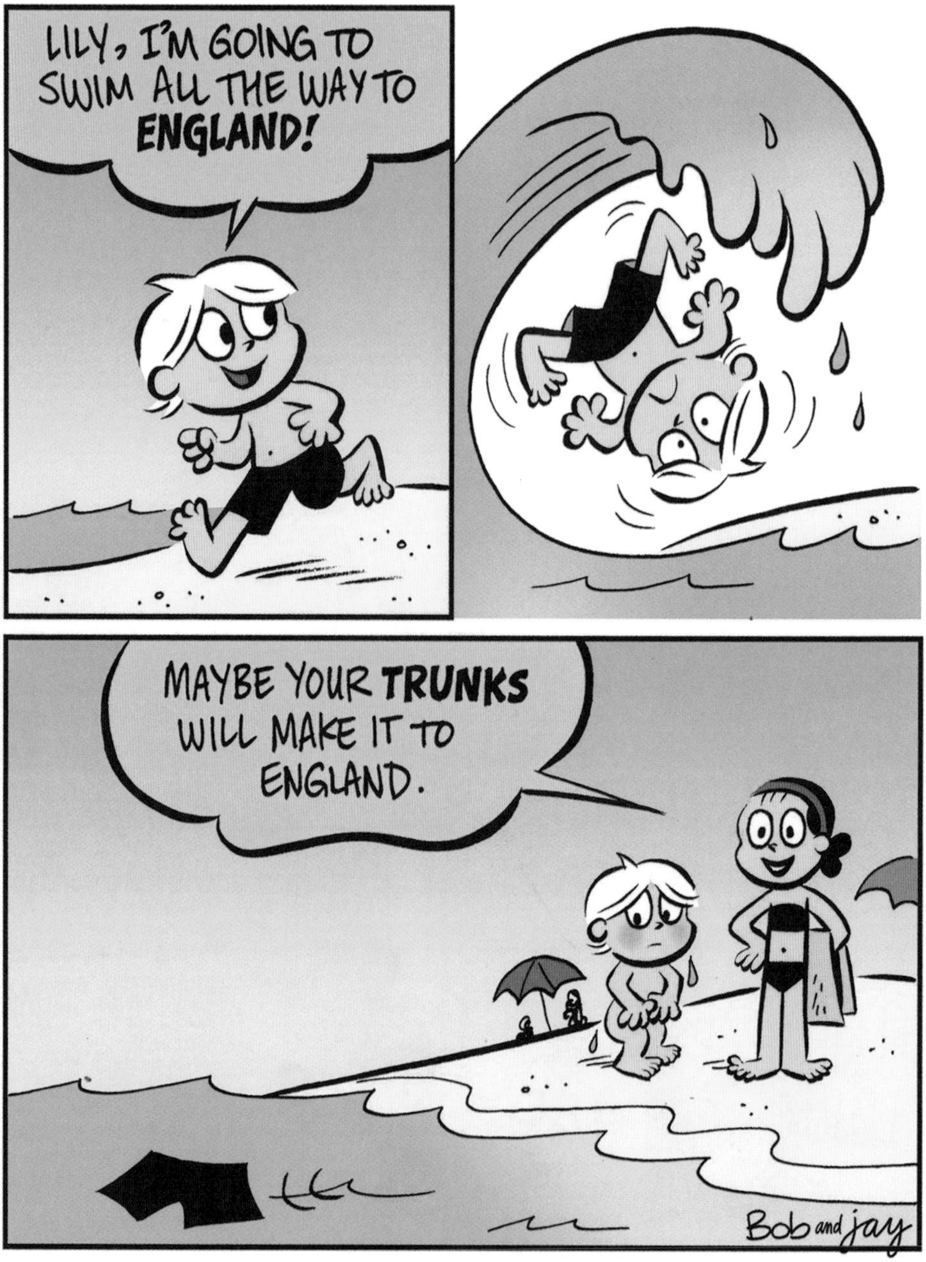
LILY, I'M GOING TO SWIM ALL THE WAY TO **ENGLAND!**
MAYBE YOUR **TRUNKS** WILL MAKE IT TO ENGLAND.
Bob and jay

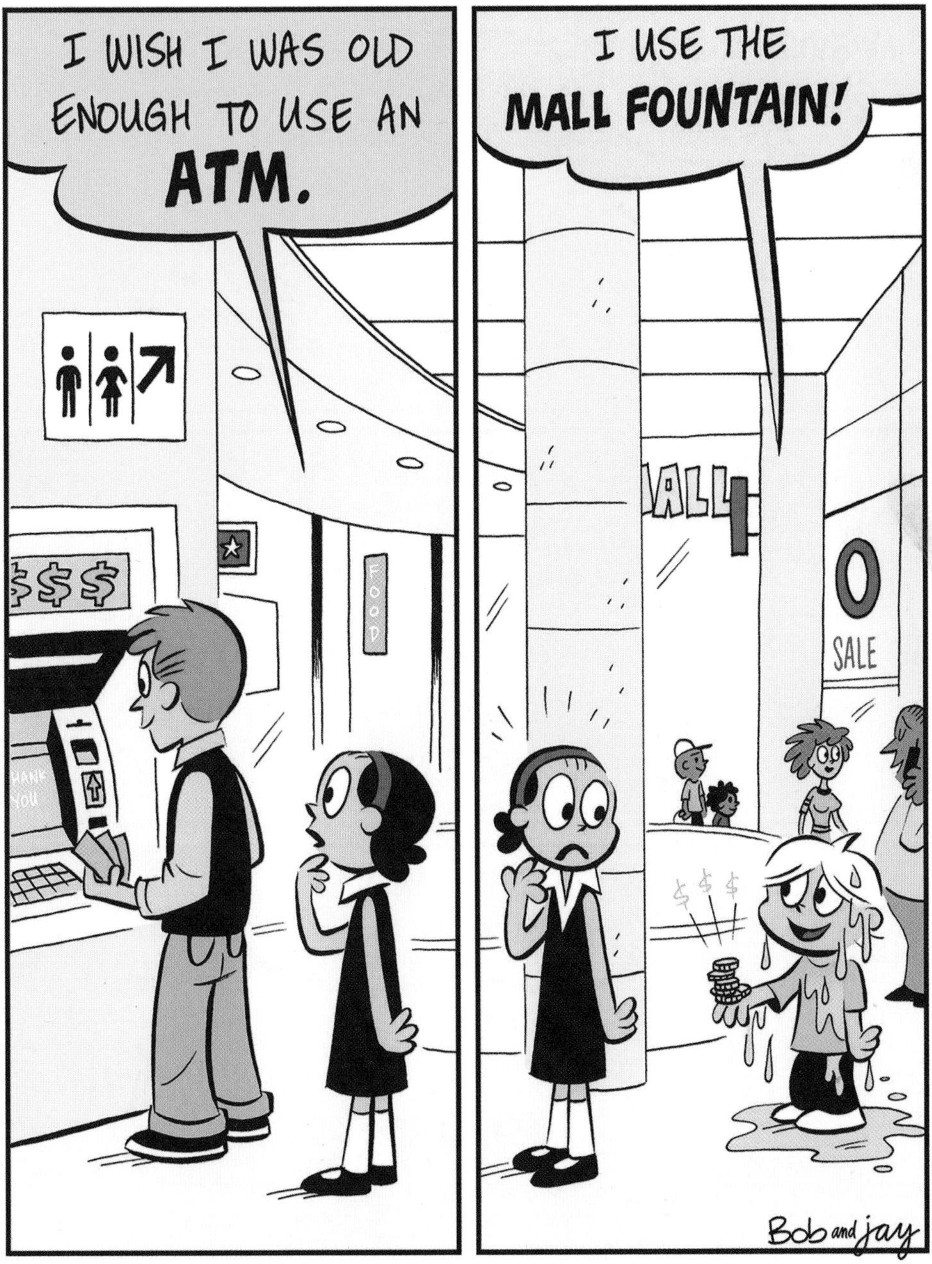
I WISH I WAS OLD ENOUGH TO USE AN **ATM.**
$$$
FOOD
HANK YOU
I USE THE **MALL FOUNTAIN!**
ALL
O
SALE
$ $ $
Bob and jay

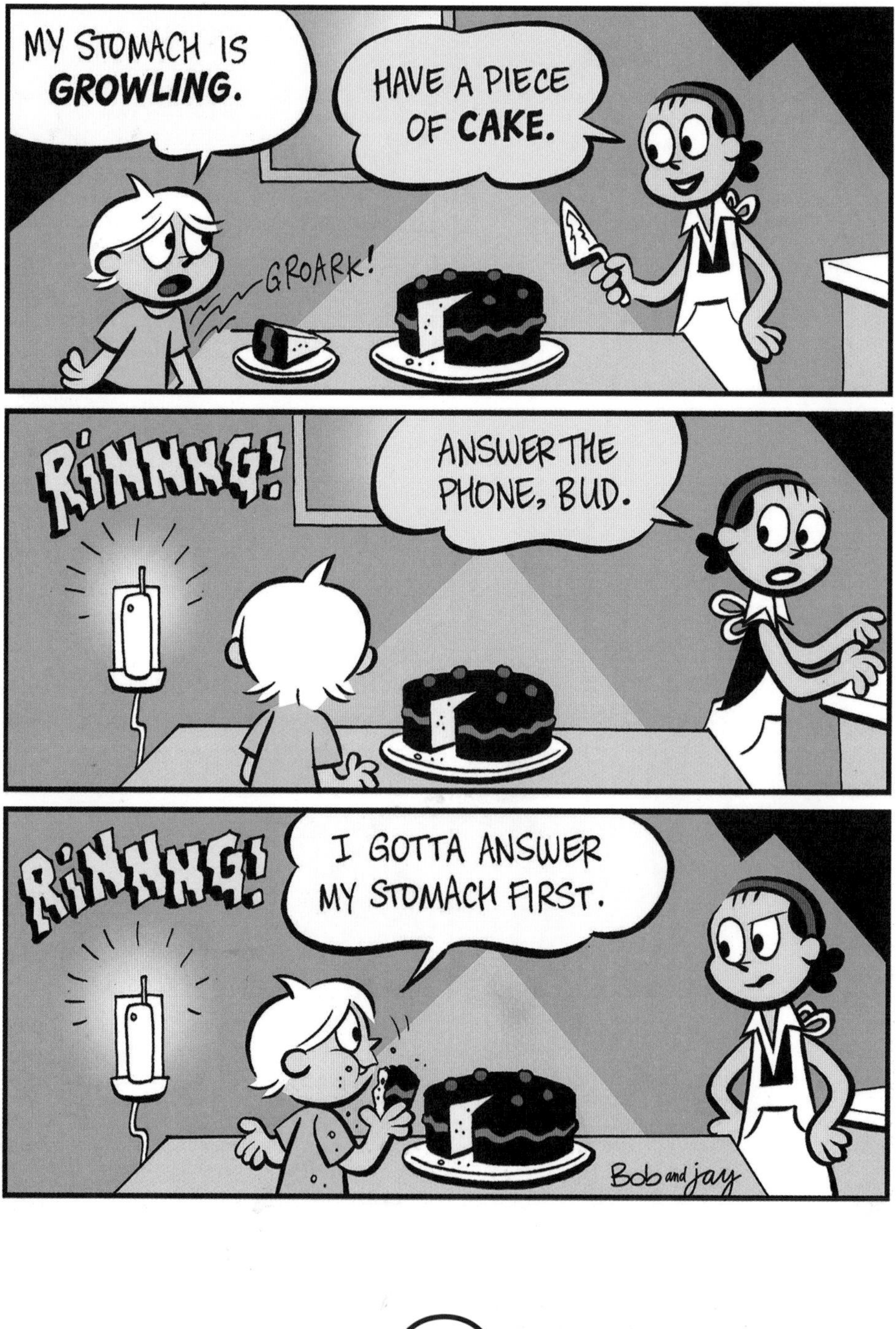
MY STOMACH IS **GROWLING.**
HAVE A PIECE OF **CAKE.**
GROARK!
RINNNG!
ANSWER THE PHONE, BUD.
RINNNG!
I GOTTA ANSWER MY STOMACH FIRST.
Bob and jay

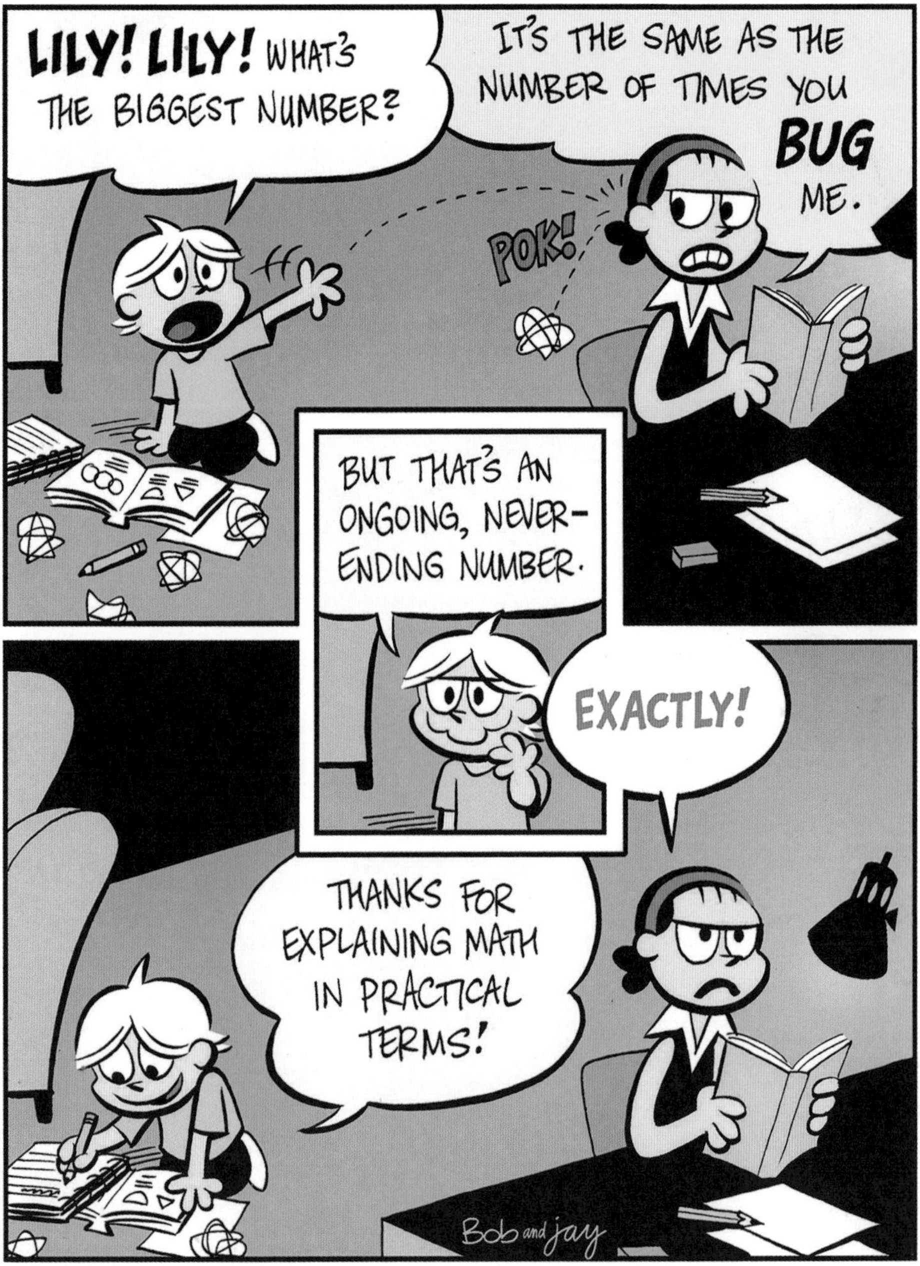
LILY! LILY! WHAT'S THE BIGGEST NUMBER?
IT'S THE SAME AS THE NUMBER OF TIMES YOU BUG ME.
POK!
BUT THAT'S AN ONGOING, NEVER-ENDING NUMBER.
EXACTLY!
THANKS FOR EXPLAINING MATH IN PRACTICAL TERMS!
Bob and jay

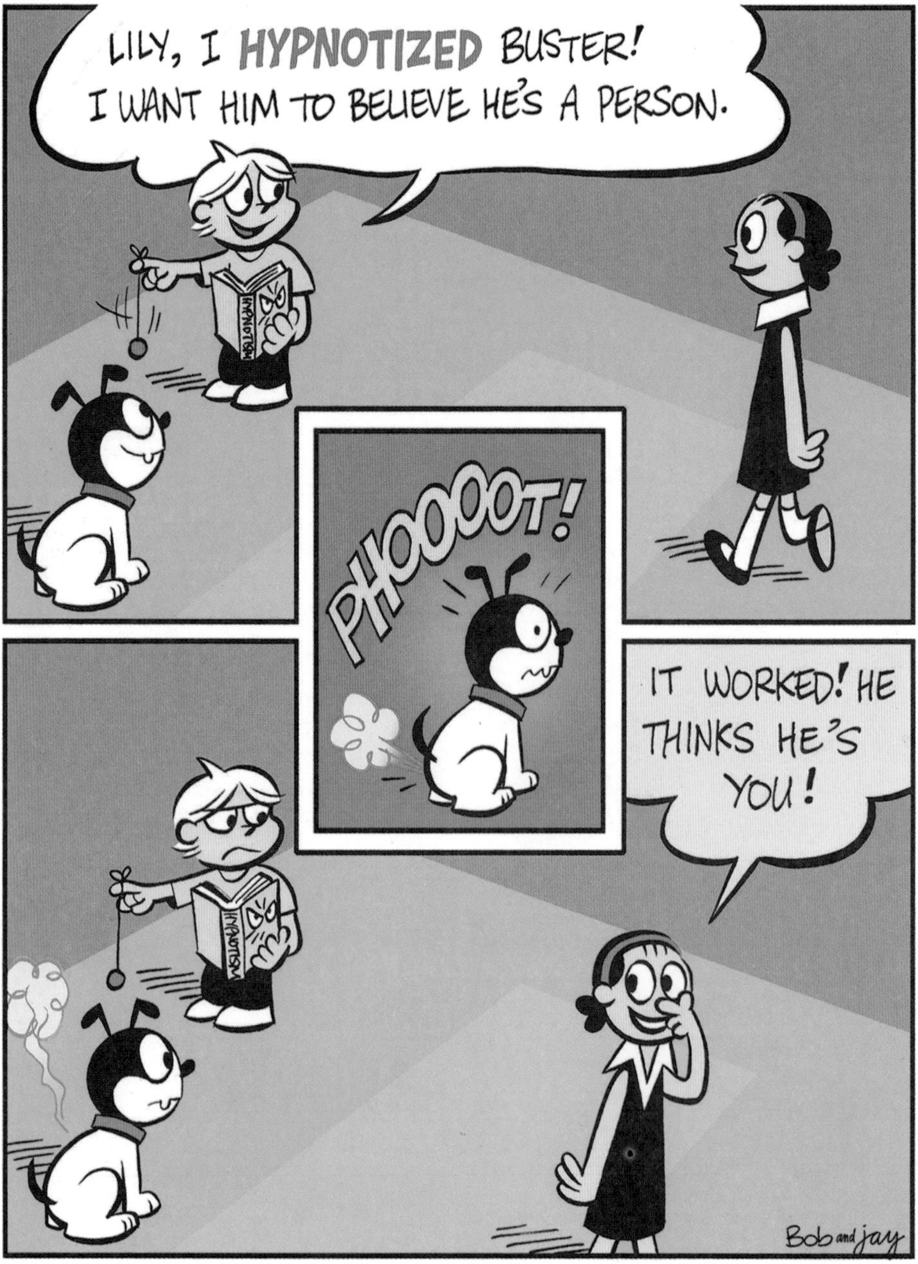
LILY, I HYPNOTIZED BUSTER! I WANT HIM TO BELIEVE HE'S A PERSON.
HYPNOTISM
PHOOOOT!
IT WORKED! HE THINKS HE'S YOU!
HYPNOTISM
Bob and jay

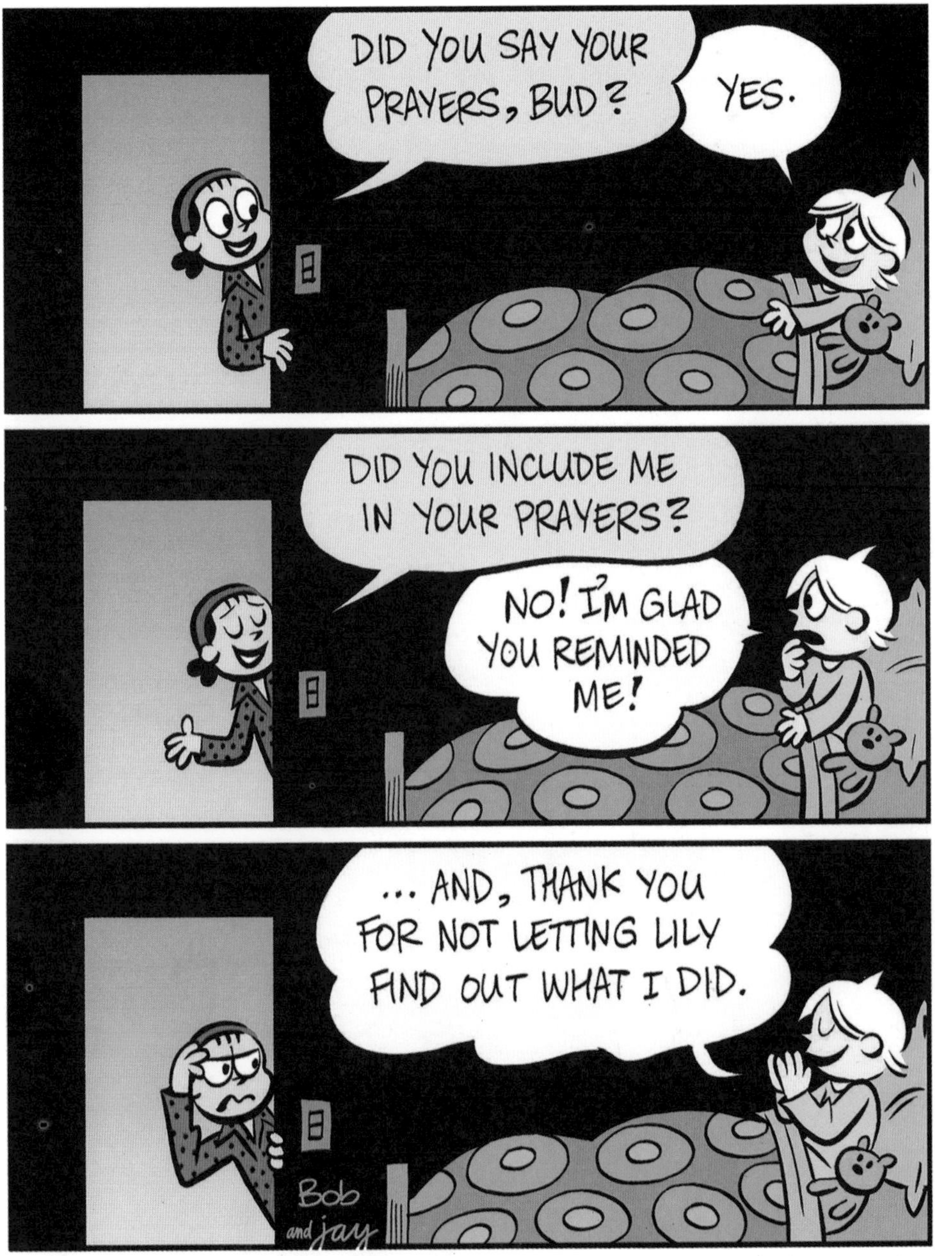
DID YOU SAY YOUR PRAYERS, BUD?
YES.
DID YOU INCLUDE ME IN YOUR PRAYERS?
NO! I'M GLAD YOU REMINDED ME!
... AND, THANK YOU FOR NOT LETTING LILY FIND OUT WHAT I DID.
Bob and jay

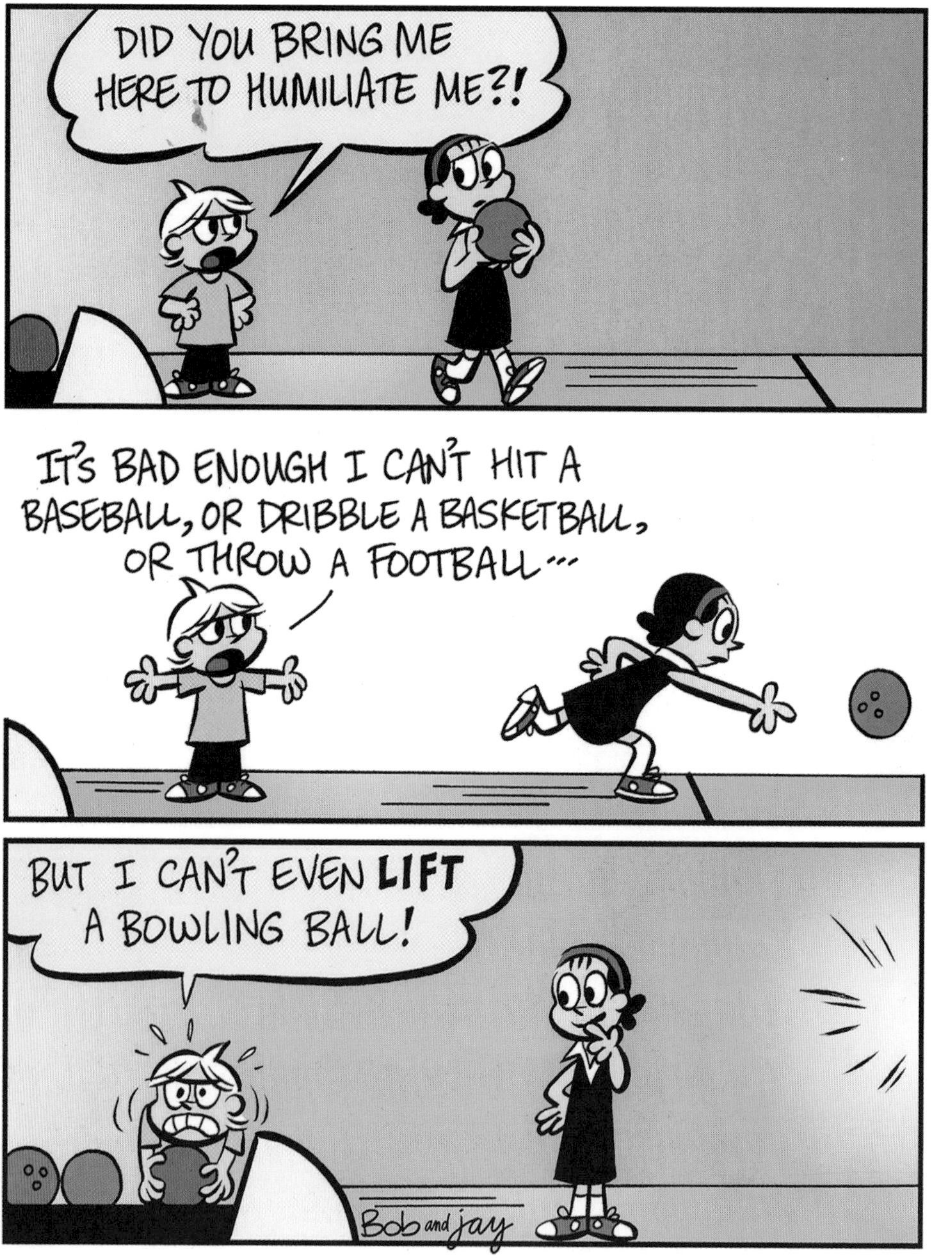
DID YOU BRING ME HERE TO HUMILIATE ME?!
IT'S BAD ENOUGH I CAN'T HIT A BASEBALL, OR DRIBBLE A BASKETBALL, OR THROW A FOOTBALL...
BUT I CAN'T EVEN **LIFT** A BOWLING BALL!
Bob and jay

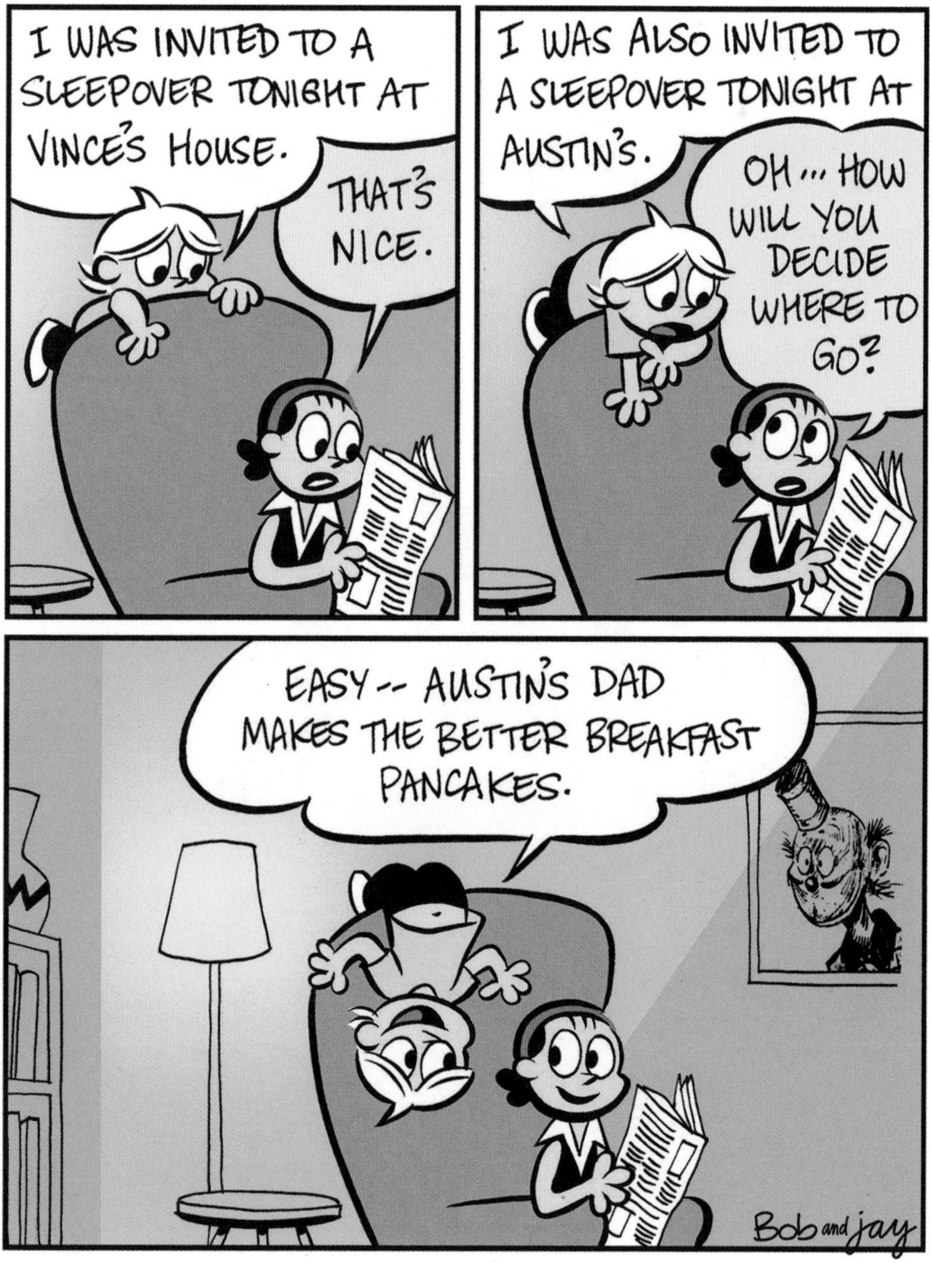
I WAS INVITED TO A SLEEPOVER TONIGHT AT VINCE'S HOUSE.
THAT'S NICE.
I WAS ALSO INVITED TO A SLEEPOVER TONIGHT AT AUSTIN'S.
OH... HOW WILL YOU DECIDE WHERE TO GO?
EASY -- AUSTIN'S DAD MAKES THE BETTER BREAKFAST PANCAKES.
Bob and jay

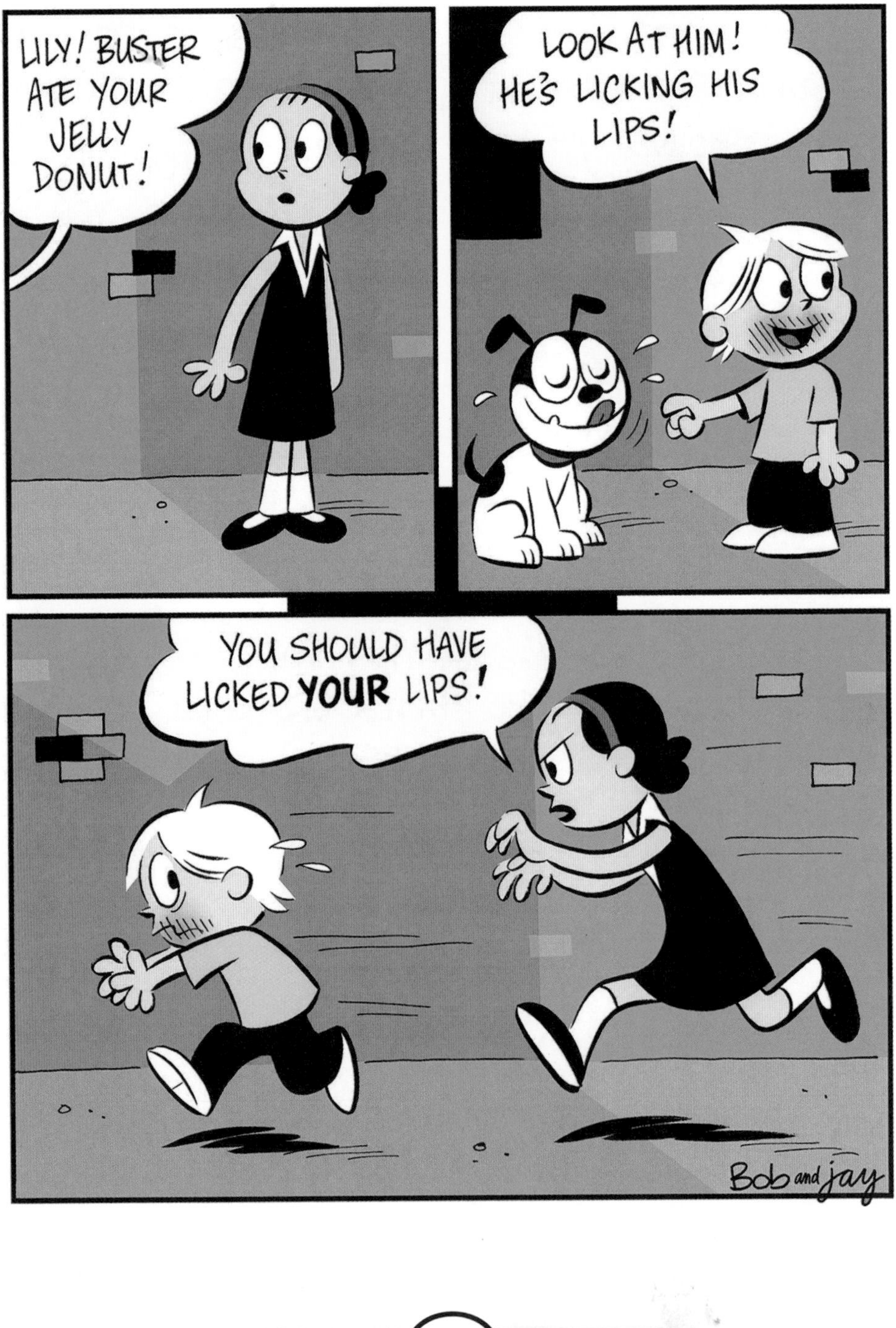
LILY! BUSTER ATE YOUR JELLY DONUT!
LOOK AT HIM! HE'S LICKING HIS LIPS!
YOU SHOULD HAVE LICKED **YOUR** LIPS!
Bob and jay

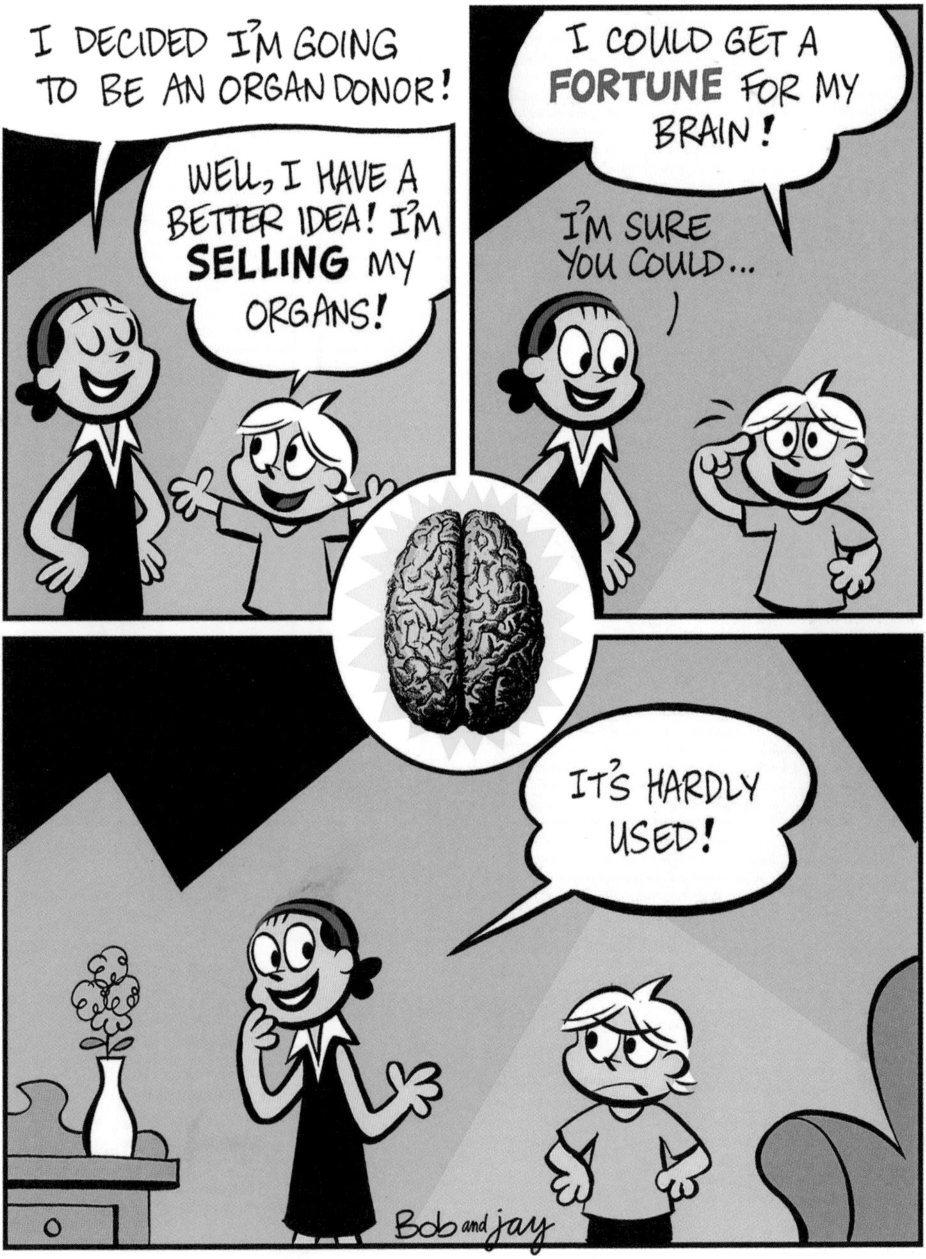
I DECIDED I'M GOING TO BE AN ORGAN DONOR!
WELL, I HAVE A BETTER IDEA! I'M SELLING MY ORGANS!
I COULD GET A FORTUNE FOR MY BRAIN!
I'M SURE YOU COULD...
IT'S HARDLY USED!
Bob and jay

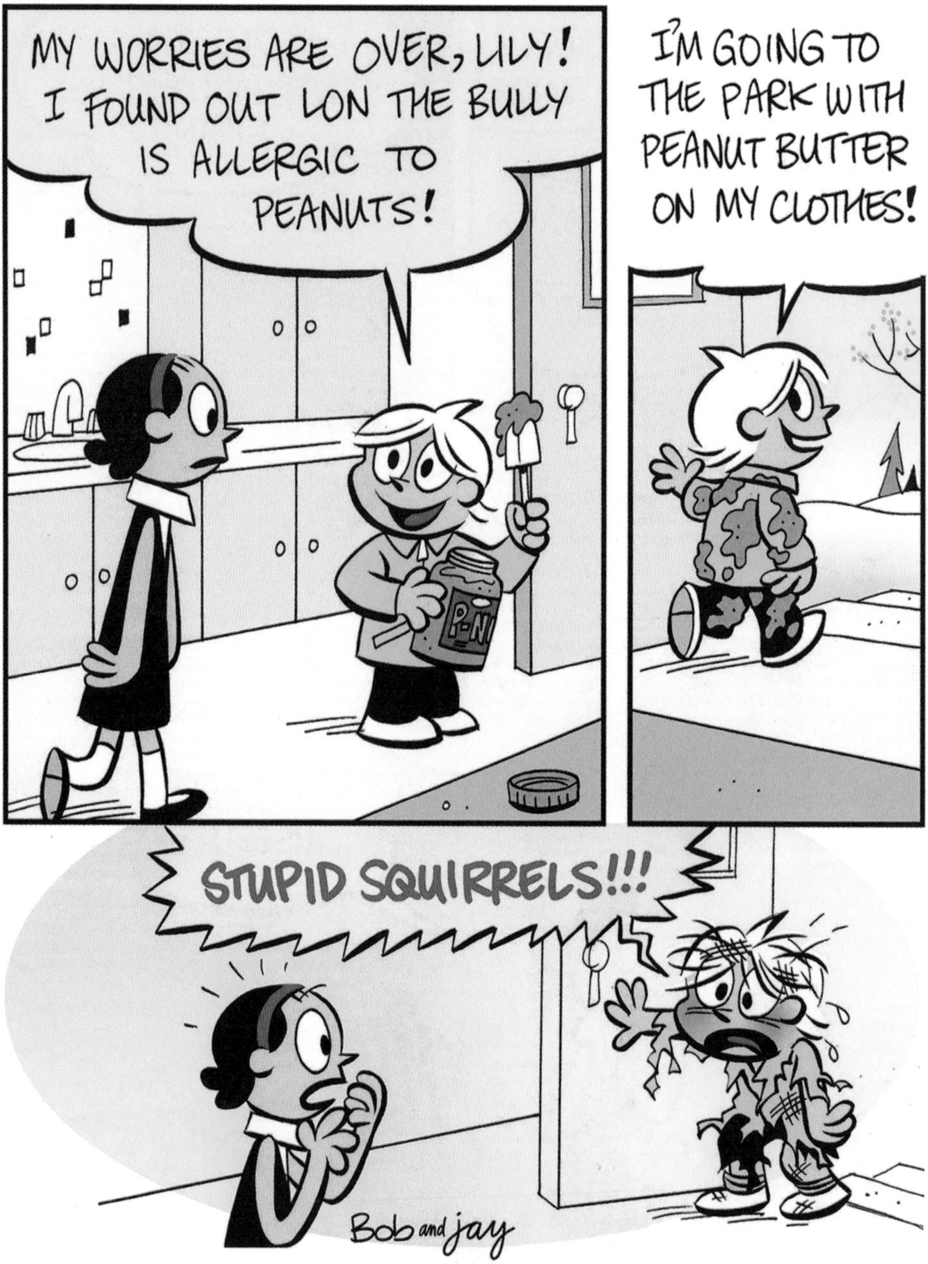
MY WORRIES ARE OVER, LILY! I FOUND OUT LON THE BULLY IS ALLERGIC TO PEANUTS!
P-NU
I'M GOING TO THE PARK WITH PEANUT BUTTER ON MY CLOTHES!
STUPID SQUIRRELS!!!
Bob and jay

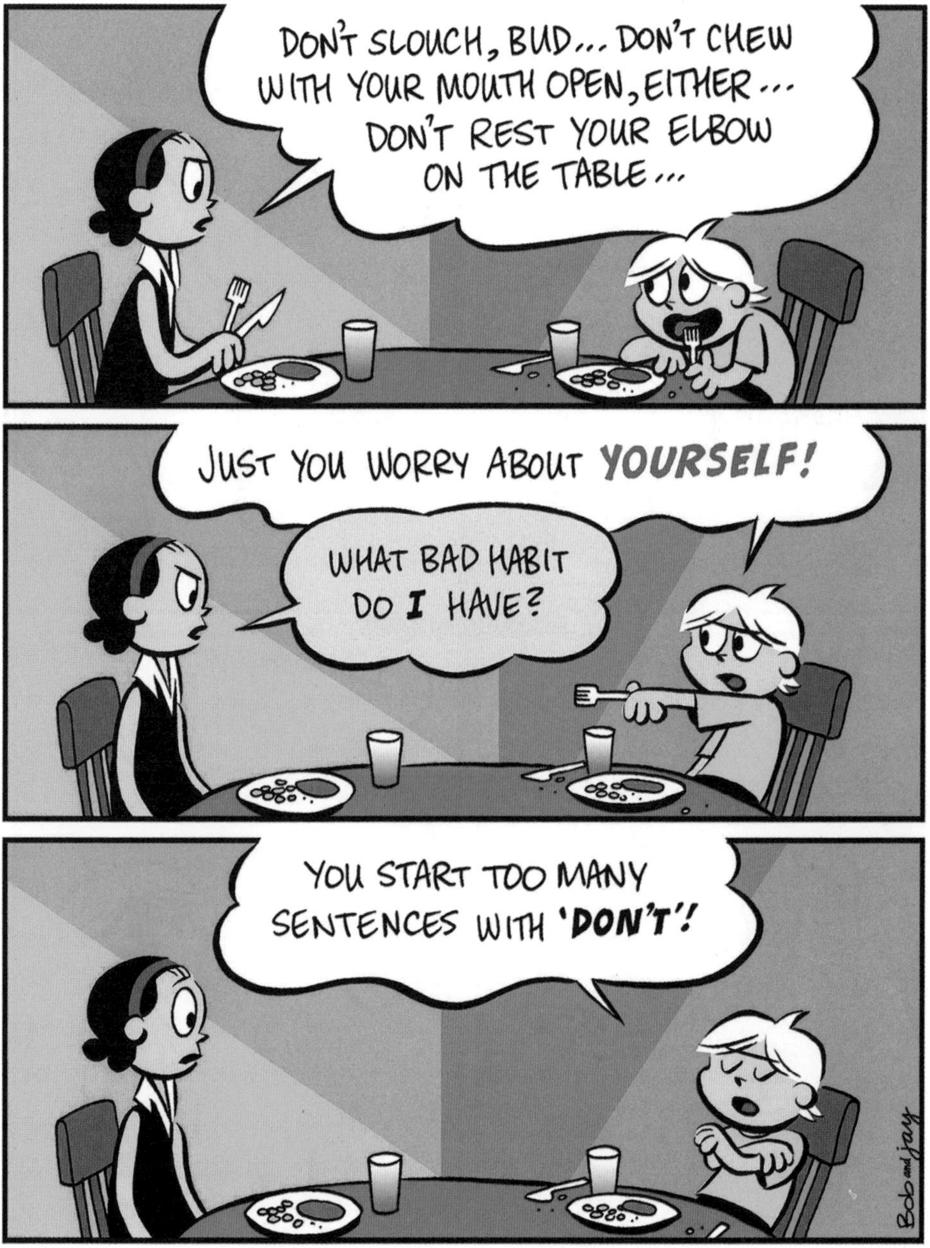
DON'T SLOUCH, BUD... DON'T CHEW WITH YOUR MOUTH OPEN, EITHER... DON'T REST YOUR ELBOW ON THE TABLE...
JUST YOU WORRY ABOUT YOURSELF!
WHAT BAD HABIT DO I HAVE?
YOU START TOO MANY SENTENCES WITH 'DON'T'!
Bob and jay

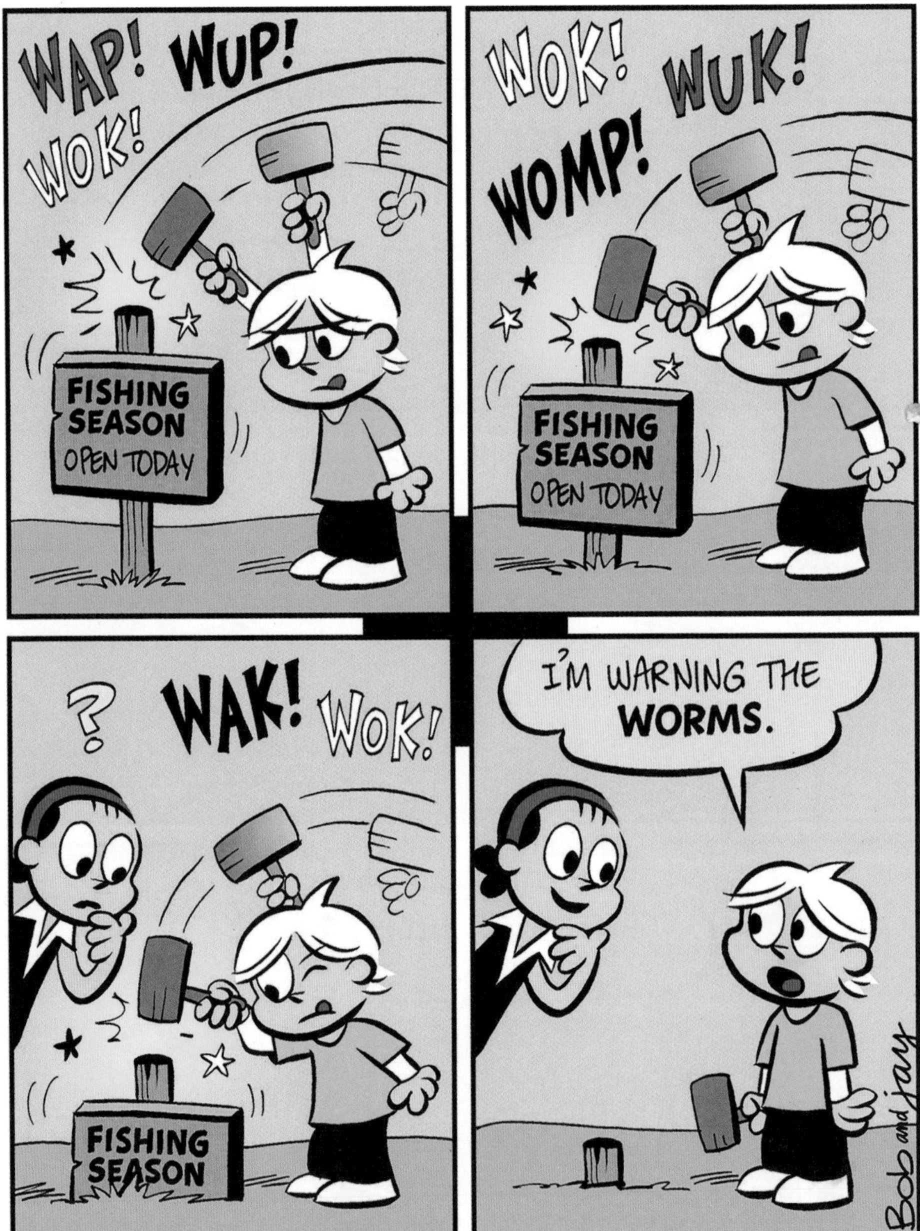

WAP! WUP!
WOK!
FISHING SEASON OPEN TODAY
WOK! WUK!
WOMP!
FISHING SEASON OPEN TODAY
?
WAK! WOK!
FISHING SEASON
I'M WARNING THE WORMS.
Bob and jay

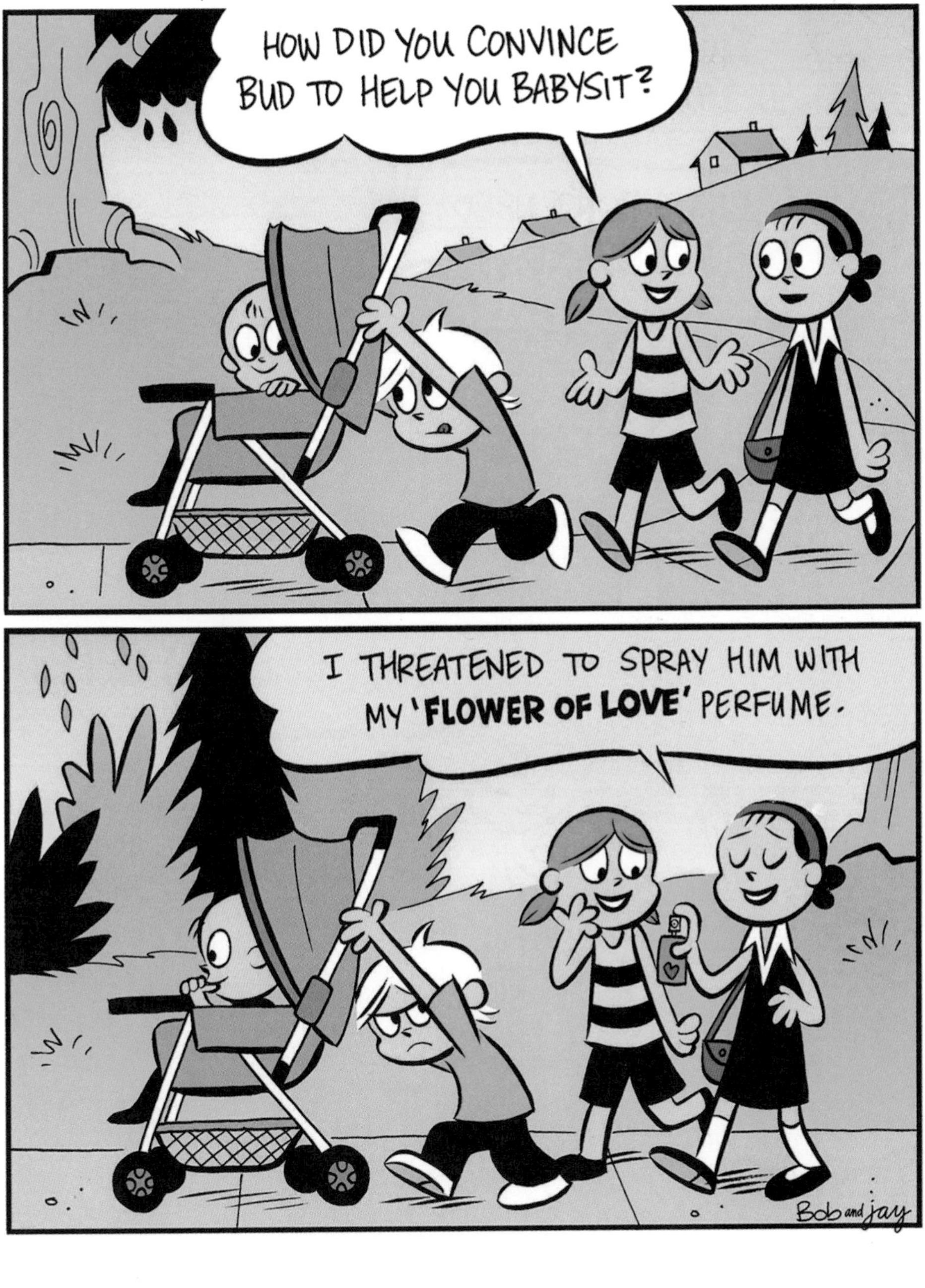
HOW DID YOU CONVINCE BUD TO HELP YOU BABYSIT?
I THREATENED TO SPRAY HIM WITH MY 'FLOWER OF LOVE' PERFUME.
Bob and jay

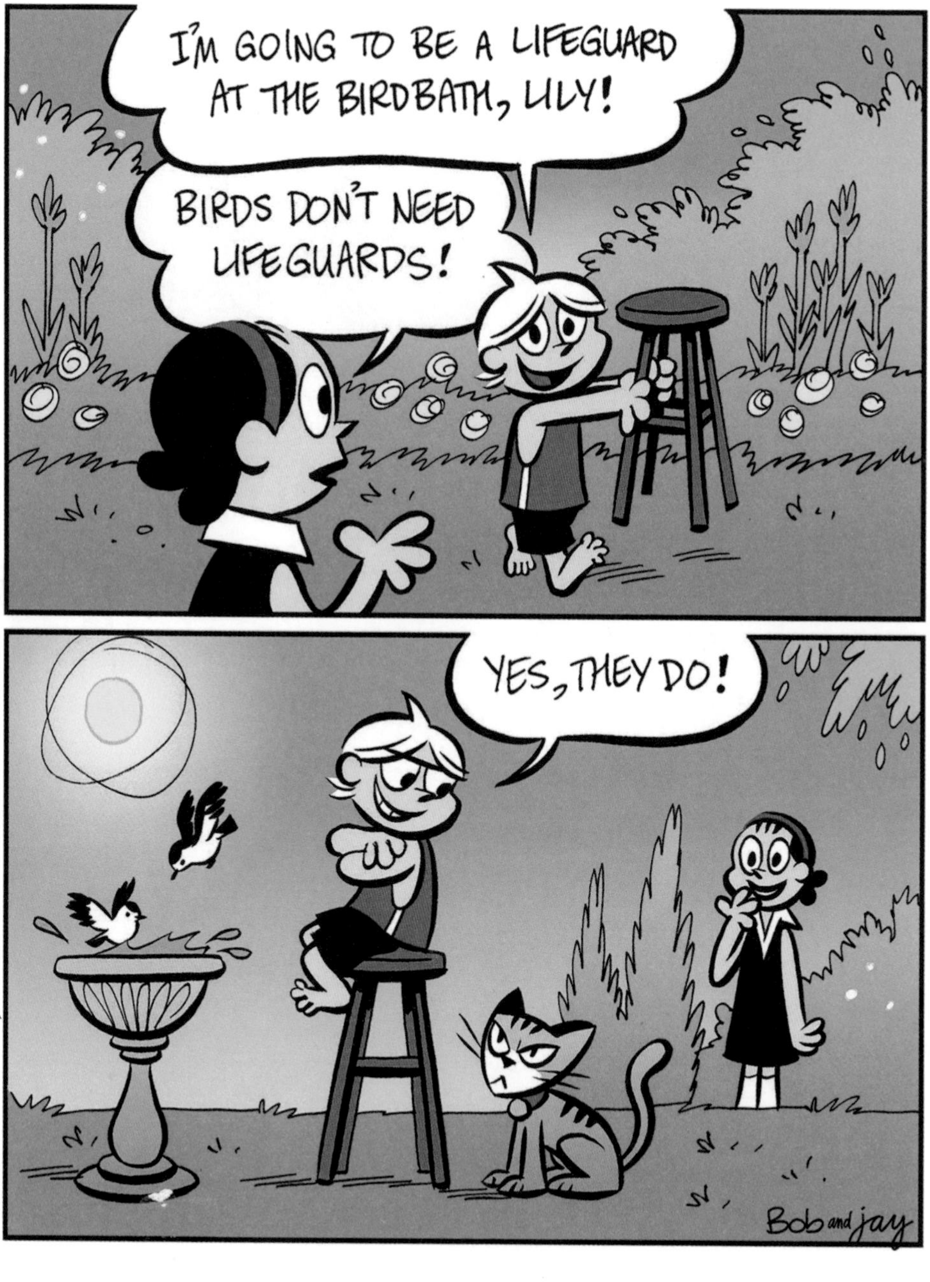
I'M GOING TO BE A LIFEGUARD AT THE BIRDBATH, LILY!
BIRDS DON'T NEED LIFEGUARDS!
YES, THEY DO!
Bob and jay

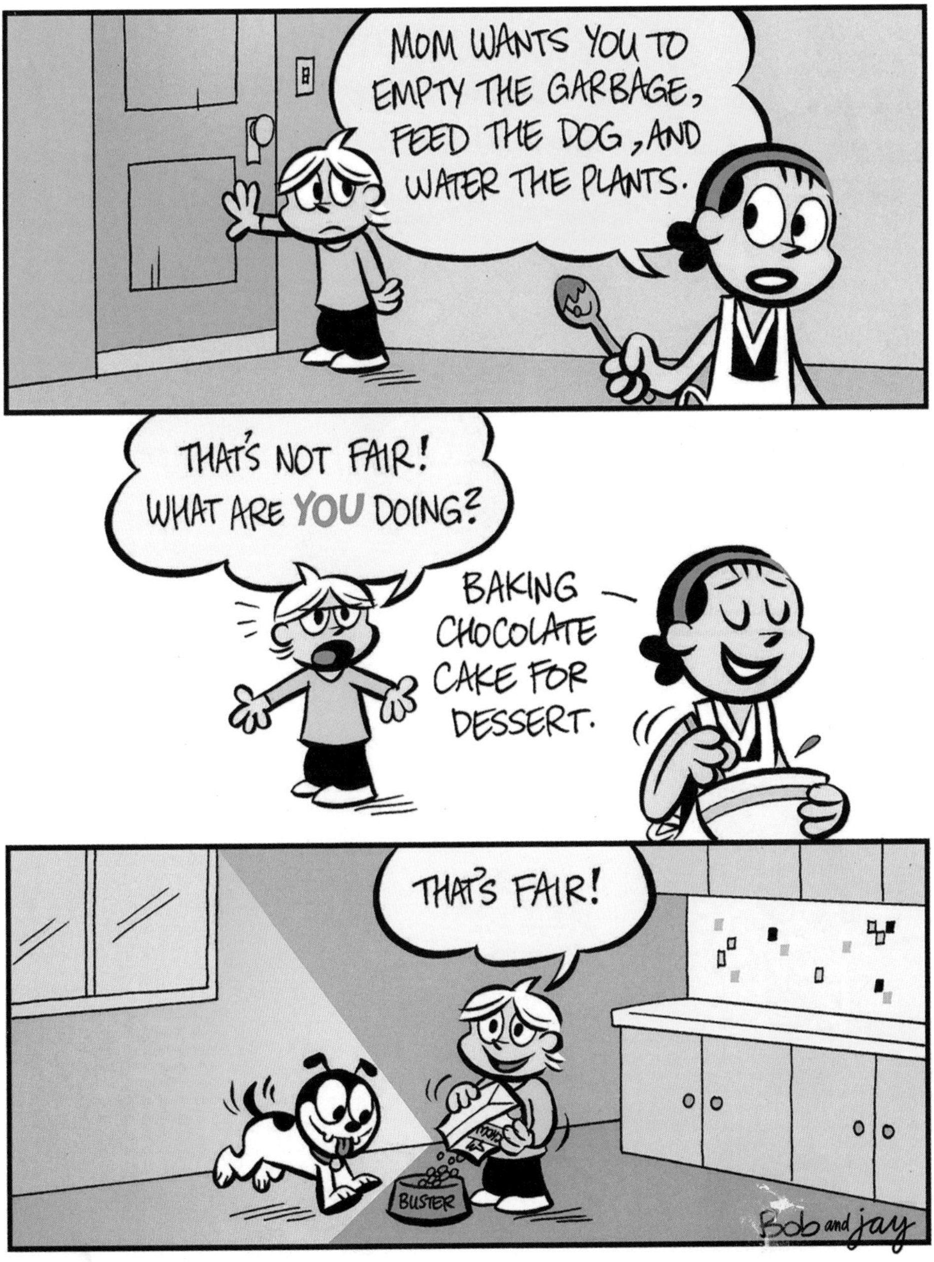
MOM WANTS YOU TO EMPTY THE GARBAGE, FEED THE DOG, AND WATER THE PLANTS.
THAT'S NOT FAIR! WHAT ARE YOU DOING?
BAKING CHOCOLATE CAKE FOR DESSERT.
THAT'S FAIR!
BUSTER
Bob and jay

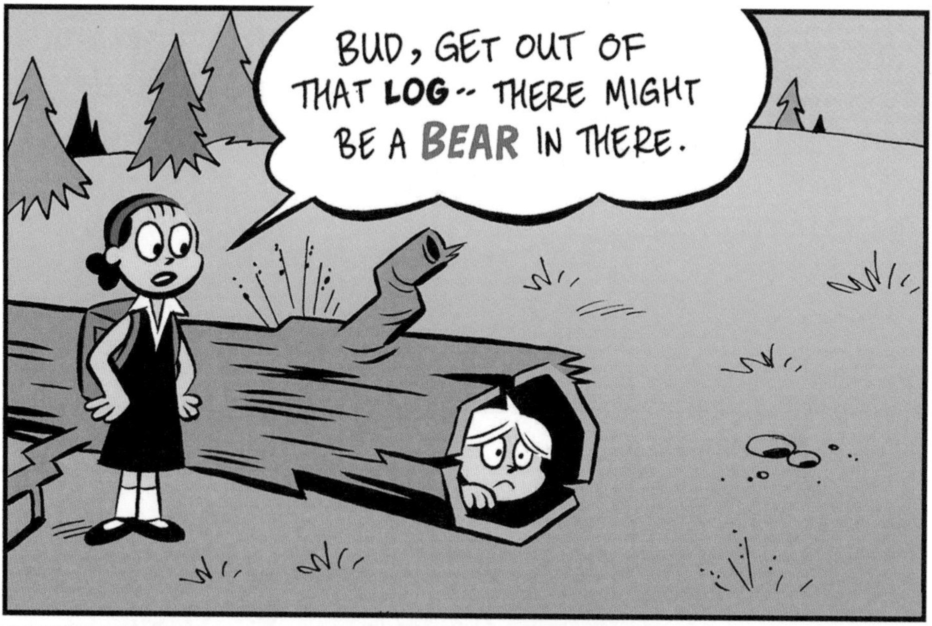
BUD, GET OUT OF THAT **LOG**-- THERE MIGHT BE A **BEAR** IN THERE.

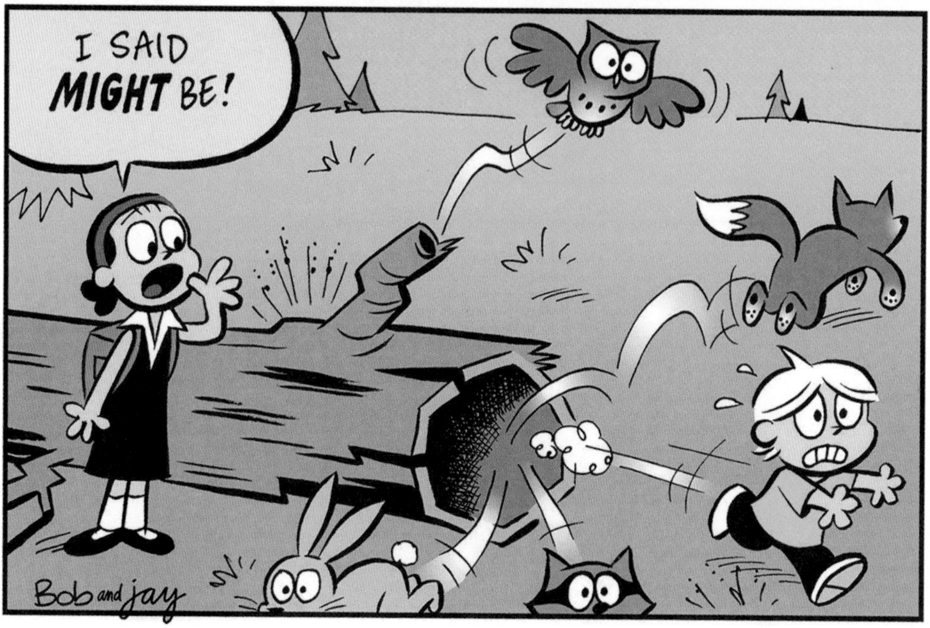
I SAID **MIGHT** BE!
Bob and jay

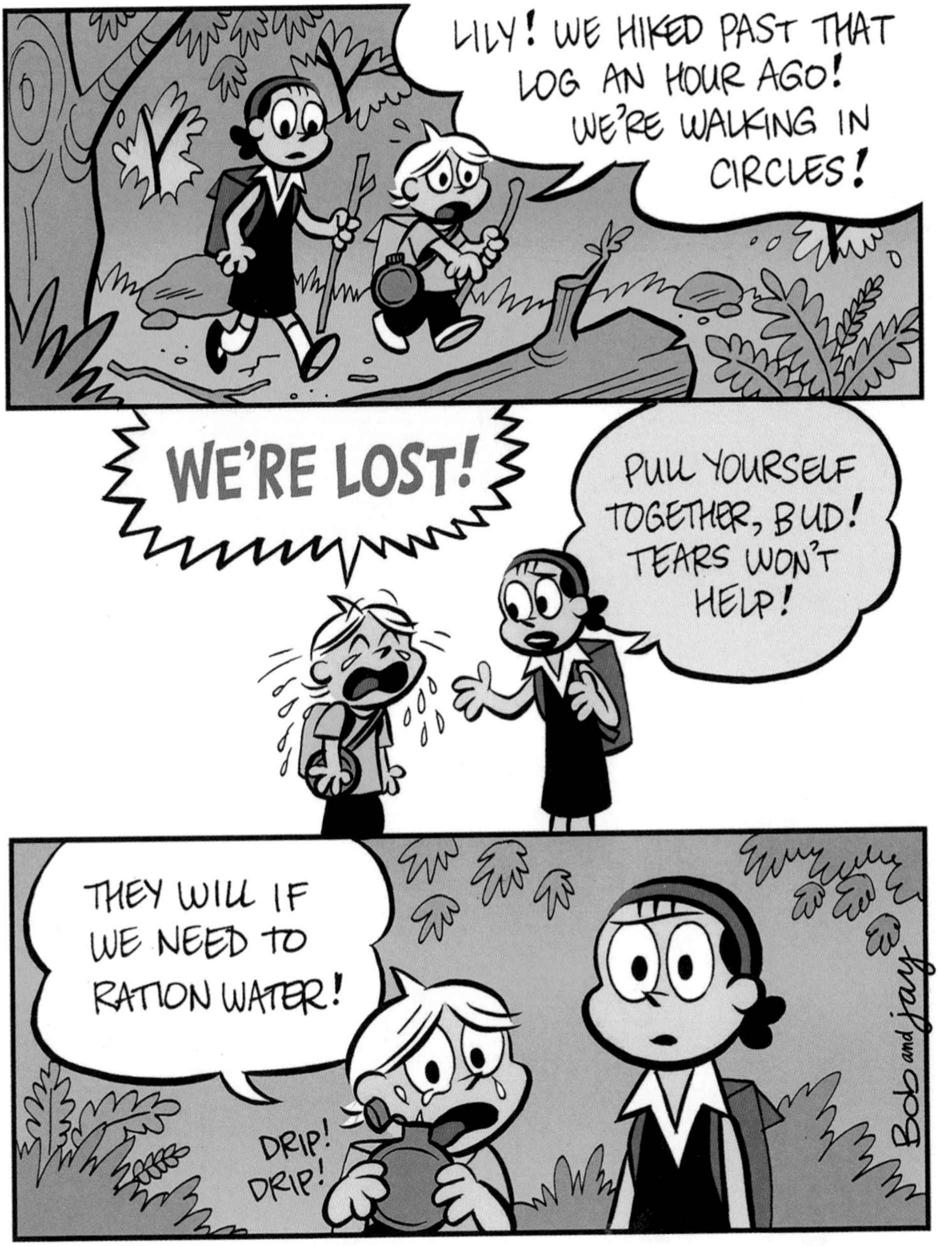
LILY! WE HIKED PAST THAT LOG AN HOUR AGO! WE'RE WALKING IN CIRCLES!
WE'RE LOST!
PULL YOURSELF TOGETHER, BUD! TEARS WON'T HELP!
THEY WILL IF WE NEED TO RATION WATER!
DRIP! DRIP!
Bob and jay

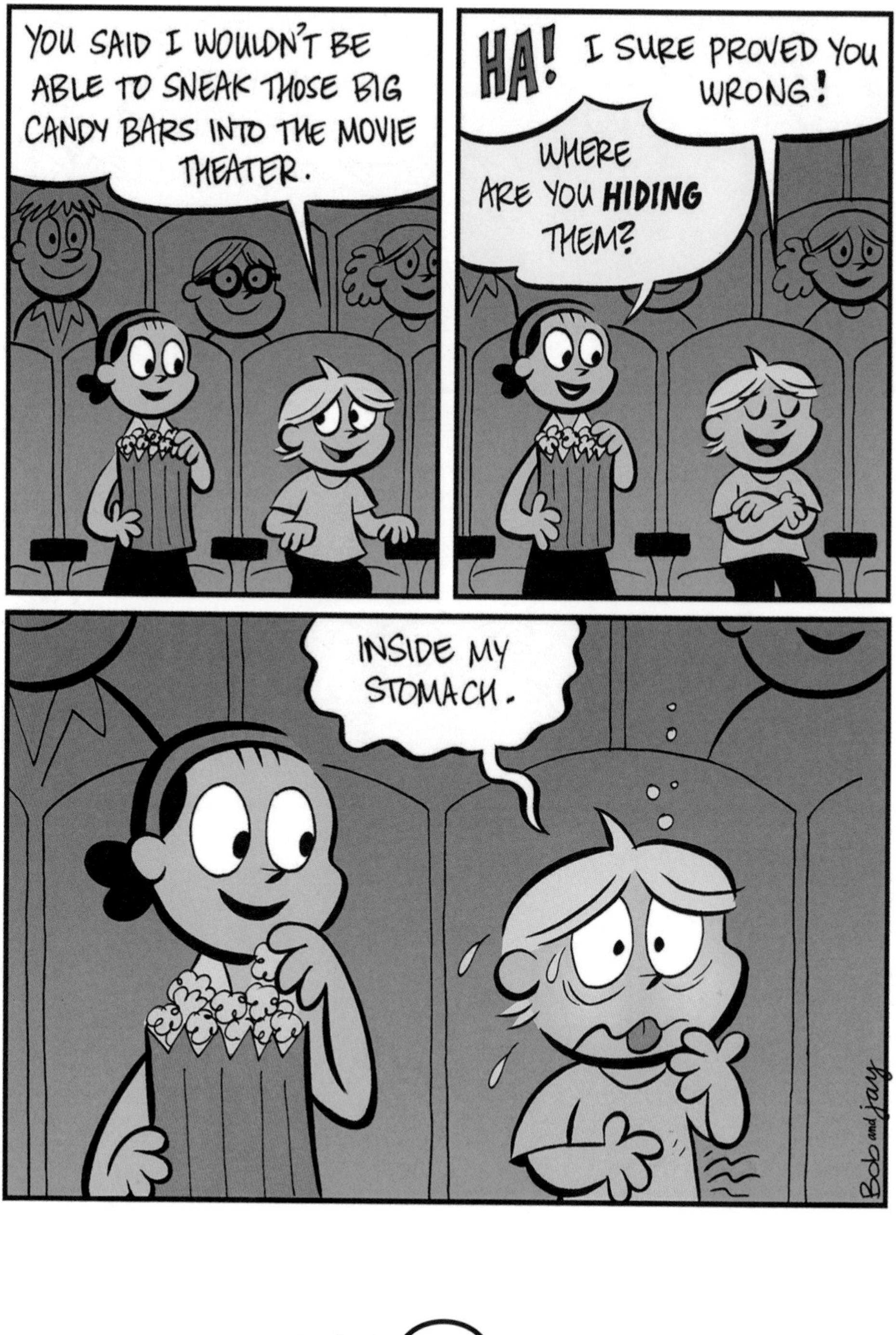
YOU SAID I WOULDN'T BE ABLE TO SNEAK THOSE BIG CANDY BARS INTO THE MOVIE THEATER.
HA! I SURE PROVED YOU WRONG!
WHERE ARE YOU **HIDING** THEM?
INSIDE MY STOMACH.
Bob and jay

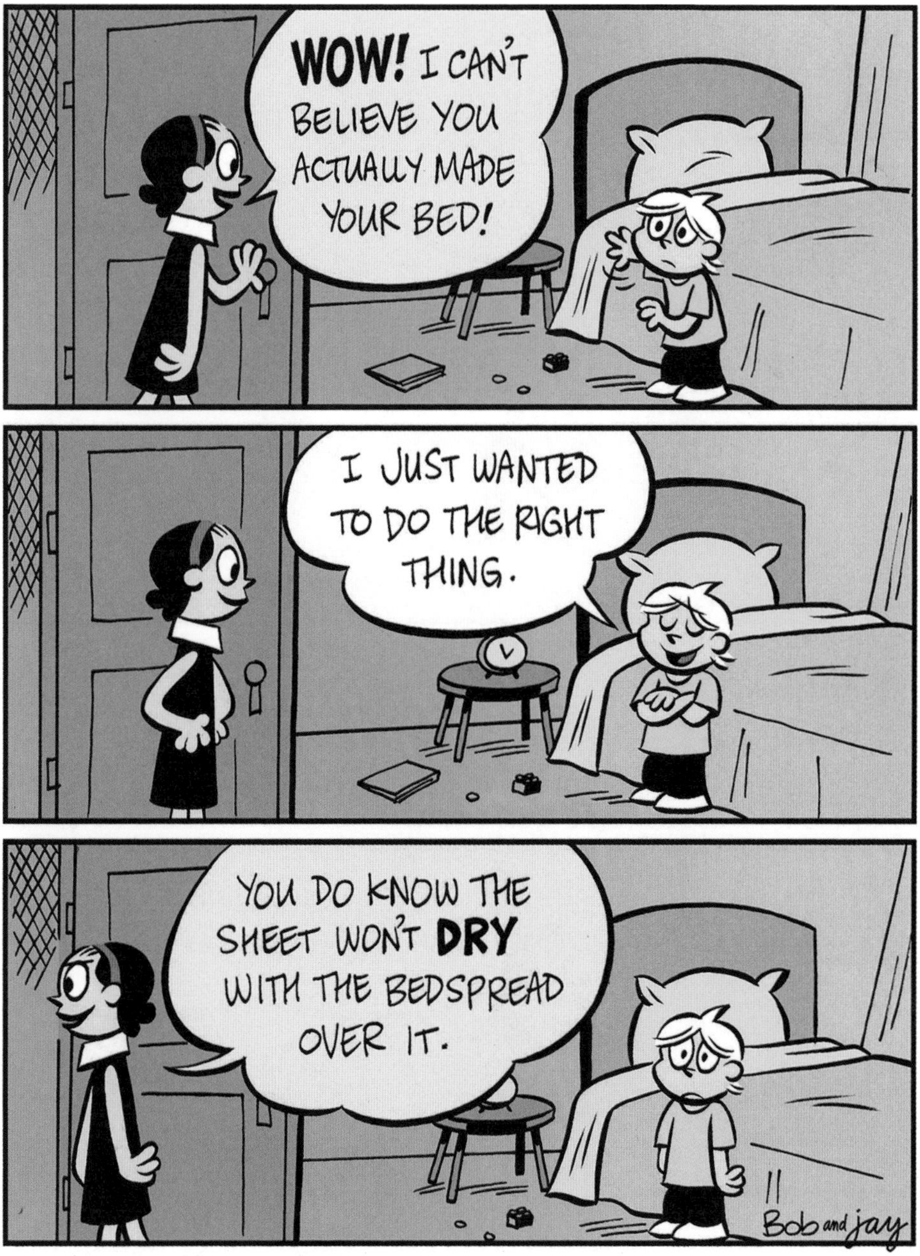
WOW! I CAN'T BELIEVE YOU ACTUALLY MADE YOUR BED!
I JUST WANTED TO DO THE RIGHT THING.
YOU DO KNOW THE SHEET WON'T DRY WITH THE BEDSPREAD OVER IT.
Bob and jay

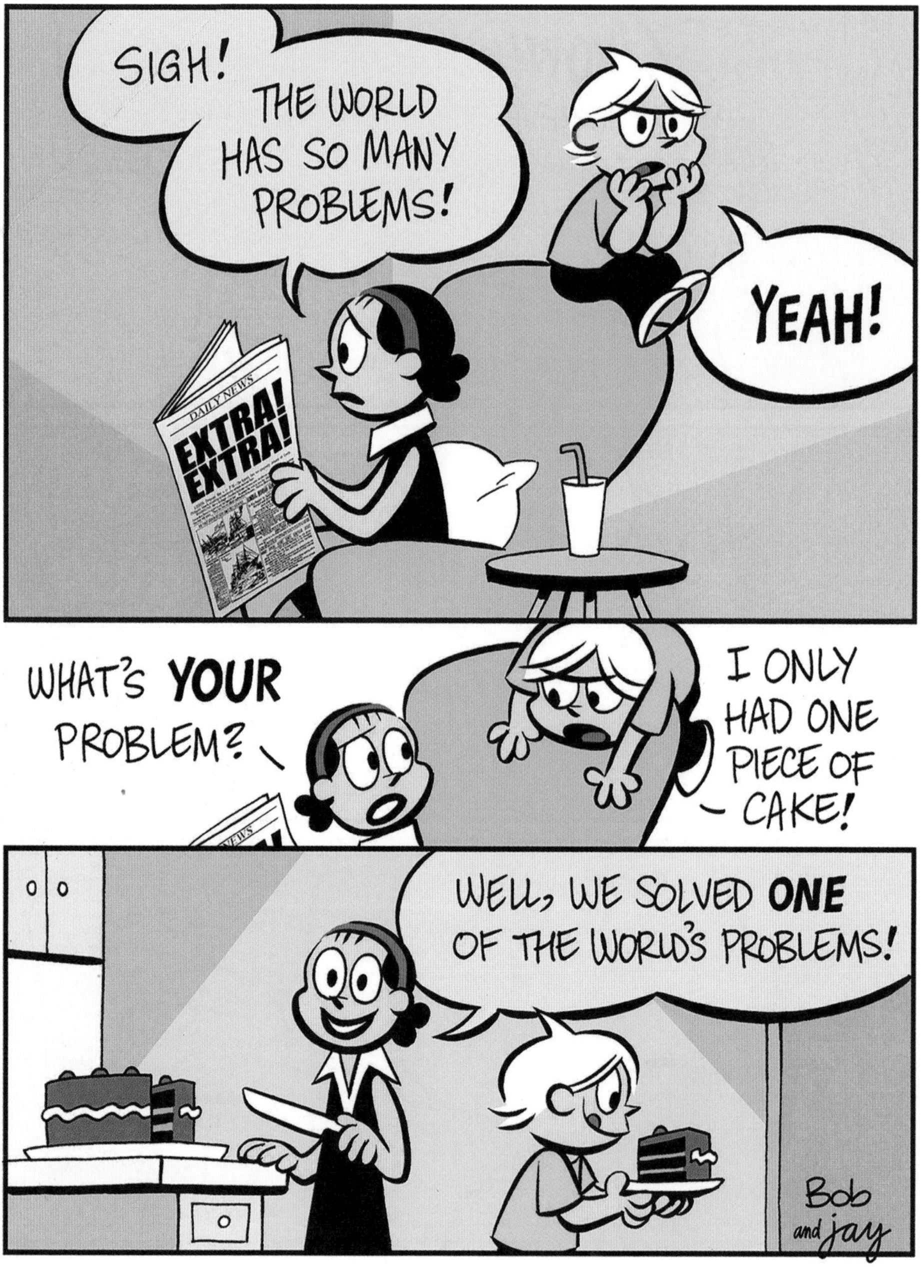
SIGH!
THE WORLD HAS SO MANY PROBLEMS!
YEAH!
DAILY NEWS
EXTRA! EXTRA!
WHAT'S **YOUR** PROBLEM?
I ONLY HAD ONE PIECE OF CAKE!
WELL, WE SOLVED **ONE** OF THE WORLD'S PROBLEMS!
Bob and jay

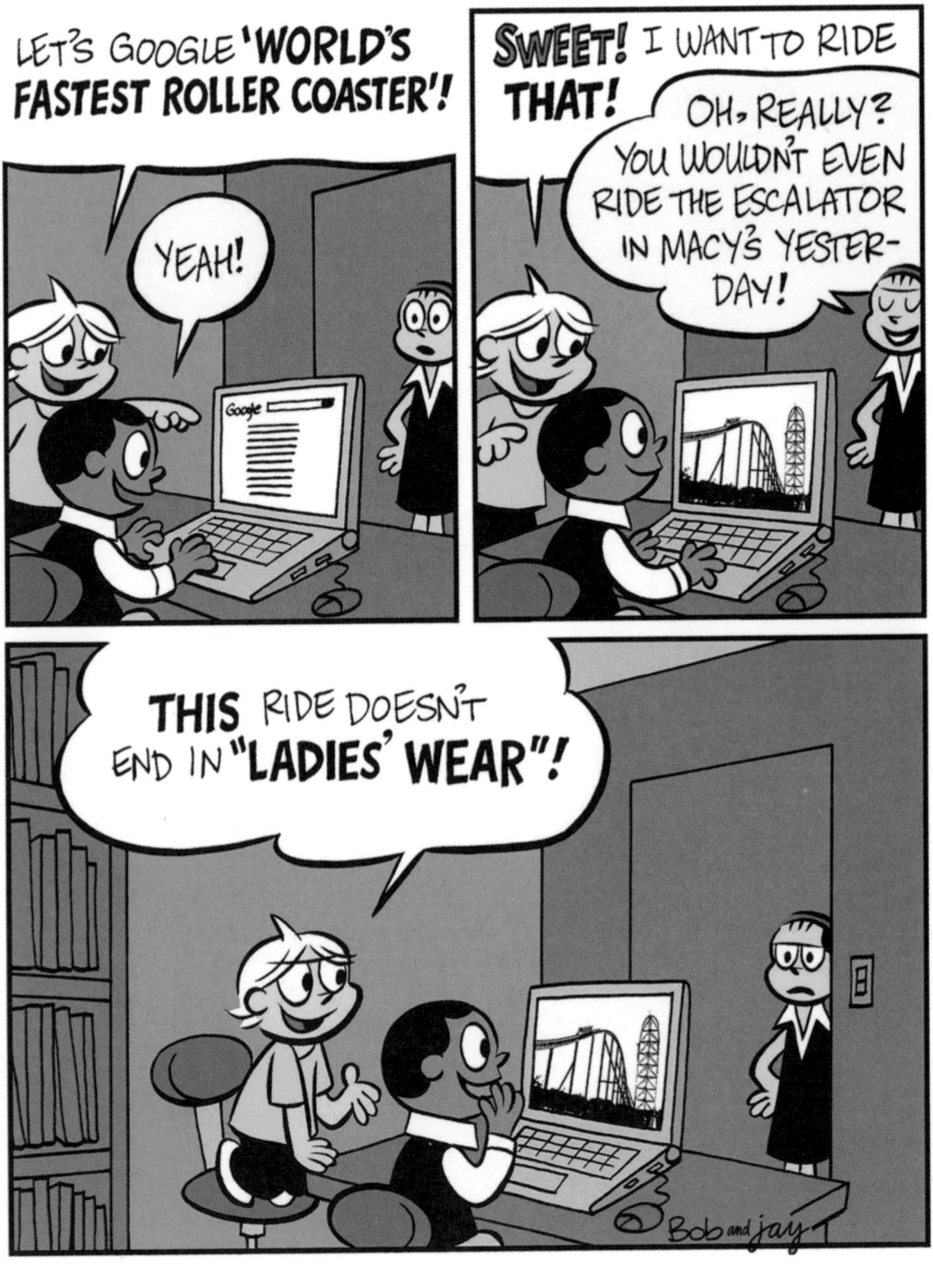

LET'S GOOGLE 'WORLD'S FASTEST ROLLER COASTER'!
YEAH!
Google
SWEET! I WANT TO RIDE THAT!
OH, REALLY? YOU WOULDN'T EVEN RIDE THE ESCALATOR IN MACY'S YESTER-DAY!
THIS RIDE DOESN'T END IN "LADIES' WEAR"!
Bob and jay

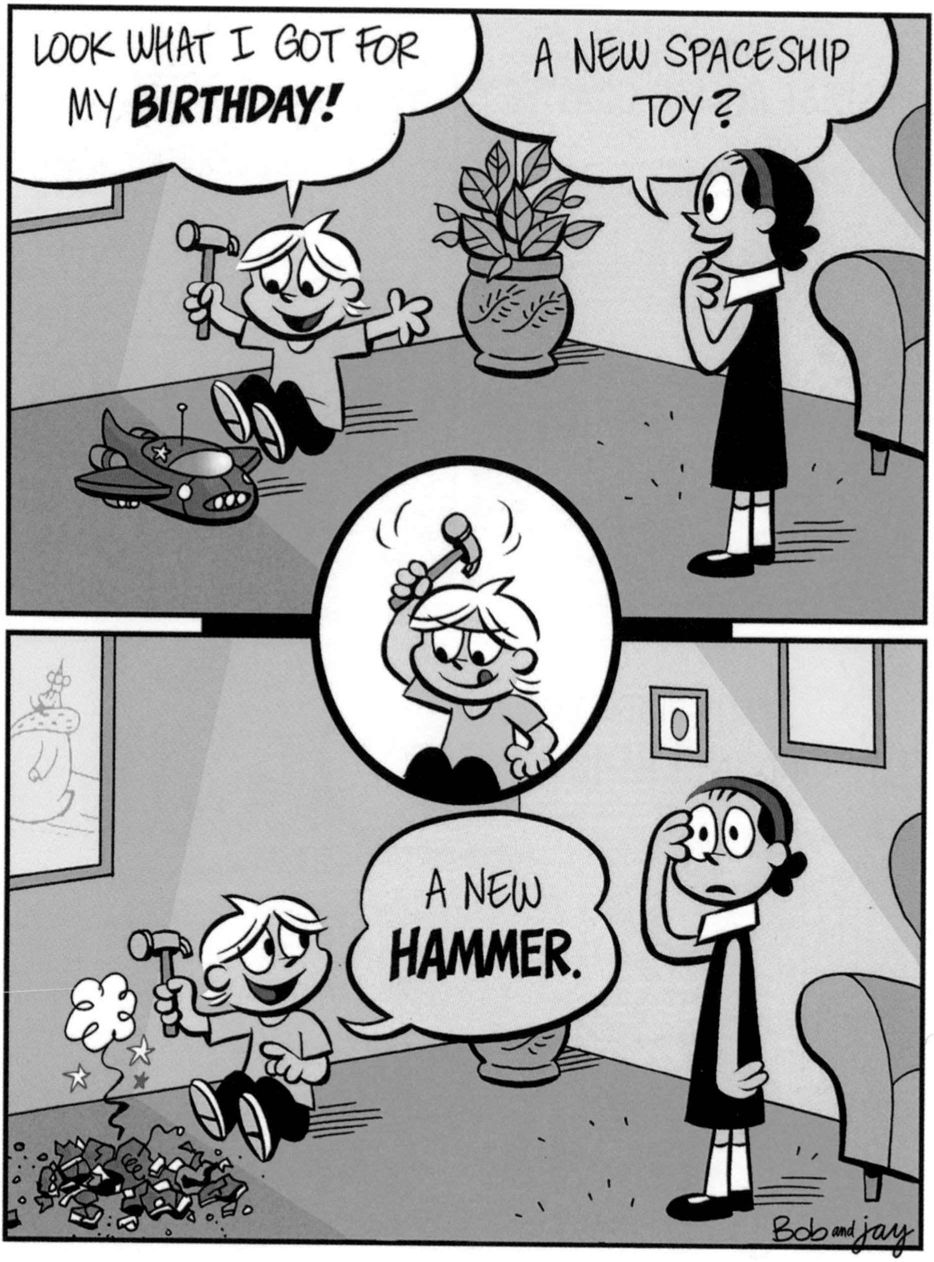
LOOK WHAT I GOT FOR MY **BIRTHDAY!**
A NEW SPACESHIP TOY?
A NEW **HAMMER.**
Bob and jay

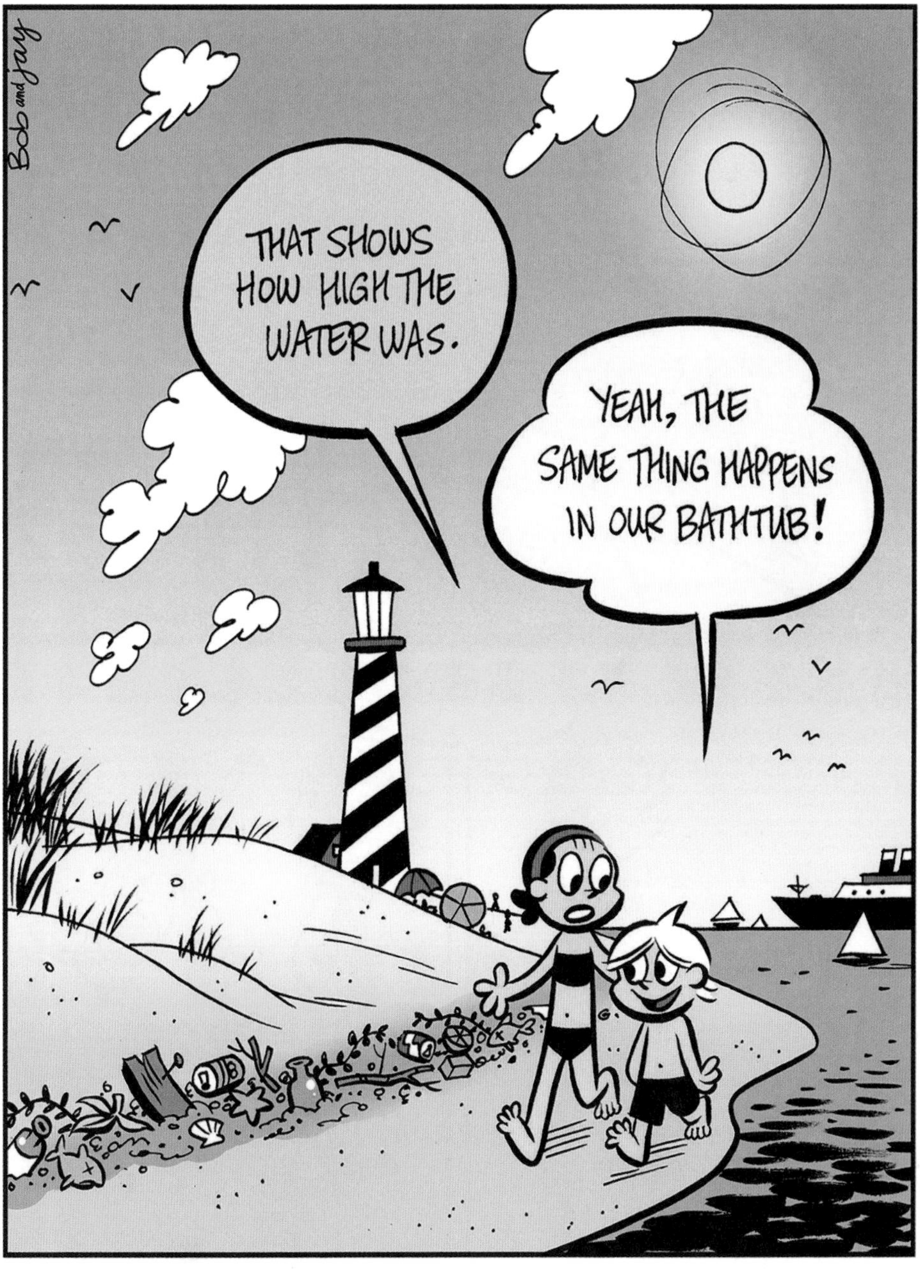
Bob and Jay
THAT SHOWS HOW HIGH THE WATER WAS.
YEAH, THE SAME THING HAPPENS IN OUR BATHTUB!

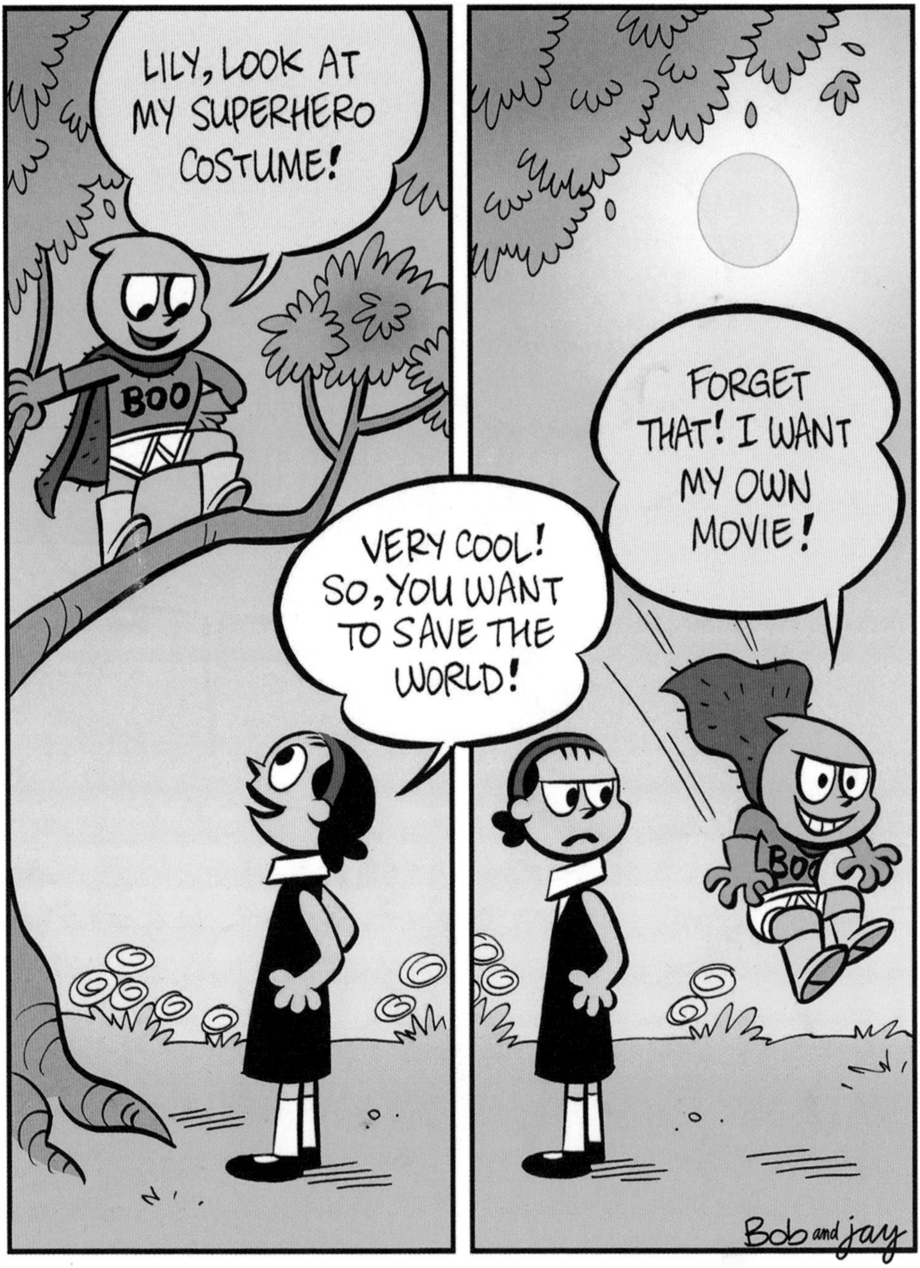
LILY, LOOK AT MY SUPERHERO COSTUME!
BOO
VERY COOL! SO, YOU WANT TO SAVE THE WORLD!
FORGET THAT! I WANT MY OWN MOVIE!
Bob and jay

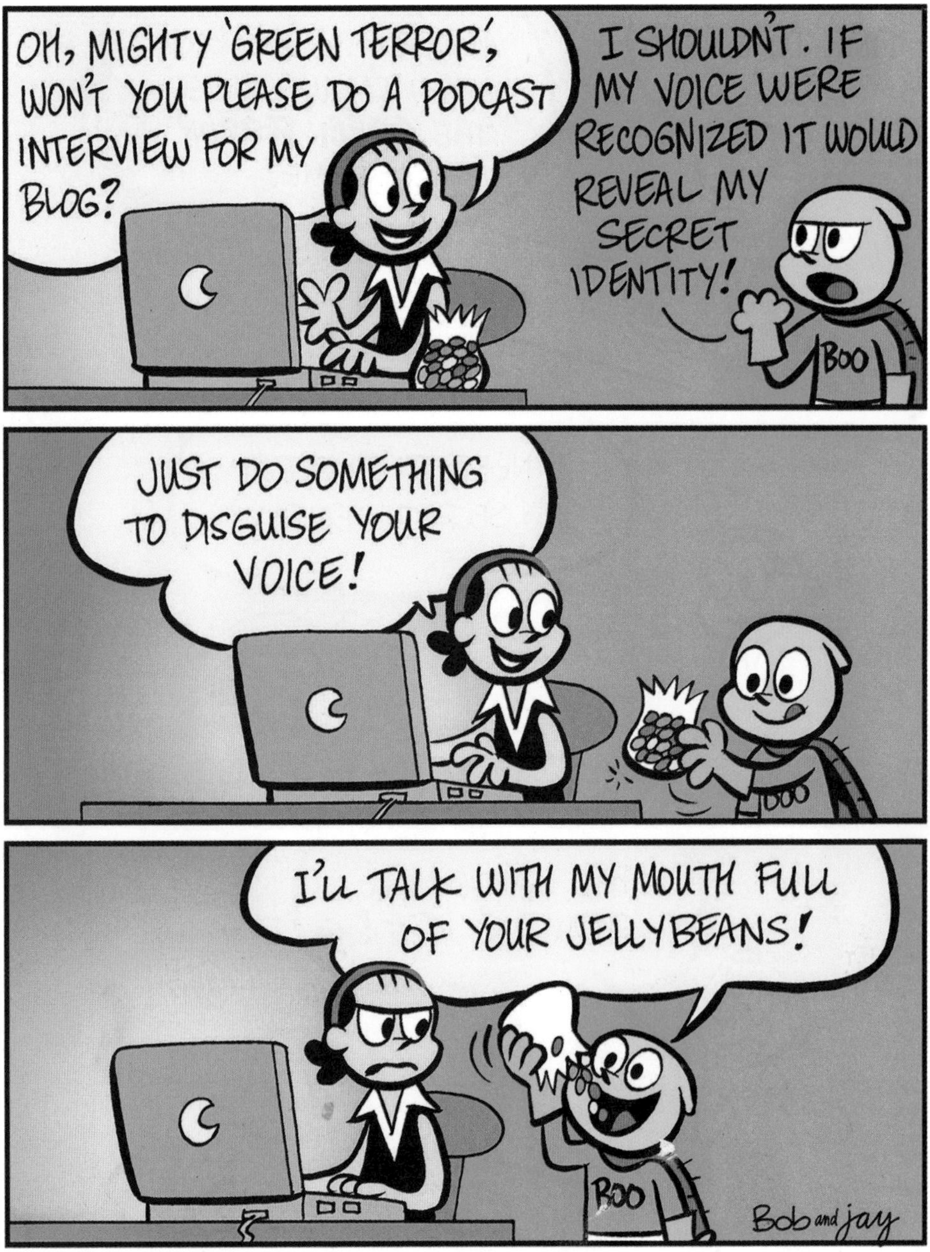
OH, MIGHTY 'GREEN TERROR', WON'T YOU PLEASE DO A PODCAST INTERVIEW FOR MY BLOG?
I SHOULDN'T. IF MY VOICE WERE RECOGNIZED IT WOULD REVEAL MY SECRET IDENTITY!
BOO
JUST DO SOMETHING TO DISGUISE YOUR VOICE!
BOO
I'LL TALK WITH MY MOUTH FULL OF YOUR JELLYBEANS!
BOO
Bob and jay

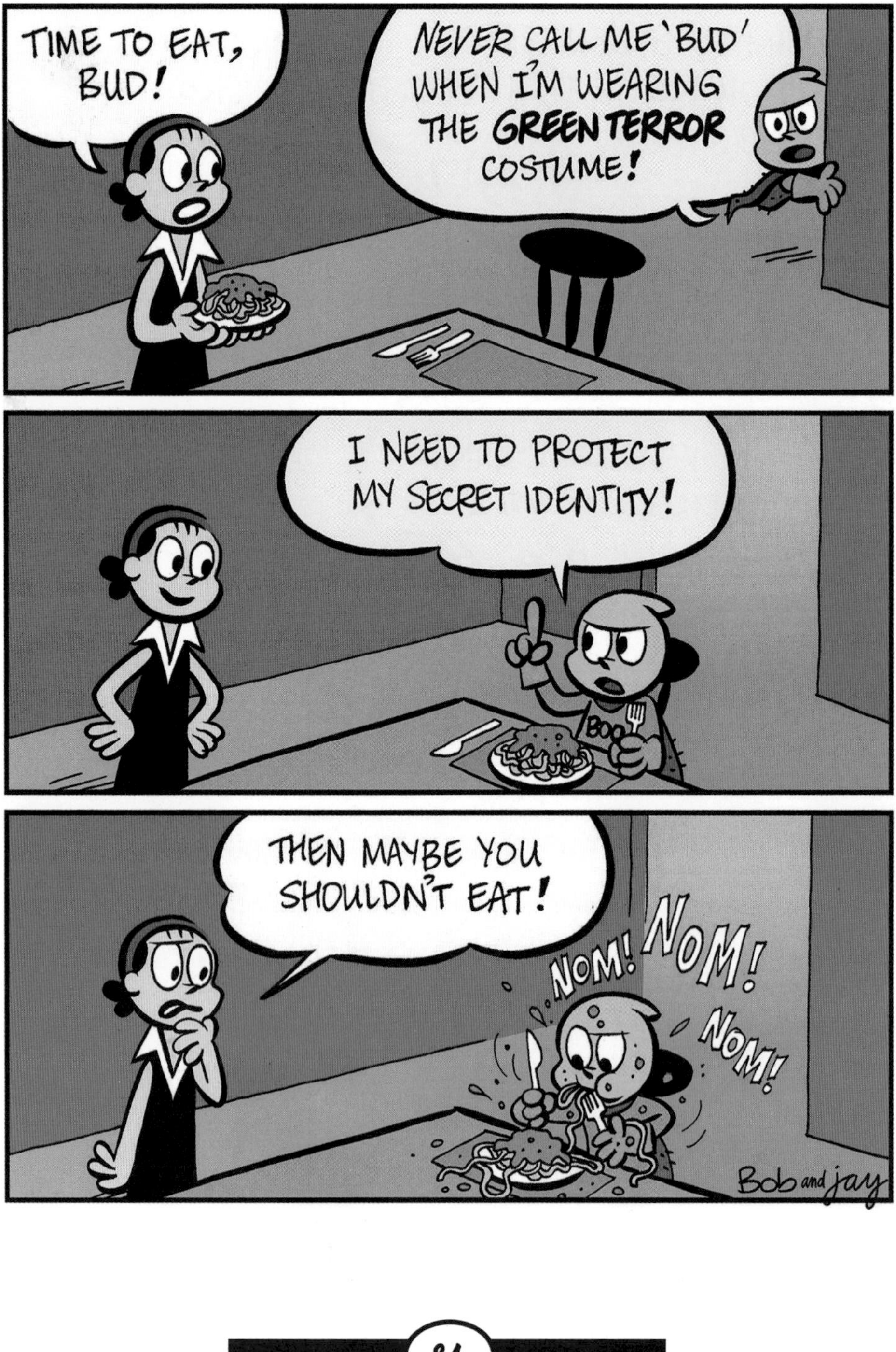
TIME TO EAT, BUD!
NEVER CALL ME 'BUD' WHEN I'M WEARING THE GREEN TERROR COSTUME!
I NEED TO PROTECT MY SECRET IDENTITY!
BOO
THEN MAYBE YOU SHOULDN'T EAT!
NOM! NOM! NOM!
Bob and jay

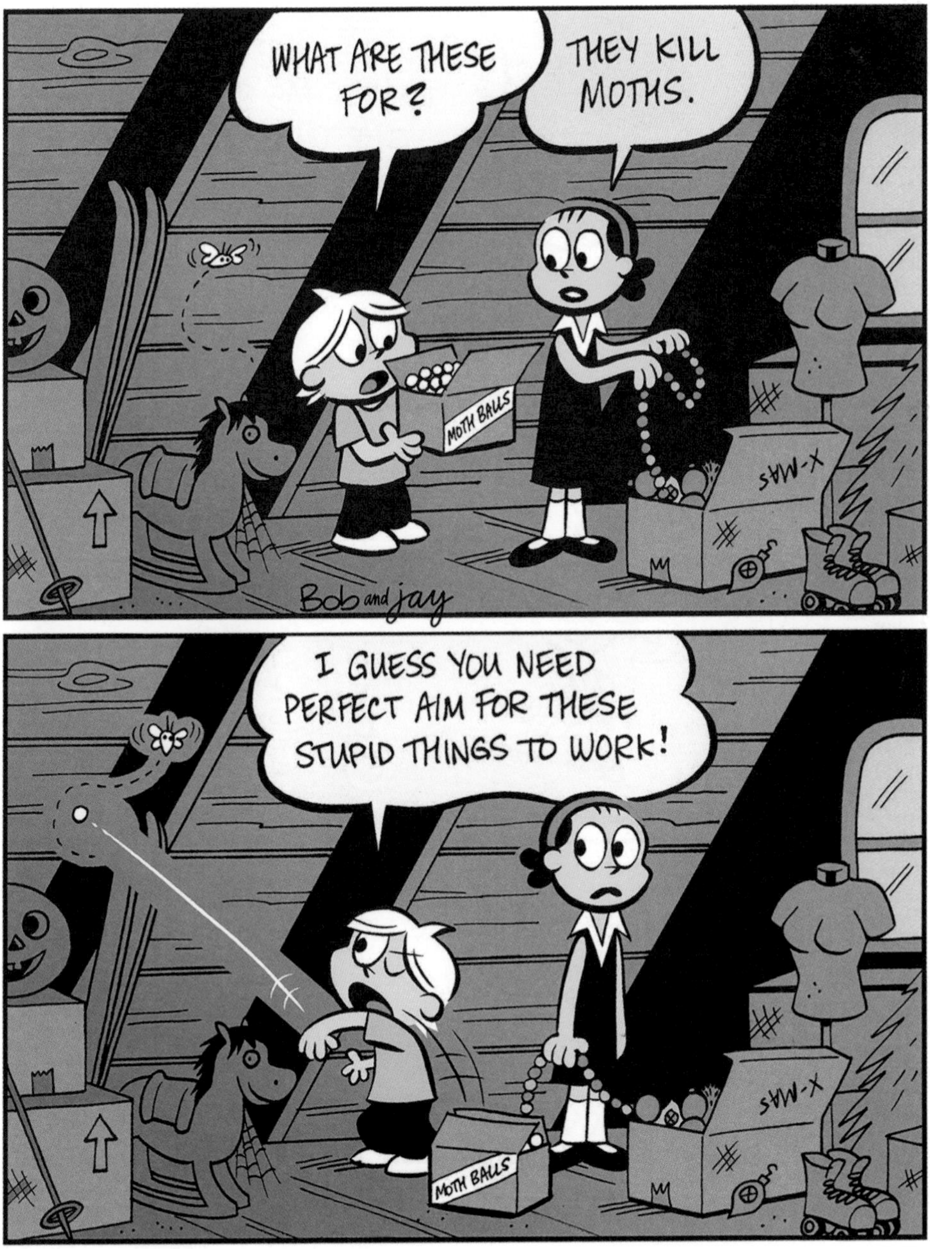
WHAT ARE THESE FOR?
THEY KILL MOTHS.
MOTH BALLS
X-MAS
Bob and jay
I GUESS YOU NEED PERFECT AIM FOR THESE STUPID THINGS TO WORK!
MOTH BALLS
X-MAS

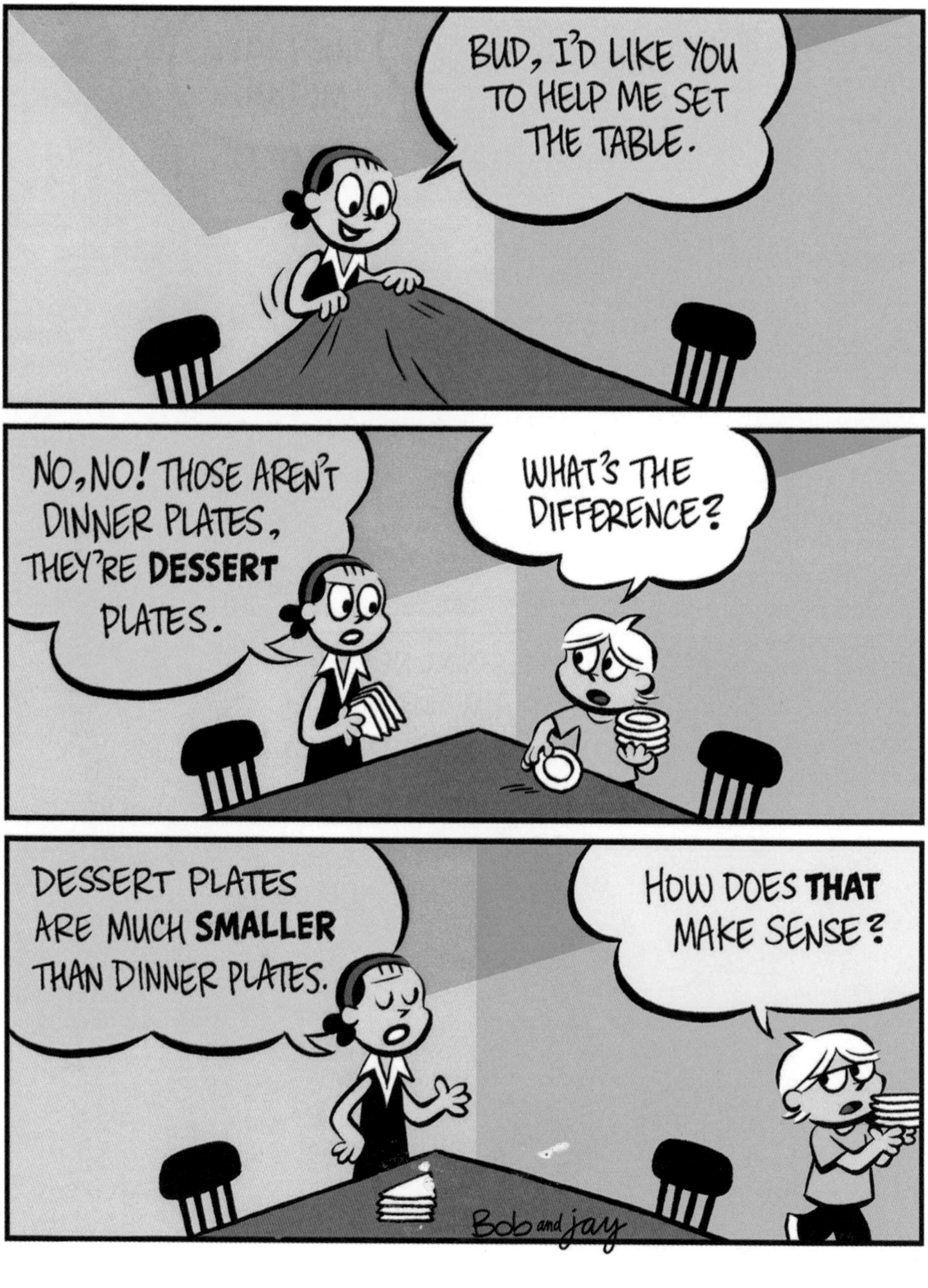
BUD, I'D LIKE YOU TO HELP ME SET THE TABLE.
NO, NO! THOSE AREN'T DINNER PLATES, THEY'RE **DESSERT** PLATES.
WHAT'S THE DIFFERENCE?
DESSERT PLATES ARE MUCH **SMALLER** THAN DINNER PLATES.
HOW DOES **THAT** MAKE SENSE?
Bob and jay

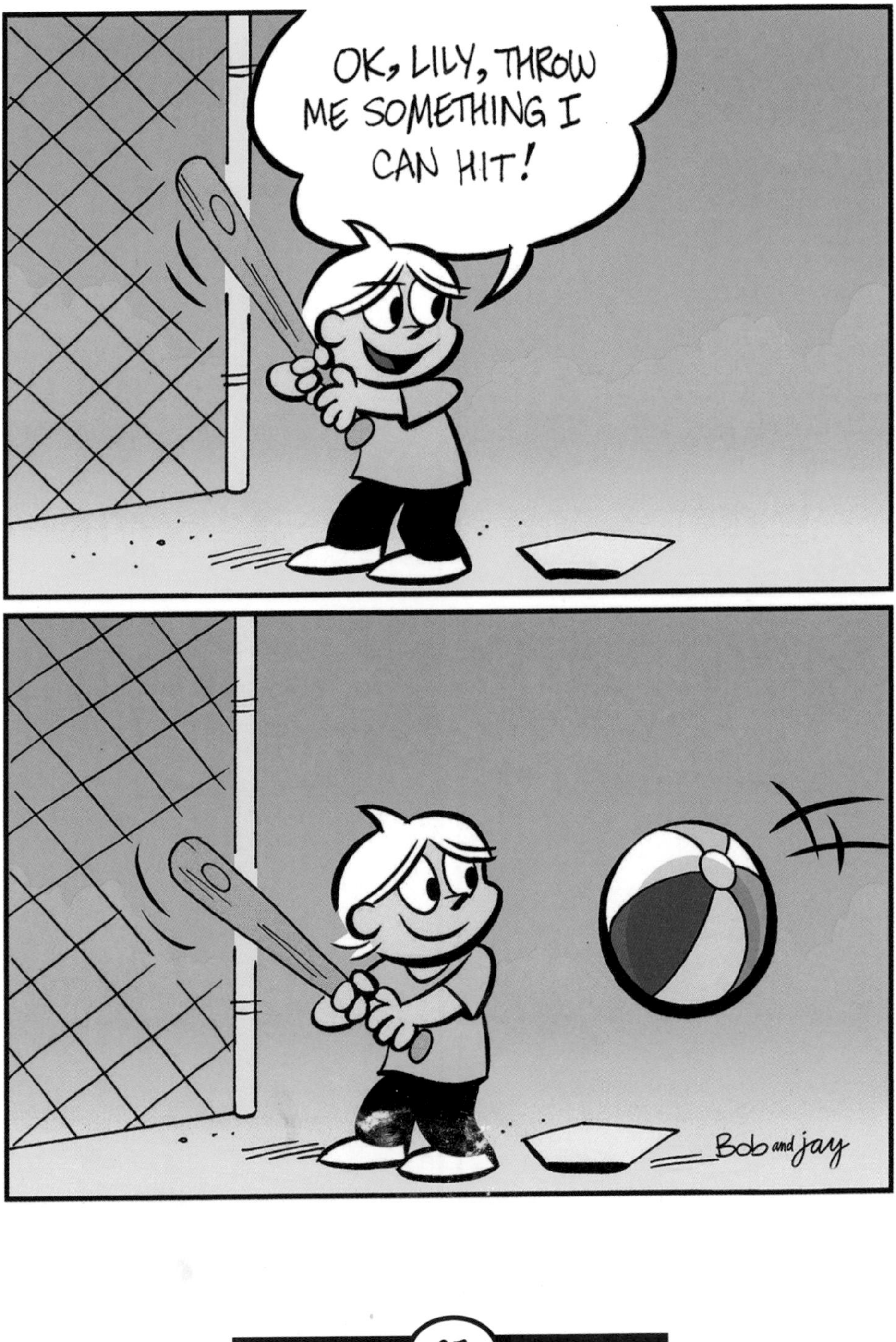
OK, LILY, THROW ME SOMETHING I CAN HIT!
Bob and jay

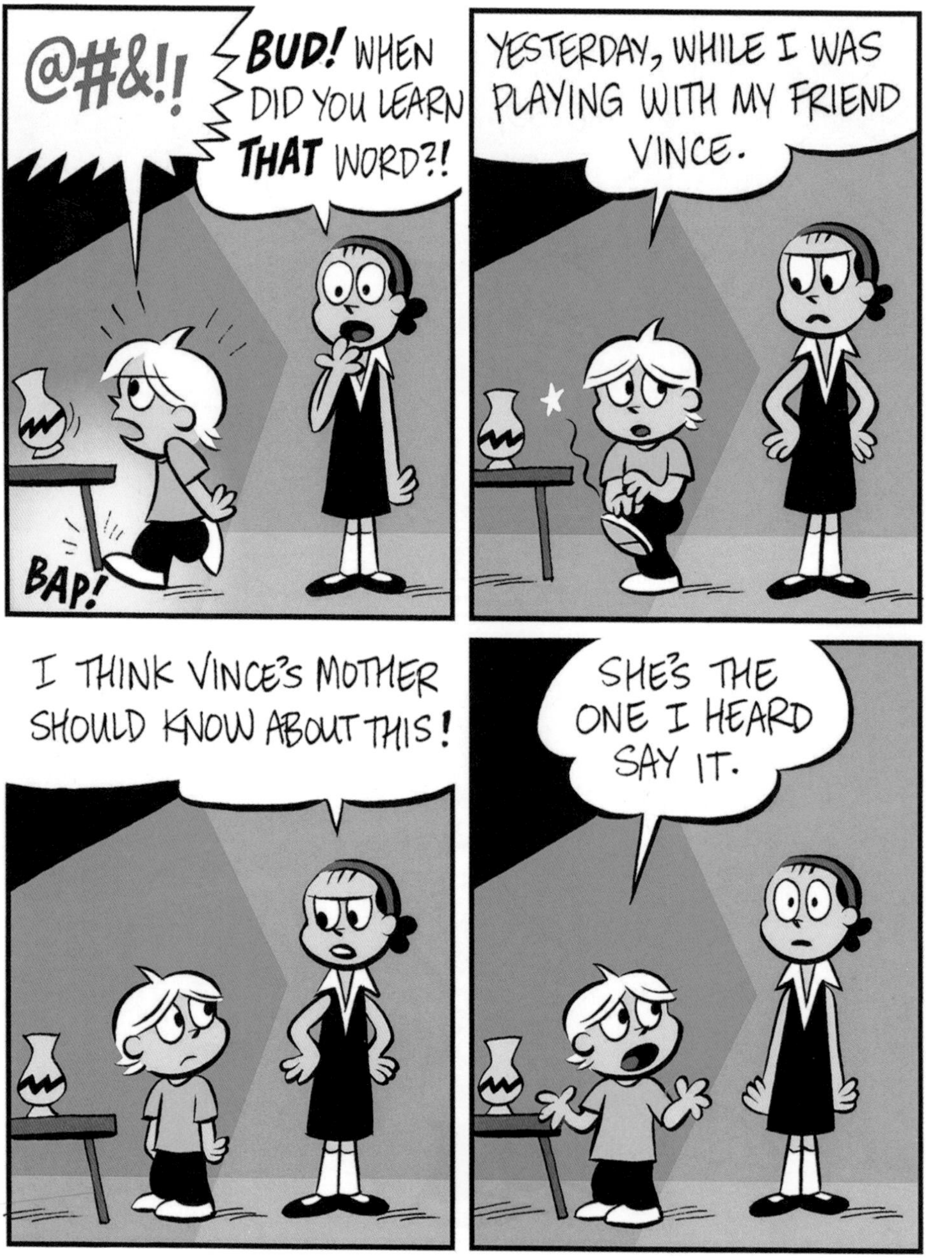

@#&!!
BUD! WHEN DID YOU LEARN THAT WORD?!
BAP!
YESTERDAY, WHILE I WAS PLAYING WITH MY FRIEND VINCE.
I THINK VINCE'S MOTHER SHOULD KNOW ABOUT THIS!
SHE'S THE ONE I HEARD SAY IT.

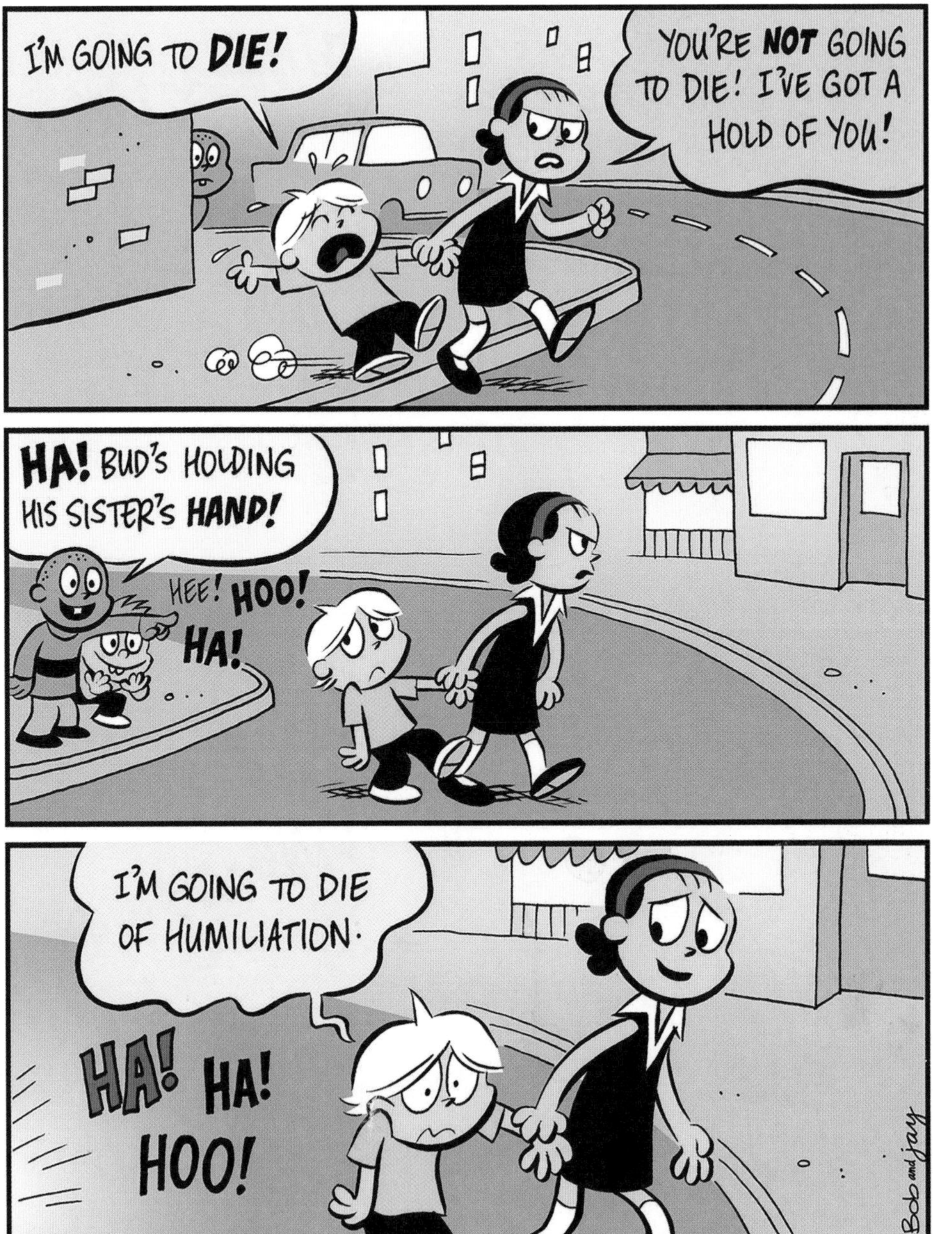
I'M GOING TO DIE!
YOU'RE NOT GOING TO DIE! I'VE GOT A HOLD OF YOU!
HA! BUD'S HOLDING HIS SISTER'S HAND!
HEE! HOO! HA!
I'M GOING TO DIE OF HUMILIATION.
HA! HA! HOO!
Bob and jay

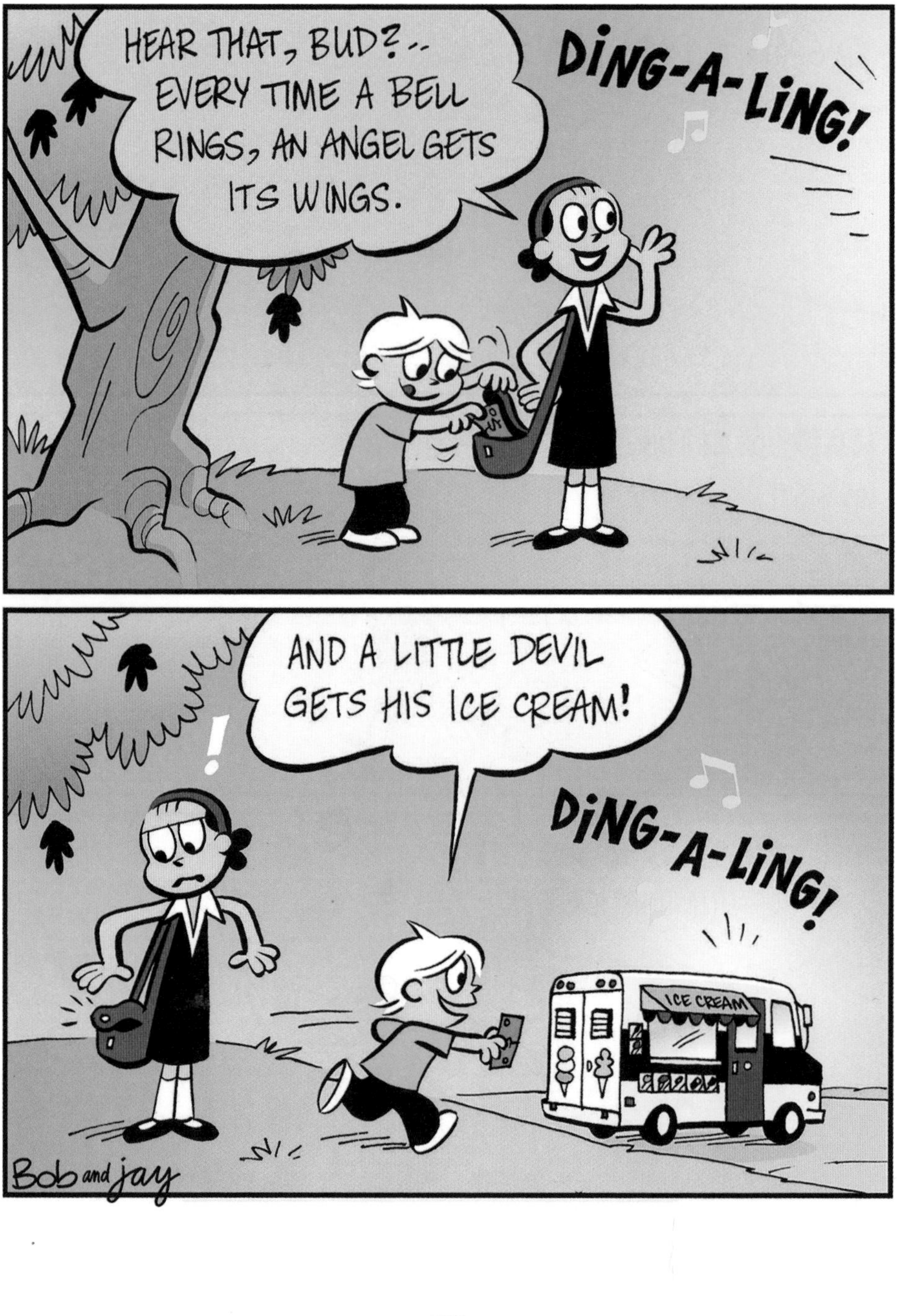
HEAR THAT, BUD?...
EVERY TIME A BELL RINGS, AN ANGEL GETS ITS WINGS.
DING-A-LING!
AND A LITTLE DEVIL GETS HIS ICE CREAM!
DING-A-LING!
ICE CREAM
Bob and jay

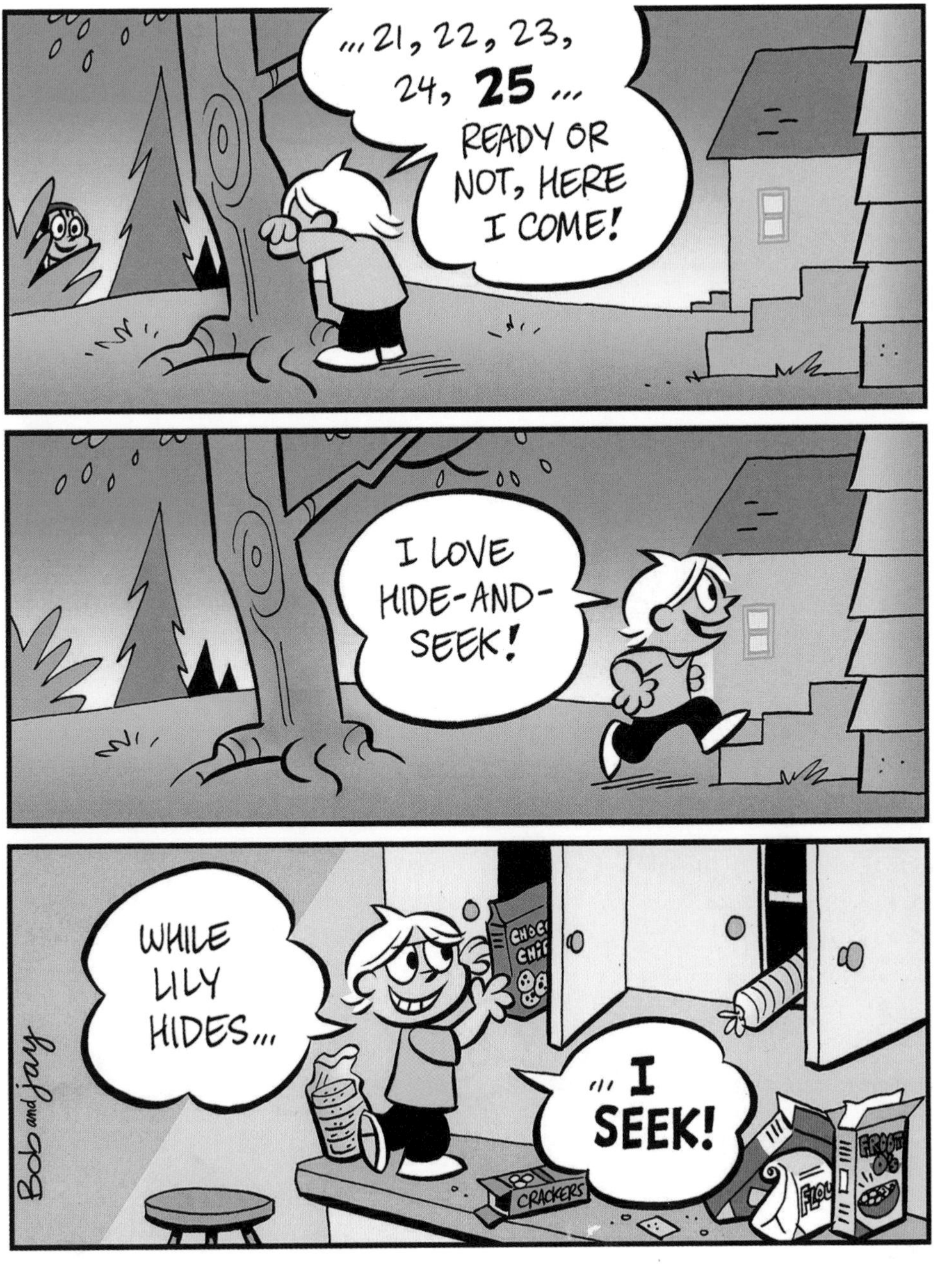
...21, 22, 23, 24, 25 ... READY OR NOT, HERE I COME!
I LOVE HIDE-AND-SEEK!
WHILE LILY HIDES...
...I SEEK!
CRACKERS
Bob and jay

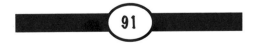

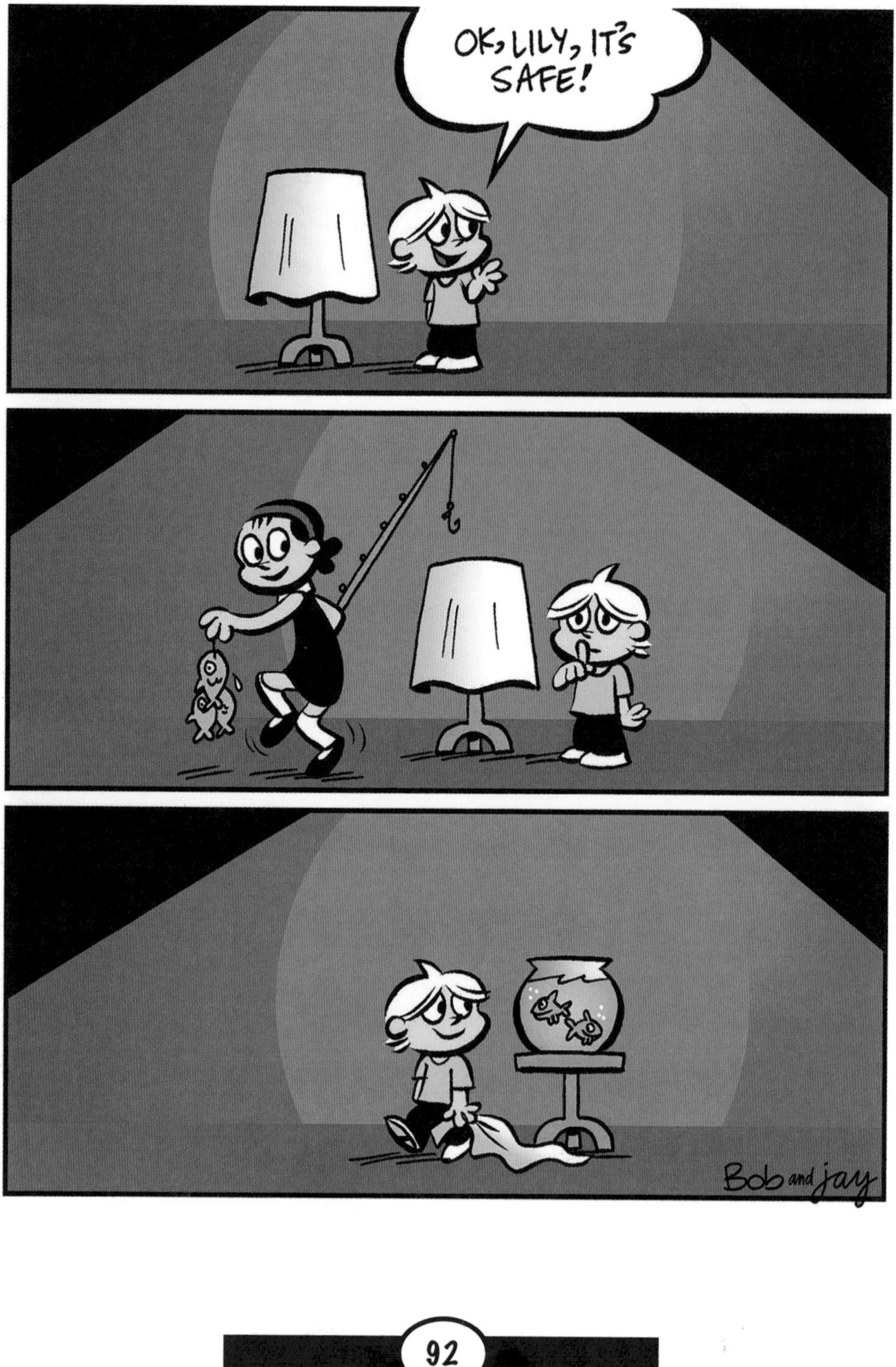
OK, LILY, IT'S SAFE!
Bob and jay

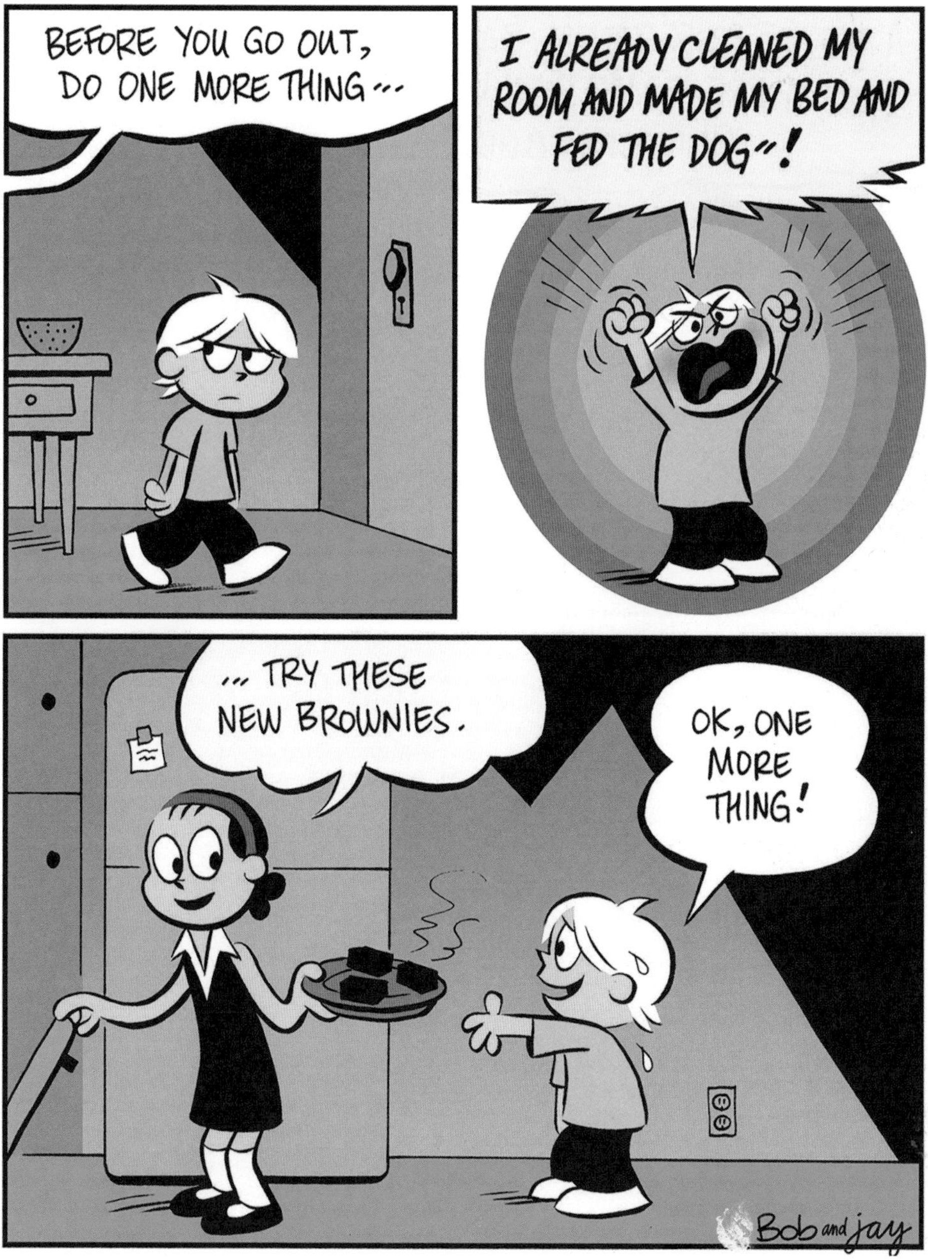
BEFORE YOU GO OUT, DO ONE MORE THING...
I ALREADY CLEANED MY ROOM AND MADE MY BED AND FED THE DOG...!
... TRY THESE NEW BROWNIES.
OK, ONE MORE THING!
Bob and jay

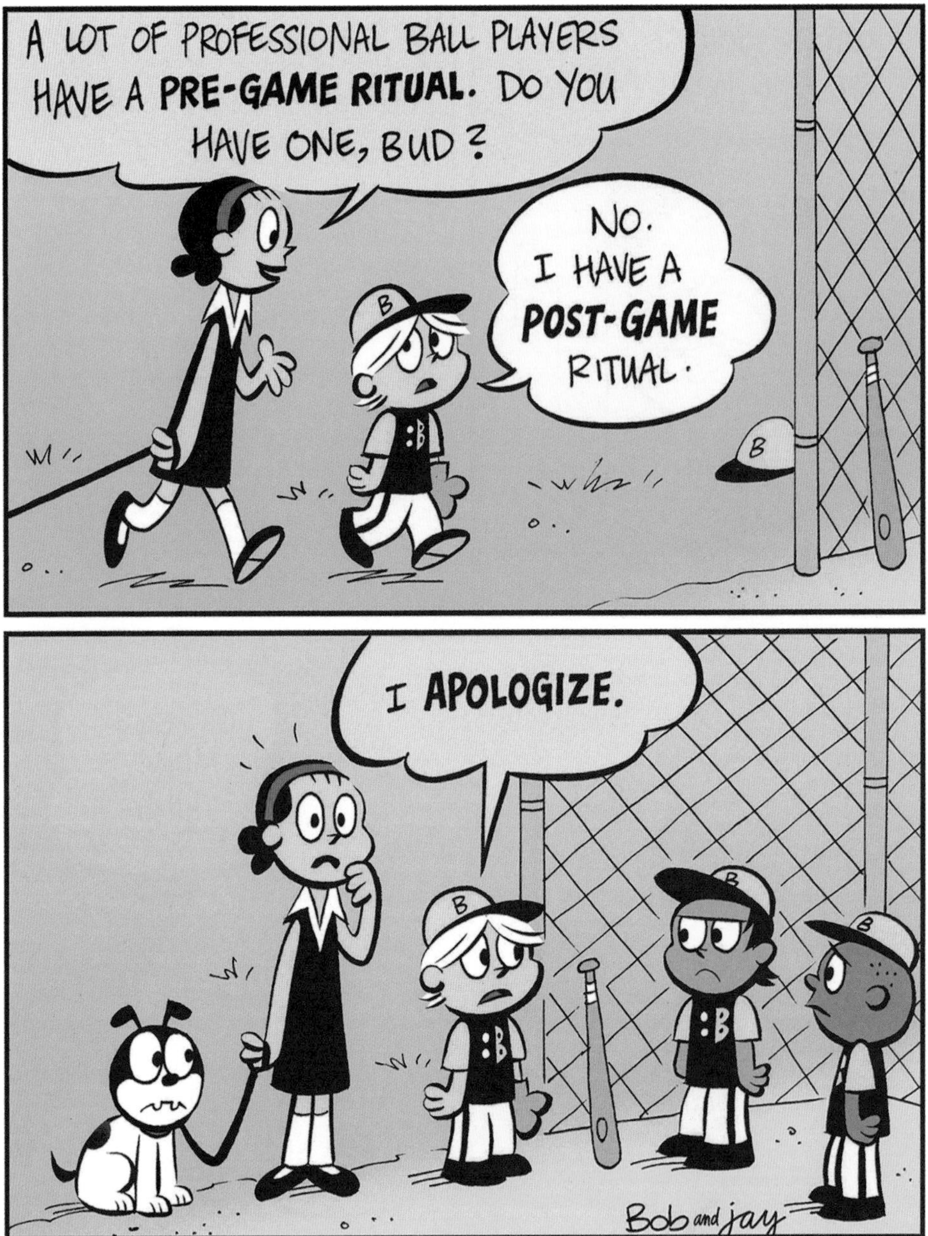
A LOT OF PROFESSIONAL BALL PLAYERS HAVE A **PRE-GAME RITUAL.** DO YOU HAVE ONE, BUD?
NO. I HAVE A **POST-GAME** RITUAL.
I **APOLOGIZE.**
Bob and jay

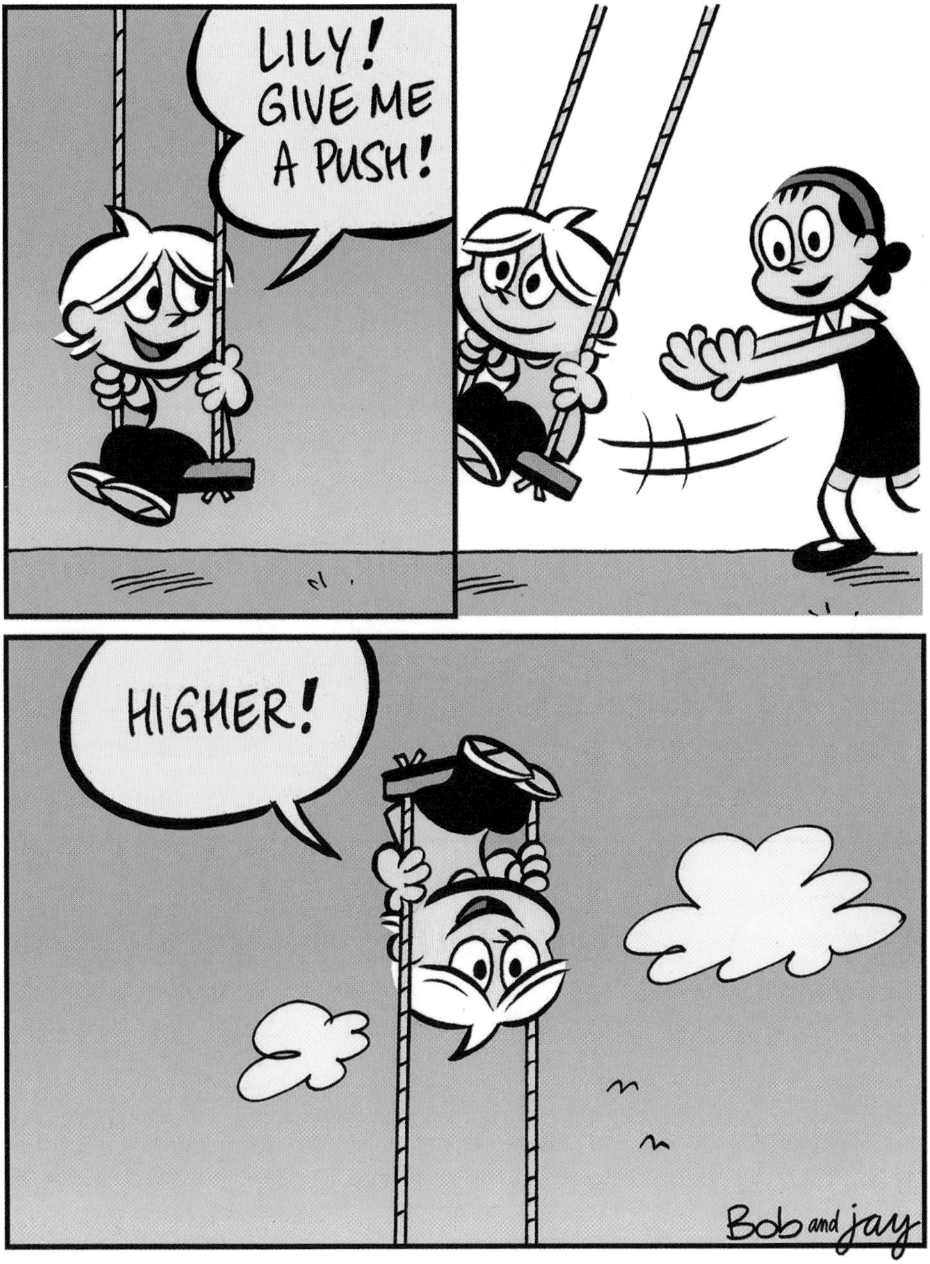
LILY! GIVE ME A PUSH!
HIGHER!
Bob and jay

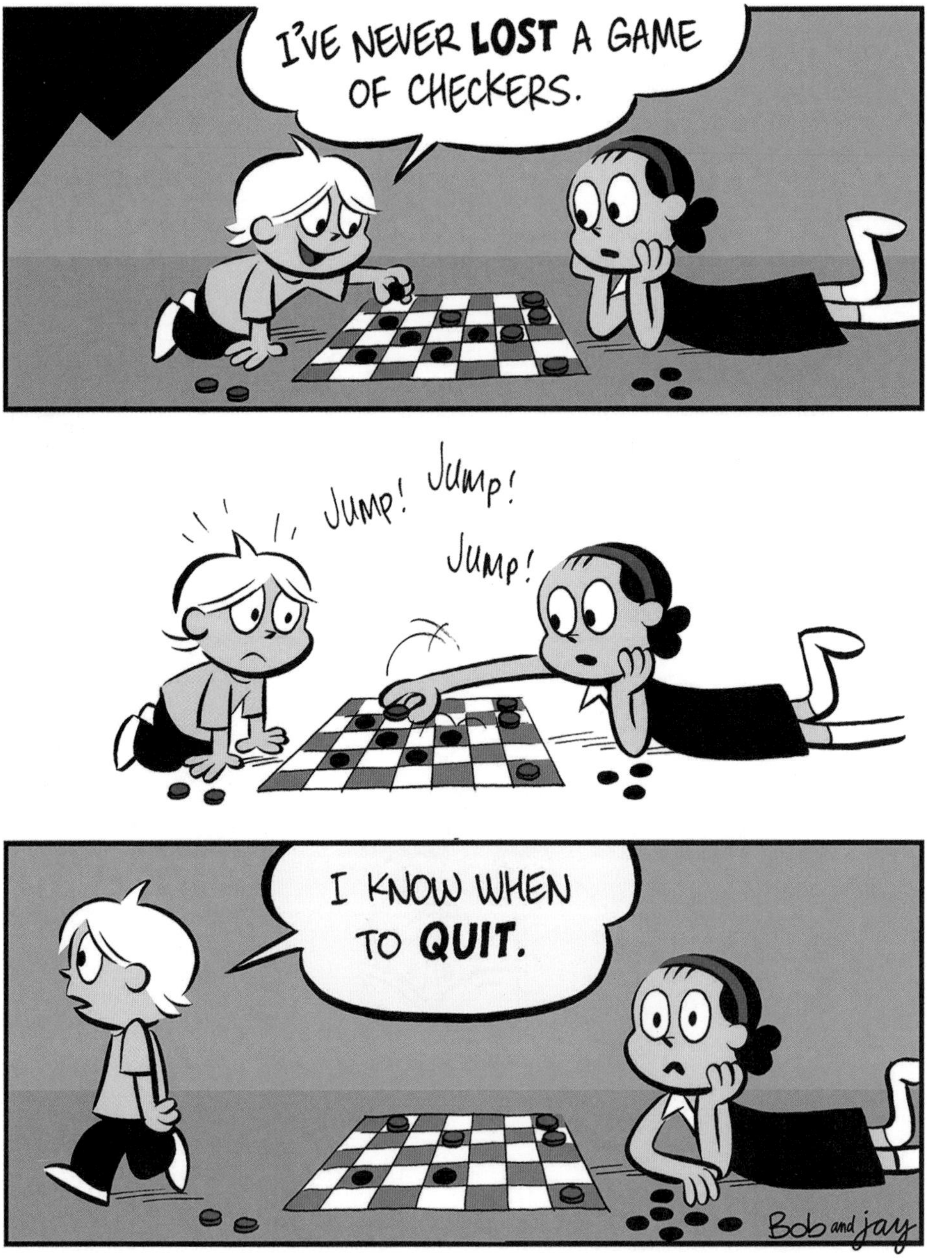
I'VE NEVER **LOST** A GAME OF CHECKERS.
JUMP! JUMP!
JUMP!
I KNOW WHEN TO **QUIT**.
Bob and jay

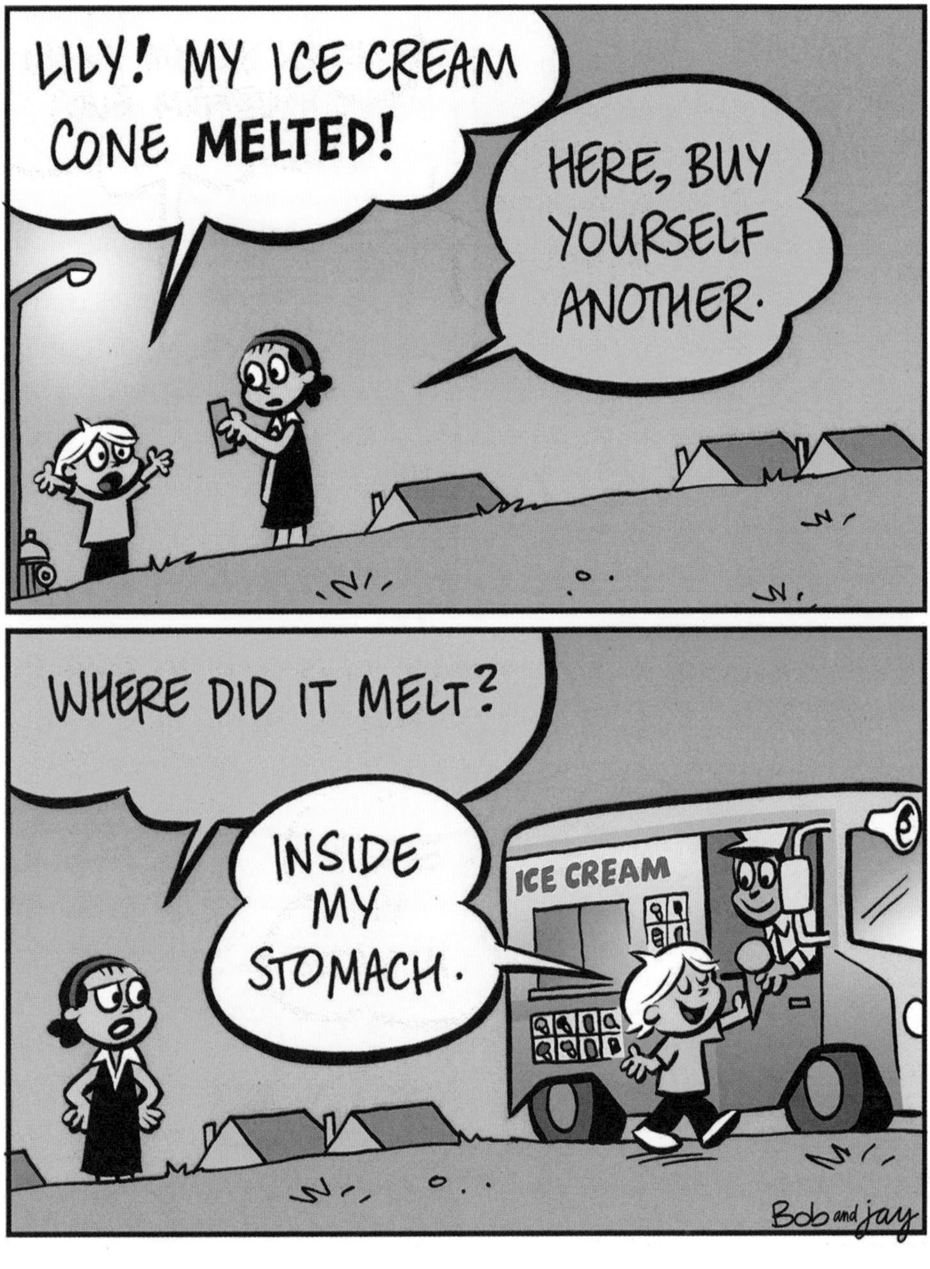
LILY! MY ICE CREAM CONE **MELTED!**
HERE, BUY YOURSELF ANOTHER.
WHERE DID IT MELT?
INSIDE MY STOMACH.
ICE CREAM
Bob and jay

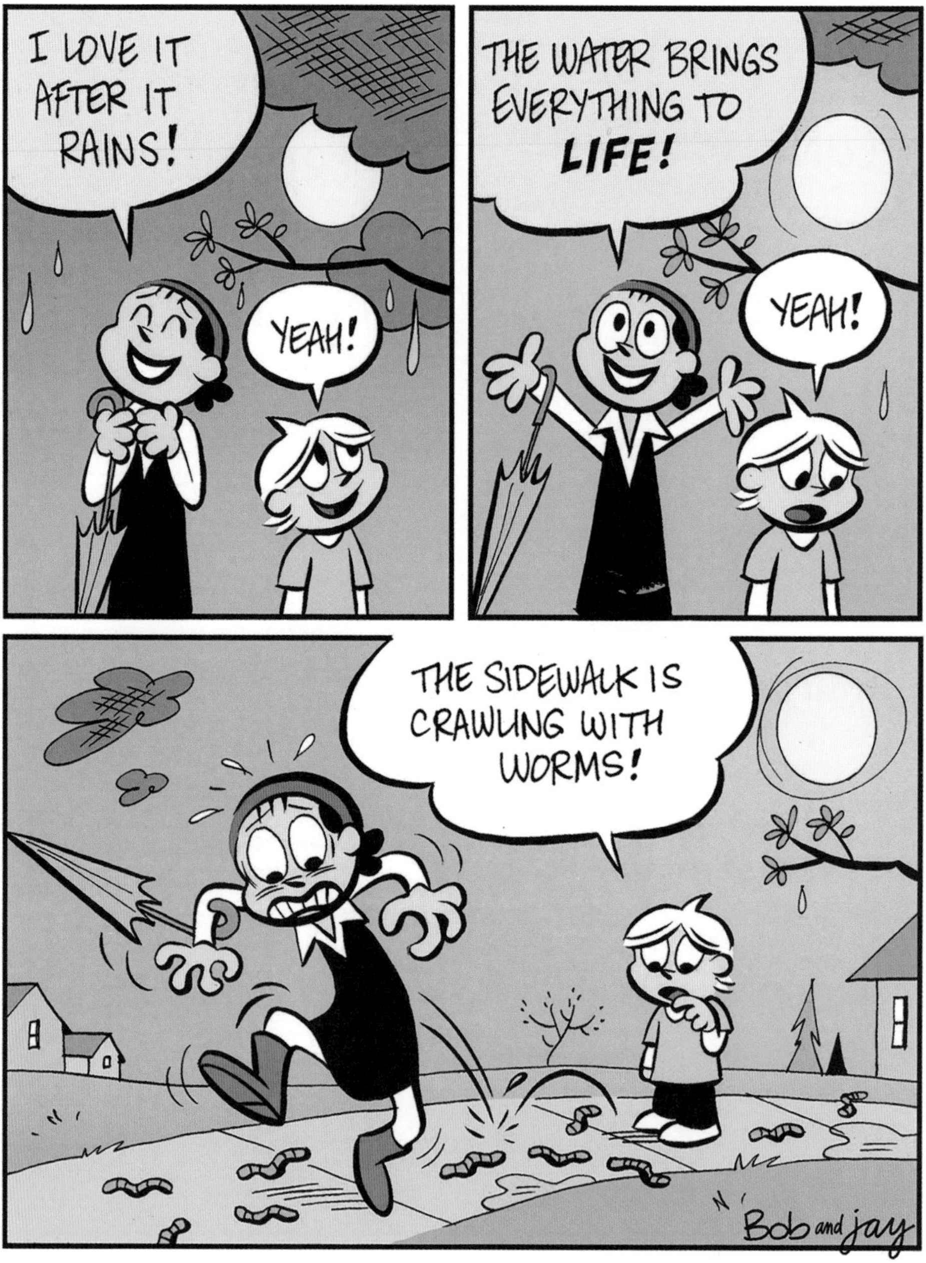
I LOVE IT AFTER IT RAINS!
YEAH!
THE WATER BRINGS EVERYTHING TO LIFE!
YEAH!
THE SIDEWALK IS CRAWLING WITH WORMS!
Bob and jay

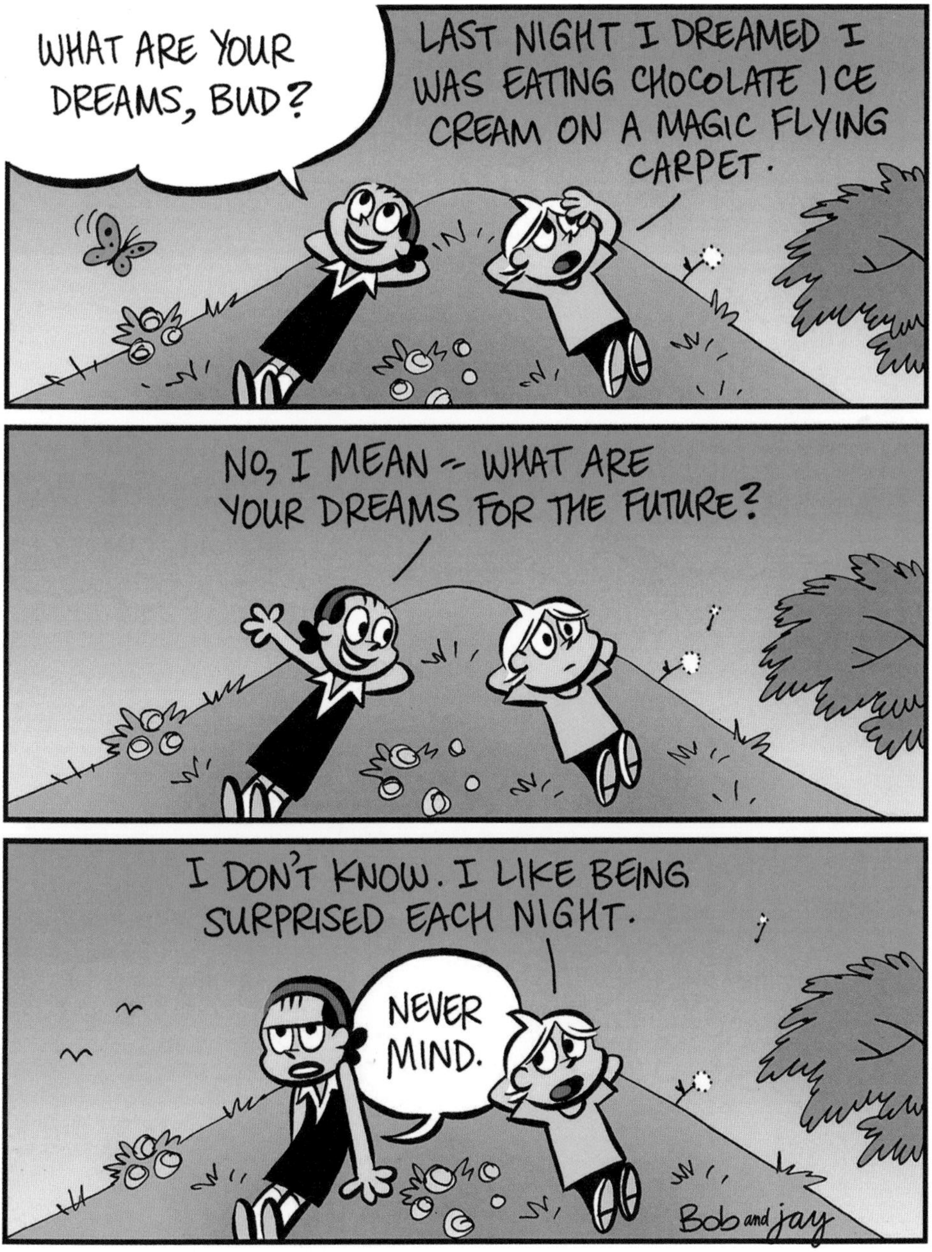
WHAT ARE YOUR DREAMS, BUD?
LAST NIGHT I DREAMED I WAS EATING CHOCOLATE ICE CREAM ON A MAGIC FLYING CARPET.
NO, I MEAN -- WHAT ARE YOUR DREAMS FOR THE FUTURE?
I DON'T KNOW. I LIKE BEING SURPRISED EACH NIGHT.
NEVER MIND.
Bob and jay

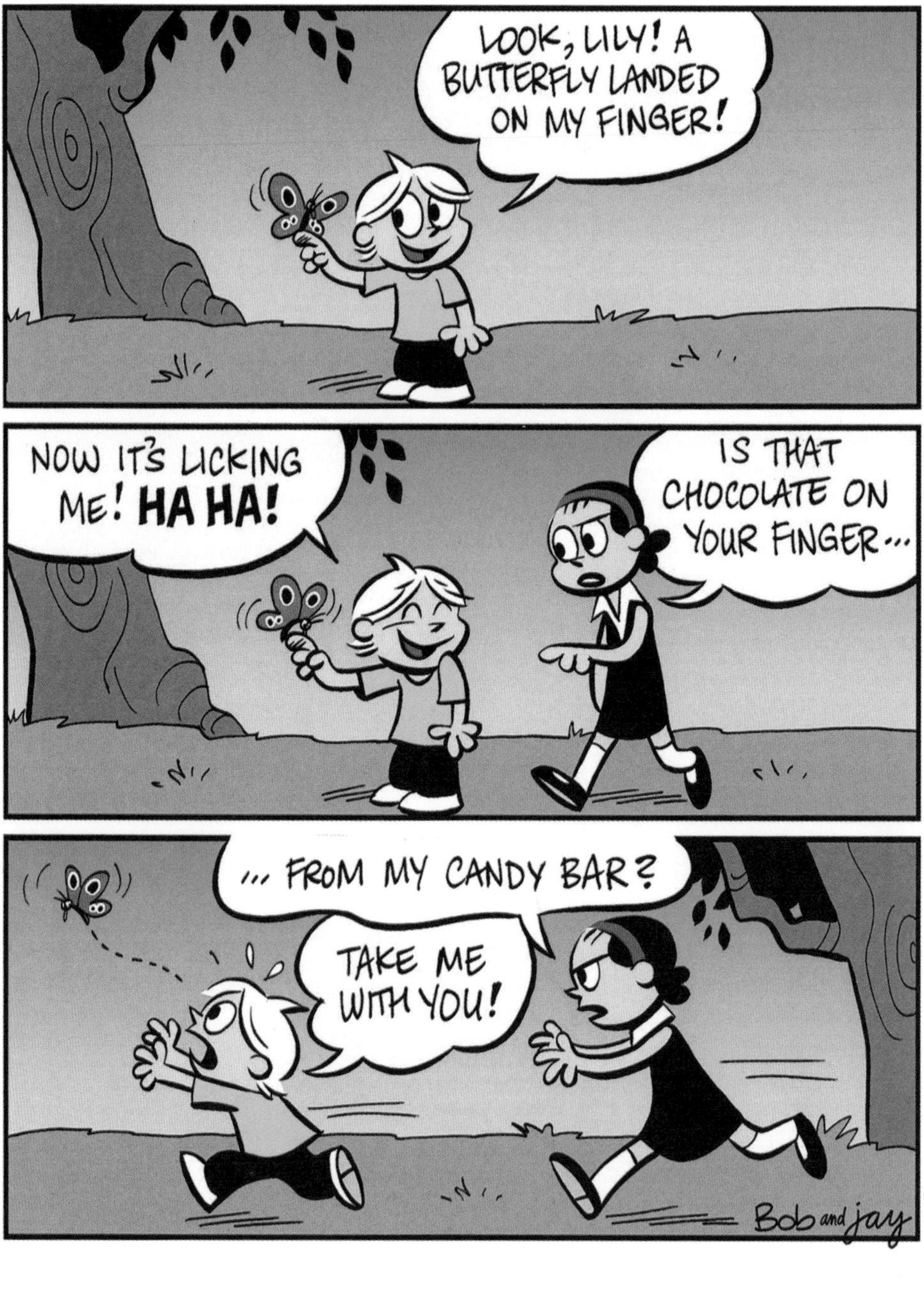
LOOK, LILY! A BUTTERFLY LANDED ON MY FINGER!
NOW IT'S LICKING ME! HA HA!
IS THAT CHOCOLATE ON YOUR FINGER...
... FROM MY CANDY BAR?
TAKE ME WITH YOU!
Bob and jay

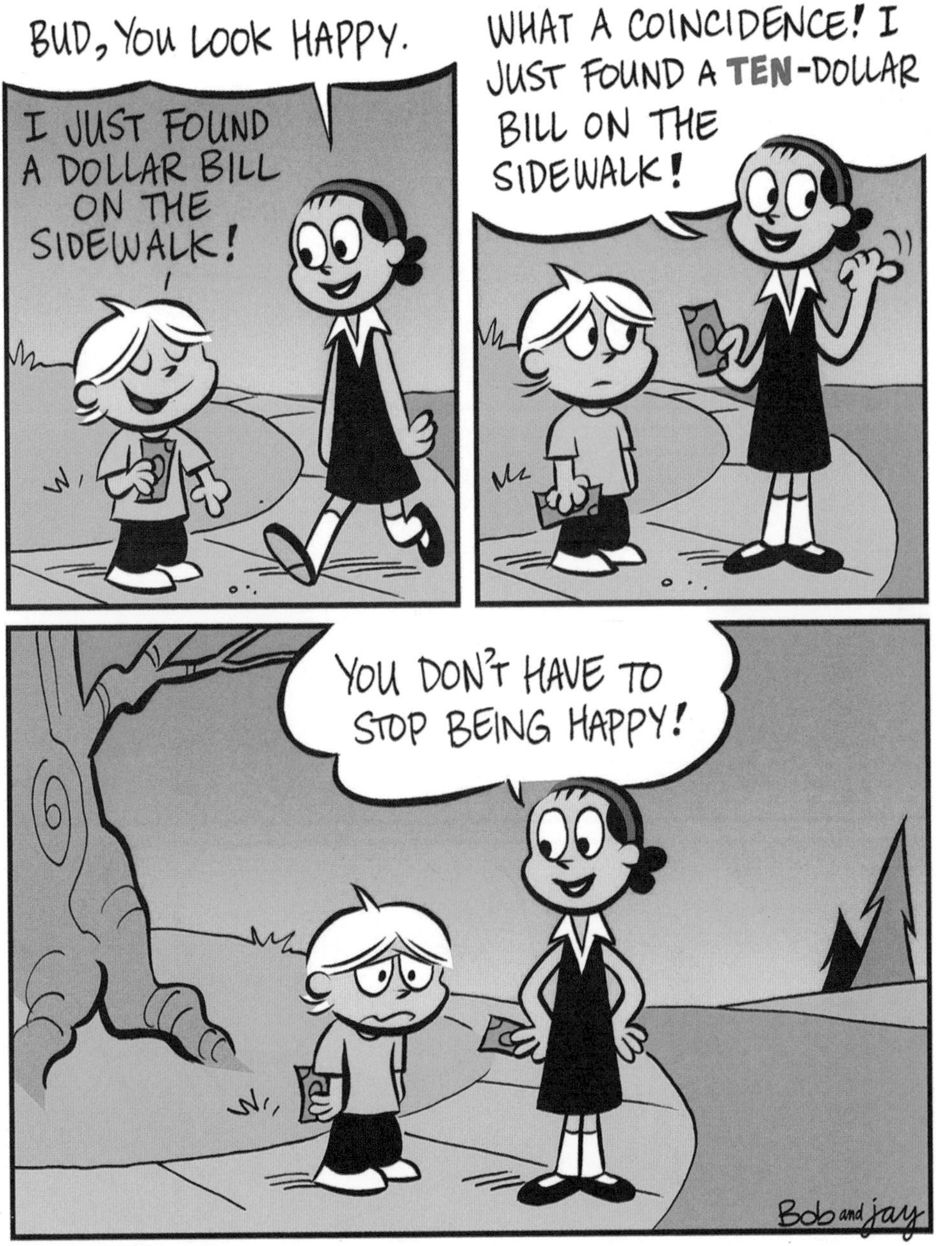
BUD, YOU LOOK HAPPY.
I JUST FOUND A DOLLAR BILL ON THE SIDEWALK!
WHAT A COINCIDENCE! I JUST FOUND A TEN-DOLLAR BILL ON THE SIDEWALK!
YOU DON'T HAVE TO STOP BEING HAPPY!
Bob and jay

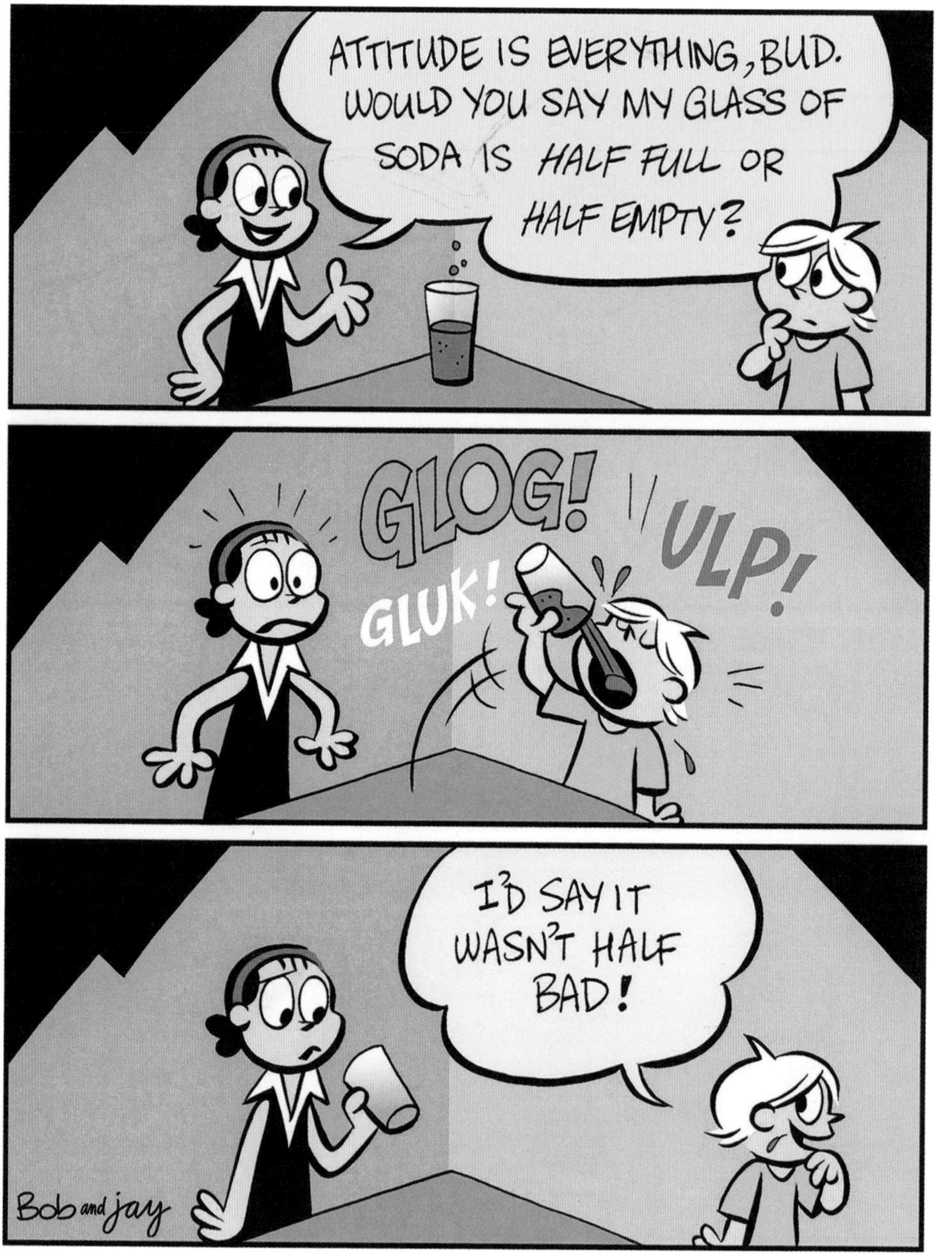
ATTITUDE IS EVERYTHING, BUD. WOULD YOU SAY MY GLASS OF SODA IS HALF FULL OR HALF EMPTY?
GLOG!
GLUK!
ULP!
I'D SAY IT WASN'T HALF BAD!
Bob and jay

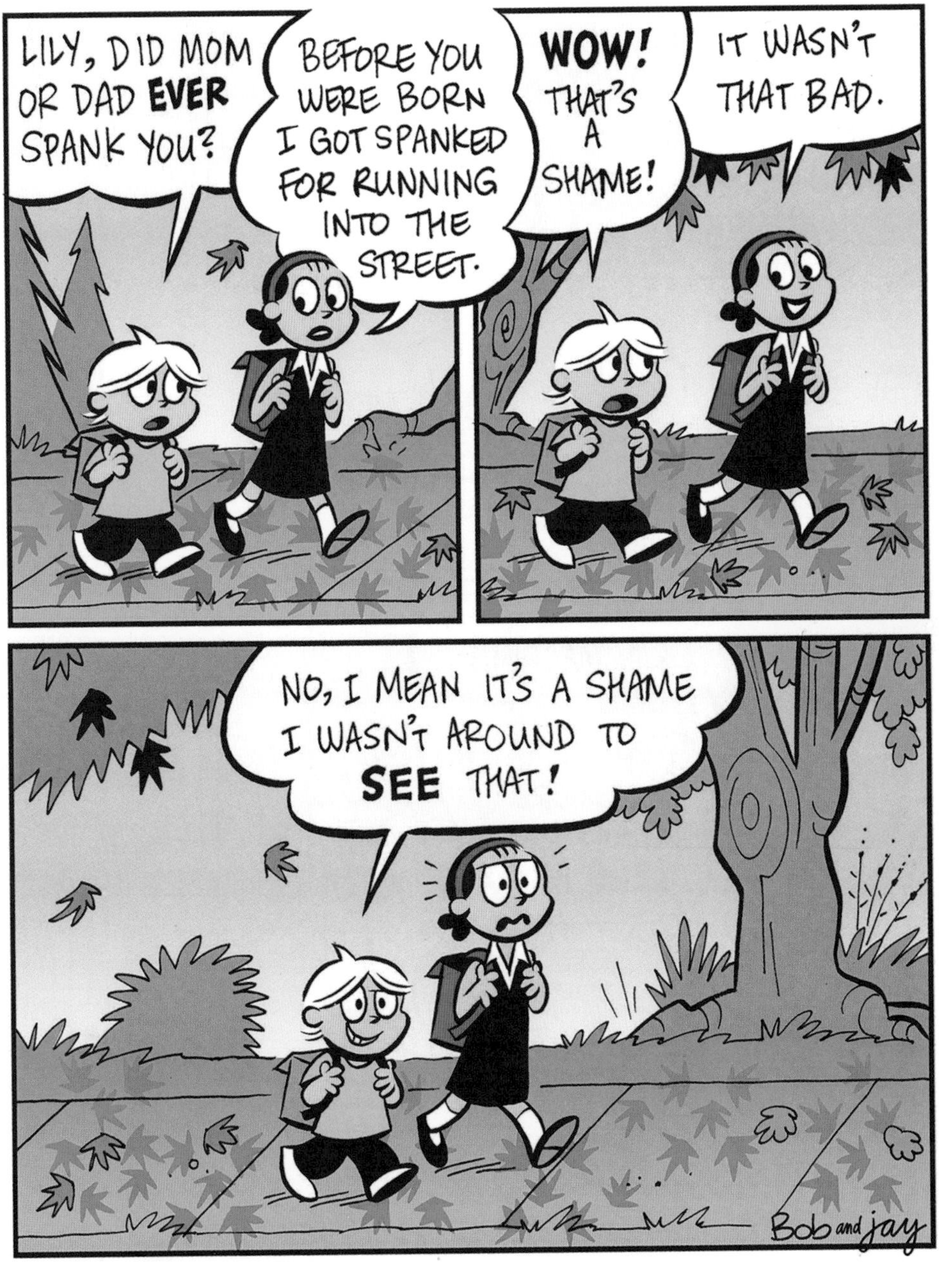
LILY, DID MOM OR DAD **EVER** SPANK YOU?
BEFORE YOU WERE BORN I GOT SPANKED FOR RUNNING INTO THE STREET.
WOW! THAT'S A SHAME!
IT WASN'T THAT BAD.
NO, I MEAN IT'S A SHAME I WASN'T AROUND TO **SEE** THAT!
Bob and jay

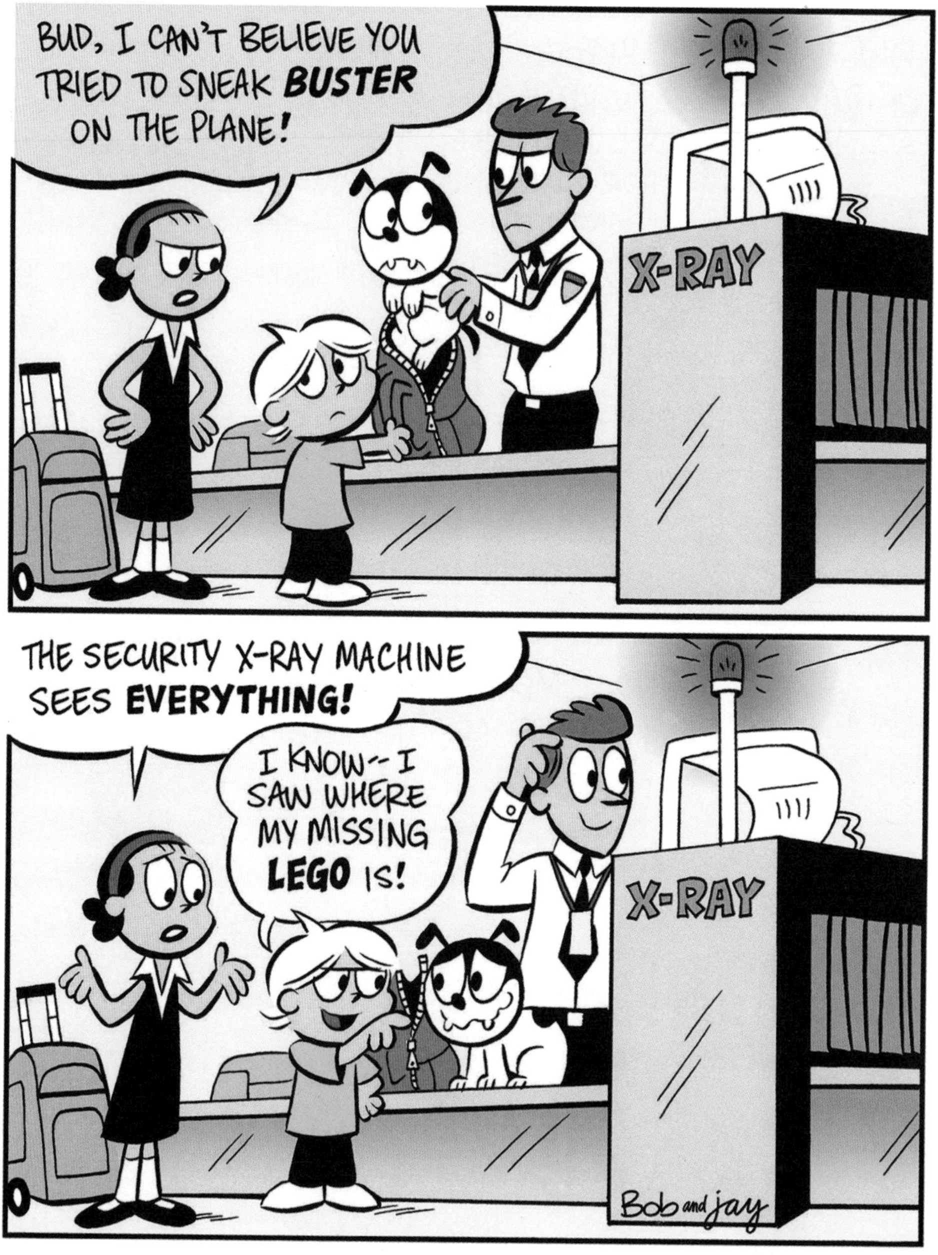
BUD, I CAN'T BELIEVE YOU TRIED TO SNEAK BUSTER ON THE PLANE!
X-RAY
THE SECURITY X-RAY MACHINE SEES EVERYTHING!
I KNOW-- I SAW WHERE MY MISSING LEGO IS!
X-RAY
Bob and jay

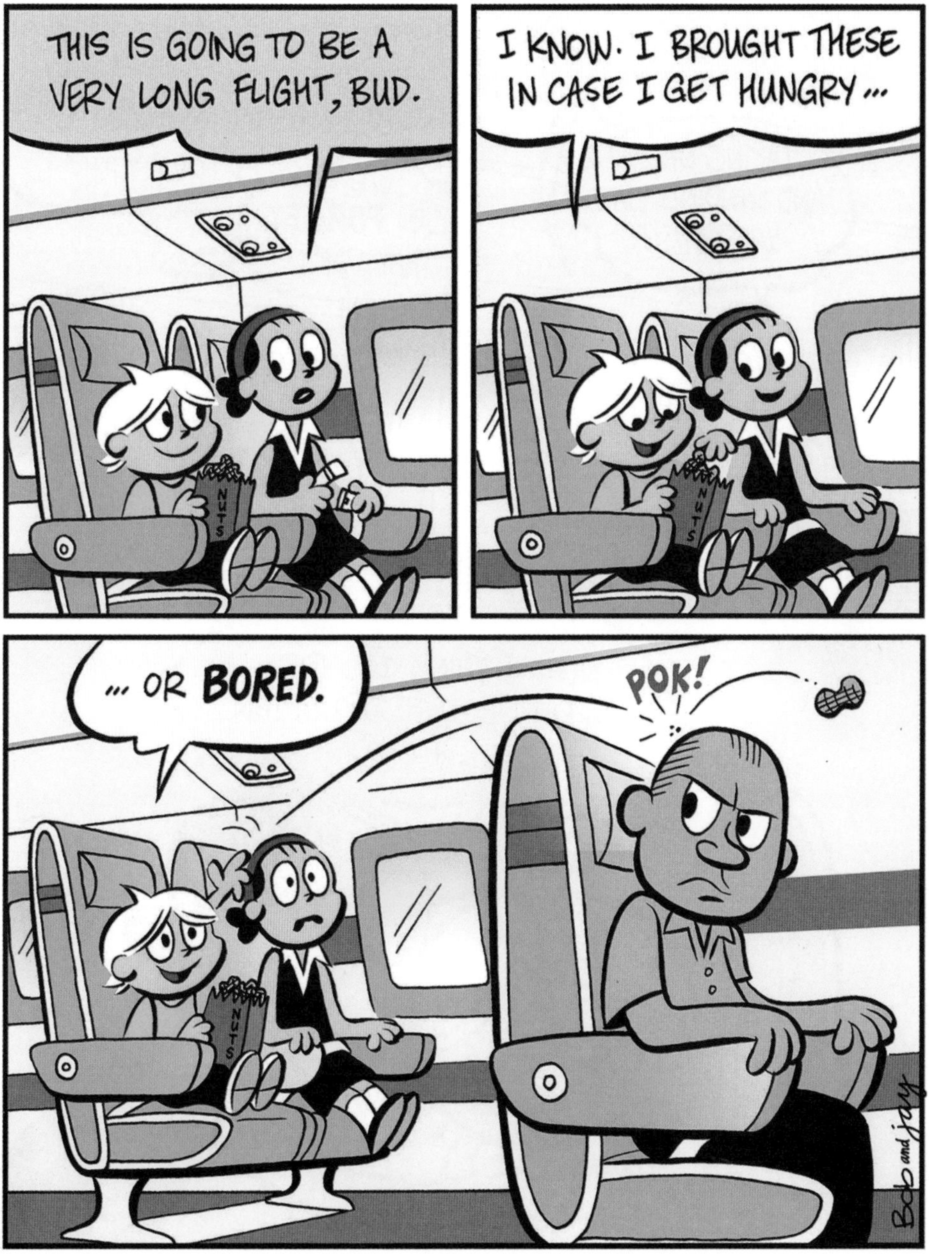
THIS IS GOING TO BE A VERY LONG FLIGHT, BUD.
NUTS
I KNOW. I BROUGHT THESE IN CASE I GET HUNGRY...
NUTS
... OR BORED.
POK!
NUTS
Bob and jay

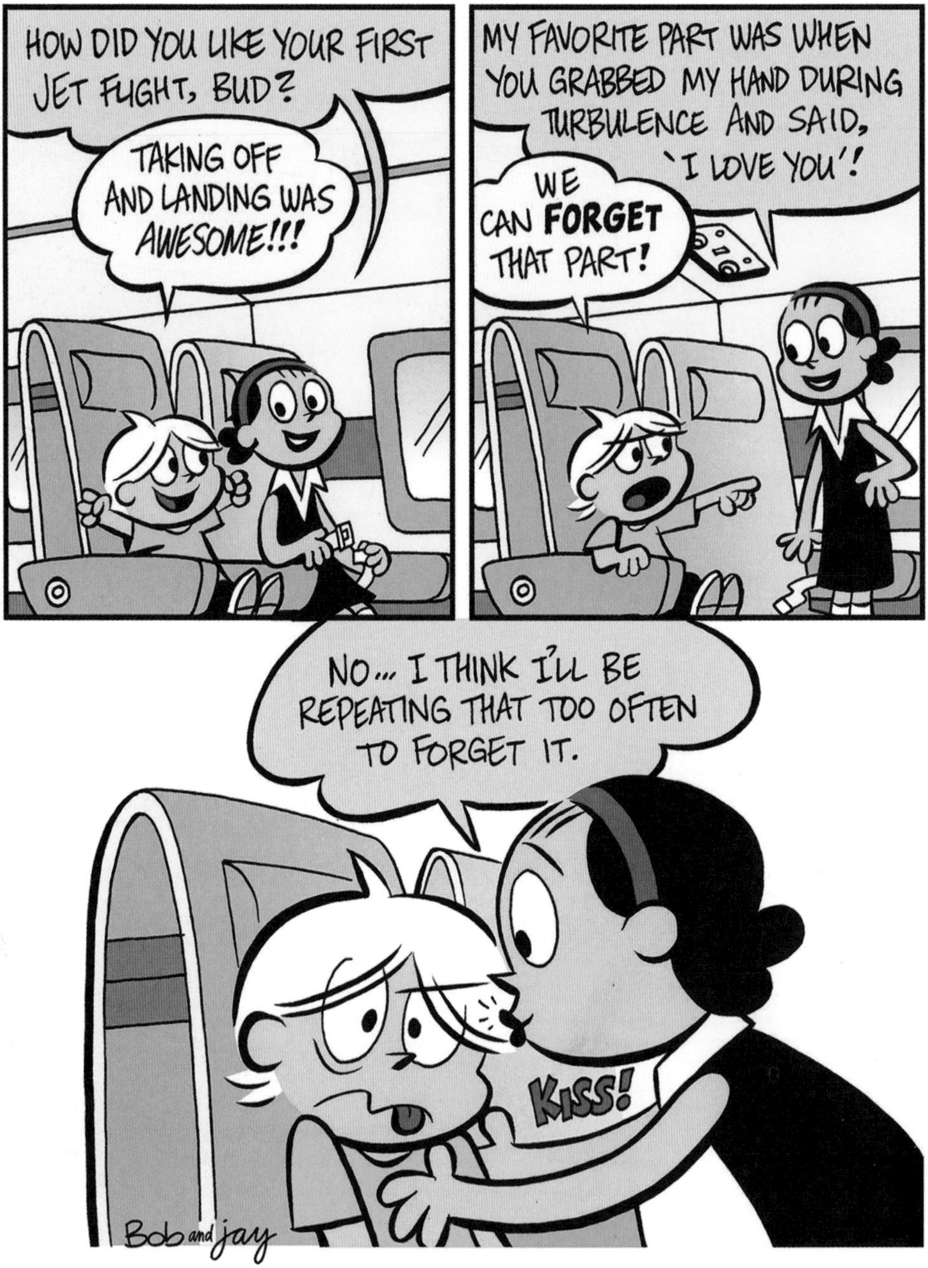
HOW DID YOU LIKE YOUR FIRST JET FLIGHT, BUD?
TAKING OFF AND LANDING WAS AWESOME!!!
MY FAVORITE PART WAS WHEN YOU GRABBED MY HAND DURING TURBULENCE AND SAID, `I LOVE YOU'!
WE CAN **FORGET** THAT PART!
NO... I THINK I'LL BE REPEATING THAT TOO OFTEN TO FORGET IT.
KISS!
Bob and jay

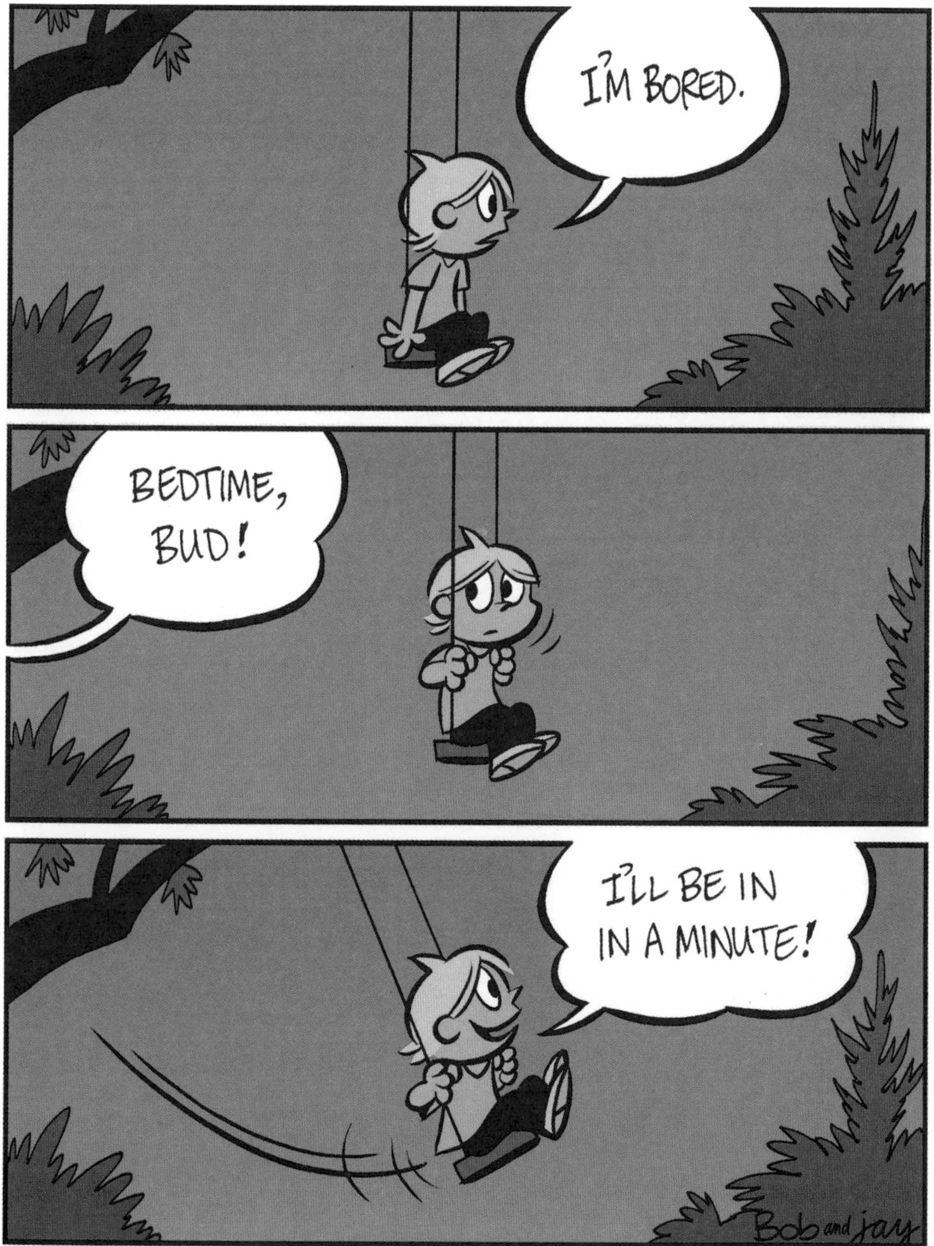
I'M BORED.
BEDTIME, BUD!
I'LL BE IN IN A MINUTE!
Bob and jay

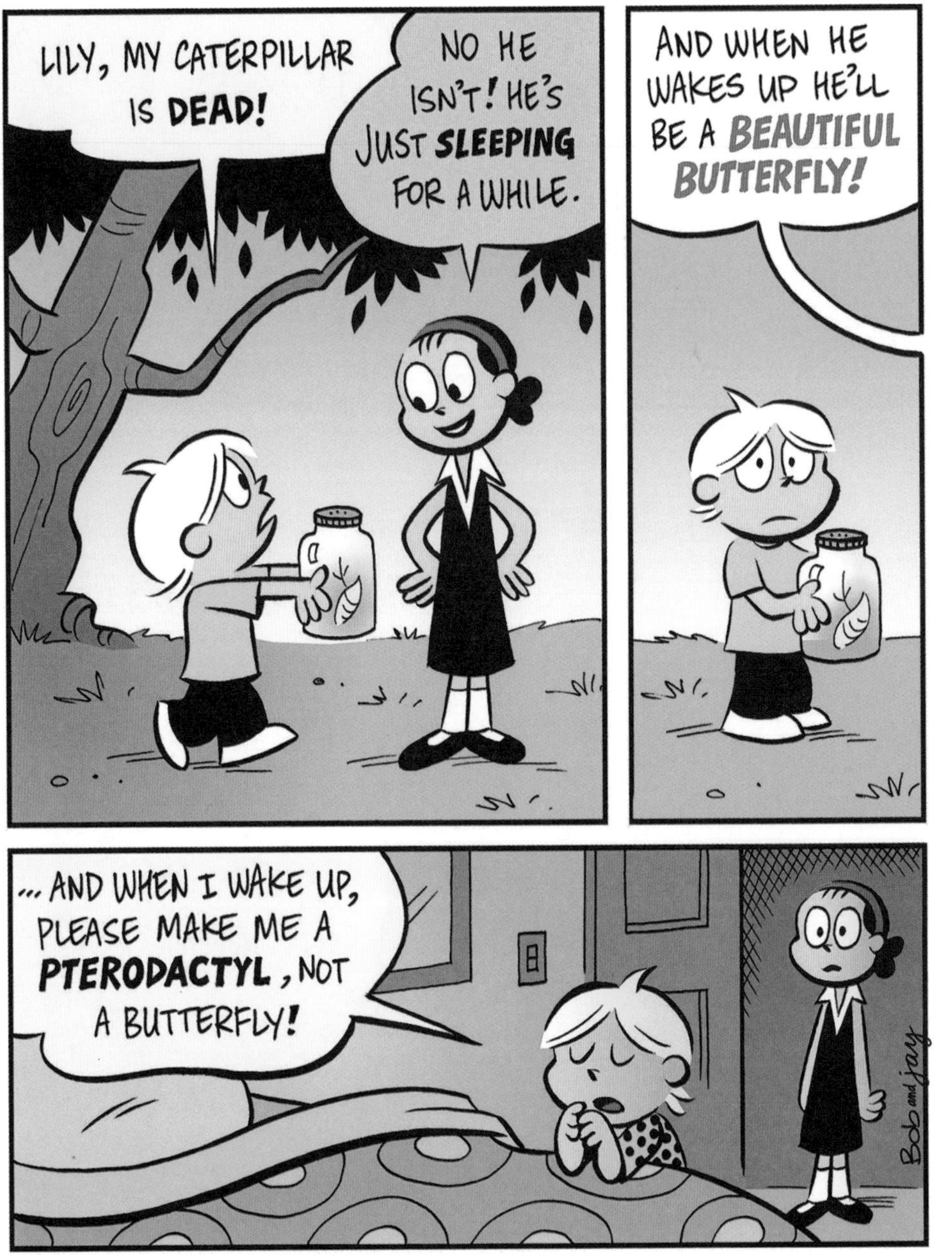
LILY, MY CATERPILLAR IS DEAD!
NO HE ISN'T! HE'S JUST SLEEPING FOR A WHILE.
AND WHEN HE WAKES UP HE'LL BE A BEAUTIFUL BUTTERFLY!
... AND WHEN I WAKE UP, PLEASE MAKE ME A PTERODACTYL, NOT A BUTTERFLY!
Bob and jay

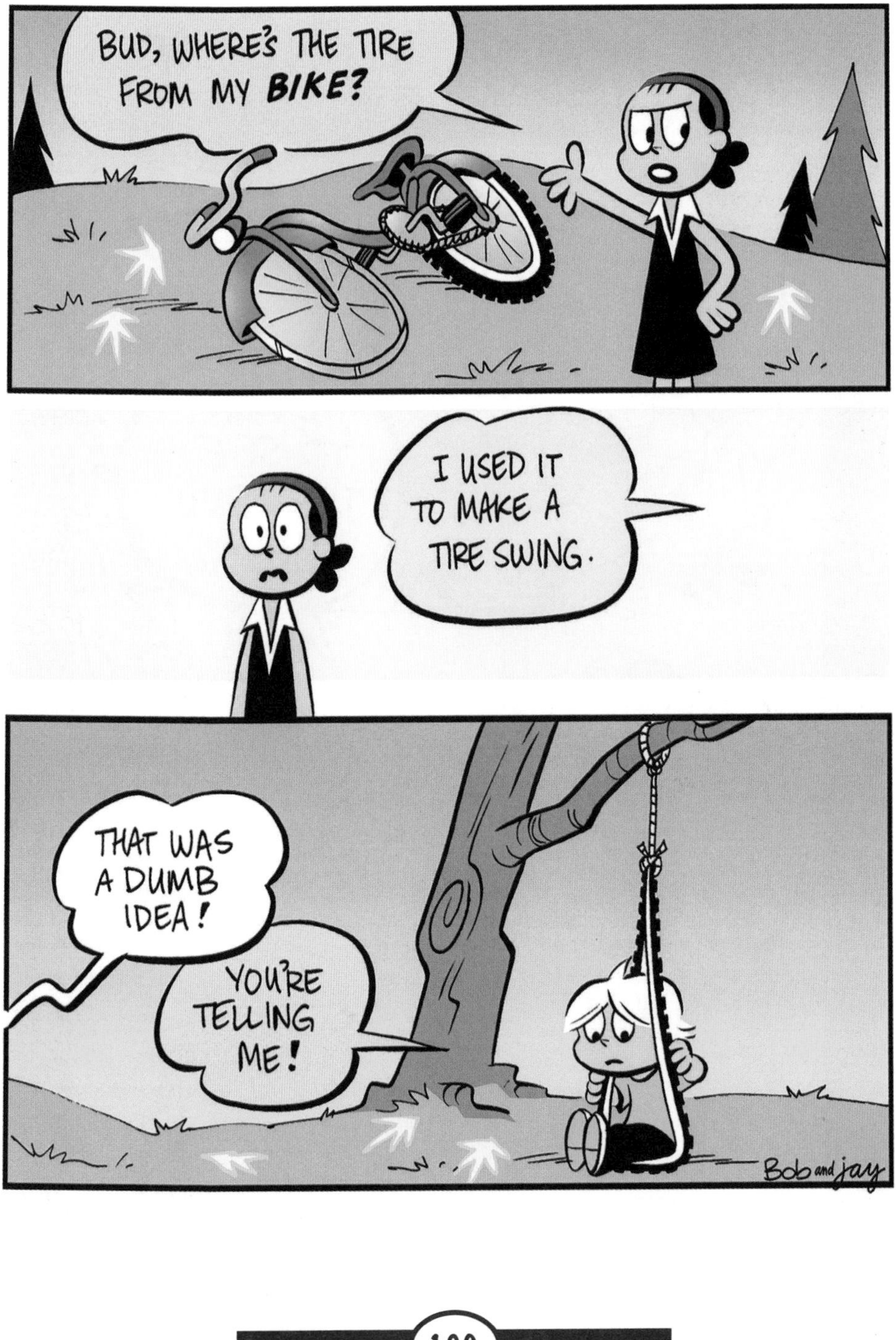
BUD, WHERE'S THE TIRE FROM MY BIKE?
I USED IT TO MAKE A TIRE SWING.
THAT WAS A DUMB IDEA!
YOU'RE TELLING ME!
Bob and jay

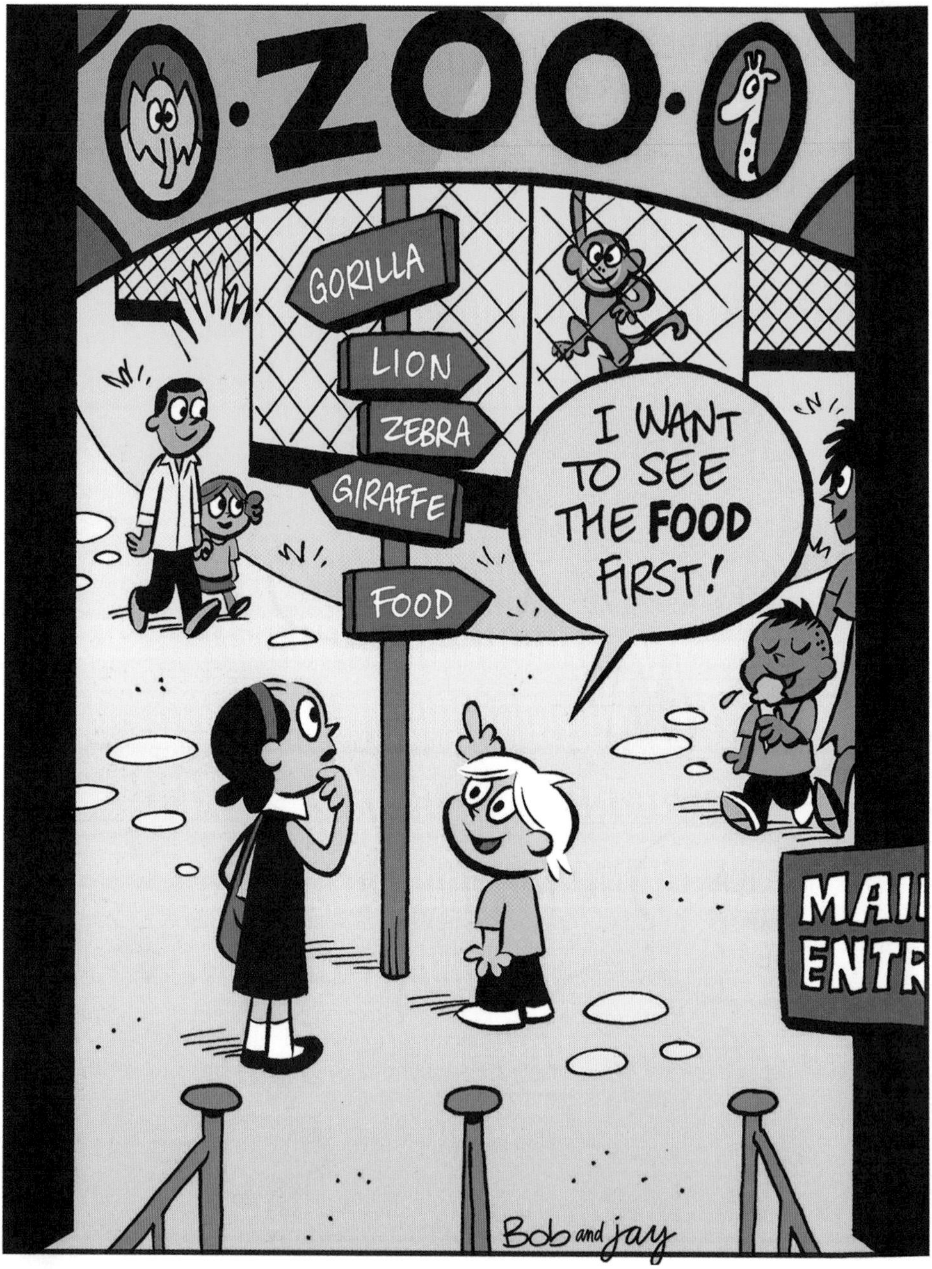
ZOO
GORILLA
LION
ZEBRA
GIRAFFE
FOOD
I WANT TO SEE THE **FOOD** FIRST!
MAI
ENTR
Bob and jay

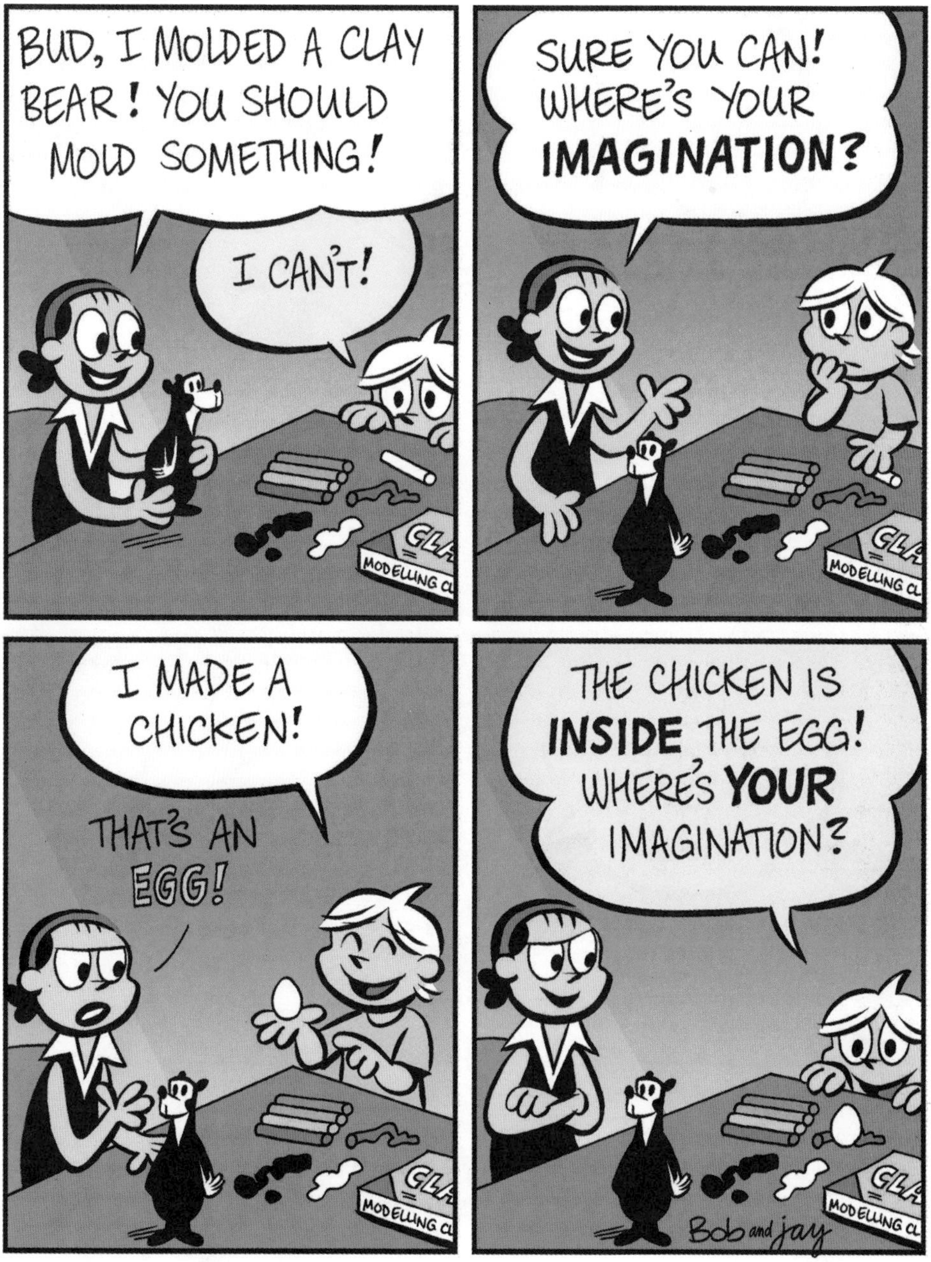
BUD, I MOLDED A CLAY BEAR! YOU SHOULD MOLD SOMETHING!
I CAN'T!
SURE YOU CAN! WHERE'S YOUR **IMAGINATION?**
I MADE A CHICKEN!
THAT'S AN EGG!
THE CHICKEN IS **INSIDE** THE EGG! WHERE'S **YOUR** IMAGINATION?
Bob and jay

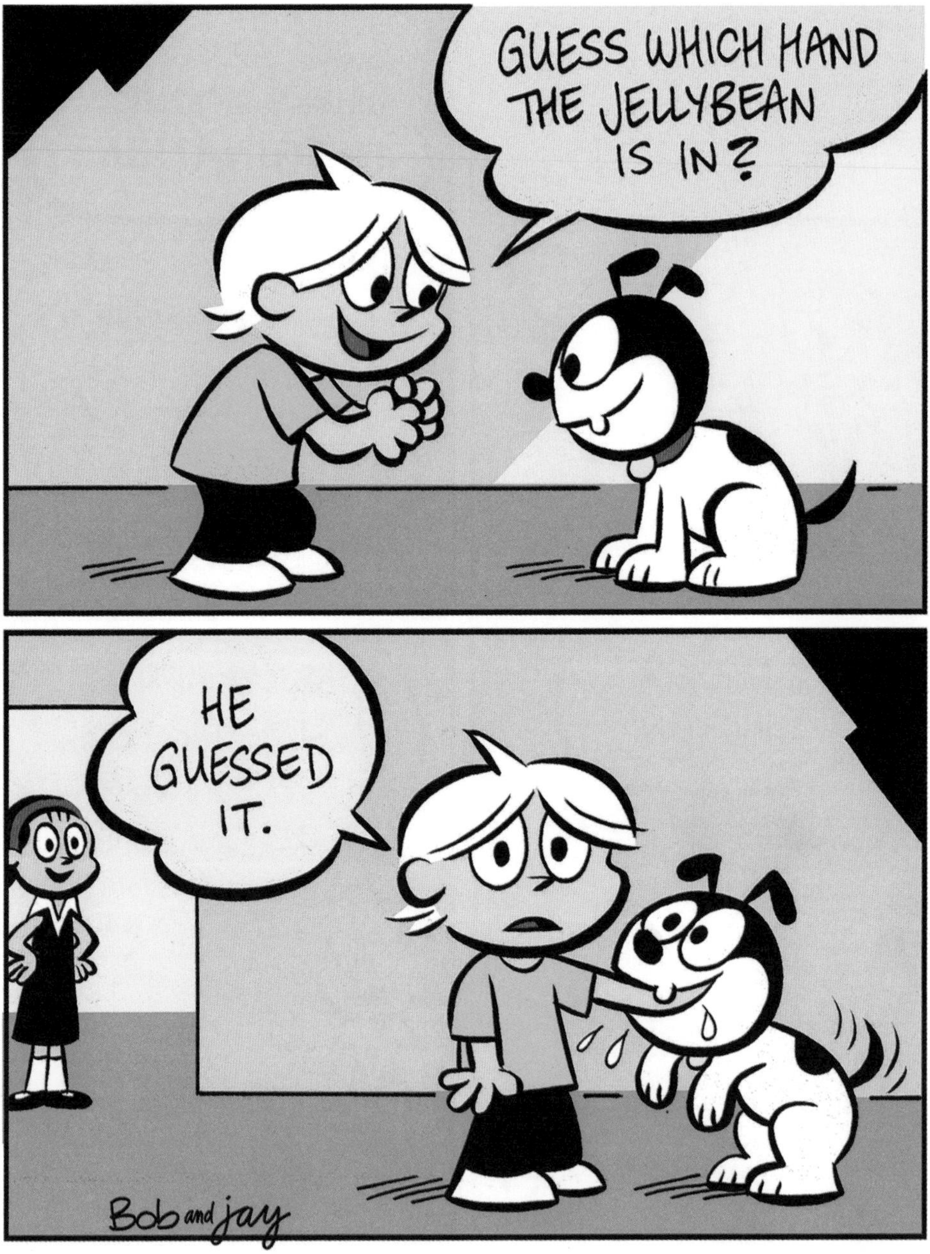
GUESS WHICH HAND THE JELLYBEAN IS IN?
HE GUESSED IT.
Bob and jay

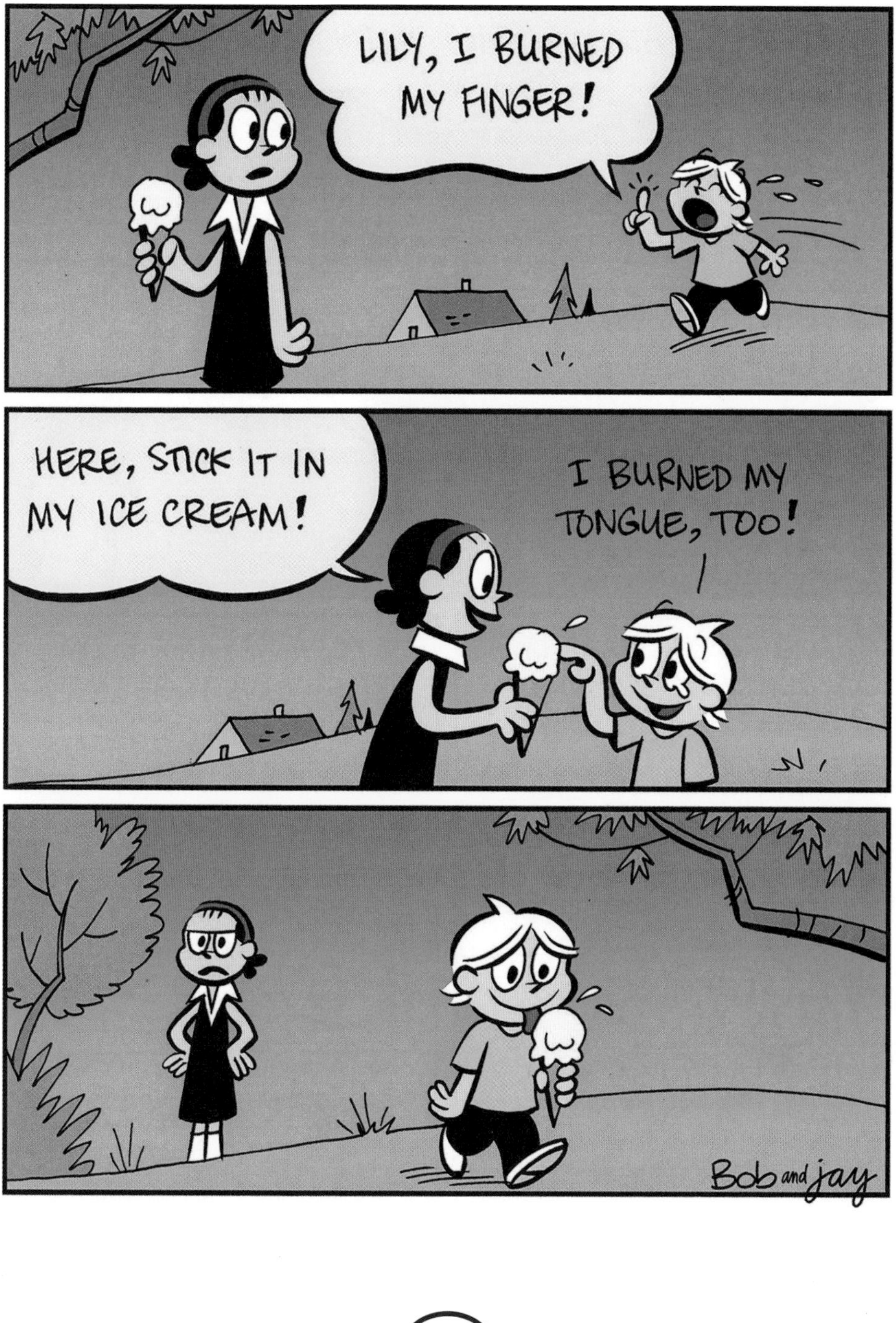
LILY, I BURNED MY FINGER!
HERE, STICK IT IN MY ICE CREAM!
I BURNED MY TONGUE, TOO!
Bob and jay

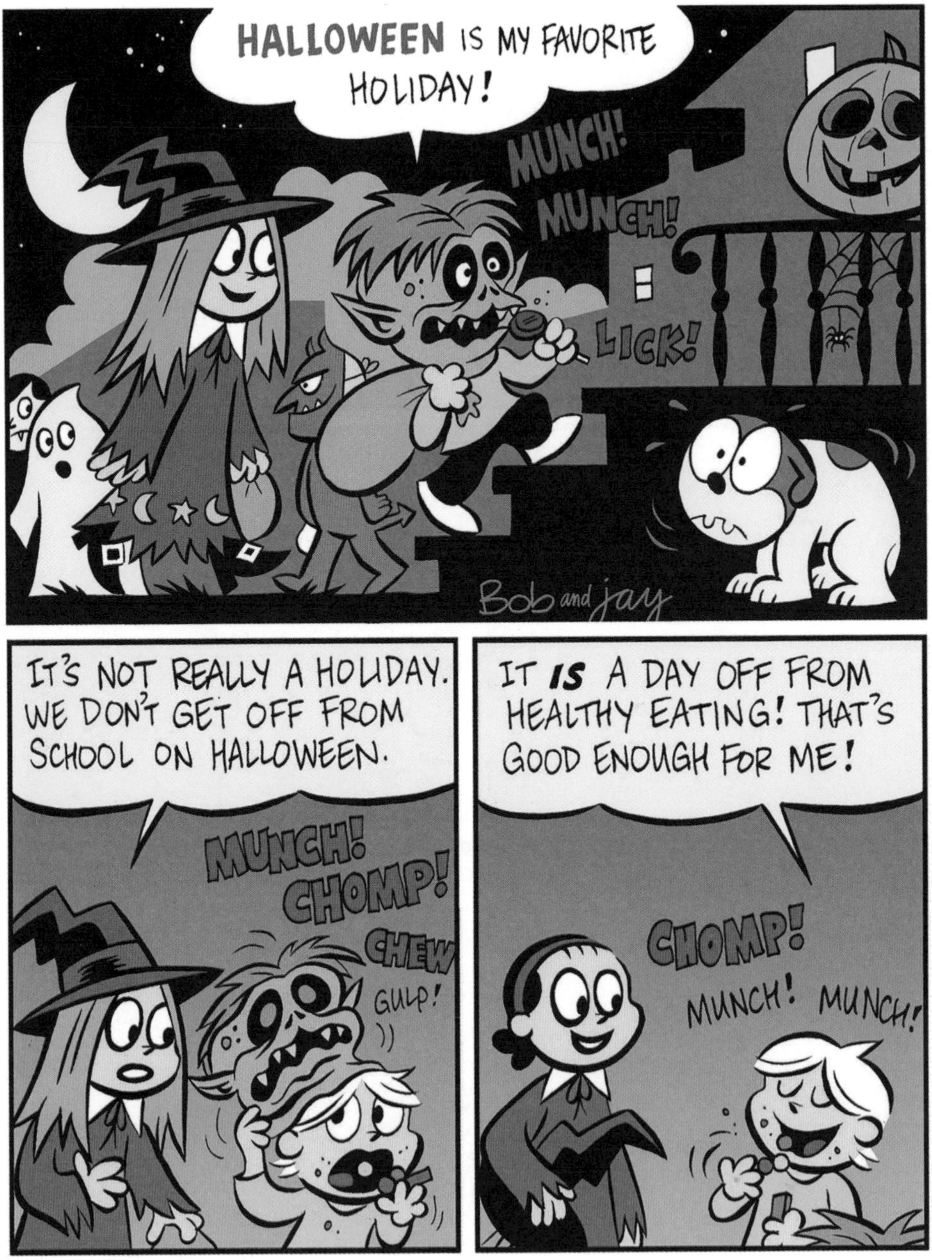
HALLOWEEN IS MY FAVORITE HOLIDAY!
MUNCH!
MUNCH!
LICK!
Bob and jay
IT'S NOT REALLY A HOLIDAY. WE DON'T GET OFF FROM SCHOOL ON HALLOWEEN.
MUNCH!
CHOMP!
CHEW
GULP!
IT IS A DAY OFF FROM HEALTHY EATING! THAT'S GOOD ENOUGH FOR ME!
CHOMP!
MUNCH!
MUNCH!

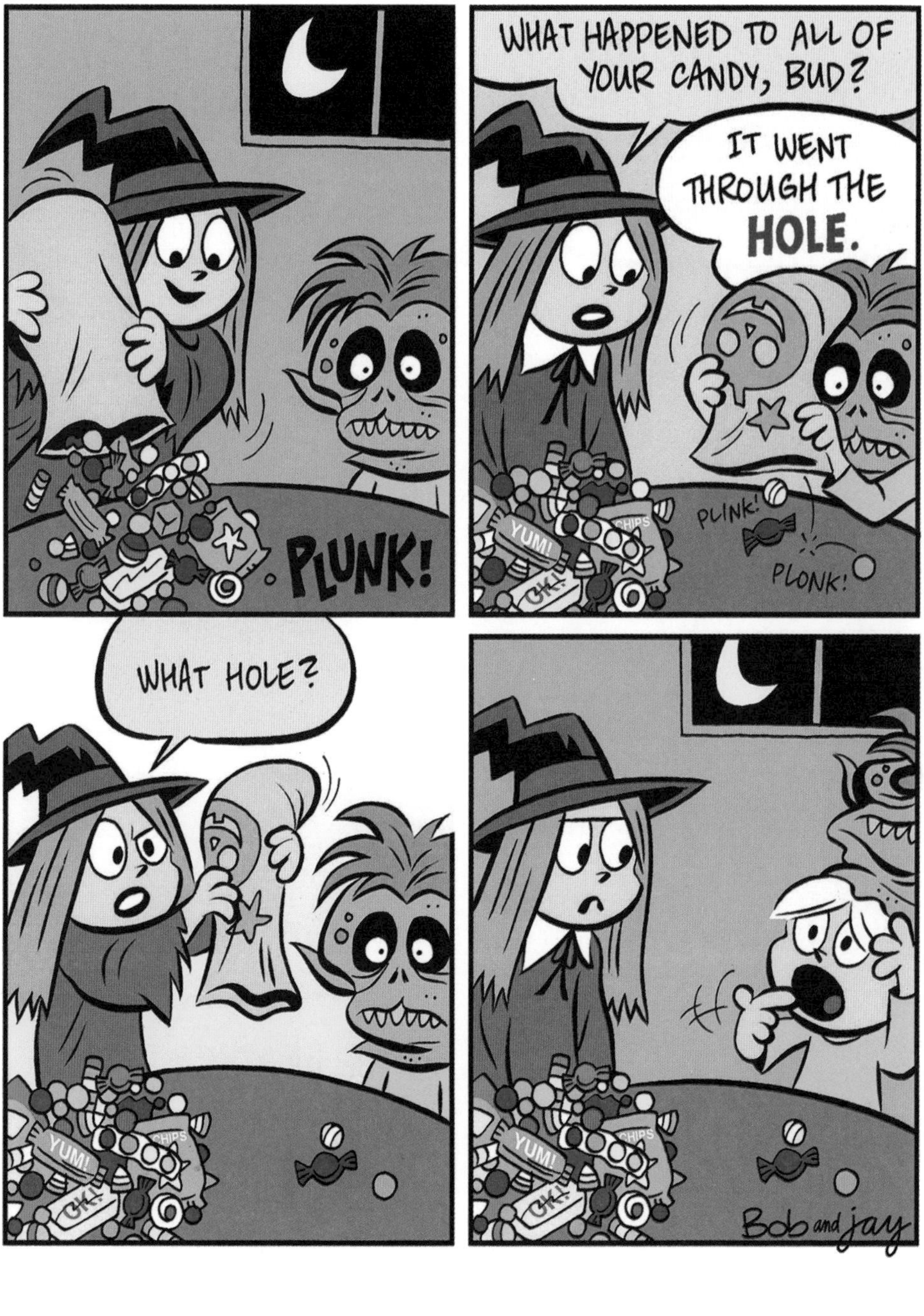
PLUNK!
WHAT HAPPENED TO ALL OF YOUR CANDY, BUD?
IT WENT THROUGH THE HOLE.
YUM!
CHIPS
PLINK!
PLONK!
WHAT HOLE?
YUM!
CHIPS
YUM!
CHIPS
Bob and jay

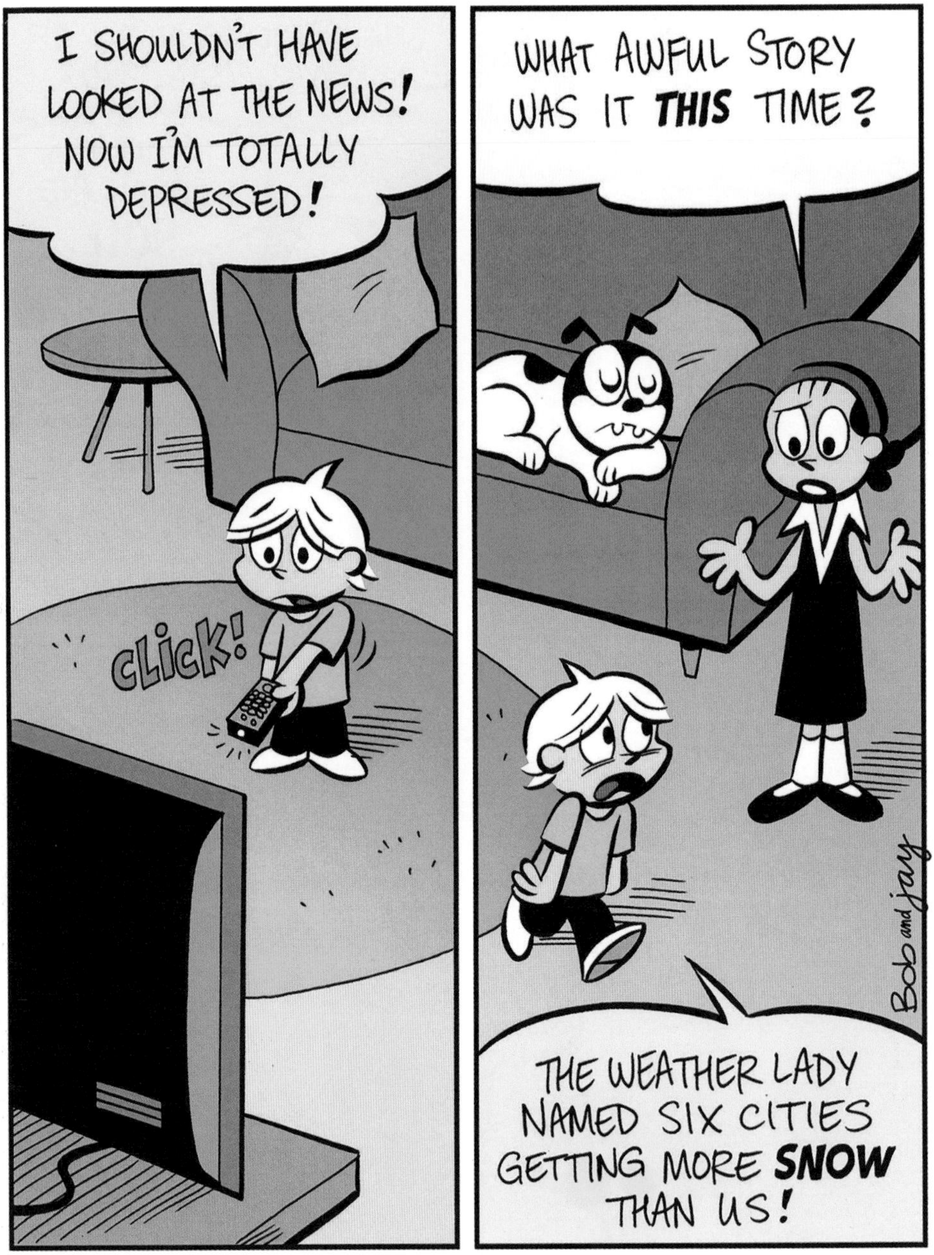
I SHOULDN'T HAVE LOOKED AT THE NEWS! NOW I'M TOTALLY DEPRESSED!
CLICK!
WHAT AWFUL STORY WAS IT **THIS** TIME?
THE WEATHER LADY NAMED SIX CITIES GETTING MORE **SNOW** THAN US!
Bob and jay

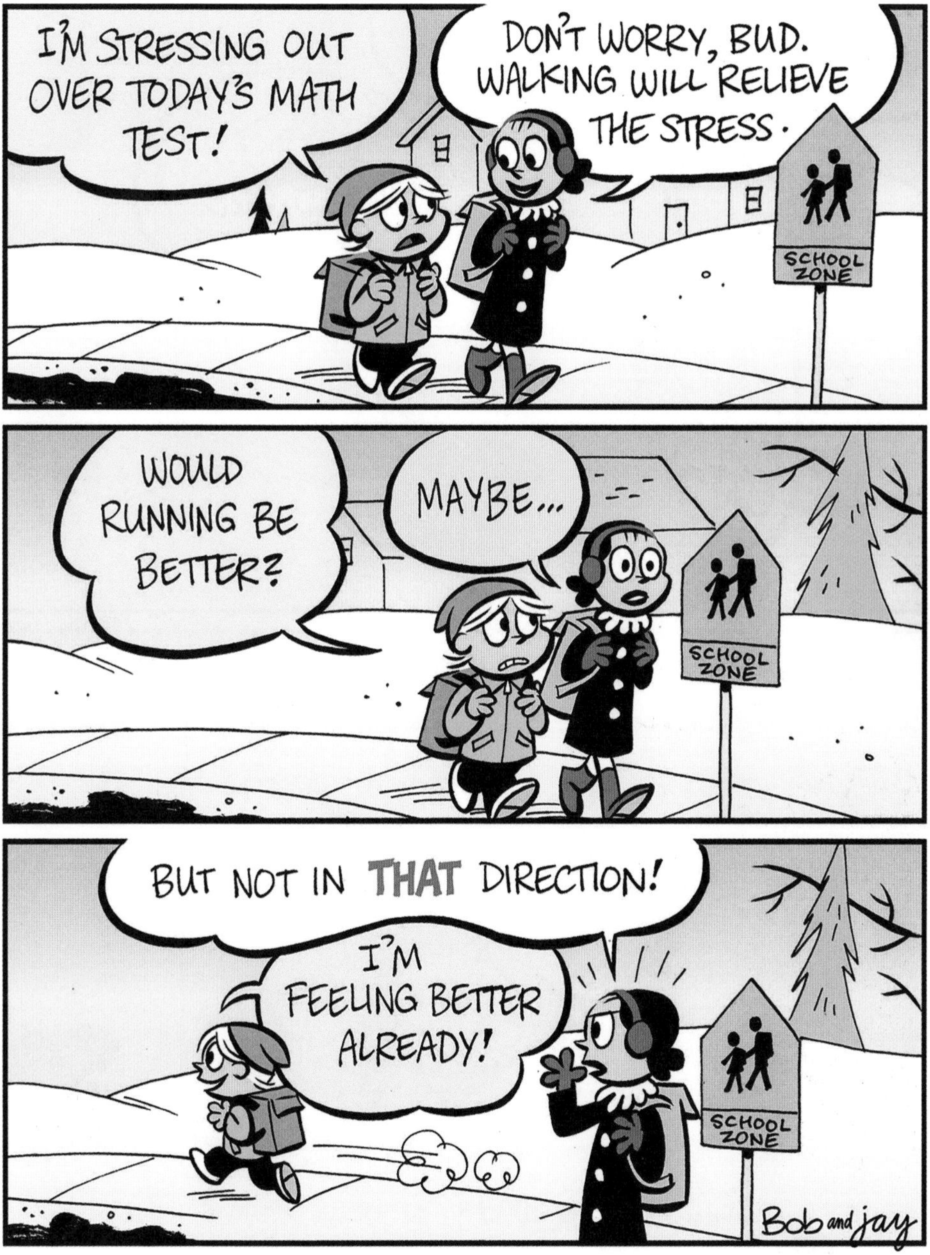
I'M STRESSING OUT OVER TODAY'S MATH TEST!
DON'T WORRY, BUD. WALKING WILL RELIEVE THE STRESS.
SCHOOL ZONE
WOULD RUNNING BE BETTER?
MAYBE...
SCHOOL ZONE
BUT NOT IN THAT DIRECTION!
I'M FEELING BETTER ALREADY!
SCHOOL ZONE
Bob and jay

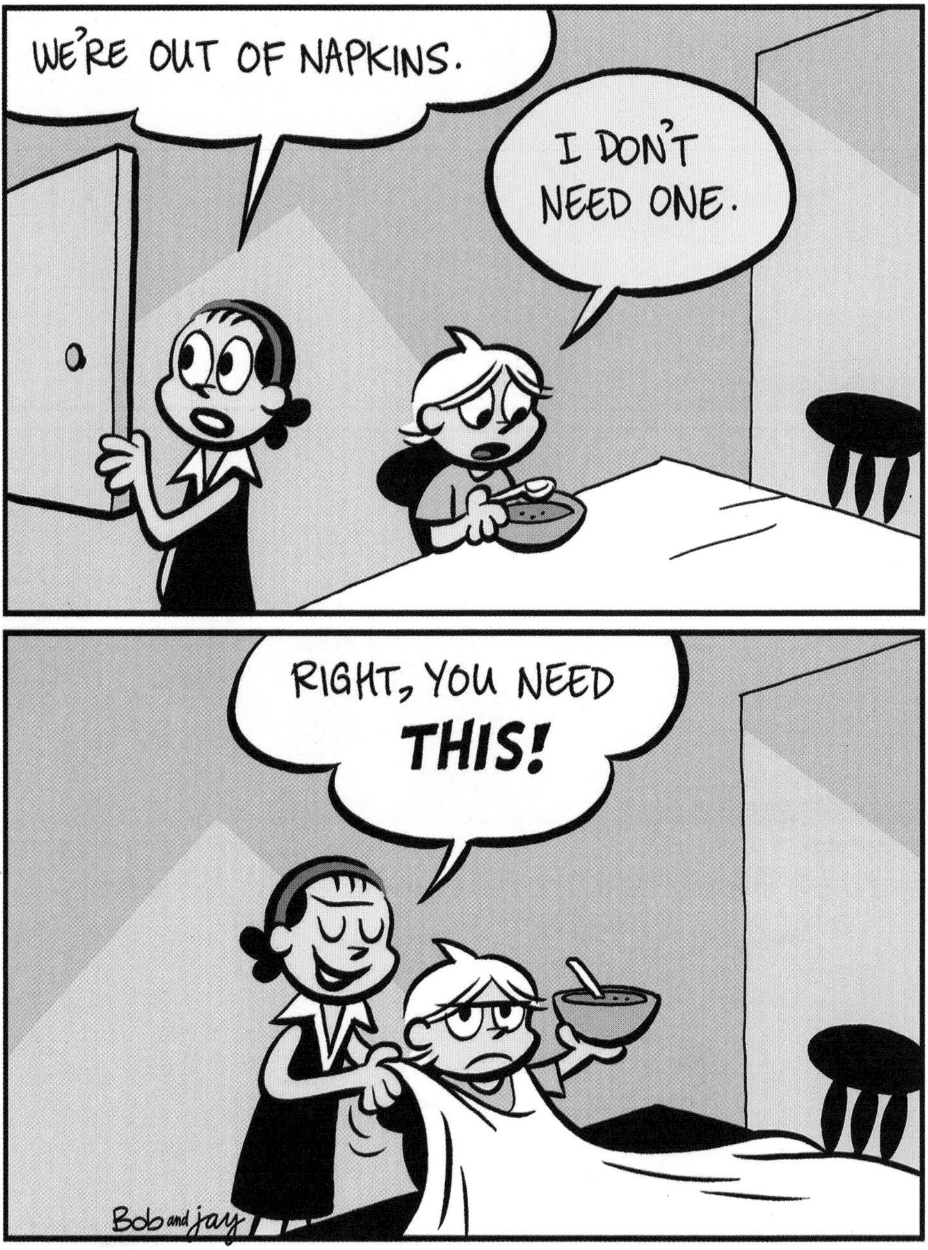
WE'RE OUT OF NAPKINS.
I DON'T NEED ONE.
RIGHT, YOU NEED THIS!
Bob and jay

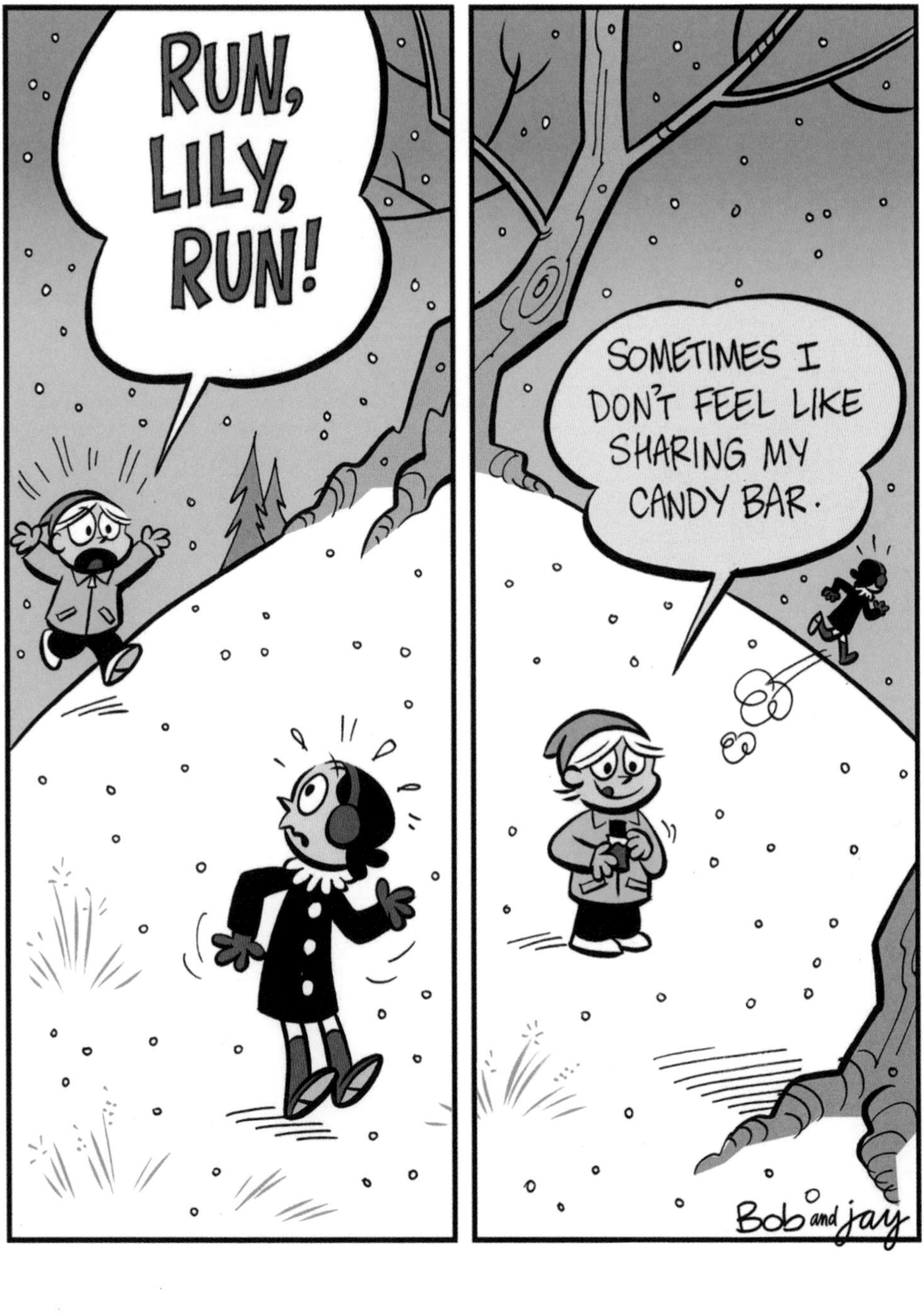
RUN, LILY, RUN!
SOMETIMES I DON'T FEEL LIKE SHARING MY CANDY BAR.
Bob and jay

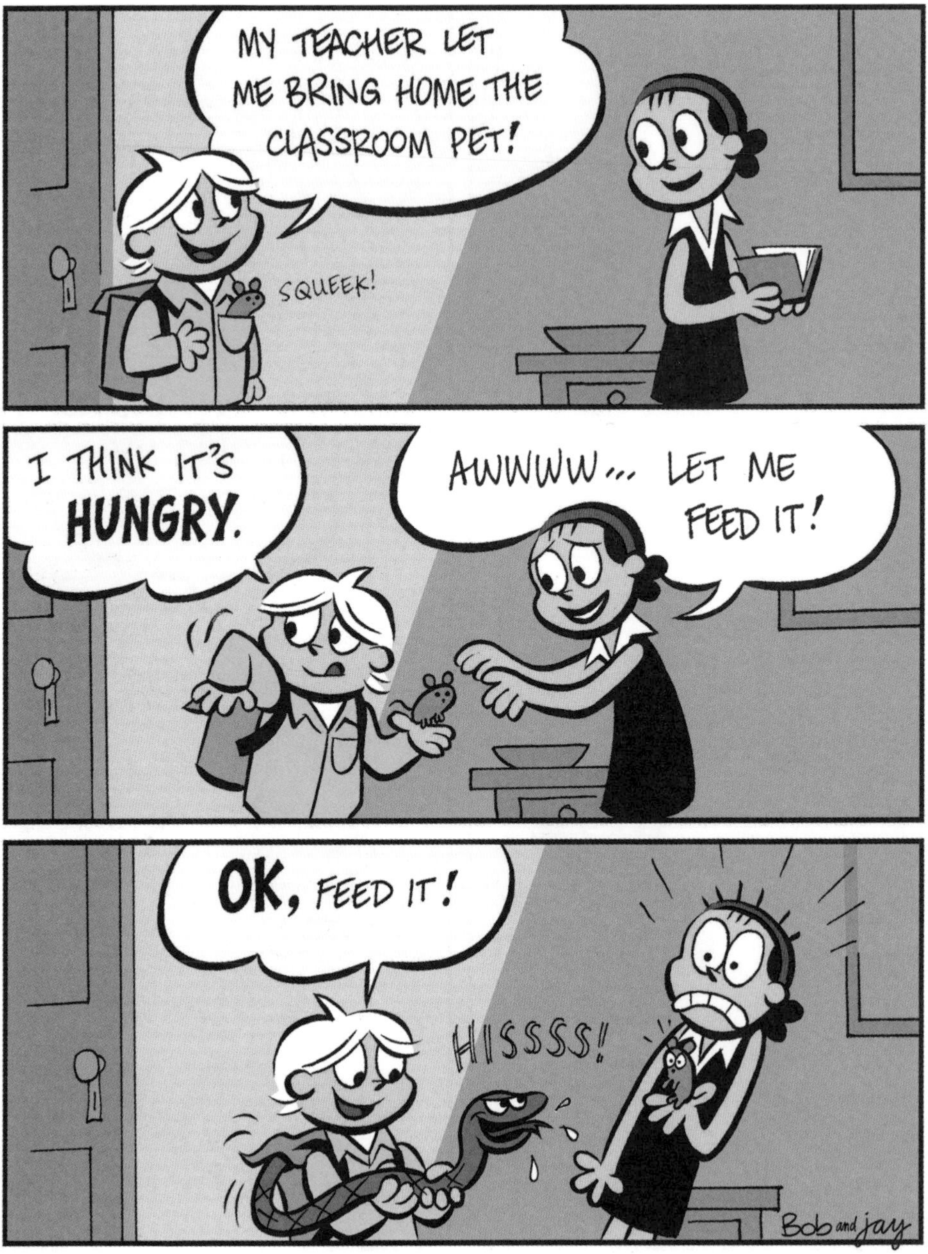
MY TEACHER LET ME BRING HOME THE CLASSROOM PET!
SQUEEK!
I THINK IT'S HUNGRY.
AWWWW... LET ME FEED IT!
OK, FEED IT!
HISSSS!
Bob and jay

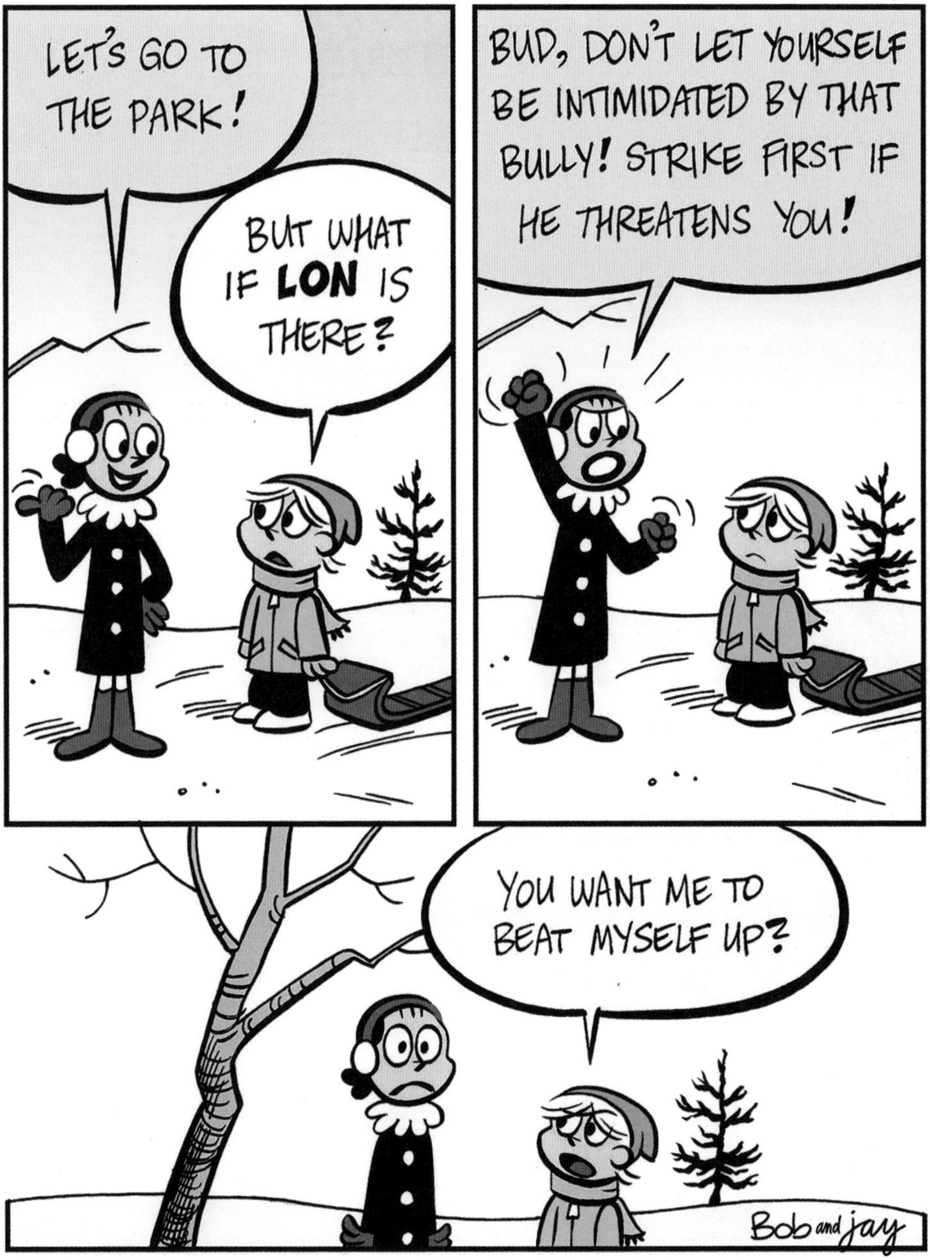
LET'S GO TO THE PARK!
BUT WHAT IF **LON** IS THERE?
BUD, DON'T LET YOURSELF BE INTIMIDATED BY THAT BULLY! STRIKE FIRST IF HE THREATENS YOU!
YOU WANT ME TO BEAT MYSELF UP?
Bob and jay

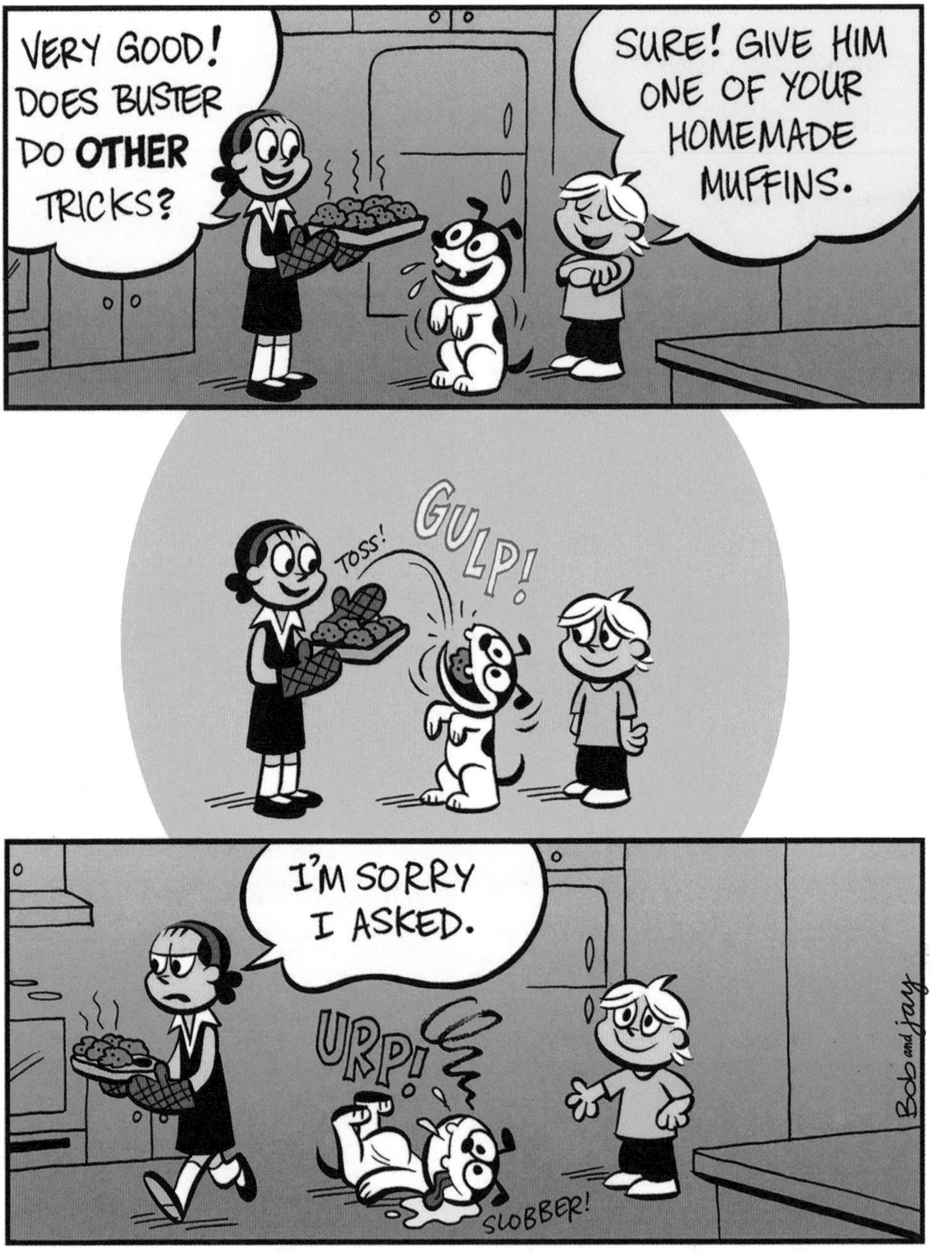
VERY GOOD! DOES BUSTER DO OTHER TRICKS?
SURE! GIVE HIM ONE OF YOUR HOMEMADE MUFFINS.
TOSS!
GULP!
I'M SORRY I ASKED.
URP!
SLOBBER!
Bob and jay

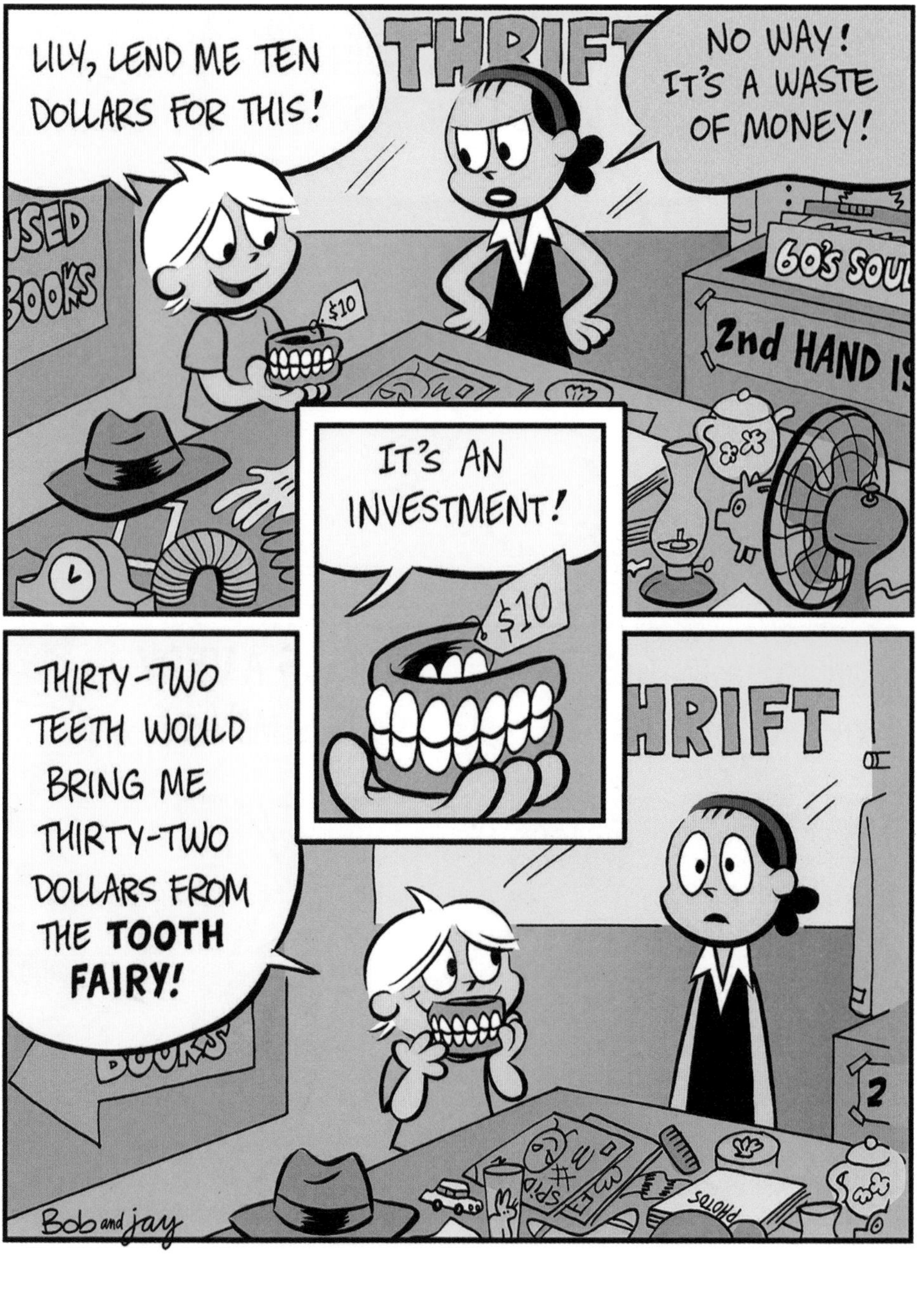
LILY, LEND ME TEN DOLLARS FOR THIS!
THRIFT
NO WAY! IT'S A WASTE OF MONEY!
USED BOOKS
$10
60'S SOUL
2nd HAND IS
IT'S AN INVESTMENT!
$10
THIRTY-TWO TEETH WOULD BRING ME THIRTY-TWO DOLLARS FROM THE TOOTH FAIRY!
HRIFT
PHOTOS
Bob and jay

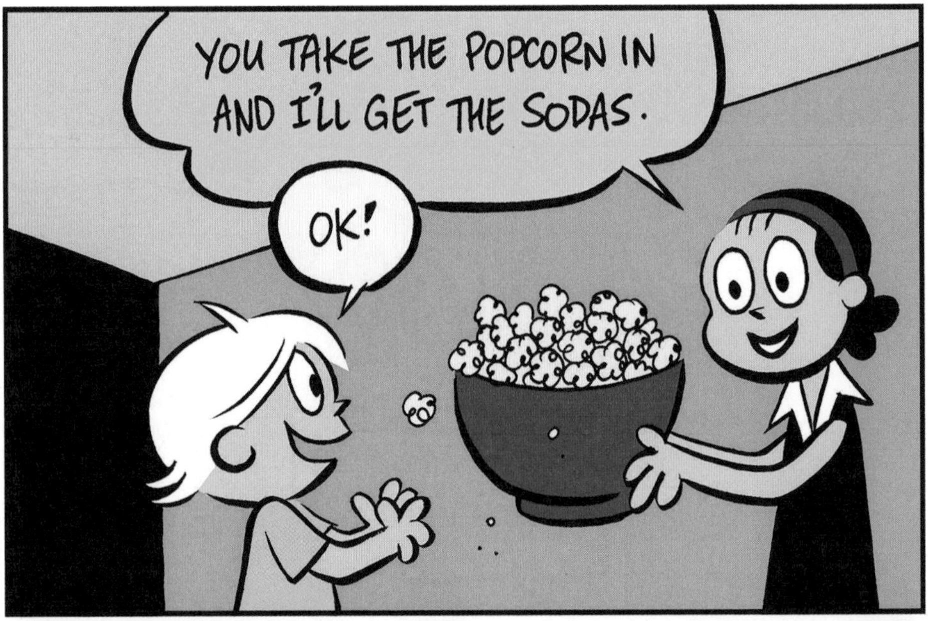
YOU TAKE THE POPCORN IN AND I'LL GET THE SODAS.
OK!

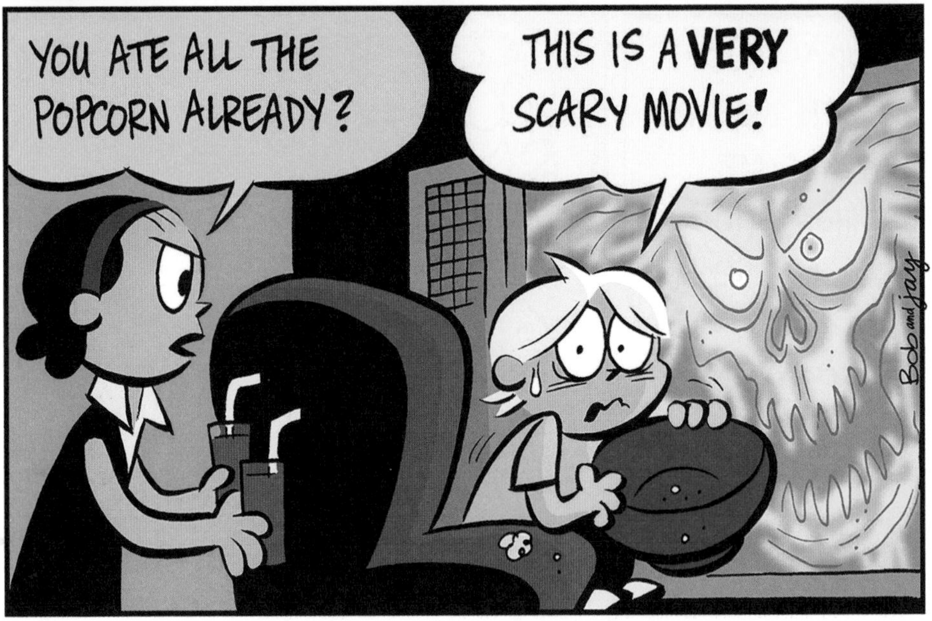
YOU ATE ALL THE POPCORN ALREADY?
THIS IS A **VERY** SCARY MOVIE!
Bob and jay

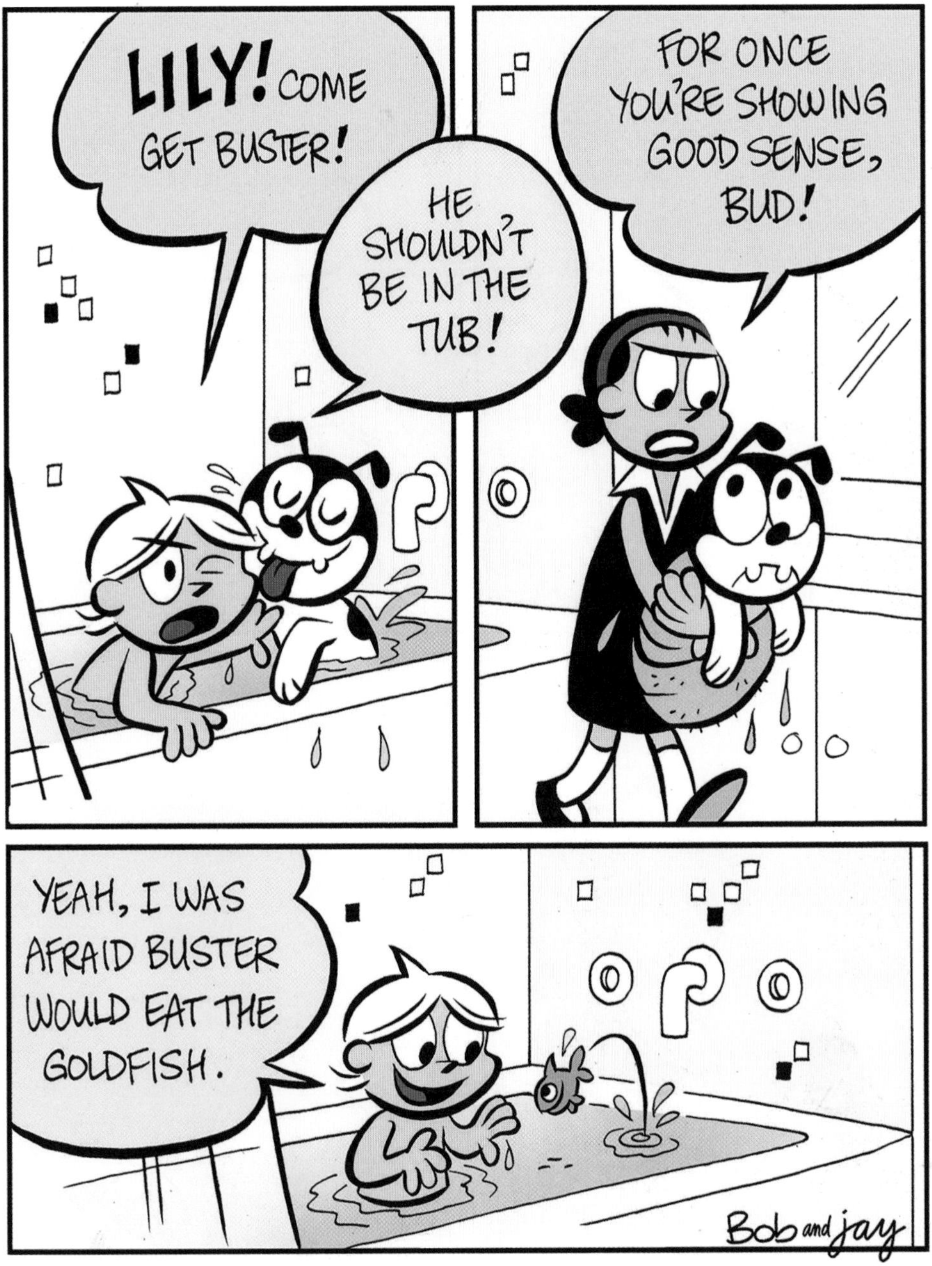
LILY! COME GET BUSTER!
HE SHOULDN'T BE IN THE TUB!
FOR ONCE YOU'RE SHOWING GOOD SENSE, BUD!
YEAH, I WAS AFRAID BUSTER WOULD EAT THE GOLDFISH.
Bob and jay

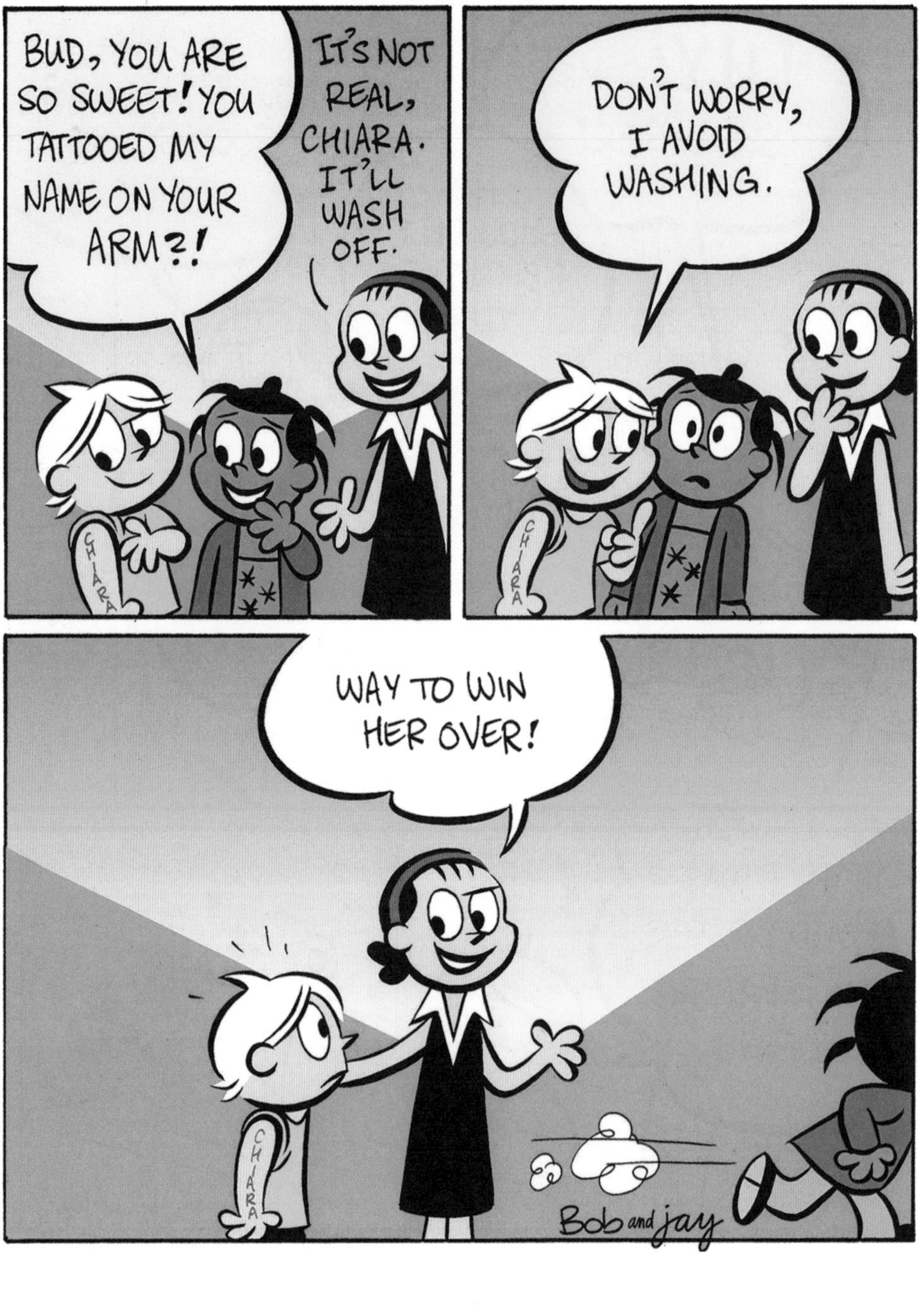
BUD, YOU ARE SO SWEET! YOU TATTOOED MY NAME ON YOUR ARM?!
IT'S NOT REAL, CHIARA. IT'LL WASH OFF.
CHIARA
DON'T WORRY, I AVOID WASHING.
CHIARA
WAY TO WIN HER OVER!
CHIARA
Bob and jay

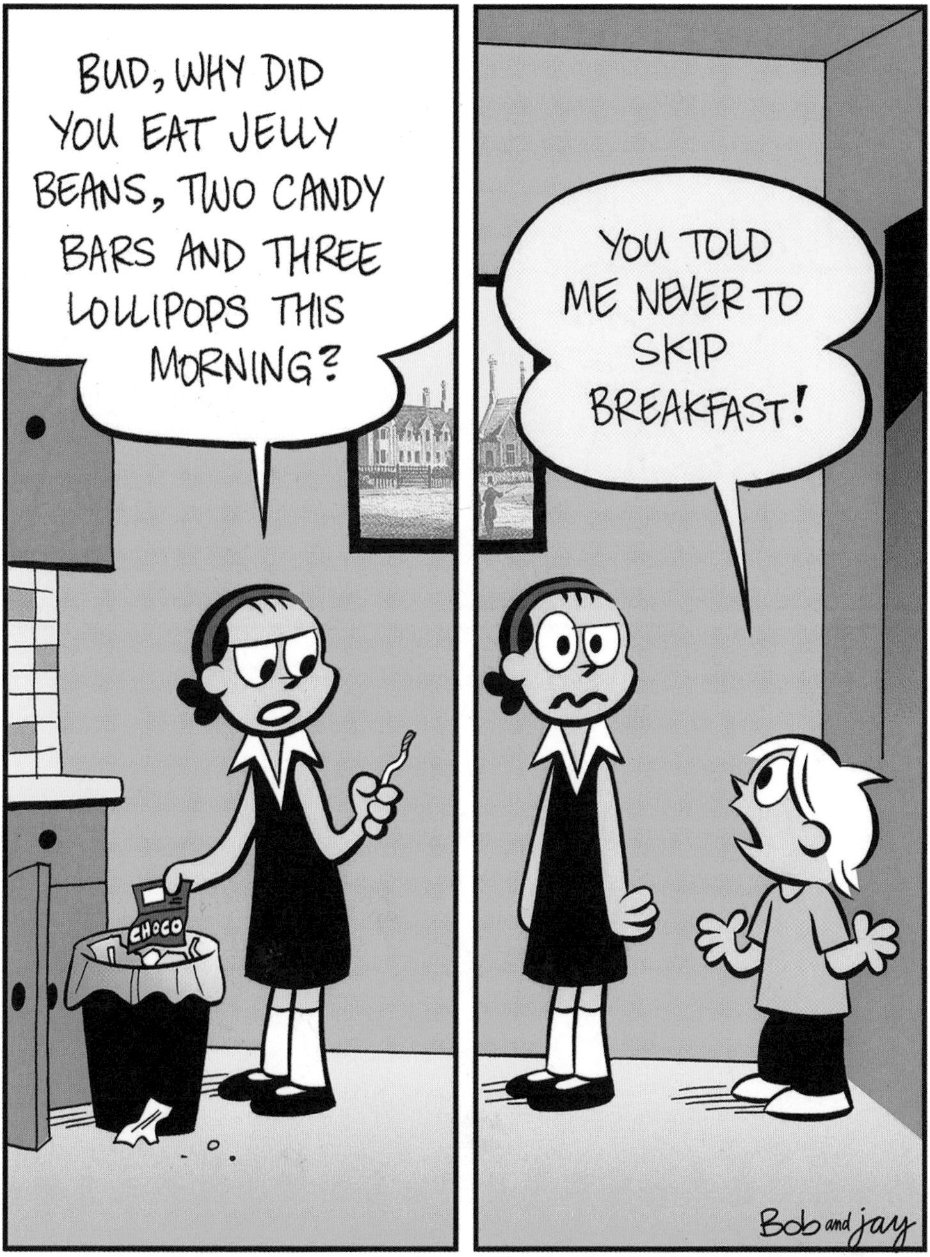
BUD, WHY DID YOU EAT JELLY BEANS, TWO CANDY BARS AND THREE LOLLIPOPS THIS MORNING?
CHOCO
YOU TOLD ME NEVER TO SKIP BREAKFAST!
Bob and jay

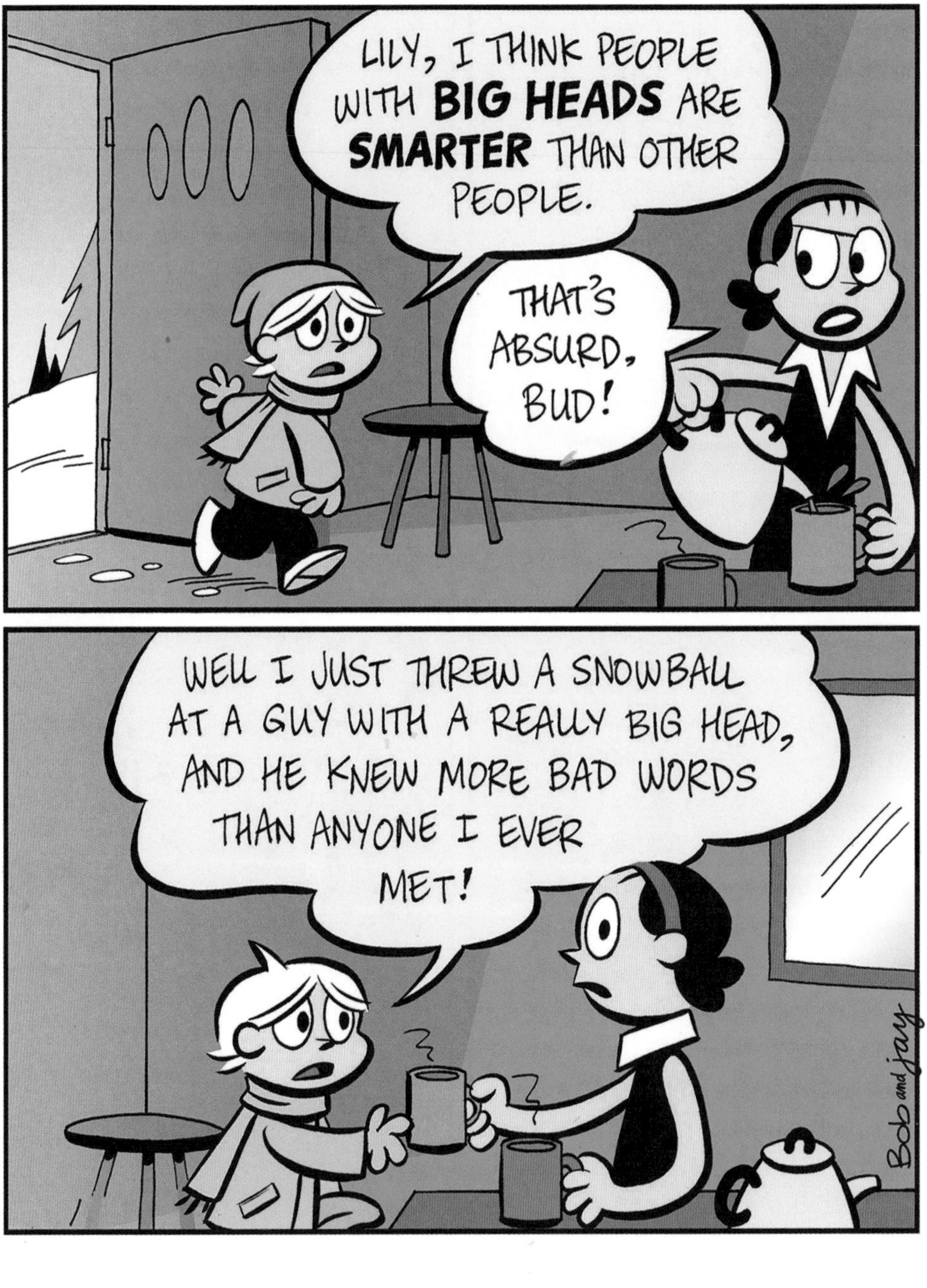
LILY, I THINK PEOPLE WITH **BIG HEADS** ARE **SMARTER** THAN OTHER PEOPLE.
THAT'S ABSURD, BUD!
WELL I JUST THREW A SNOWBALL AT A GUY WITH A REALLY BIG HEAD, AND HE KNEW MORE BAD WORDS THAN ANYONE I EVER MET!
Bob and jay

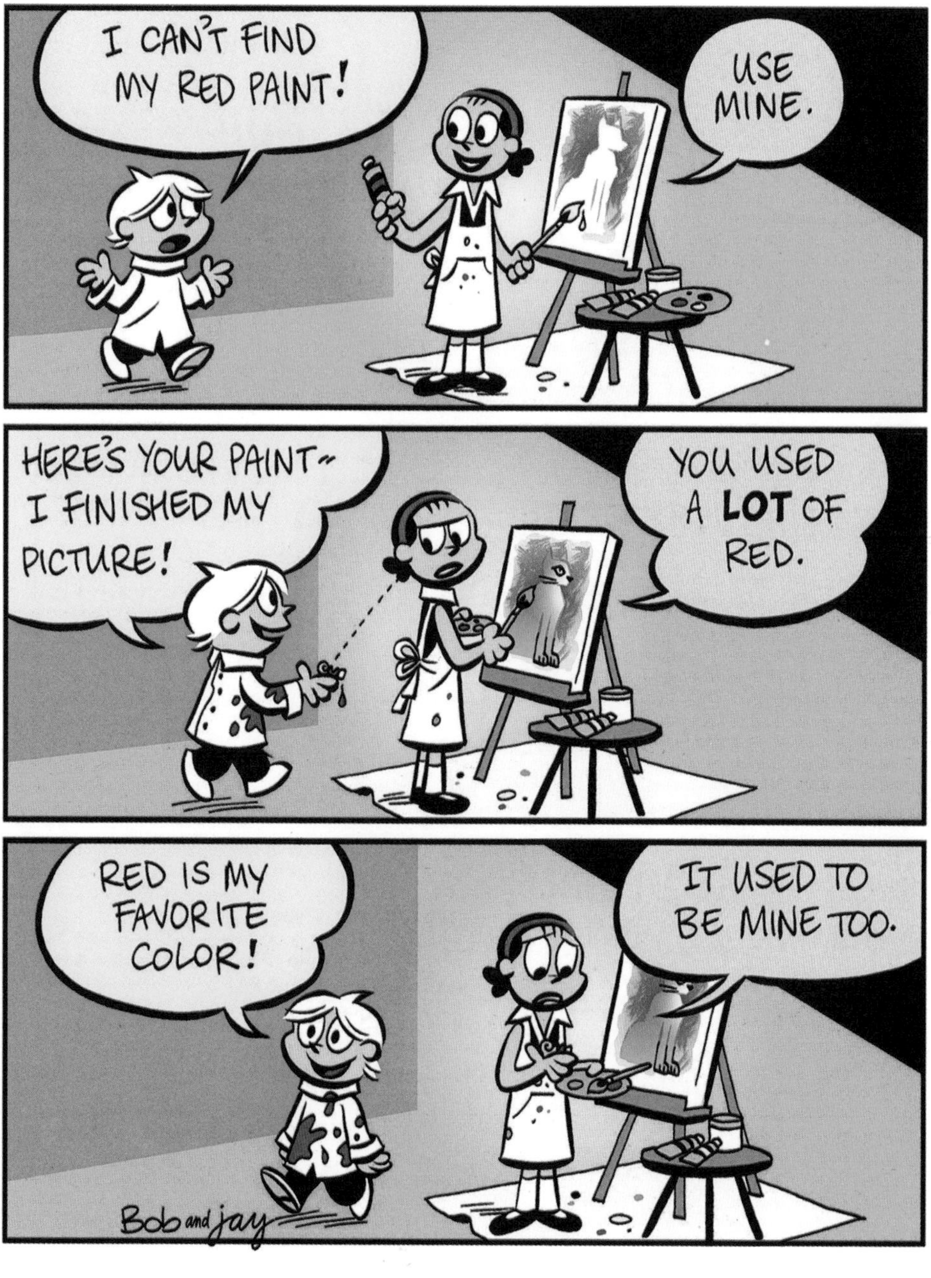
I CAN'T FIND MY RED PAINT!
USE MINE.
HERE'S YOUR PAINT~ I FINISHED MY PICTURE!
YOU USED A **LOT** OF RED.
RED IS MY FAVORITE COLOR!
IT USED TO BE MINE TOO.
Bob and jay

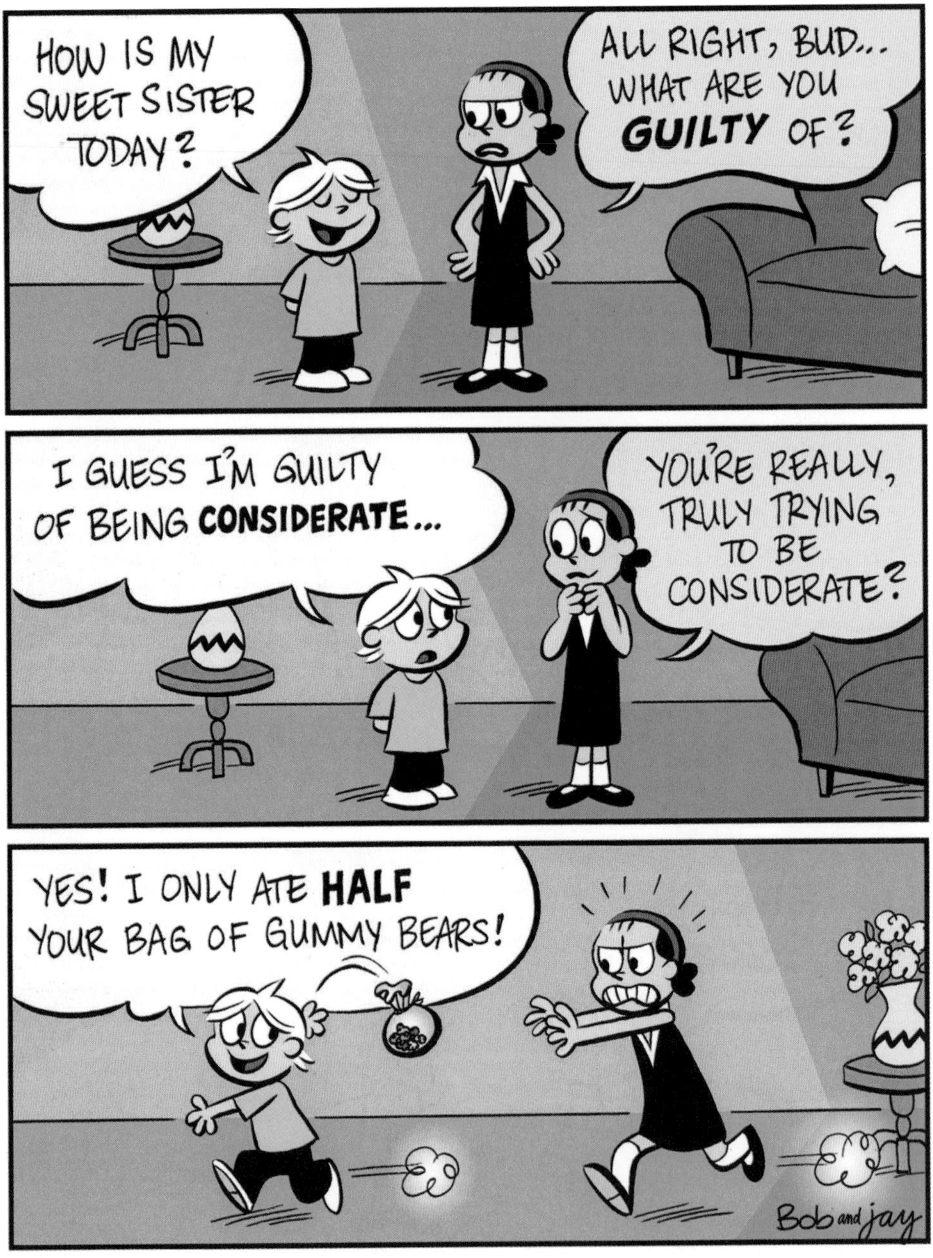
HOW IS MY SWEET SISTER TODAY?
ALL RIGHT, BUD... WHAT ARE YOU **GUILTY** OF?
I GUESS I'M GUILTY OF BEING **CONSIDERATE**...
YOU'RE REALLY, TRULY TRYING TO BE CONSIDERATE?
YES! I ONLY ATE **HALF** YOUR BAG OF GUMMY BEARS!
Bob and jay

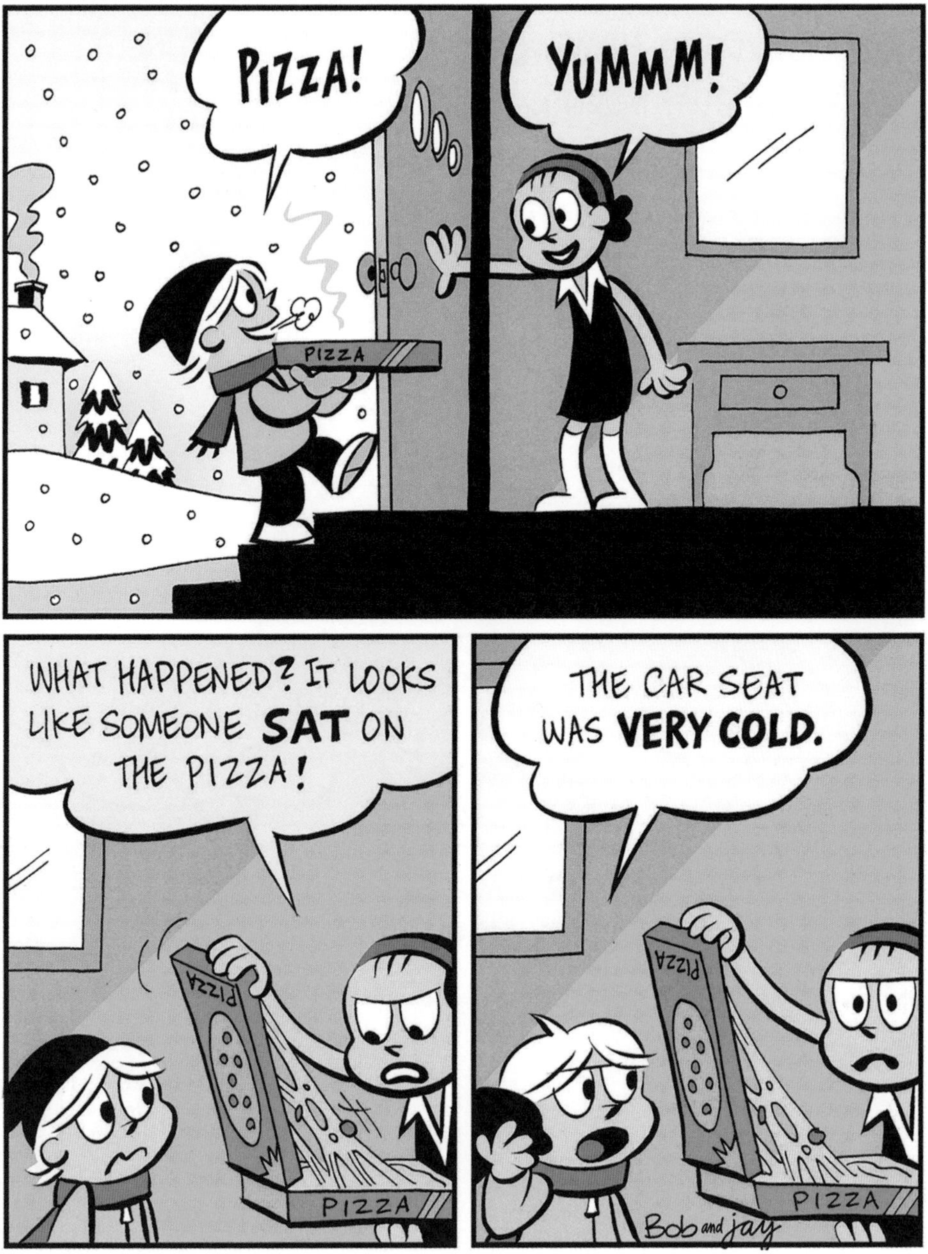
PIZZA!
PIZZA
YUMMM!
WHAT HAPPENED? IT LOOKS LIKE SOMEONE **SAT** ON THE PIZZA!
PIZZA
PIZZA
THE CAR SEAT WAS **VERY COLD.**
PIZZA
PIZZA
Bob and jay

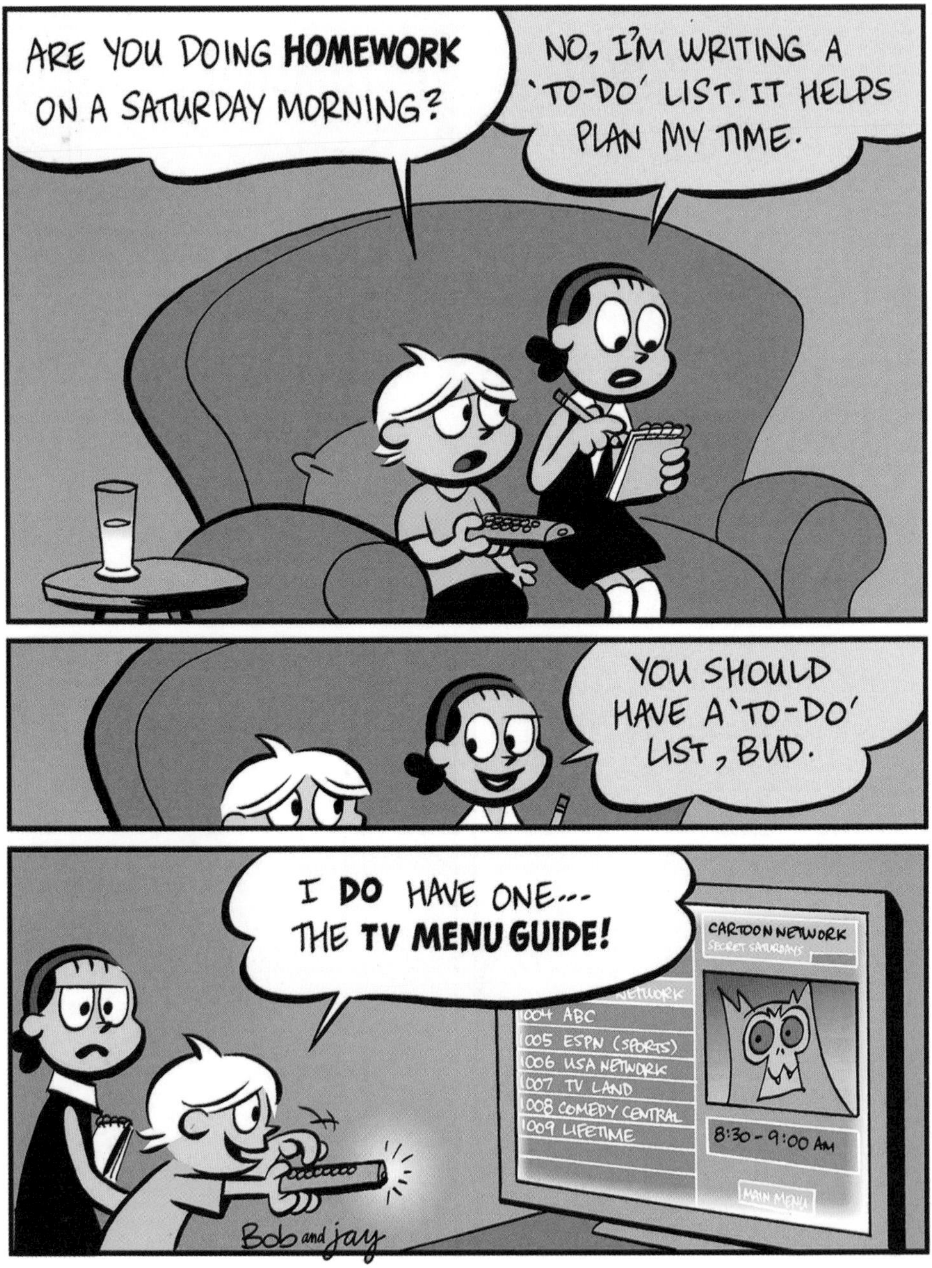
ARE YOU DOING **HOMEWORK** ON A SATURDAY MORNING?
NO, I'M WRITING A 'TO-DO' LIST. IT HELPS PLAN MY TIME.
YOU SHOULD HAVE A 'TO-DO' LIST, BUD.
I **DO** HAVE ONE--- THE **TV MENU GUIDE!**
CARTOON NETWORK
SECRET SATURDAYS
1004 ABC
1005 ESPN (SPORTS)
1006 USA NETWORK
1007 TV LAND
1008 COMEDY CENTRAL
1009 LIFETIME
8:30 - 9:00 AM
MAIN MENU
Bob and jay

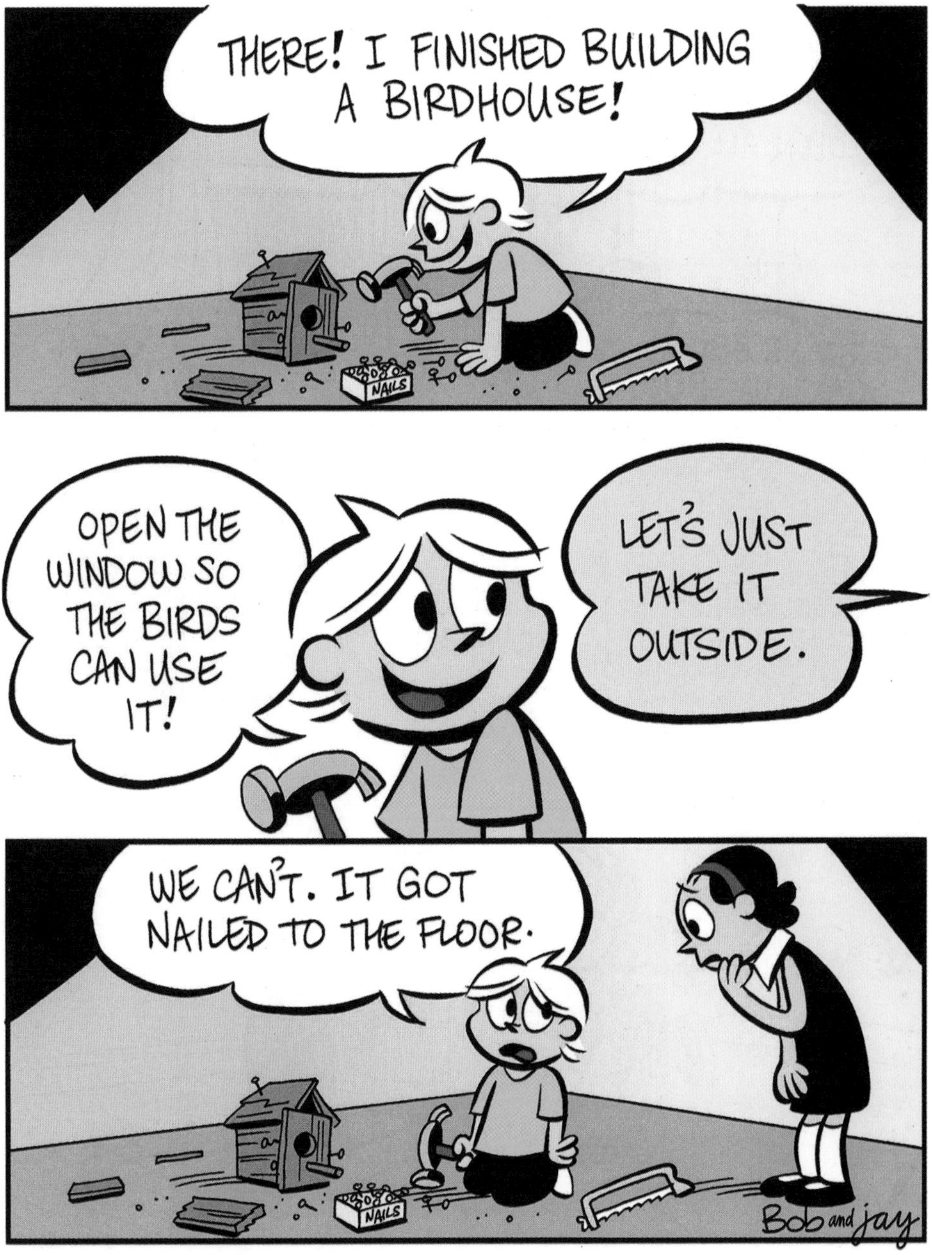
THERE! I FINISHED BUILDING A BIRDHOUSE!
NAILS
OPEN THE WINDOW SO THE BIRDS CAN USE IT!
LET'S JUST TAKE IT OUTSIDE.
WE CAN'T. IT GOT NAILED TO THE FLOOR.
NAILS
Bob and jay

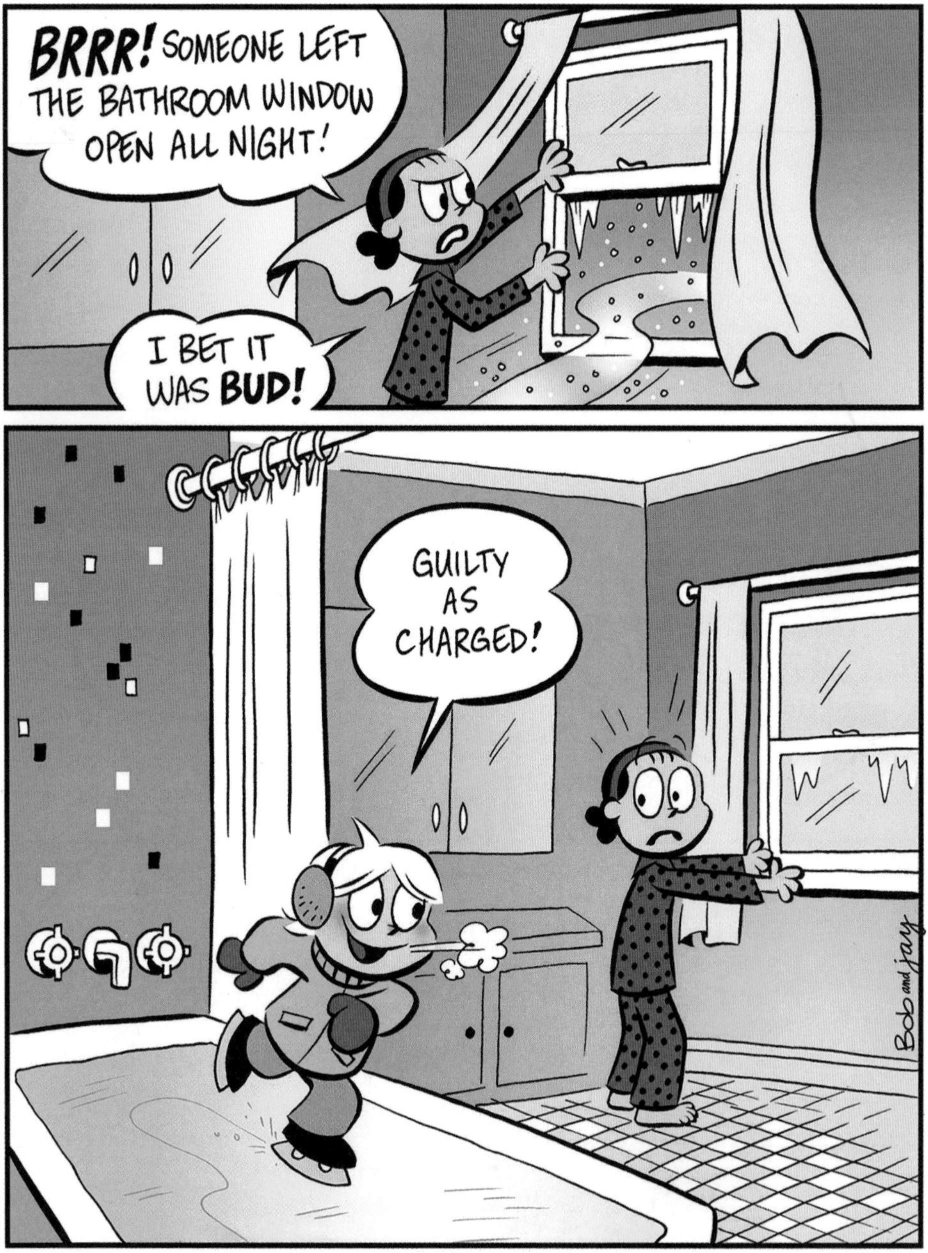
BRRR! SOMEONE LEFT THE BATHROOM WINDOW OPEN ALL NIGHT!
I BET IT WAS BUD!
GUILTY AS CHARGED!
Bob and jay

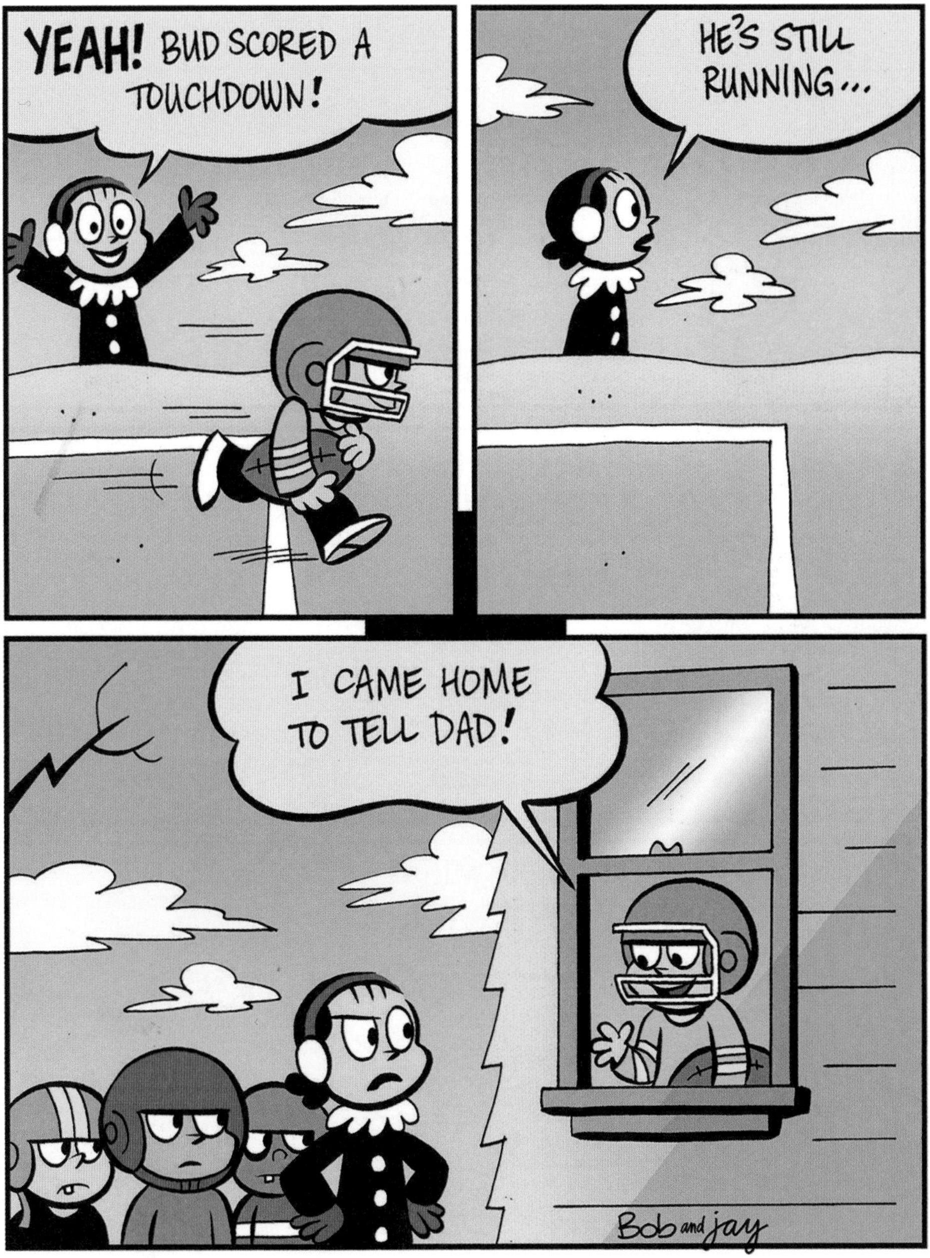
YEAH! BUD SCORED A TOUCHDOWN!
HE'S STILL RUNNING...
I CAME HOME TO TELL DAD!
Bob and jay

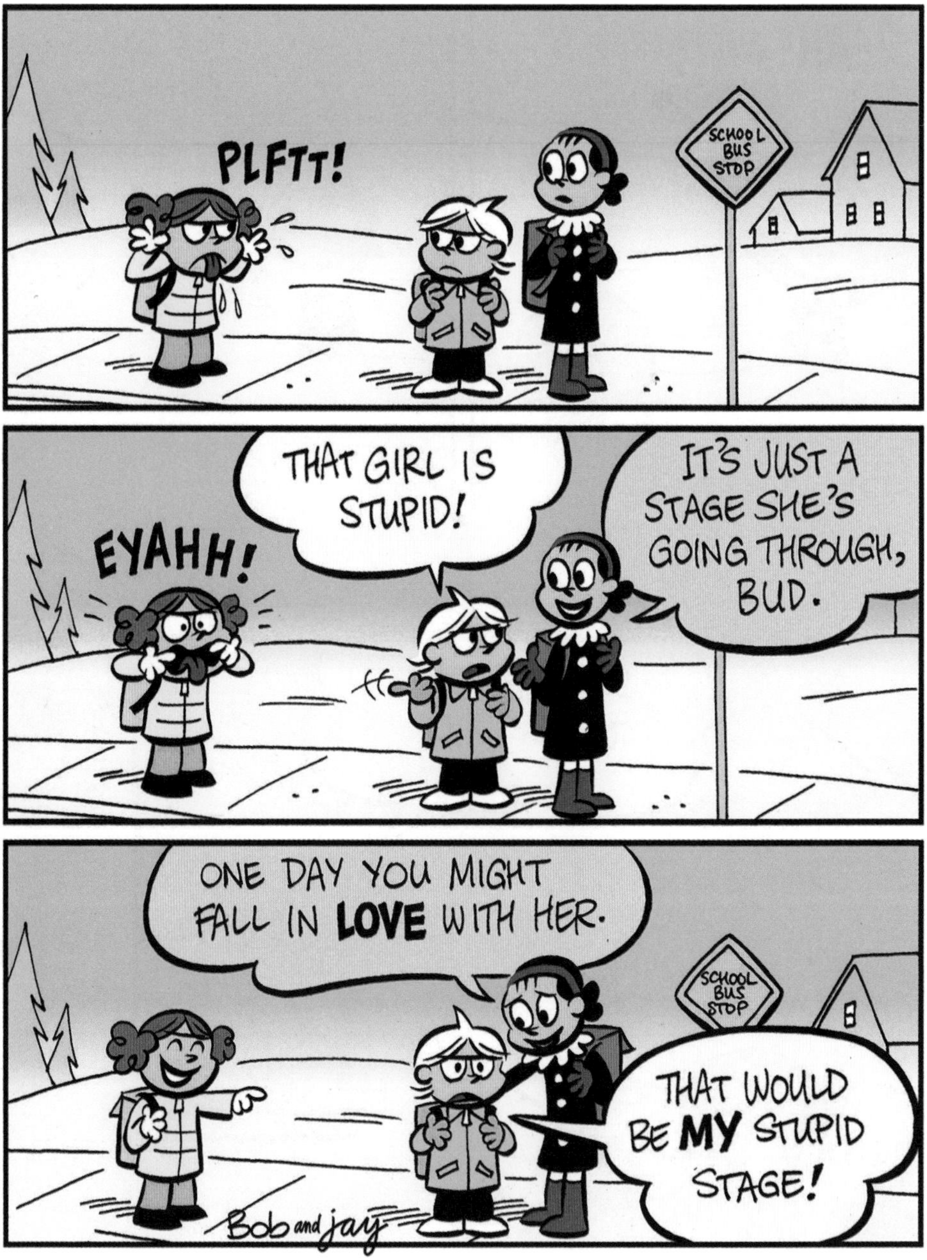
PLFTT!
SCHOOL BUS STOP
EYAHH!
THAT GIRL IS STUPID!
IT'S JUST A STAGE SHE'S GOING THROUGH, BUD.
ONE DAY YOU MIGHT FALL IN **LOVE** WITH HER.
SCHOOL BUS STOP
THAT WOULD BE **MY** STUPID STAGE!
Bob and jay

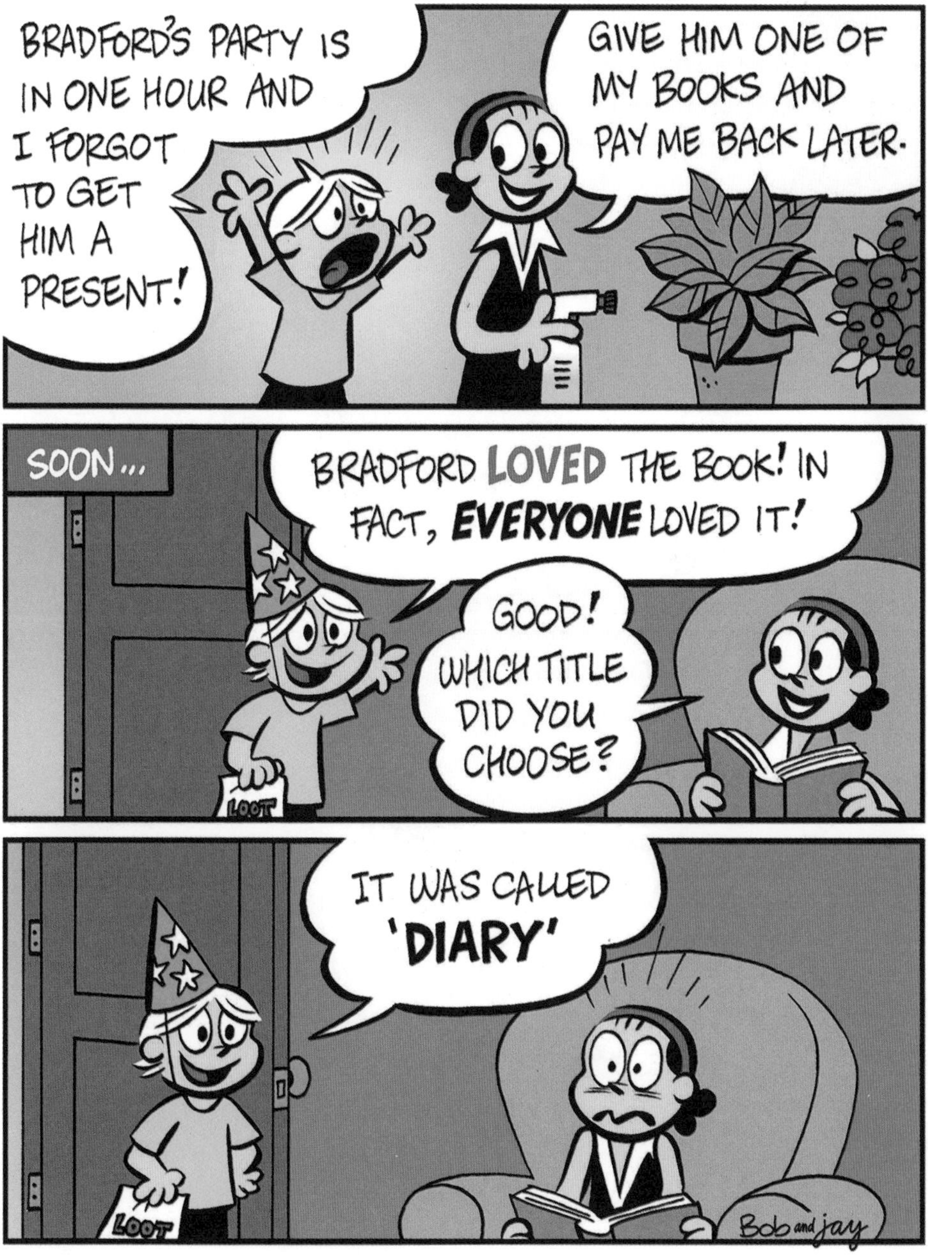
BRADFORD'S PARTY IS IN ONE HOUR AND I FORGOT TO GET HIM A PRESENT!
GIVE HIM ONE OF MY BOOKS AND PAY ME BACK LATER.
SOON...
BRADFORD LOVED THE BOOK! IN FACT, EVERYONE LOVED IT!
GOOD! WHICH TITLE DID YOU CHOOSE?
LOOT
IT WAS CALLED 'DIARY'
LOOT
Bob and jay

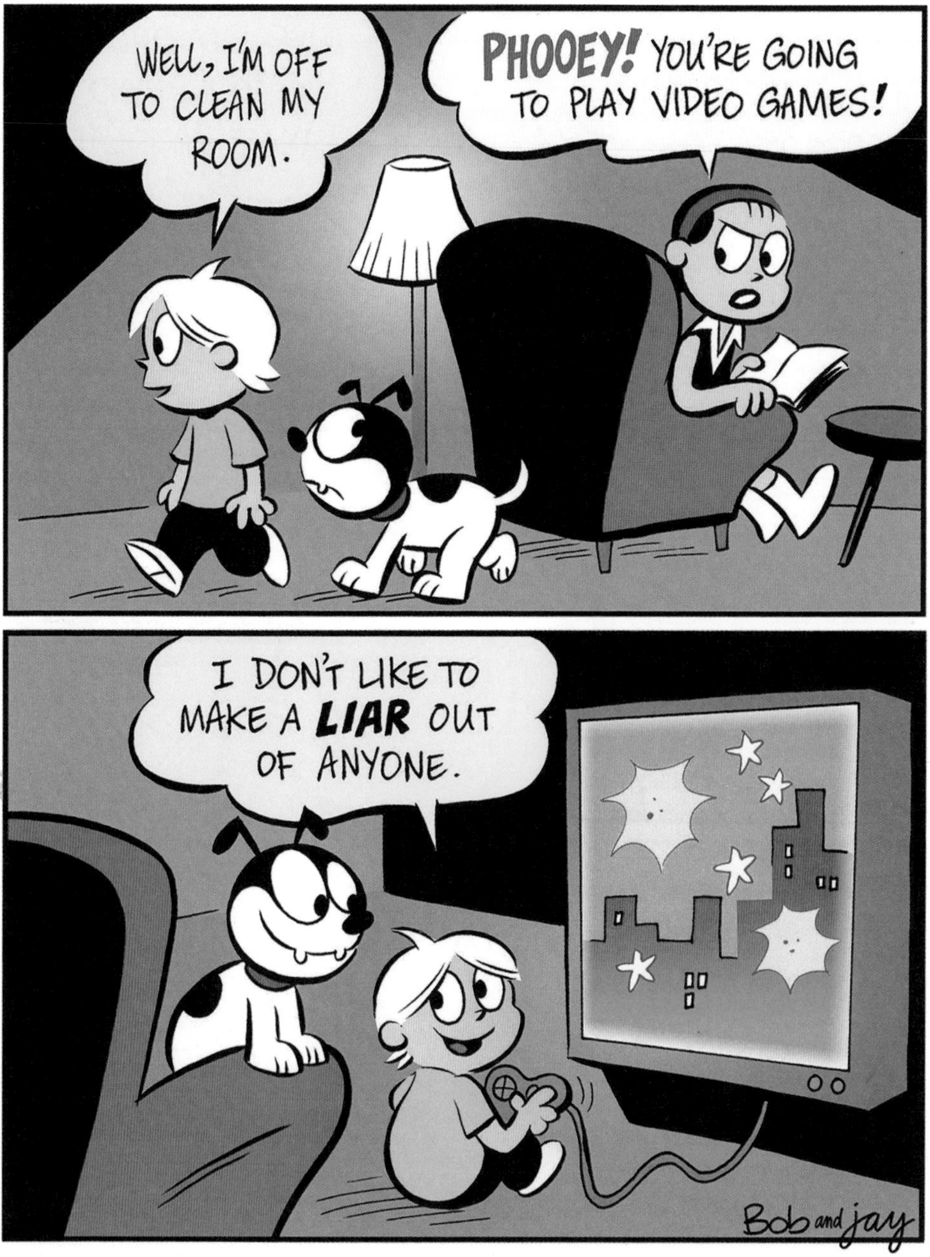
WELL, I'M OFF TO CLEAN MY ROOM.
PHOOEY! YOU'RE GOING TO PLAY VIDEO GAMES!
I DON'T LIKE TO MAKE A LIAR OUT OF ANYONE.
Bob and jay

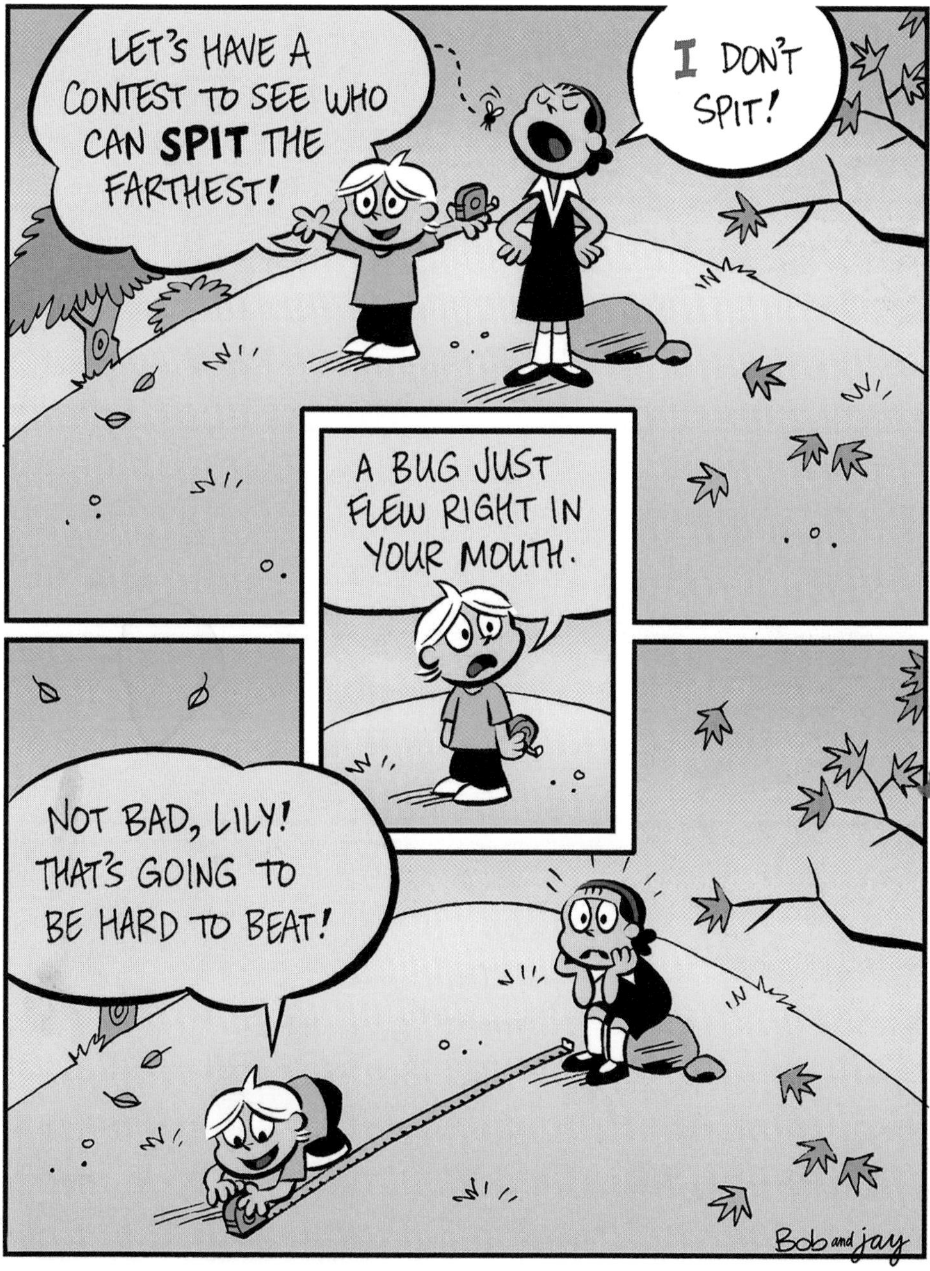
LET'S HAVE A CONTEST TO SEE WHO CAN SPIT THE FARTHEST!
I DON'T SPIT!
A BUG JUST FLEW RIGHT IN YOUR MOUTH.
NOT BAD, LILY! THAT'S GOING TO BE HARD TO BEAT!
Bob and jay

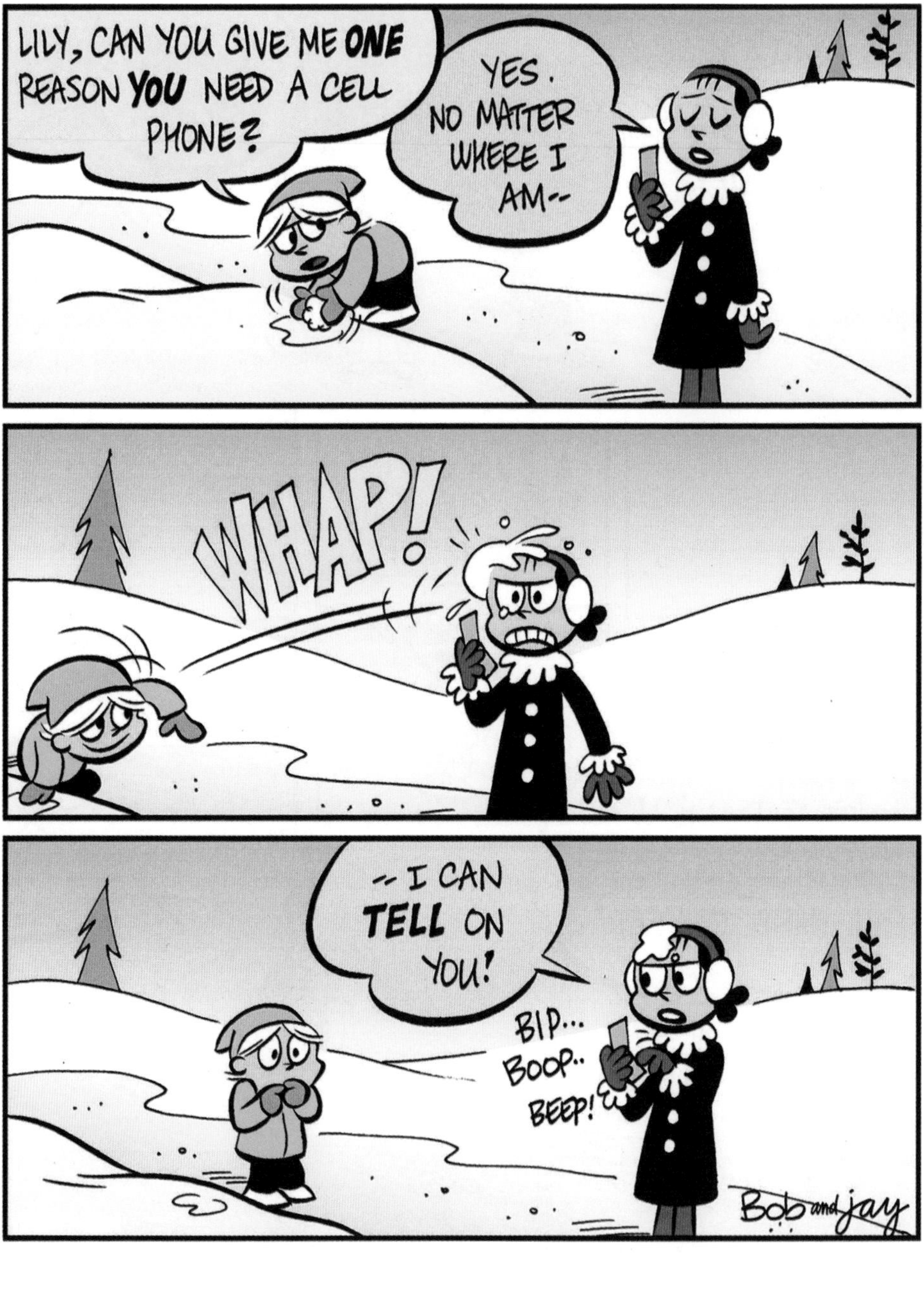
LILY, CAN YOU GIVE ME **ONE** REASON **YOU** NEED A CELL PHONE?
YES. NO MATTER WHERE I AM--
WHAP!
--I CAN **TELL** ON YOU!
BIP... BOOP.. BEEP!
Bob and jay

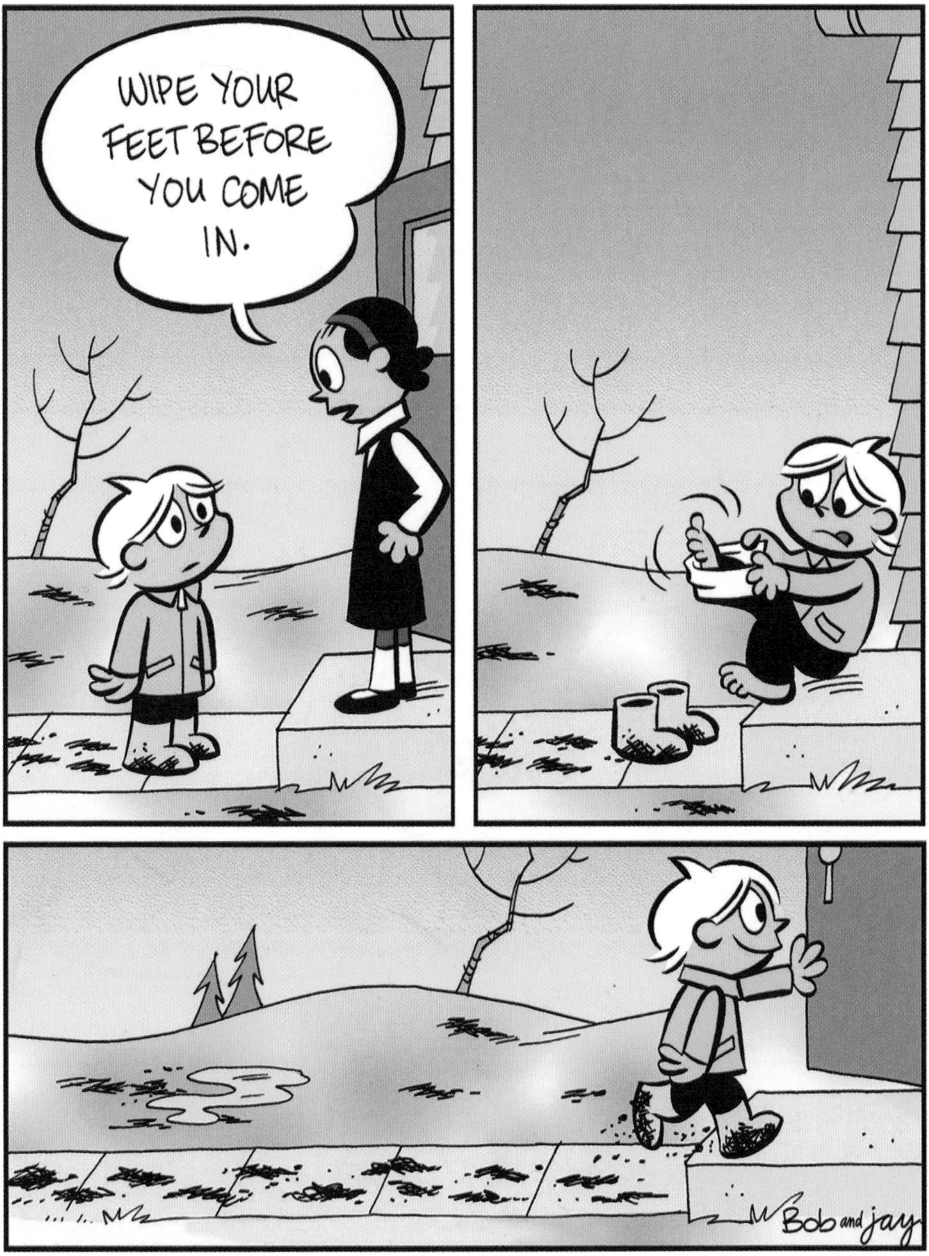
WIPE YOUR FEET BEFORE YOU COME IN.
Bob and jay

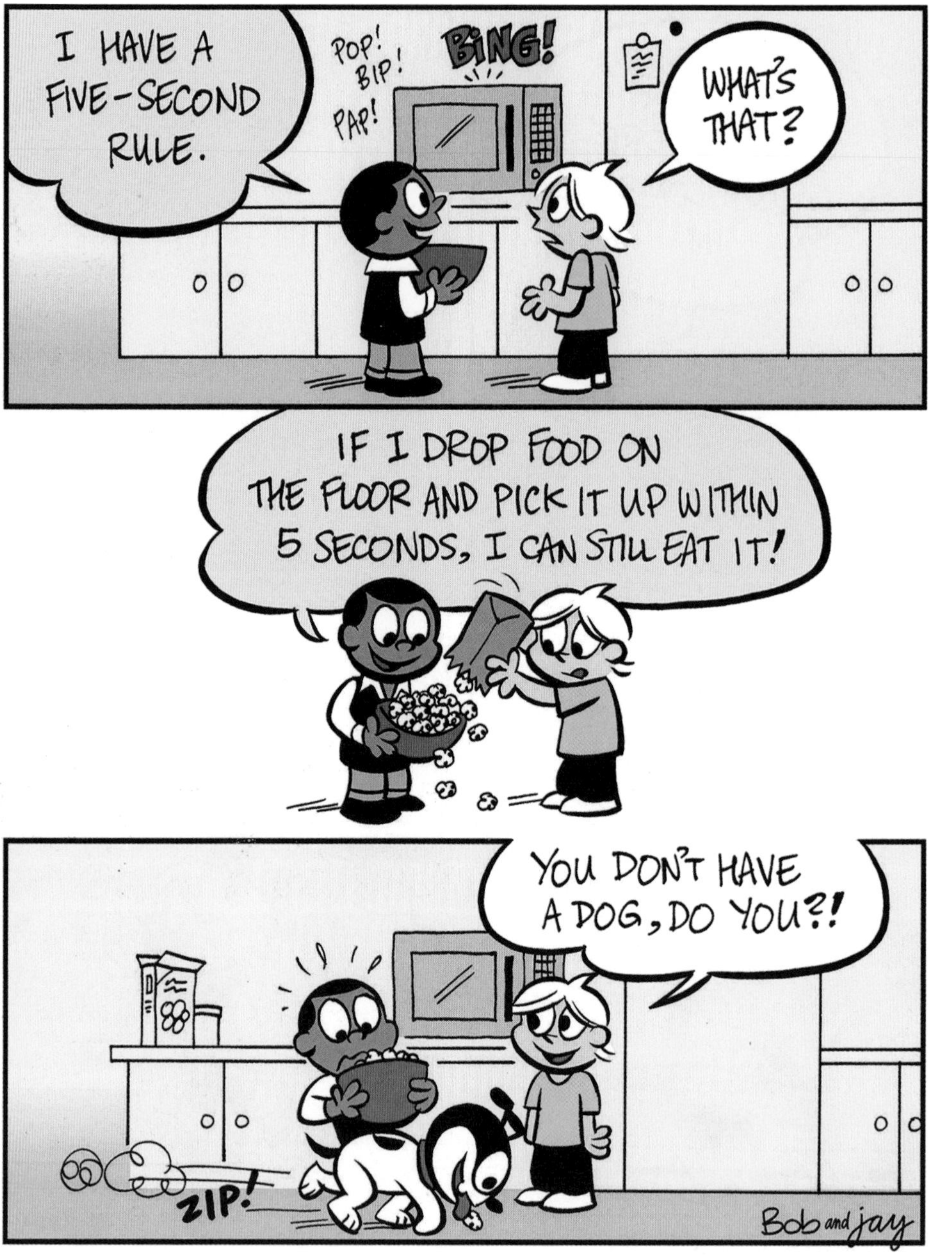
I HAVE A FIVE-SECOND RULE.
POP! BIP! PAP!
BING!
WHAT'S THAT?
IF I DROP FOOD ON THE FLOOR AND PICK IT UP WITHIN 5 SECONDS, I CAN STILL EAT IT!
YOU DON'T HAVE A DOG, DO YOU?!
ZIP!
Bob and jay

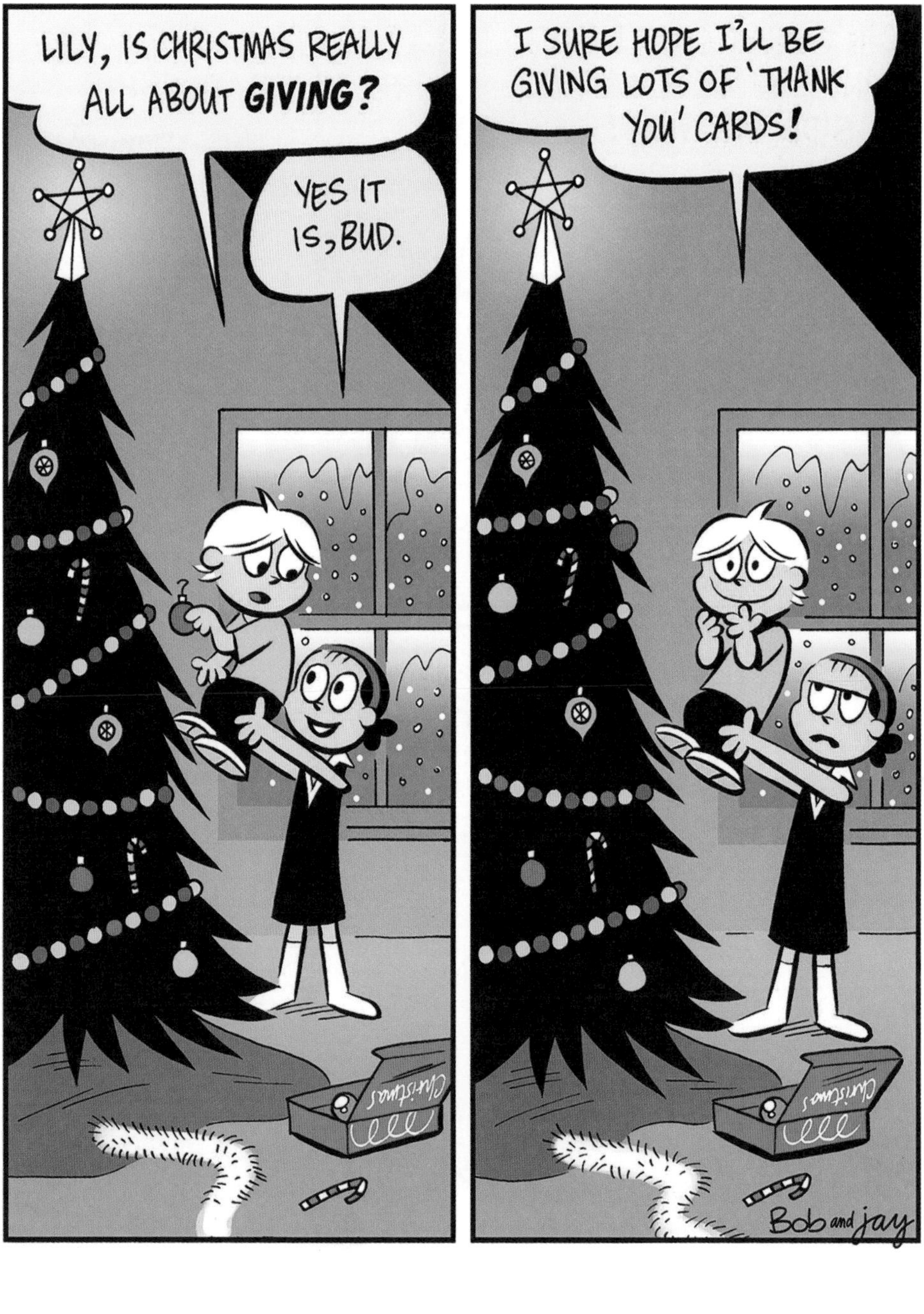
LILY, IS CHRISTMAS REALLY ALL ABOUT GIVING?
YES IT IS, BUD.
I SURE HOPE I'LL BE GIVING LOTS OF 'THANK YOU' CARDS!
Christmas
Bob and jay

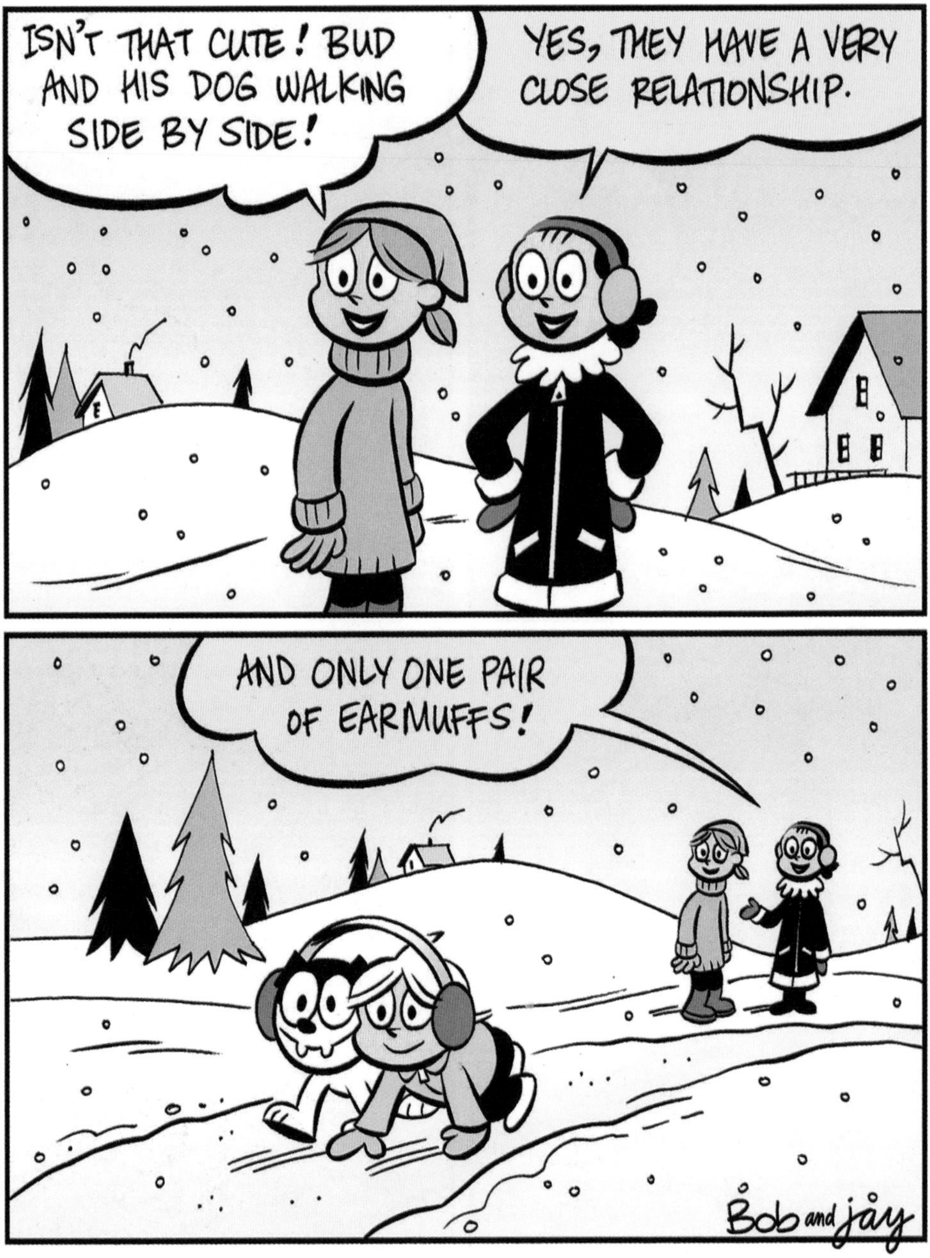
ISN'T THAT CUTE! BUD AND HIS DOG WALKING SIDE BY SIDE!
YES, THEY HAVE A VERY CLOSE RELATIONSHIP.
AND ONLY ONE PAIR OF EARMUFFS!
Bob and jay

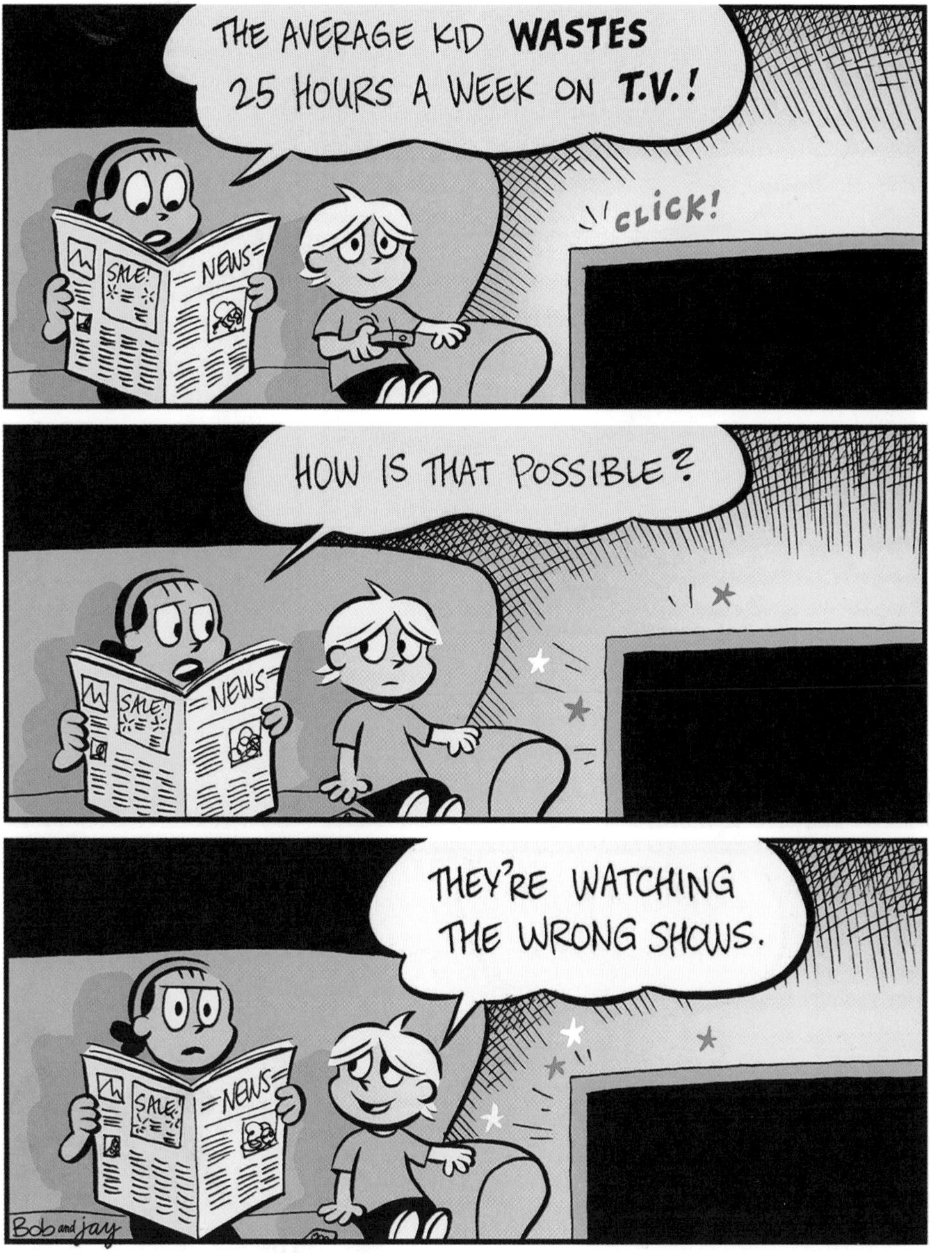
THE AVERAGE KID WASTES 25 HOURS A WEEK ON T.V.!
CLICK!
SALE!
NEWS
HOW IS THAT POSSIBLE?
THEY'RE WATCHING THE WRONG SHOWS.
Bob and jay

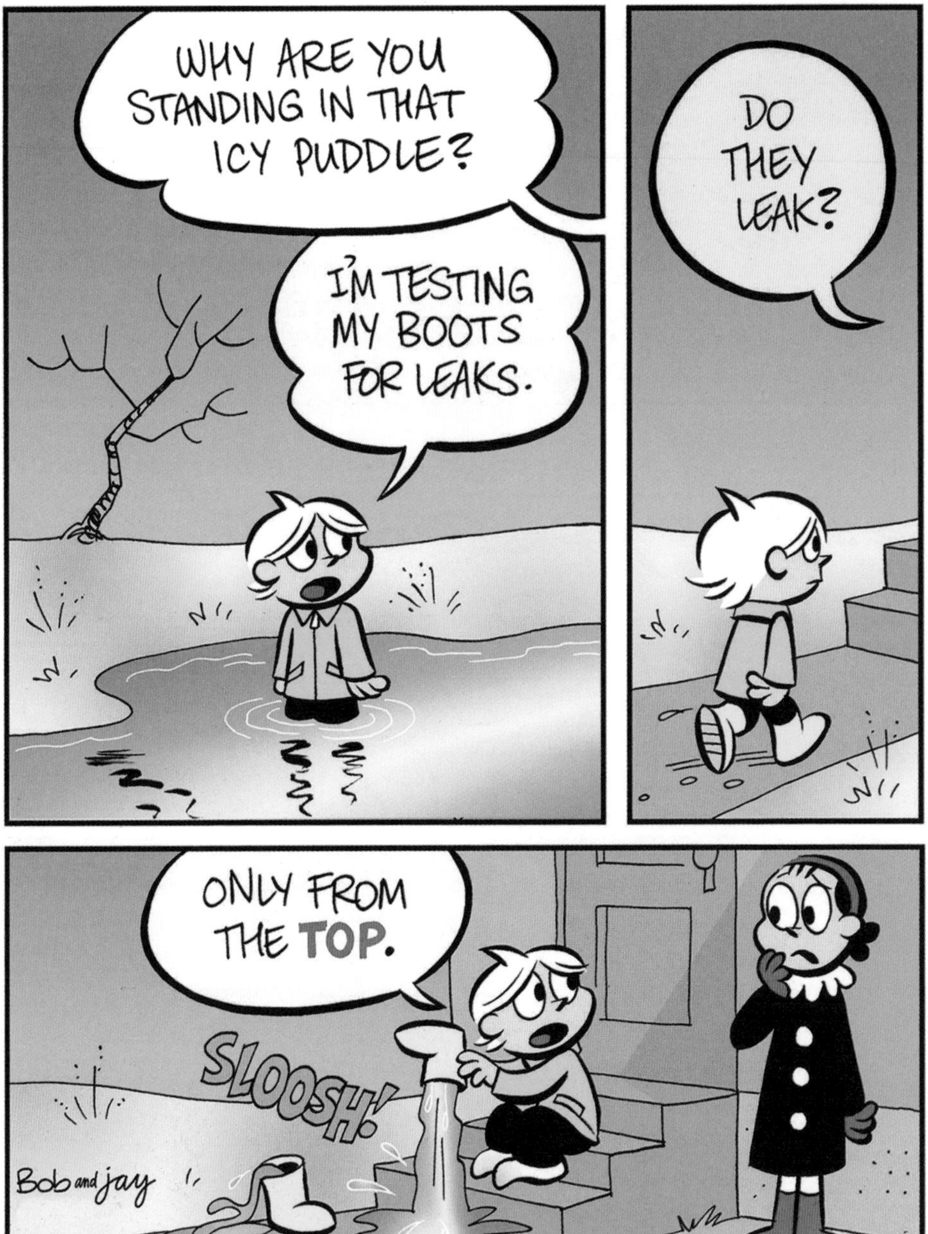
WHY ARE YOU STANDING IN THAT ICY PUDDLE?
I'M TESTING MY BOOTS FOR LEAKS.
DO THEY LEAK?
ONLY FROM THE **TOP.**
SLOOSH!
Bob and jay

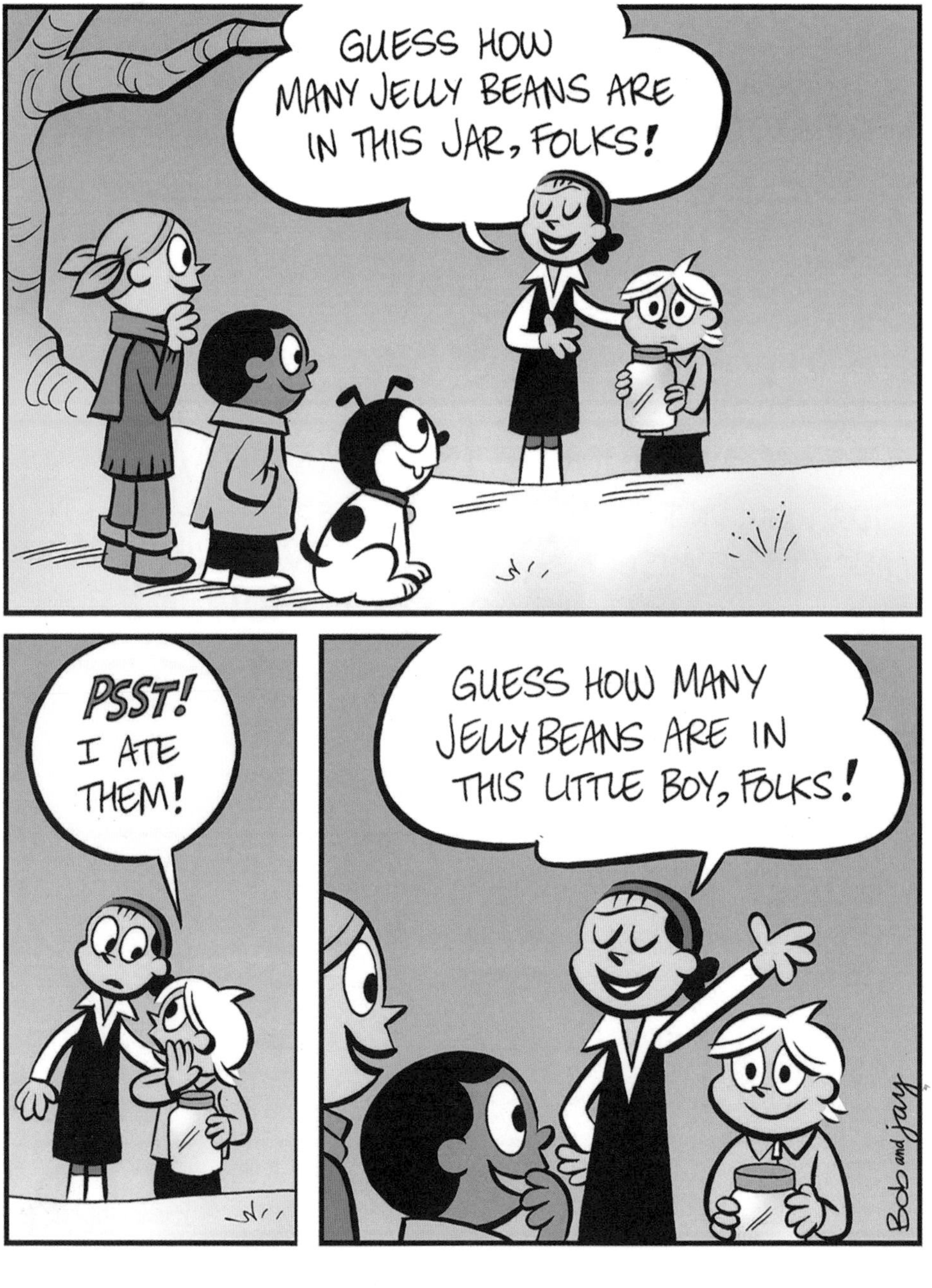
GUESS HOW MANY JELLY BEANS ARE IN THIS JAR, FOLKS!
PSST! I ATE THEM!
GUESS HOW MANY JELLY BEANS ARE IN THIS LITTLE BOY, FOLKS!
Bob and jay

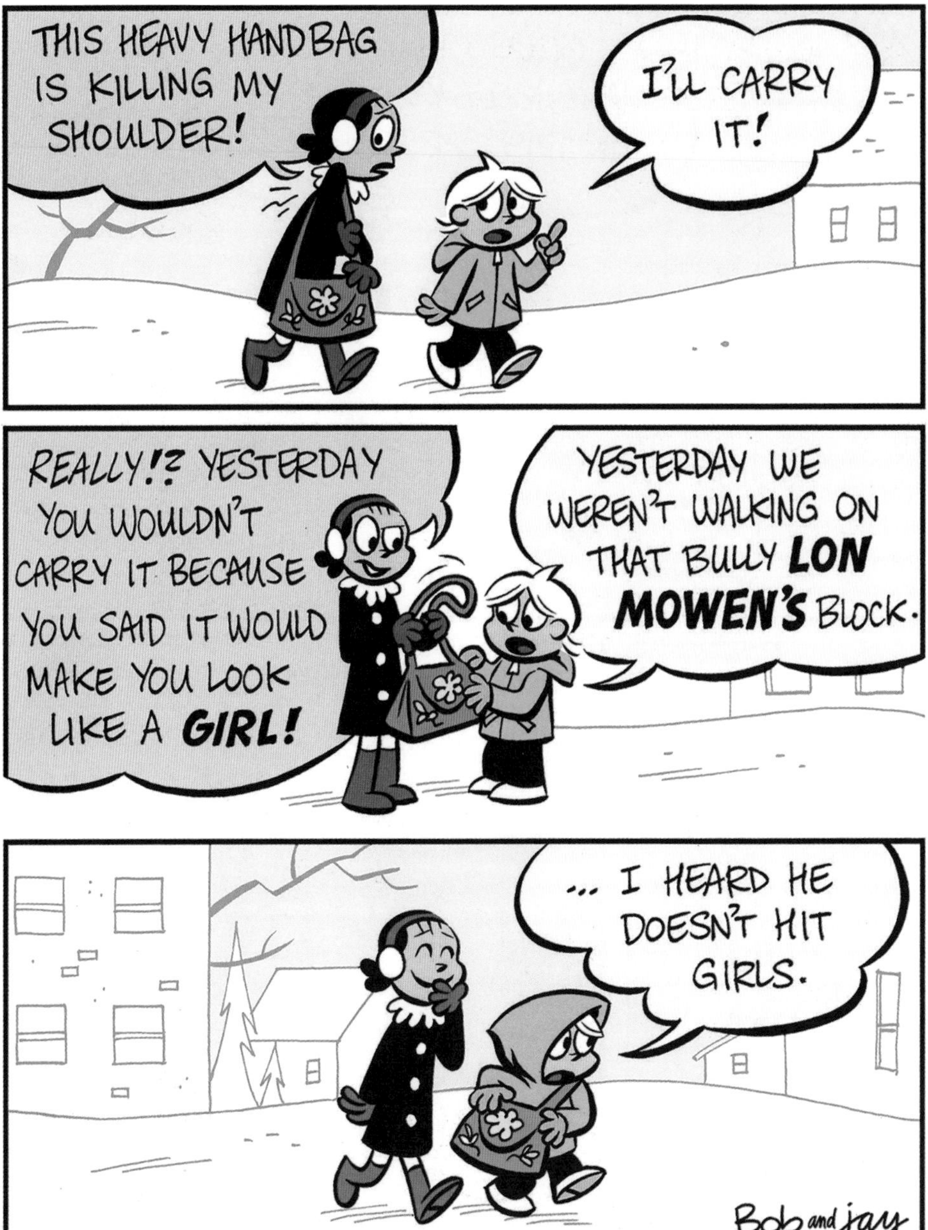
THIS HEAVY HANDBAG IS KILLING MY SHOULDER!
I'LL CARRY IT!
REALLY!? YESTERDAY YOU WOULDN'T CARRY IT BECAUSE YOU SAID IT WOULD MAKE YOU LOOK LIKE A **GIRL!**
YESTERDAY WE WEREN'T WALKING ON THAT BULLY **LON MOWEN'S** BLOCK.
... I HEARD HE DOESN'T HIT GIRLS.
Bob and jay

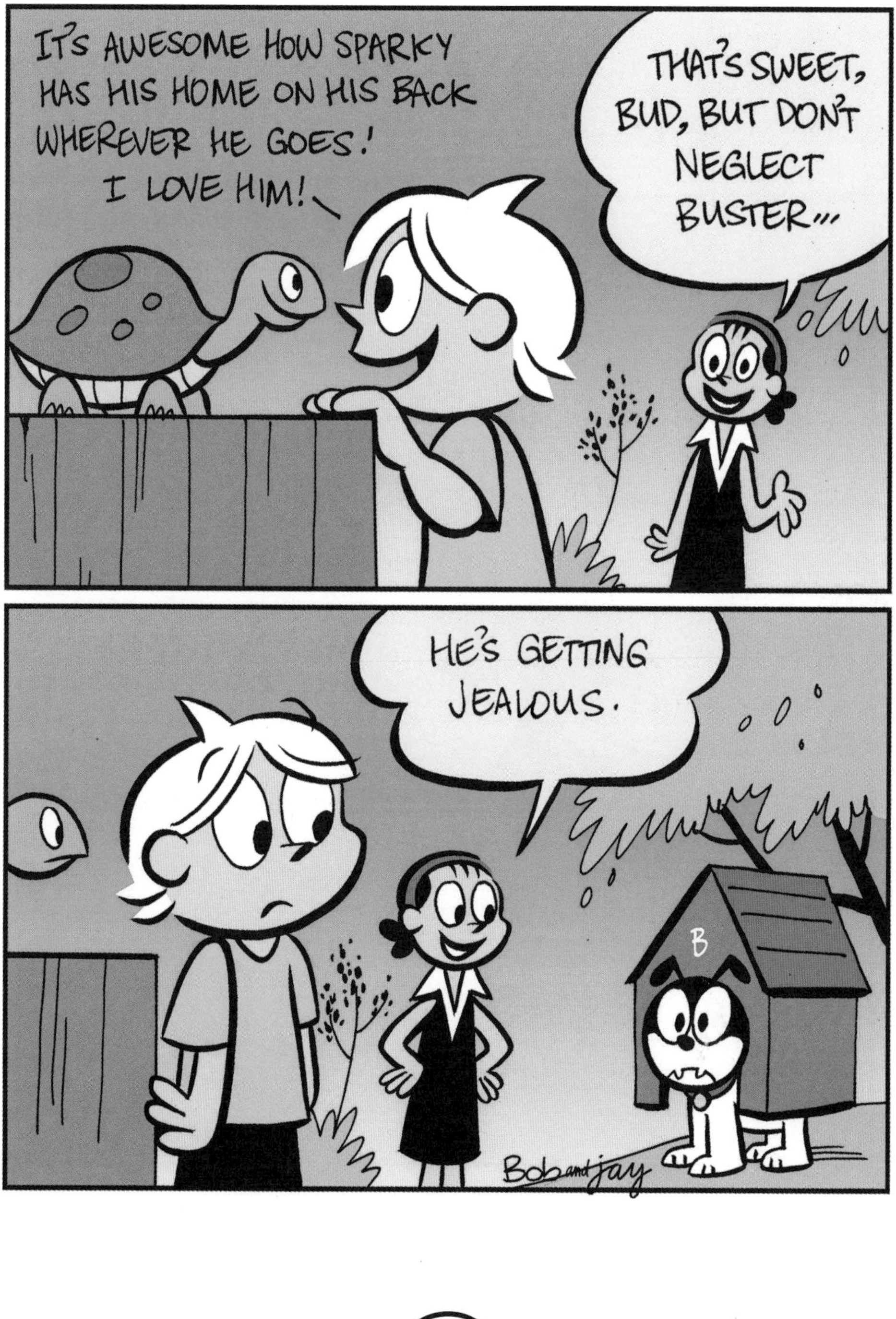
IT'S AWESOME HOW SPARKY HAS HIS HOME ON HIS BACK WHEREVER HE GOES! I LOVE HIM!
THAT'S SWEET, BUD, BUT DON'T NEGLECT BUSTER...
HE'S GETTING JEALOUS.
B
Bob and jay

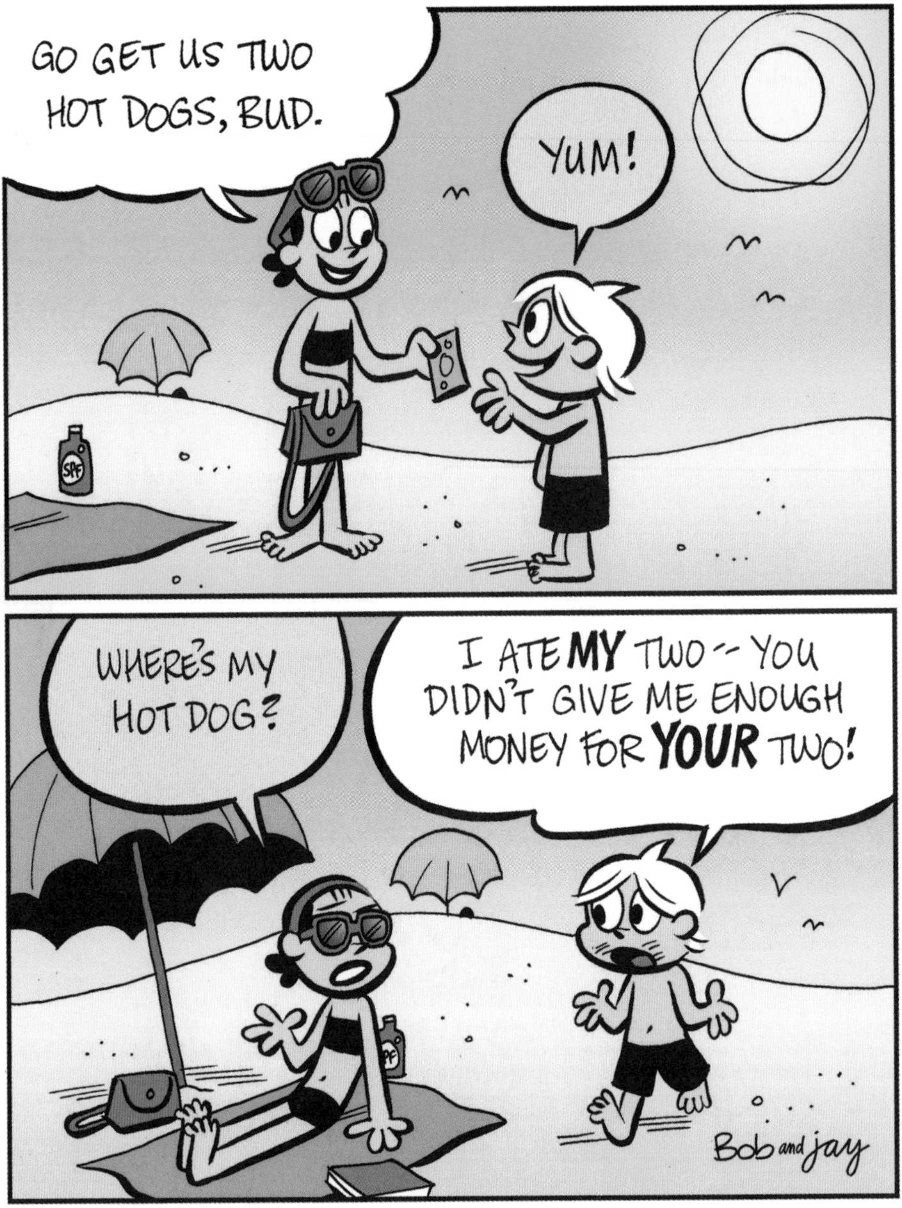
GO GET US TWO HOT DOGS, BUD.
YUM!
SPF
WHERE'S MY HOT DOG?
I ATE **MY** TWO -- YOU DIDN'T GIVE ME ENOUGH MONEY FOR **YOUR** TWO!
Bob and jay

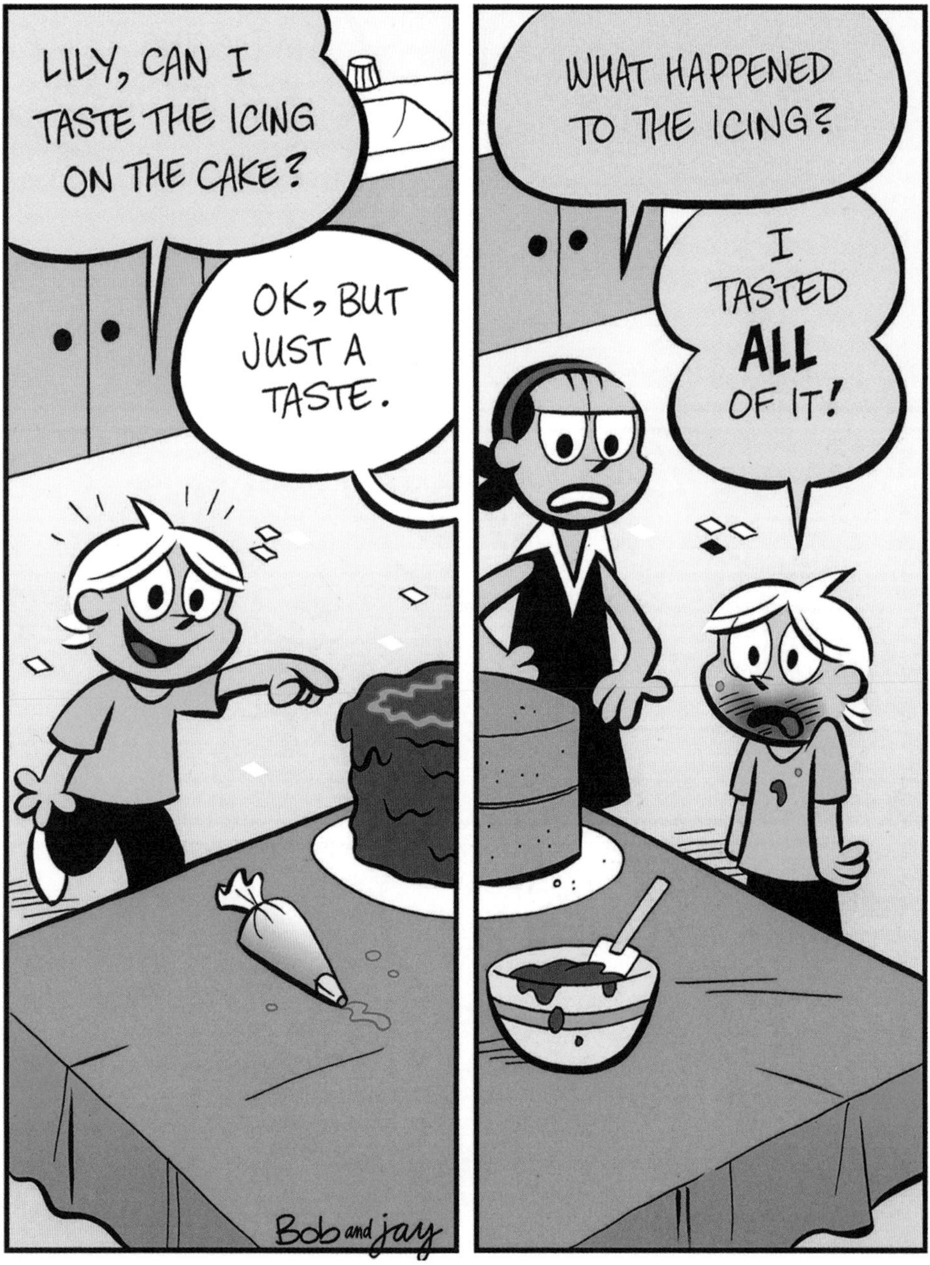
LILY, CAN I TASTE THE ICING ON THE CAKE?
OK, BUT JUST A TASTE.
Bob and jay
WHAT HAPPENED TO THE ICING?
I TASTED **ALL** OF IT!

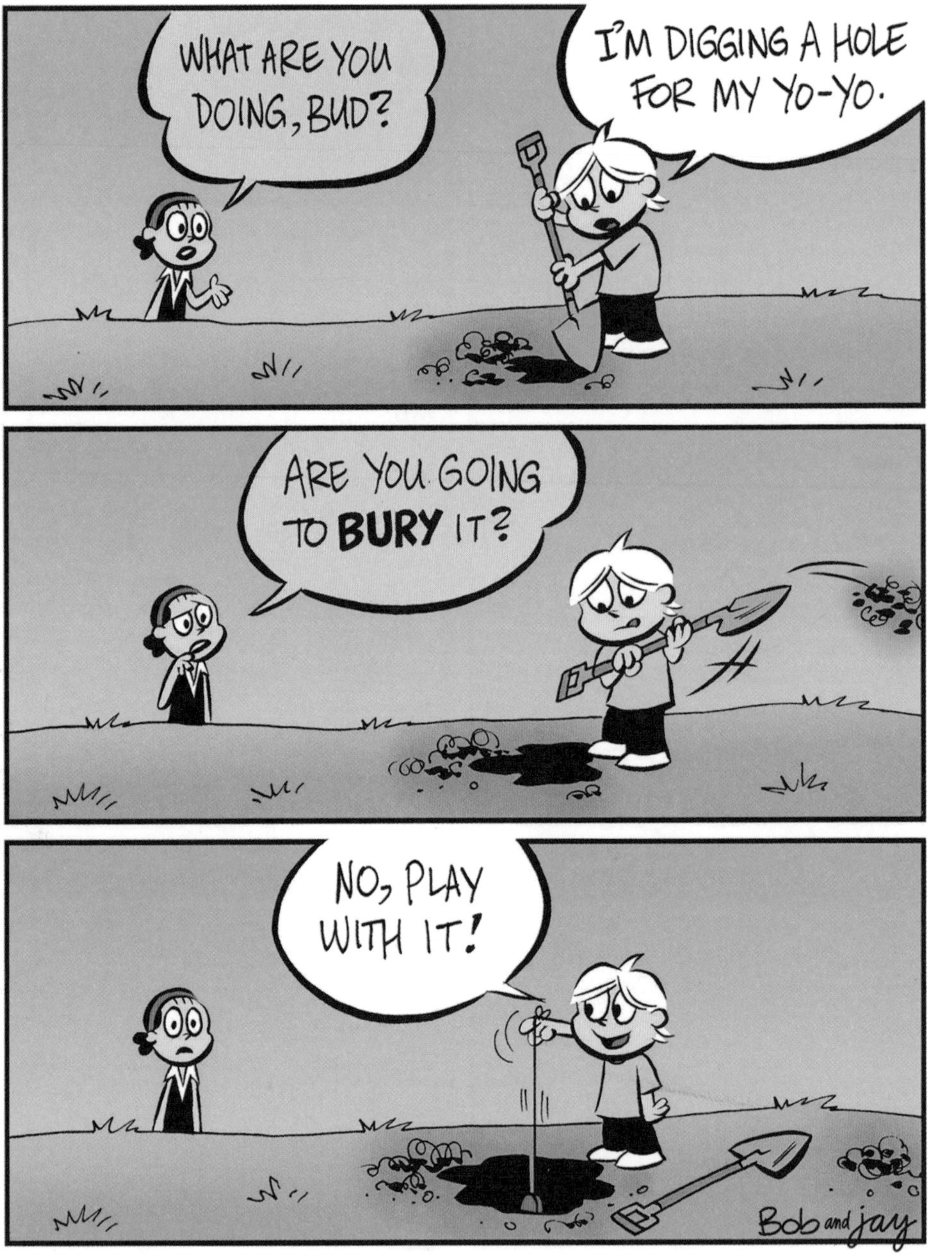
WHAT ARE YOU DOING, BUD?
I'M DIGGING A HOLE FOR MY YO-YO.
ARE YOU GOING TO **BURY** IT?
NO, PLAY WITH IT!
Bob and jay

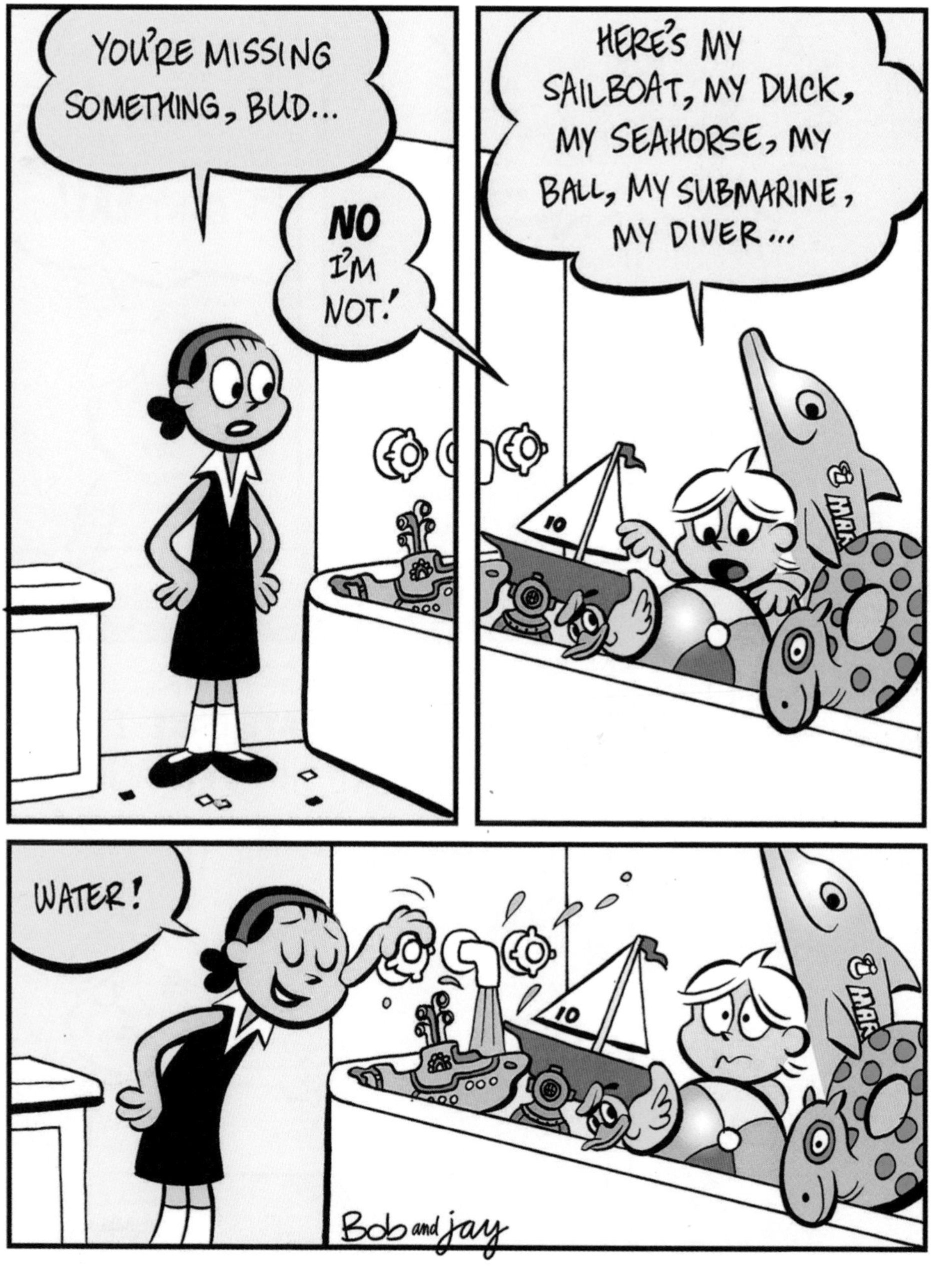
YOU'RE MISSING SOMETHING, BUD...
NO I'M NOT!
HERE'S MY SAILBOAT, MY DUCK, MY SEAHORSE, MY BALL, MY SUBMARINE, MY DIVER...
WATER!
Bob and jay

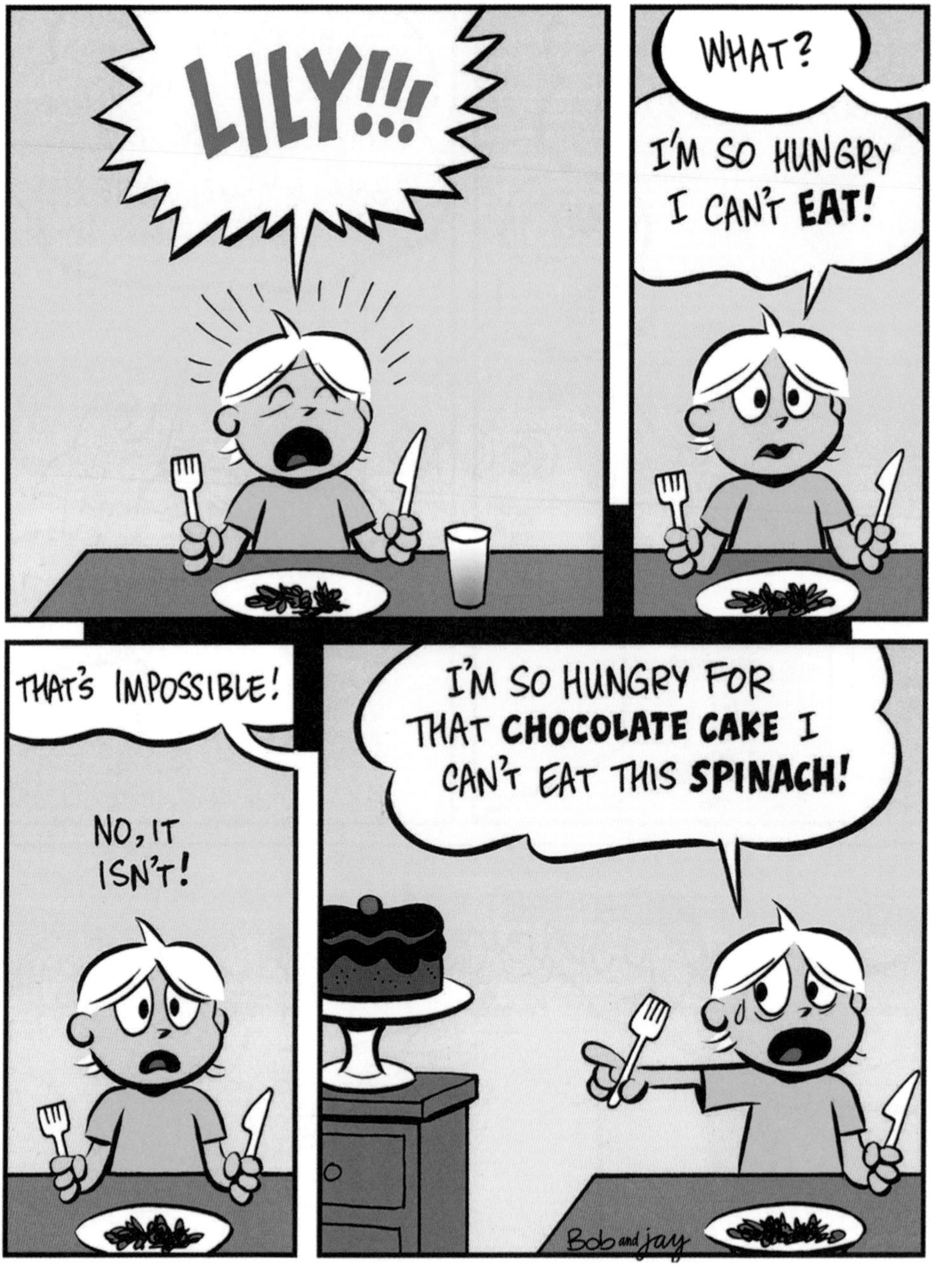
LILY!!!
WHAT?
I'M SO HUNGRY I CAN'T EAT!
THAT'S IMPOSSIBLE!
NO, IT ISN'T!
I'M SO HUNGRY FOR THAT CHOCOLATE CAKE I CAN'T EAT THIS SPINACH!
Bob and jay

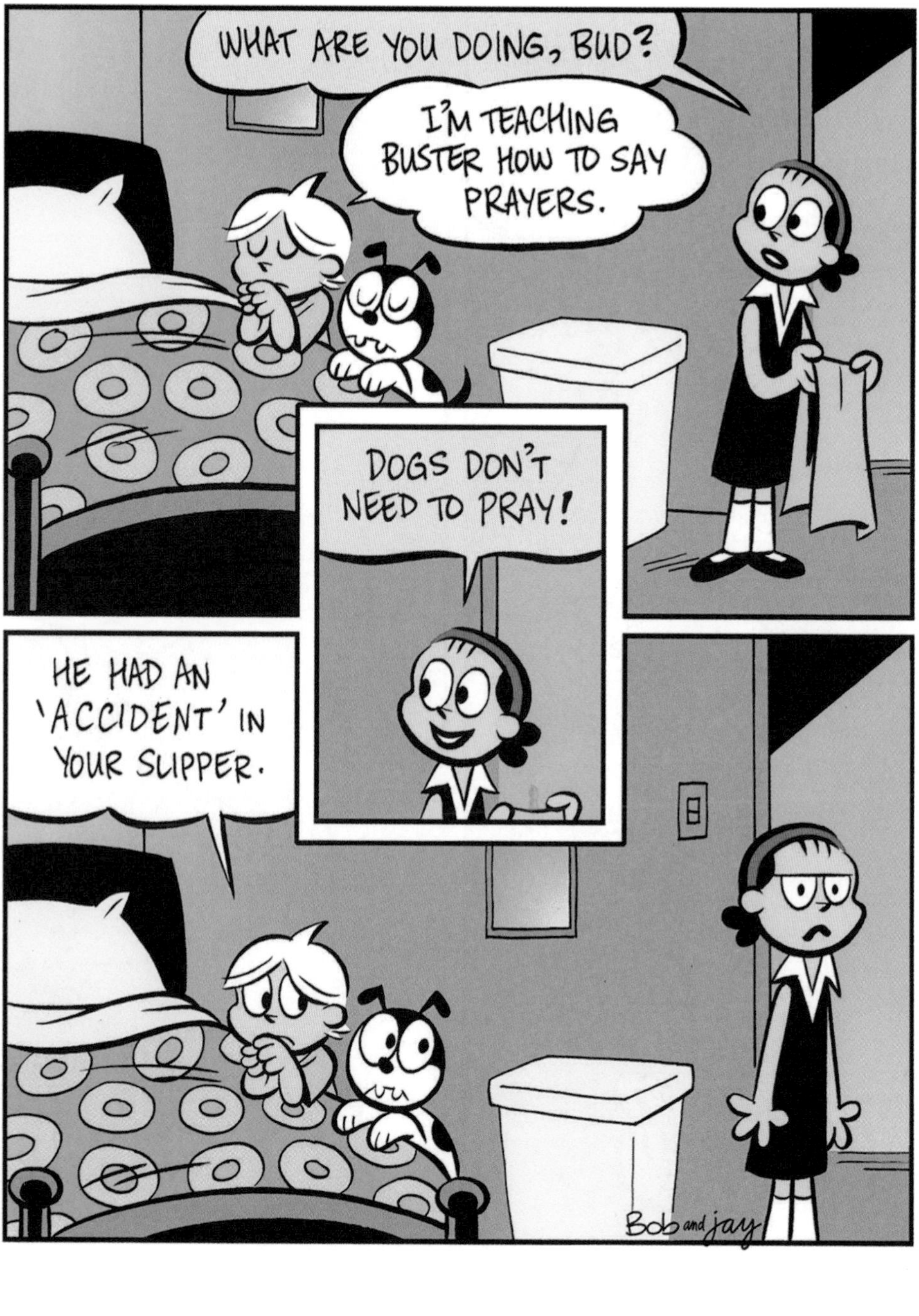
WHAT ARE YOU DOING, BUD?
I'M TEACHING BUSTER HOW TO SAY PRAYERS.
DOGS DON'T NEED TO PRAY!
HE HAD AN 'ACCIDENT' IN YOUR SLIPPER.
Bob and jay

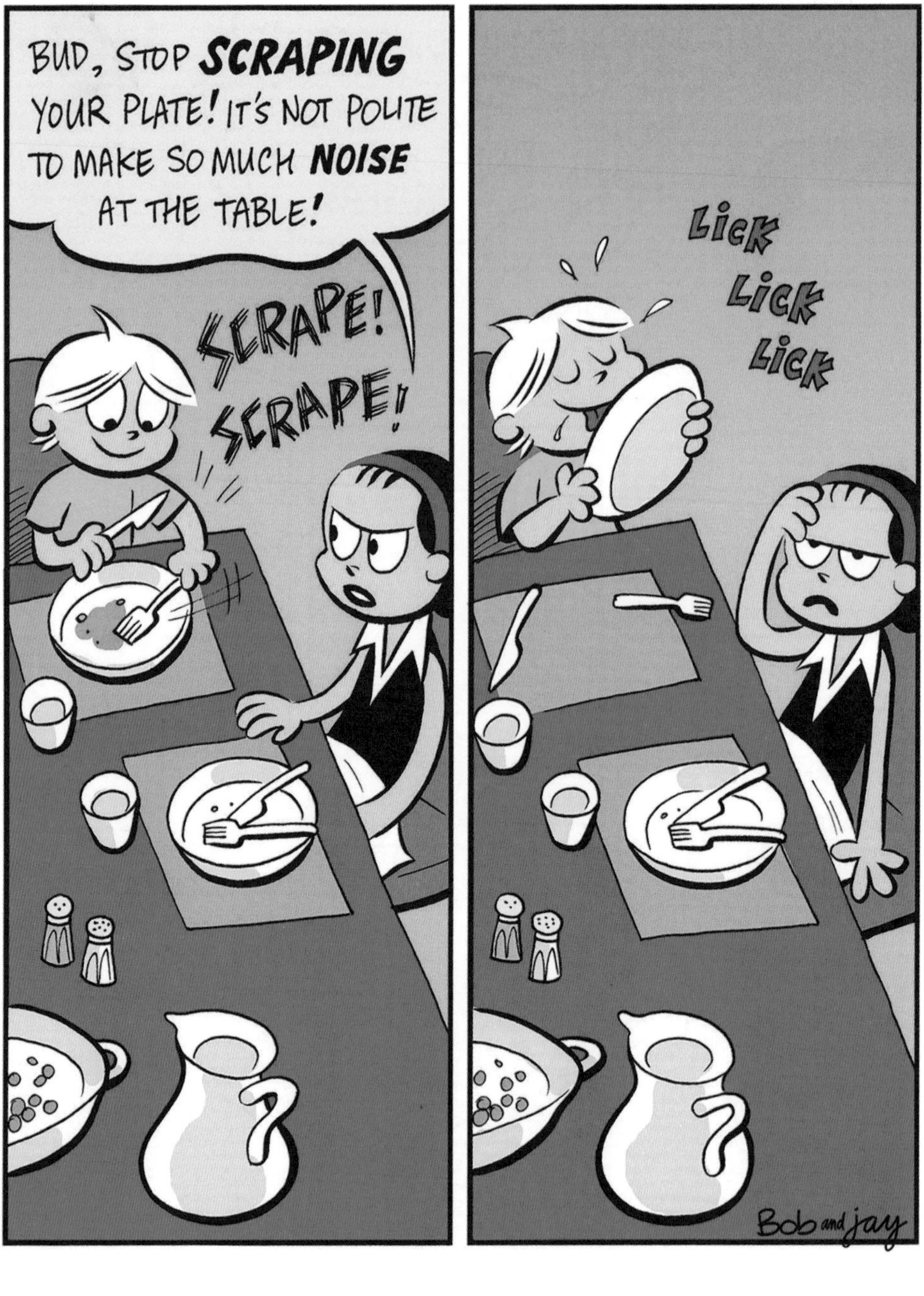
BUD, STOP **SCRAPING** YOUR PLATE! IT'S NOT POLITE TO MAKE SO MUCH **NOISE** AT THE TABLE!
SCRAPE! SCRAPE!
LICK LICK LICK
Bob and jay

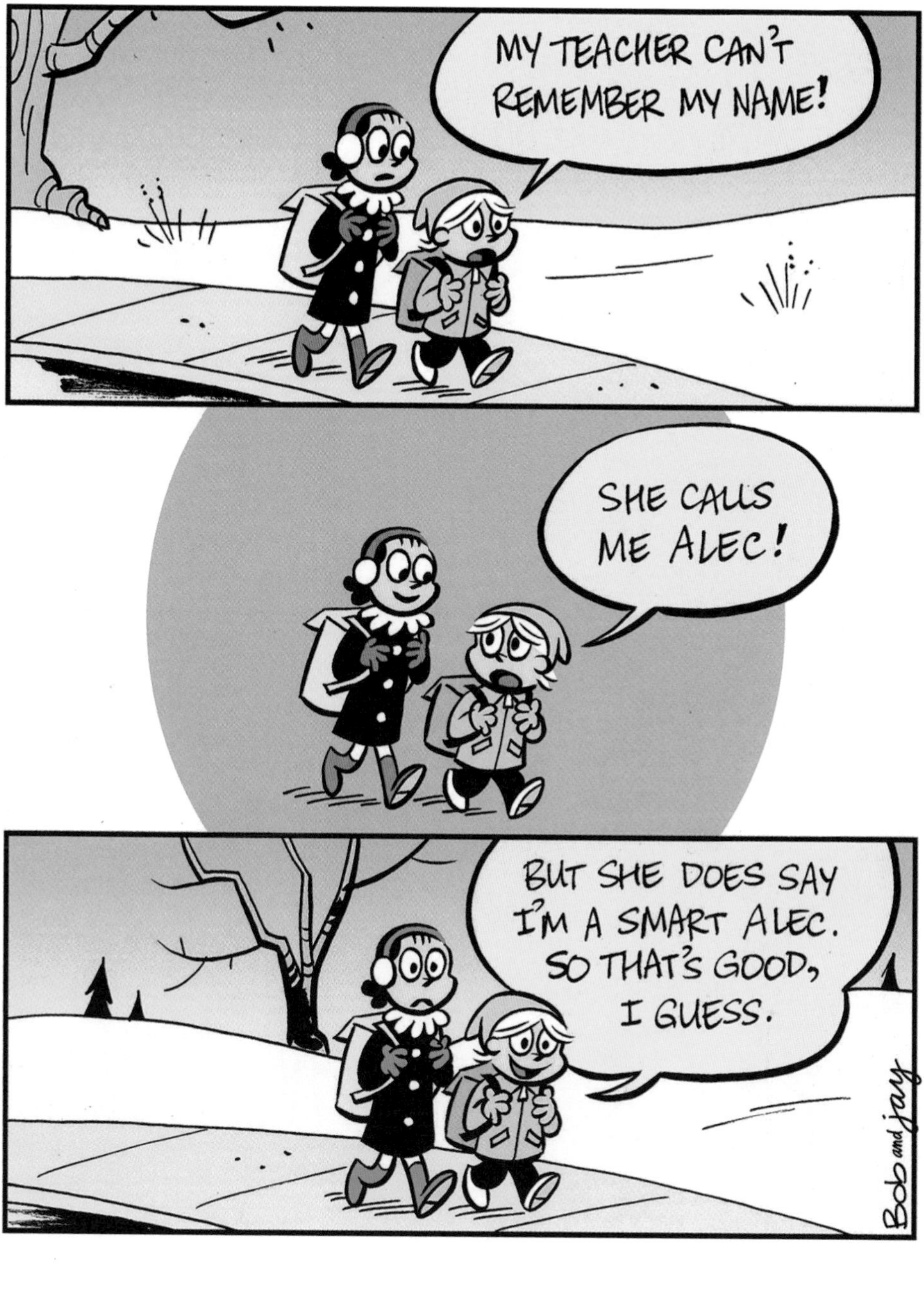
MY TEACHER CAN'T REMEMBER MY NAME!
SHE CALLS ME ALEC!
BUT SHE DOES SAY I'M A SMART ALEC. SO THAT'S GOOD, I GUESS.
Bob and jay

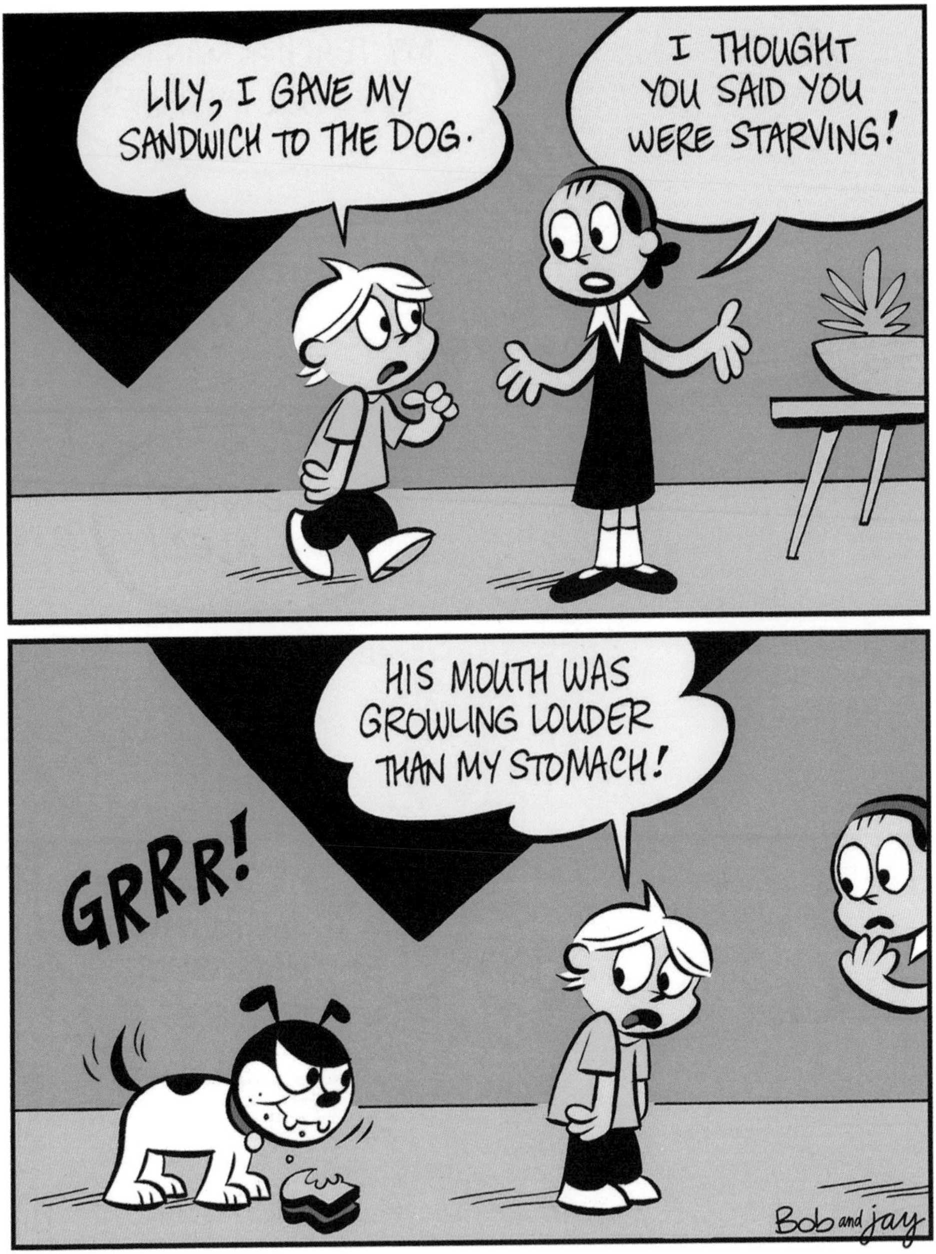
LILY, I GAVE MY SANDWICH TO THE DOG.
I THOUGHT YOU SAID YOU WERE STARVING!
HIS MOUTH WAS GROWLING LOUDER THAN MY STOMACH!
GRRR!
Bob and jay

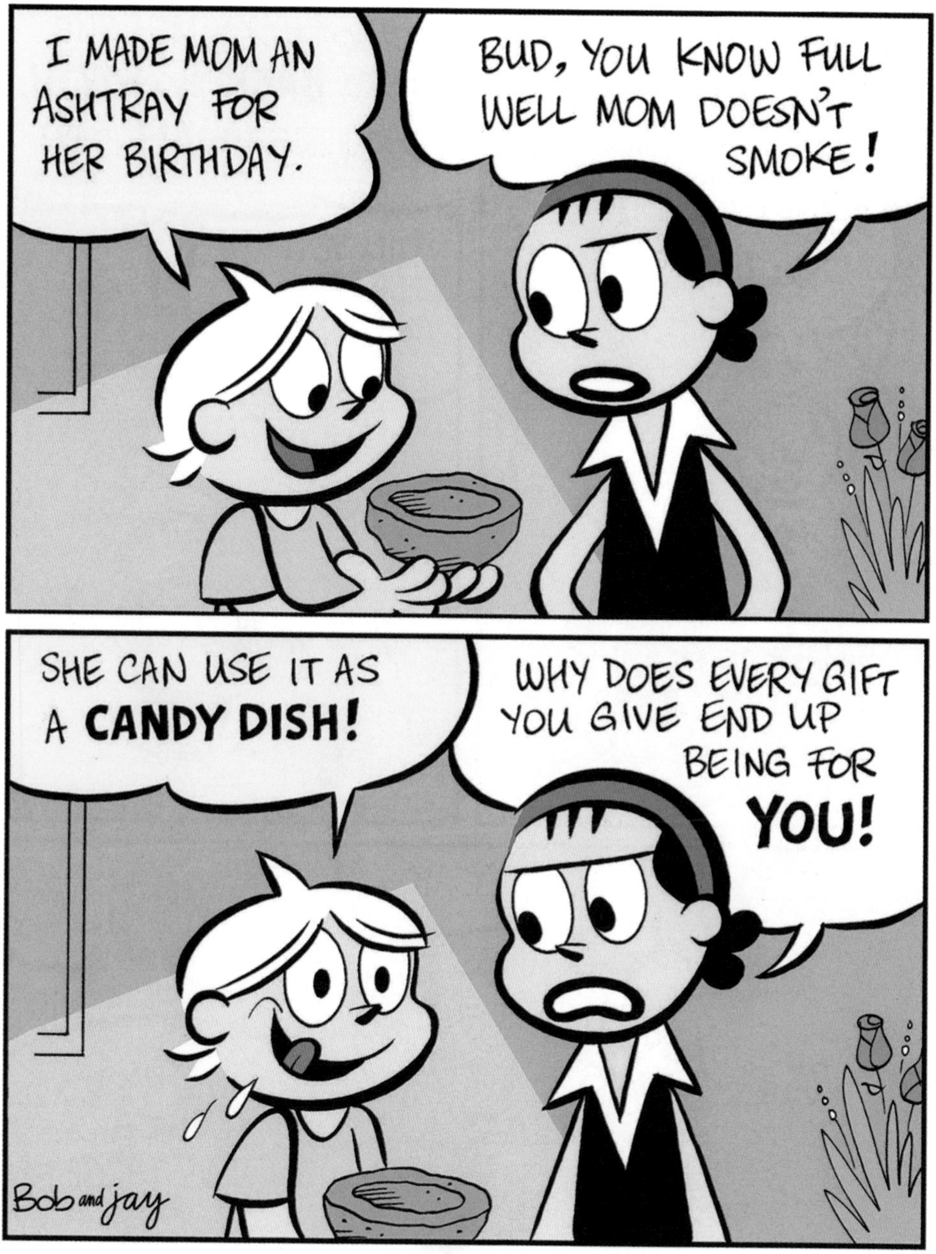
I MADE MOM AN ASHTRAY FOR HER BIRTHDAY.
BUD, YOU KNOW FULL WELL MOM DOESN'T SMOKE!
SHE CAN USE IT AS A **CANDY DISH!**
WHY DOES EVERY GIFT YOU GIVE END UP BEING FOR **YOU!**
Bob and jay

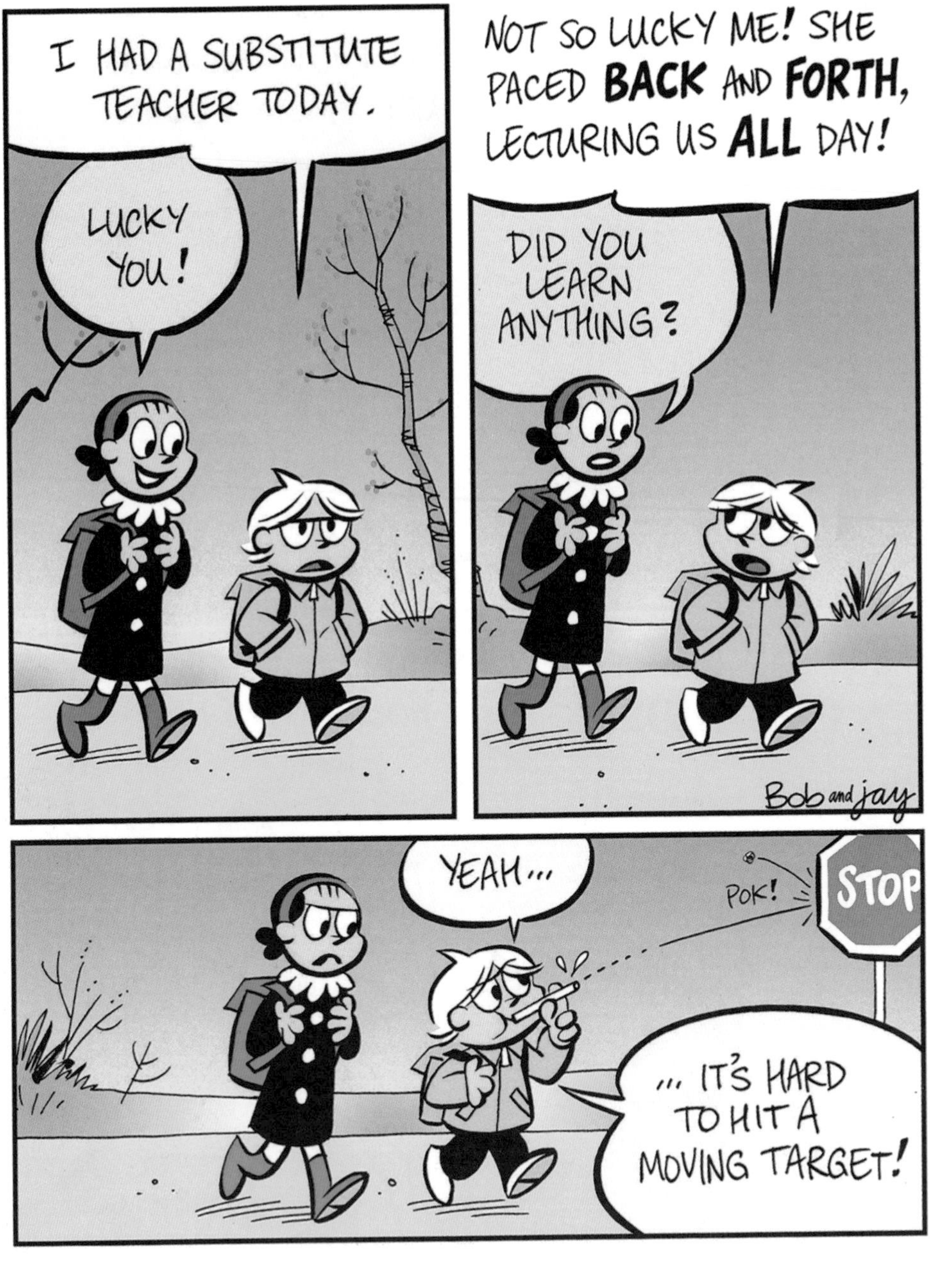
I HAD A SUBSTITUTE TEACHER TODAY.
LUCKY YOU!
NOT SO LUCKY ME! SHE PACED **BACK** AND **FORTH**, LECTURING US **ALL** DAY!
DID YOU LEARN ANYTHING?
Bob and jay
YEAH...
POK!
STOP
... IT'S HARD TO HIT A MOVING TARGET!

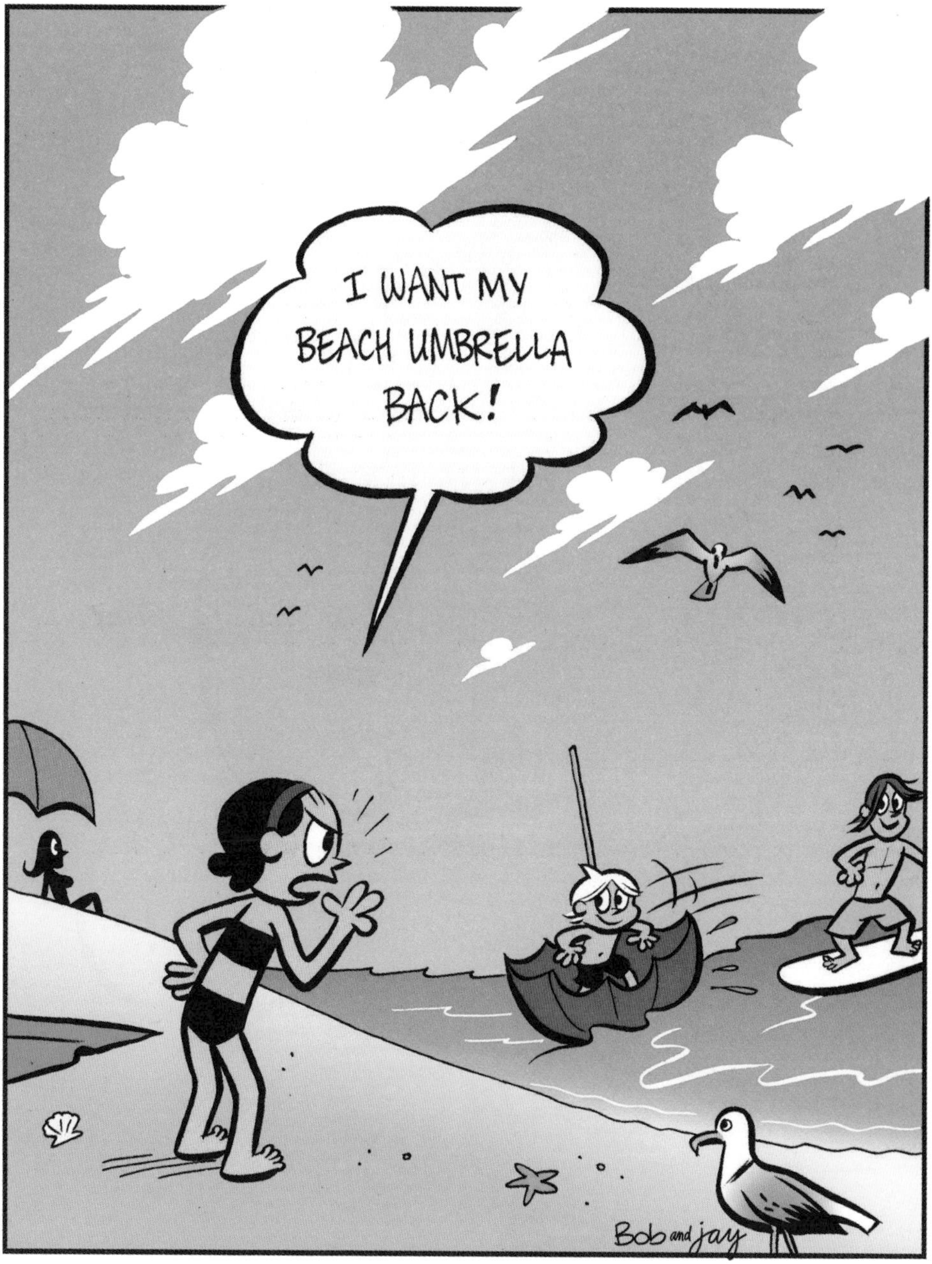
I WANT MY BEACH UMBRELLA BACK!
Bob and jay

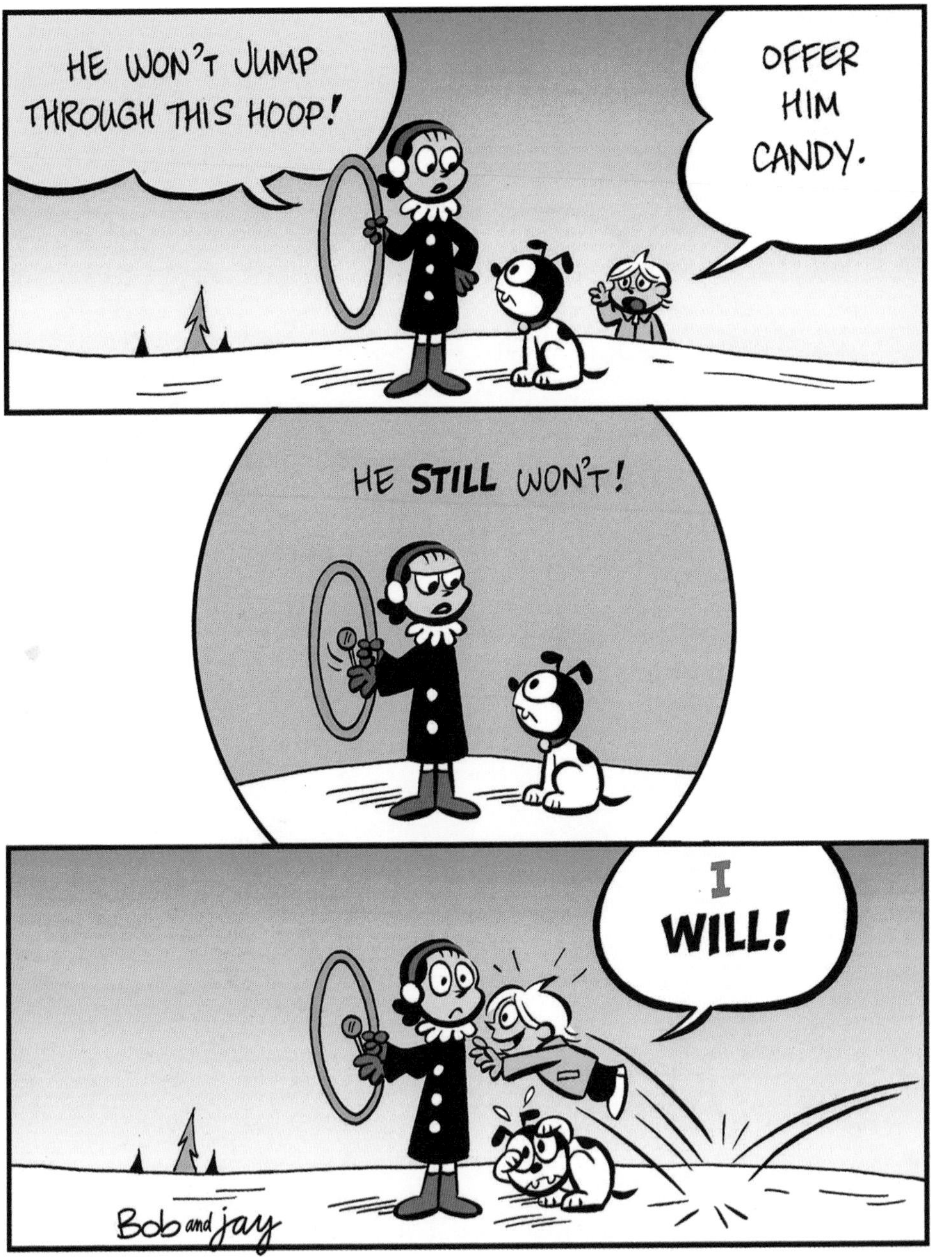
HE WON'T JUMP THROUGH THIS HOOP!
OFFER HIM CANDY.
HE STILL WON'T!
I WILL!
Bob and jay

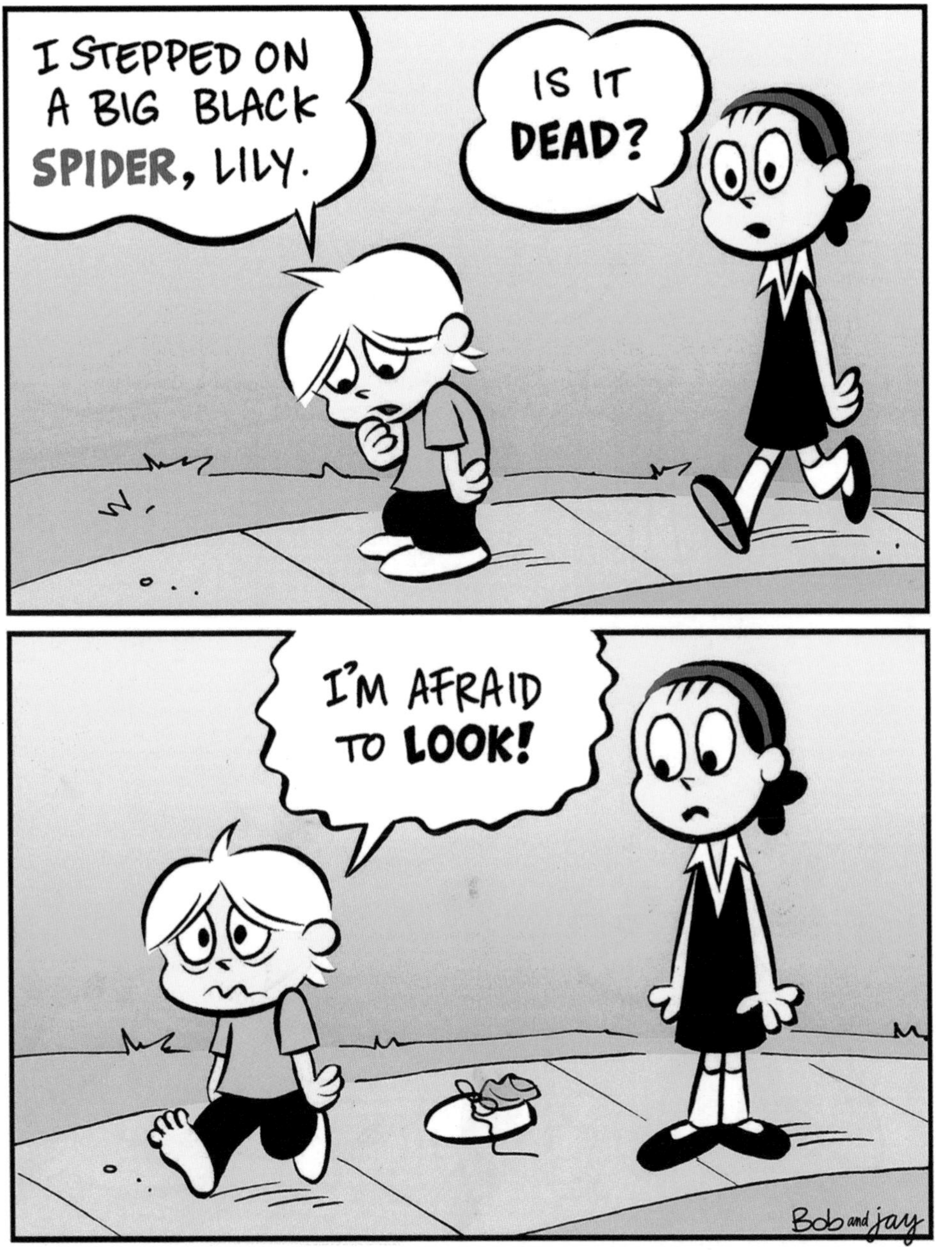
I STEPPED ON A BIG BLACK SPIDER, LILY.
IS IT DEAD?
I'M AFRAID TO LOOK!
Bob and jay

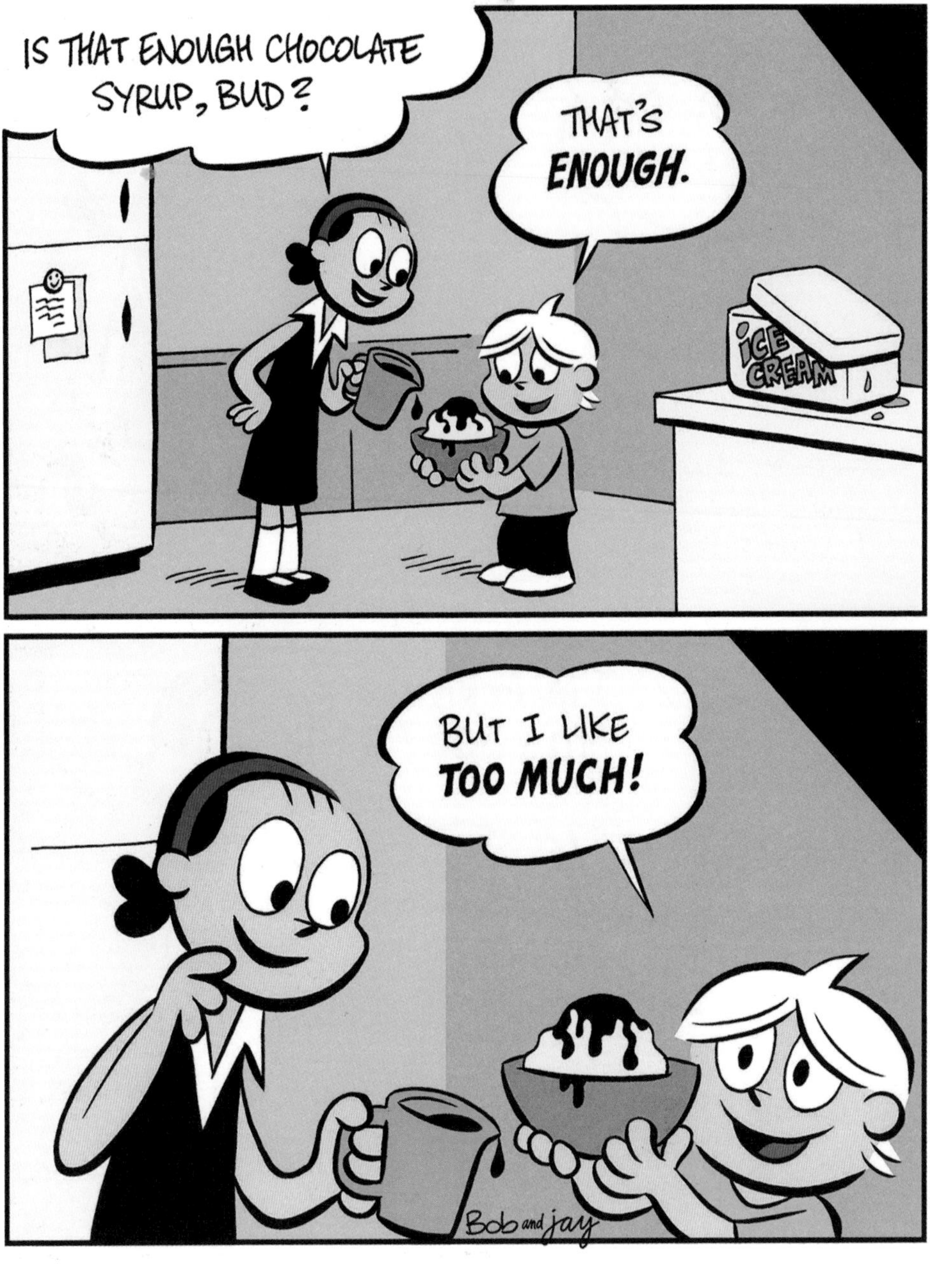
IS THAT ENOUGH CHOCOLATE SYRUP, BUD?
THAT'S ENOUGH.
ICE CREAM
BUT I LIKE TOO MUCH!
Bob and jay

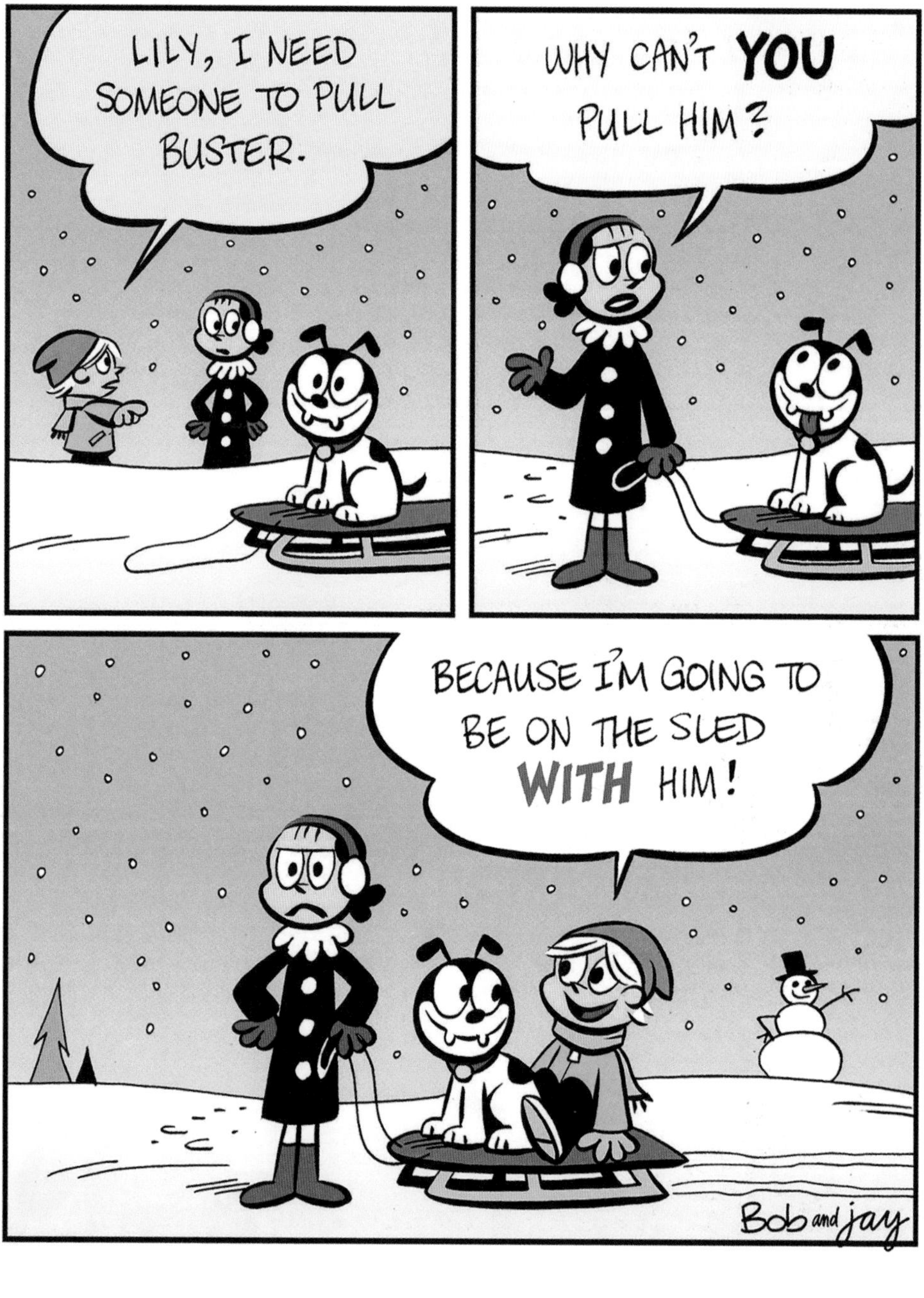
LILY, I NEED SOMEONE TO PULL BUSTER.
WHY CAN'T YOU PULL HIM?
BECAUSE I'M GOING TO BE ON THE SLED WITH HIM!
Bob and jay

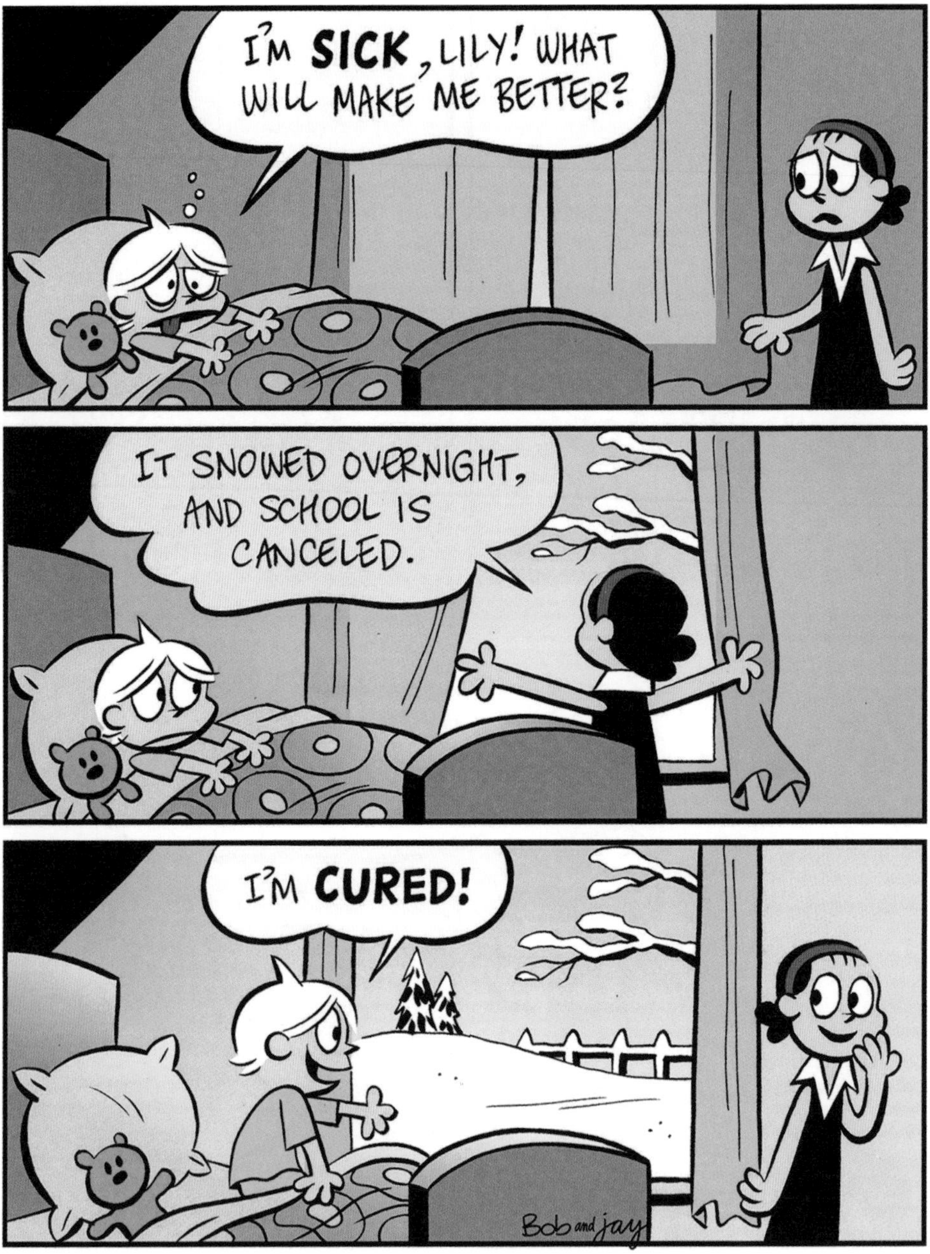
I'M **SICK**, LILY! WHAT WILL MAKE ME BETTER?
IT SNOWED OVERNIGHT, AND SCHOOL IS CANCELED.
I'M **CURED!**
Bob and jay

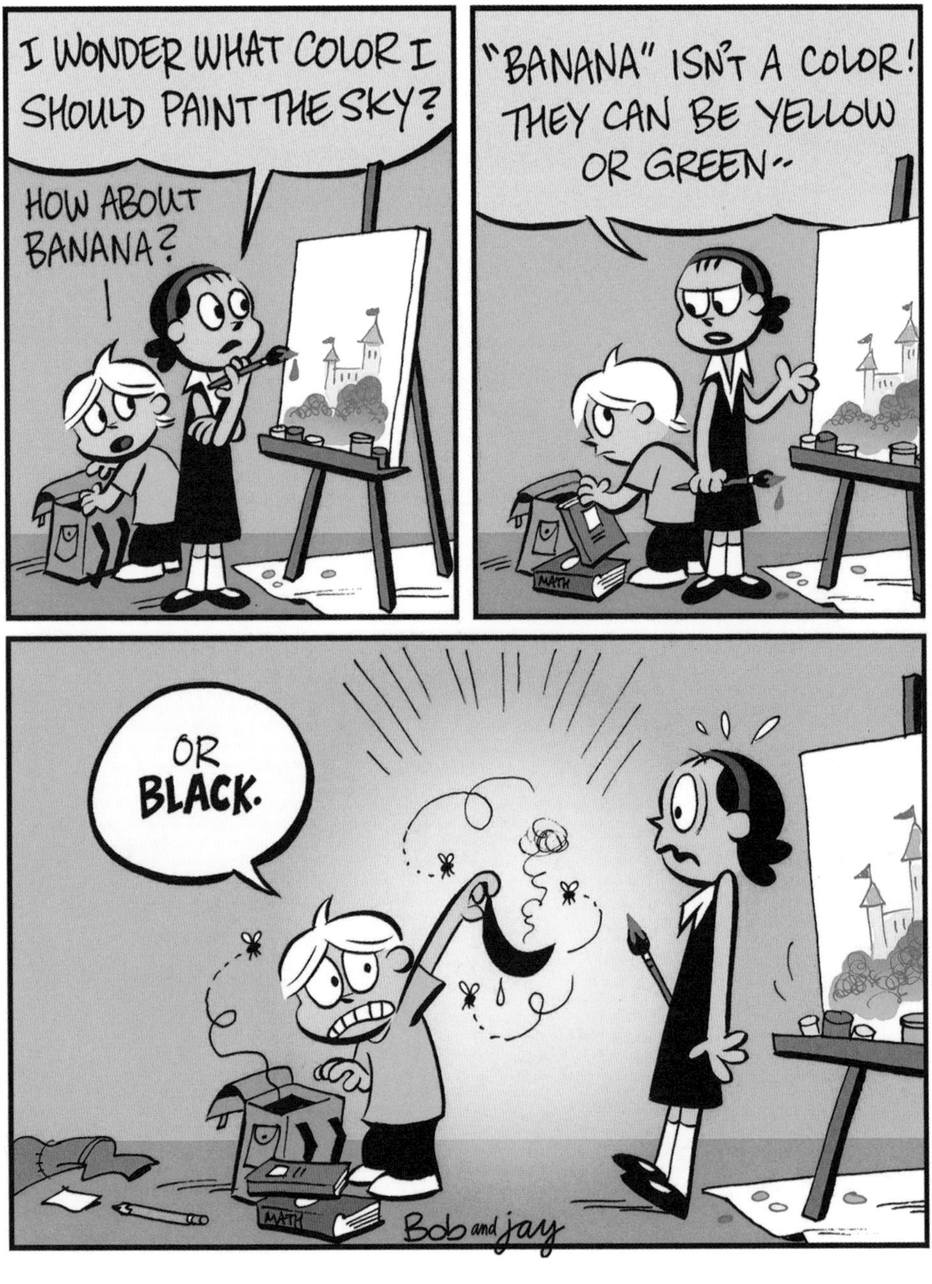
I WONDER WHAT COLOR I SHOULD PAINT THE SKY?
HOW ABOUT BANANA?
"BANANA" ISN'T A COLOR! THEY CAN BE YELLOW OR GREEN--
OR BLACK.
MATH
MATH
Bob and jay

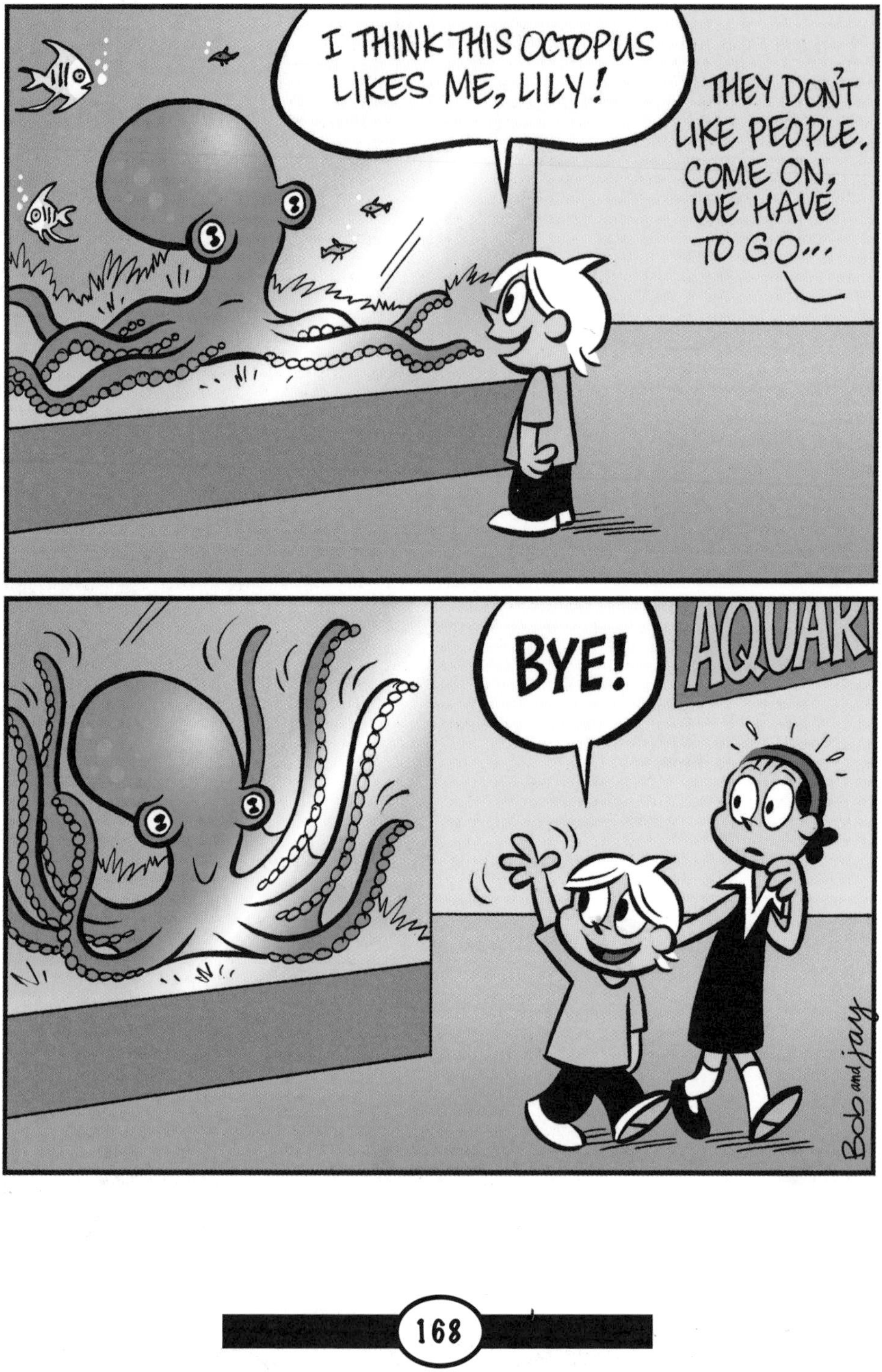
I THINK THIS OCTOPUS LIKES ME, LILY!
THEY DON'T LIKE PEOPLE. COME ON, WE HAVE TO GO...
BYE!
AQUAR
Bob and jay

MORE TO EXPLORE!

JOIN LILY AND BUD TO SPOT SIX DIFFERENCES IN THE FOLLOWING FOUR PUZZLES.

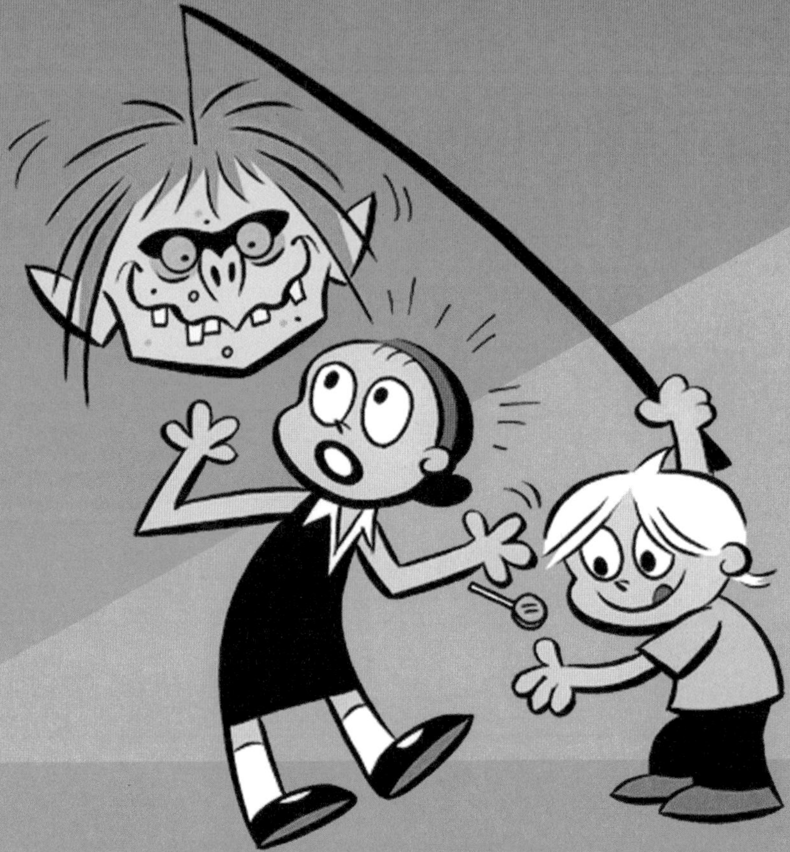

(SOLUTIONS ARE ON PAGE 174)

Oh, Brother!

Spot Six Differences

HELP!
BUD?!!
THE HOT SAND WAS BURNING MY FEET.
Bob and jay

HELP!
BUD?!
THE HOT SAND WAS BURNING MY FEET.
Bob and jay

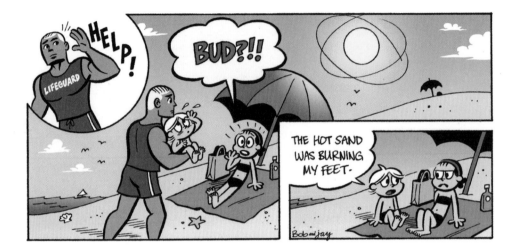

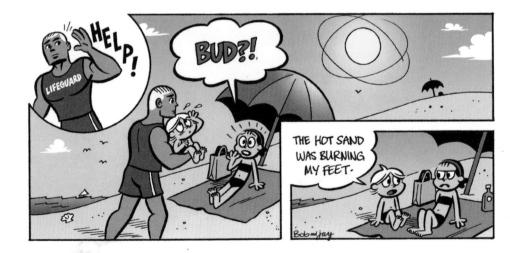

Oh, Brother!
Spot Six Differences

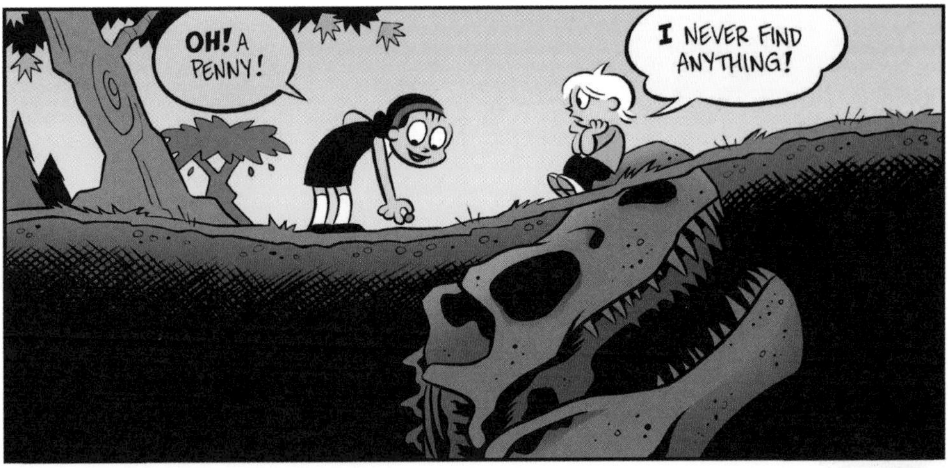
OH! A PENNY!
I NEVER FIND ANYTHING!

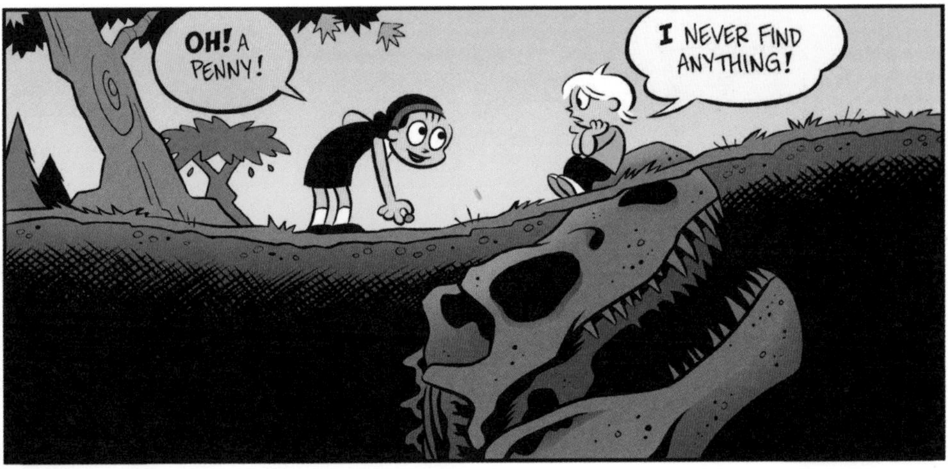
OH! A PENNY!
I NEVER FIND ANYTHING!

Oh, Brother!
Spot Six Differences

YOUR SUPPER IS GETTING COLD, BUD!
I'M HAVING TOO MUCH FUN FLYING MY KITE!
Bob and jay
YOU GO EAT. I'LL KEEP IT FLYING FOR YOU.
THIS **IS** FUN!
I THOUGHT YOU WERE GOING TO EAT.
I **CAN'T** EAT IF YOU'RE HAVING FUN FLYING MY KITE!

YOUR SUPPER IS GETTING COLD, BUD!
I'M HAVING TOO MUCH FUN FLYING MY KITE!
Bob and jay
YOU GO EAT. I'LL KEEP IT FLYING FOR YOU.
THIS **IS** FUN!
I THOUGHT YOU WERE GOING TO EAT.
I **CAN'T** EAT IF YOU'RE HAVING FUN FLYING MY KITE!

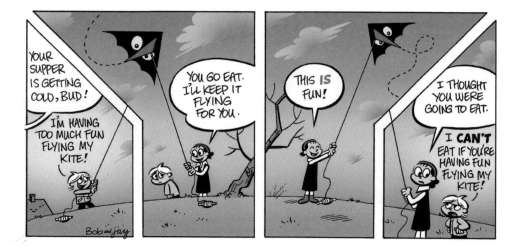

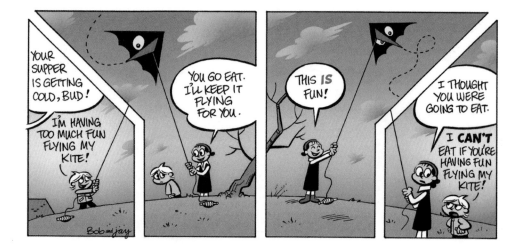

Oh, Brother!

Spot Six Differences

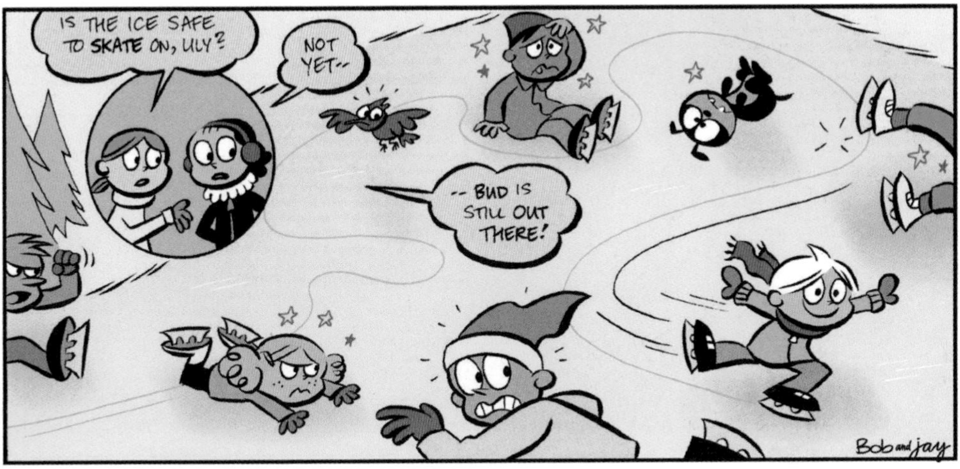
IS THE ICE SAFE TO SKATE ON, ULY?
NOT YET--
-- BUD IS STILL OUT THERE!
Bob and jay

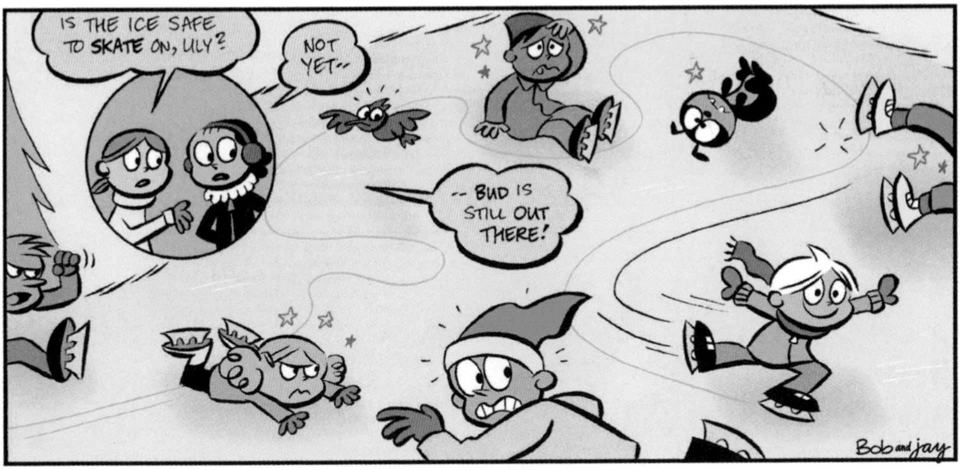
IS THE ICE SAFE TO SKATE ON, ULY?
NOT YET--
-- BUD IS STILL OUT THERE!
Bob and jay

SOLUTIONS

1. EXCLAMATION POINT
2. DRAWSTRING
3. STARFISH
4. BIRD
5. SUNSCREEN
6. CLOUD

HELP!
LIFEGUARD
BUD?!
THE HOT SAND WAS BURNING MY FEET.
Bob and Jay

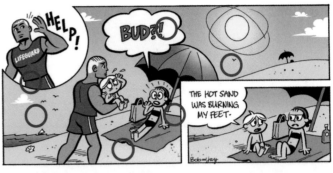

1. FOSSIL TOOTH
2. BUD'S SHOES
3. LEAF
4. GRASS
5. LILY'S EYES
6. SOCKS

OH! A PENNY!
I NEVER FIND ANYTHING!

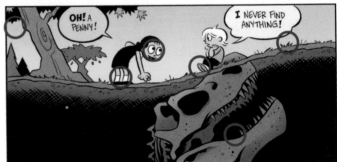

1. HEART AND INITIALS ON TREE
2. LILY'S HAIR
3. CHIMNEY
4. STRING
5. EYEBROWS
6. KITE

YOUR SUPPER IS GETTING COLD, BUD!
I'M HAVING TOO MUCH FUN FLYING MY KITE!
YOU GO EAT. I'LL KEEP IT FLYING FOR YOU.
THIS IS FUN!
I THOUGHT YOU WERE GOING TO EAT.
I CAN'T EAT IF YOU'RE HAVING FUN FLYING MY KITE!
Bob and Jay

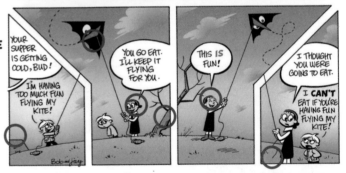

1. BUD'S SCARF
2. GIRL'S FRECKLES
3. STAR
4. BIRD FEET
5. DOG'S TAIL
6. TREE

IS THE ICE SAFE TO SKATE ON, LILY?
NOT YET--
--BUD IS STILL OUT THERE!
Bob and Jay

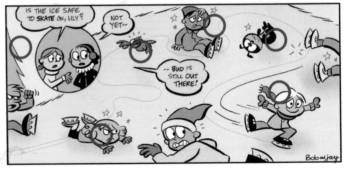

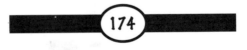

Check out these and other books at ampkids.com

SNOOPY
CONTACT!
PULL-OUT POSTER PLUS FLIP-BOOK ANIMATION
A PEANUTS Collection

STINKY CECIL
IN OPERATION POND RESCUE
PAIGE BRADDOCK

the MUTTS Winter diaries
PATRICK McDONNELL

Unicorn on a Roll
Another Phoebe and her Unicorn Adventure
Dana Simpson

big NATE
WELCOME TO MY WORLD
FULL COLOR Plus PULL-OUT POSTER
by LINCOLN PEIRCE

big NATE'S
GREATEST HITS
by LINCOLN PEIRCE

SKIP SCHOOL, FLY TO SPACE
Rockitt Shipp
New York Times Bestselling Author
Stephan T. Pastis
A Pearls Before Swine Collection

THE G-MAN SUPER JOURNAL
Awesome Origins
Chris Giarrusso

MARK TATULLI
#1
"A surefire hit and an absolute scream!"
DESMOND PUCKET
Makes Monster Magic

Also available:

Teaching and activity guides for each title.

AMP! Comics for Kids books make reading FUN!

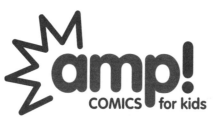

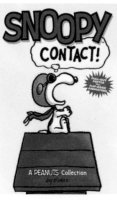

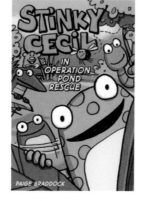

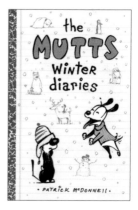

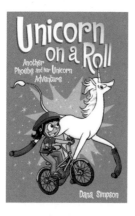

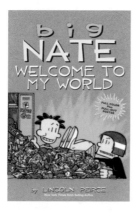

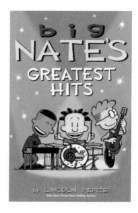

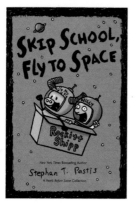

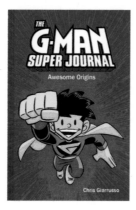

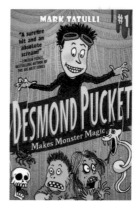

Andrews McMeel Publishing, LLC
an Andrews McMeel Universal company
1130 Walnut Street, Kansas City, Missouri 64106

www.andrewsmcmeel.com

15 16 17 18 19 SDB 10 9 8 7 6 5 4 3 2 1

ISBN: 978-1-4494-7225-2

Library of Congress Control Number: 2015943415

Made by:
Shenzhen Donnelley Printing Company Ltd.
Address and location of manufacturer:
No. 47, Wuhe Nan Road, Bantian Ind. Zone,
Shenzhen China, 518129
1st Printing - 7/27/15

ATTENTION: SCHOOLS AND BUSINESSES

Andrews McMeel books are available at quantity discounts with bulk purchase for educational, business, or sales promotional use. For information, please e-mail the Andrews McMeel Publishing Special Sales Department: specialsales@amuniversal.com.